Edwin Hodder

George Fife Angas

Father and Founder of South Australia

Edwin Hodder

George Fife Angas
Father and Founder of South Australia

ISBN/EAN: 9783337005085

Printed in Europe, USA, Canada, Australia, Japan

Cover: Foto ©Raphael Reischuk / pixelio.de

More available books at **www.hansebooks.com**

GEORGE FIFE ANGAS

FATHER AND FOUNDER OF SOUTH AUSTRALIA.

BY

EDWIN HODDER,

AUTHOR OF "THE LIFE AND WORK OF THE SEVENTH EARL OF SHAFTESBURY,"
"THE LIFE OF SAMUEL MORLEY," ETC.

WITH ETCHED PORTRAIT BY H. MANESSE.

London:

HODDER AND STOUGHTON,

27, PATERNOSTER ROW.

—

MDCCCXCI.

UNWIN BROTHERS, THE GRESHAM PRESS, CHILWORTH AND LONDON.

PREFACE.

In the rush and whirl of modern life, men who once occupied prominent places, and whose names were familiar throughout the land, are so apt to be forgotten, that it is not improbable some may ask the question, "Who was George Fife Angas?"

Forty-one years having elapsed since he left England to reside in Australia, and twelve years since he died, the question is justifiable, and I answer it at once.

He was one of the Fathers and Founders of South Australia; he originated the South Australian Company, the Bank of South Australia, the National Provincial Bank of England, and the Union Bank of Australia; he fought the battle of the slaves in Honduras and the Mosquito Coast, and obtained an Act of Parliament for their emancipation; he circumvented a reigning monarch and stayed a despotic religious persecution; his foresight and shrewdness won for Great Britain the possession of New Zealand as a colony; he realised a large fortune, lost it in pure philanthropy, and, after years of poverty and distress, regained it fourfold through the reckless land pur-

chases of an adventurer; he established the first
Sunday School Union in the North of England,
was one of the founders of the British and Foreign
Sailors' Society and other well-known institutions,
and was, fifty years ago, one of the leading
" philanthropists " of this country.

My chief concern in the preparation of this volume
has been to show what manner of man he was who
accomplished all this, and the material at my disposal
has been embarrassing in its richness. The only
restraint laid upon me has been the knowledge that
he was from first to last a man to whom religion
was the Alpha and Omega of life, and it would have
been expressly contrary to his wish that any attempt
should be made to tell his life-story unless this
aspect of his character were put in the forefront of
the narrative.

I am under great obligation to the members of
Mr. Angas's family to the third . generation for
placing information at my disposal and otherwise
assisting me, but more especially to his son, the
Hon. J. H. Angas, of Collingrove, Angaston, South
Australia, at whose request I have undertaken this
work, and who has rendered me invaluable aid, not
only in reading and revising the manuscript and
proofs, but in various other ways.

My thanks are also due to the Rev. Dr. Angus of
Regent's Park College, to the late Rev. Professor
Evans of New College, and Mrs. Evans ; and to the
Rev. H. Hussey of South Australia, who was for

many years private secretary to Mr. Angas, and compiled with great skill and industry voluminous material to which I have had unrestricted access. I am also indebted to the valuable library of the Royal Colonial Institute, which has been available to me for reference.

Whatever place Mr. Angas may take in the annals of this country, his name will be an abiding monument in South Australia; and when the history of that colony is written, it will be found that he must occupy a very prominent position in its records.

EDWIN HODDER.

St. Aubyns, Shortlands, Kent.
August, 1891.

CONTENTS.

CHAPTER VII.

PERSECUTION, AND WHAT CAME OF IT.

CHAPTER VIII.

HOW NEW ZEALAND BECAME A BRITISH COLONY.

CHAPTER IX.

A RECKLESS PURCHASE.

CHAPTER X.

A CRISIS.

CHAPTER XI.

IN DEEP WATERS.

CHAPTER XII.

SOUTHWARD HO!

CHAPTER XIII.

LIFE IN ADELAIDE.

CHAPTER XIV.

IN THE LEGISLATIVE COUNCIL.

CHAPTER XV.

HOME AND COLONIAL AFFAIRS.

CHAPTER XVI.

PERSONAL AND DOMESTIC.

CHAPTER XVII.

LENGTHENING SHADOWS.

CHAPTER XVIII.

DEATH AND CHARACTERISTICS.

CHAPTER I.

Caleb Angas—Ancestry—Early Struggles for Religious Freedom—Archibald, Ninth Earl of Angus, and his Times—Alexander Angus settles in Newcastle—Family History—Birth of George Fife Angas—State of the Times—Newcastle as it Was and Is—Boyhood—Choosing a Career—An arduous Journey—Starting a Benevolent Society—In London—The art of Carriage-building—Inner Life and Character—Keeping a Journal—Personal Religion—Marriage.

TOWARDS the end of last century there lived and flourished in the town of Newcastle-upon-Tyne, one Caleb Angas, an extensive coach manufacturer and shipowner. He was a shrewd, intelligent, and far-seeing man, with a cool head and a warm heart, and, from the enthusiasm and energy he threw into everything he undertook, he obtained for himself a position of some importance, not only in the town and county, but wherever his influence was felt. He conducted his affairs with prudence and discretion; made men his study as well as things, and took his part in the activities of life with the determination to do his duty as a good citizen and an honourable man.

Blessed with an iron constitution, inherited from

2

generations of men who had lived long past the
allotted threescore years and ten, and animated by
a simple faith, the legacy of Puritan ancestors, he
lived in the midst of his large and united family,
cherishing a laudable ambition for the future of
himself and of them.

Although Caleb Angas did not trouble himself
much about ancestry, yet it was to him a perfectly
justifiable pride and pleasure to know that he bore
a name which held an important place in Scottish
history, and that he could trace his lineage to
generations of Angus's who had made their mark
on the Borders, and especially in Northumberland.
Moreover, he had the satisfaction of knowing that
for two centuries his direct ancestors had borne a
consistent and conspicuous part in the religious
history of the times in which they lived, uniformly
on the side opposed to Episcopacy.

It may not be uninteresting to glance briefly at
some phases of this family and religious history.

The translation of the Scriptures into the vulgar
tongue inaugurated, both for Scotland and England,
a great moral and religious revolution. On the
4th of February, 1526, the first copy of the New
Testament, translated and printed abroad in English,
arrived in Britain, and from that day may be traced
the increasing progress of the Protestant Reformation, in no country taking deeper and firmer root
than in Scotland. The whole nation was convulsed
by the vain attempt of Rome to arrest the circula-

tion of the Bible, to stop the preaching and crush the truths of the gospel.

Presbyterianism, brought by John Knox from Geneva, where it was in operation under Calvin, was introduced into Scotland about 1560, and it remained the national faith, although King James I. subsequently elected to sit by the favour of Episcopacy on the English throne.

Among those who took a consistent part on the side of religious freedom in the long and arduous struggles of those times was Archibald, Ninth Earl of Angus. He was a man "after a godly sort," of whom it is recorded : "His mind was ever, even in the midst of Business, wholly bent to God-ward, and would have been glad to have been freed from all Thoughts and Affairs which had any Mixture of Earthly Things." *   But he could not remain in-

---

* It is recorded of this Earl of Angus that in the English Court he was kindly received and honourably entertained by the liberality of Queen Elizabeth, and that "being of so great Hope and Expectation, conceived by the Appearance of his present Virtues, his Wisdom, Discretion, and Towardliness, which made him acceptable to all, and begot Love and Favour, both from her Majesty and her Counsillors that then guided the State, such as Sir Robert Dudley, Earl of Leicester, Sir Francis Walsingham, secretary ; and more especially he procured the liking of him who is ever to be remembered with Honour, Sir Philip Sidney ; like Disposition, in Courtesy of Nature, and Equality of Age, did so knit their hearts together that Sir Philip failed not, as often as affairs would permit him, to visit him, insomuch that he did scarce suffer any one Day to slip, whereof he did not spend the most Part in his Company. He was then in Travail, or had brought forth rather (though not polished and refined as now it is), his so beautiful and universally accepted

active when he saw "the Romish party labouring
to undermine the true Reformed Religion and such
as had been Instruments to establish it, upon whose
Ruin these new Men did endeavour to build their
preferment, so that none could with surety live in
any honourable Place as a good Patriot, but behoved
to take Part with them that strove for Religion and
undergo the like Hazard as they did." *

Angus, therefore, joined with the lords against
the courtiers, and suffered in consequence. For, in
the Parliament "kept at Edinburgh, on the 22nd of
May, 1584, the Earl of Angus and Mar, the Earl
of Gowry, and the Master of Glamis, with divers
barons and others, their associates, were forfeited;
the order of Church Government by Presbyterians,
Synods, and General Assemblies, which had been
received and publickly allowed in Scotland, all Men
swearing and subscribing thereto, and the Oath
translated into divers languages with great approbation of Foreign Reformed Churches, and no small
Commendation of King and Country, forbidden and
prohibited and termed unlawful Conventicles—and in
place thereof the office of Bishops was reared up
again and erected."

Thereupon the Earl of Angus and his associates,
with their estates confiscated, were removed by

Birth, his Arcadia. He delighted much to impart it to Angus, and
Angus took as much pleasure to be partaker thereof."

* "The History of the House and Race of Douglas and Angus,"
written by Mr. David Hume, of Godscroft, Edinburgh, 1748.

English interference to Newcastle, where they were joined by many like-minded persons, who were entirely supported by the Earl until his means failed, when he said cheerfully, "Now it is gone, and fare it well. I never looked that it should have done so much good."

Eventually the lords were removed to Norwich, and thence to London, where, as they could not obtain a "Scot's Church" for which they had sued they met for worship in the Tower, "a privileged Place and without the jurisdiction of the Bishops." Here, amongst other exercises, "Mr. Andrew Melvil read Lectures in Latin upon the Old Testament, beginning at Genesis, which were much frequented, and the Earl of Angus was a diligent Auditor, and a painful Repeater of them for his own Use and Contentment."

We need not follow any further the history of the Earl of Angus, whose career was closed in the year 1588.

One Alexander Angus, who came to Newcastle about the year 1584, when Archibald, Ninth Earl of Angus, banished from Scotland, was living in that town, was undoubtedly a "forebear" of our Caleb, and although the genealogical registers preserved by Caleb do not clearly make out that Alexander was closely related to the Earl, there is no doubt he was of the same clan, and probably of the same sturdy stock. This Alexander Angus, to whom Caleb could trace back his pedigree in an unbroken line, settled at Raw-house, near Hexham, in the county of Northumberland, where, although suffering many serious pecuniary losses, he farmed his estate so carefully that he succeeded in preserving it to his family, in whose possession it has remained for many generations. From him sprang a very numerous family, of which some fifteen hundred names have been preserved, and Caleb was of the fifth generation. They continued to live in the North of England, and gained renown principally as agriculturists and graziers. One remarkable fact in connection with them was that scarcely an individual of this numerous house had ever "belonged to the Episcopacy," and, although many attempts had been made to root them out of the county of Northumberland on the ground of their Nonconformity, every such effort failed. From generation to generation they kept up, with primitive simplicity and great regularity, the Christian ordinances of Baptism and the Lord's Supper.

Henry Angus, of Raw-house, was the first of that name in the North of England who professed the religious principles of the Calvinistic Baptists, which principles have been retained by many later members of the Angus family. Until the fourth generation, the spelling of the surname was uniformly Angus, but for some unexplained reason it was changed by John Angus, of Dotland, Hexham, the father of Caleb, to *Angas*.

On the 1st of May, 1789, there was born to the house of Caleb Angas, in St. John's Lane, Newcastle, a seventh son, George Fife Angas, the subject of the present memoir. The world's affairs, in which he was destined to take so important a part, were in a troubled state at that time, and if we take a rapid glance at some of them, it will assist us to fix in our minds certain landmarks of history which may be useful as we pursue the narrative of a life within whose span occurred many of the most stirring events of modern times.

In England, Wellington was but just out of his teens, and Samuel Johnson had been dead only four and a half years. The serious illness of George III. had led Pitt to prepare a Bill for a limited and restricted Regency, rendered unnecessary by the recovery of the King. The great Evangelical revival had not yet borne its fruits ; the Bible Society and other important religious and philanthropic institutions were not founded; the emancipation of the negroes was still far distant ; there was hardly any visible indication of the existence of that sweeping current of political feeling which brought in its train such great reforms. Unsuccessful attempts had been made to obtain the repeal of the Test and Corporation Acts, and Protestant Dissenters were only allowed the same privileges as Roman Catholics. In Ireland, affairs were in their chronic state of disturbance, and the Irish Parliament had invited the Prince of Wales to assume the government, in the

hope that the presence of royalty and the semblance
of a King might induce the people to settle down
quietly.

France was in a distracted state; the revolu-
.tionary spirit was abroad, and signs of the
approaching tempest were becoming day by day
more ominous, but it wanted more than two
months of the time for the breaking of the storm
which swept away the Bastille and inaugurated the
First French Revolution.

In Germany, the Emperor Joseph II. was contending against the revolutionary risings in that
country, and had appealed to France for assistance
to keep the smouldering embers from bursting into
flames. Austria, Russia, Turkey, Denmark, Sweden,
and Norway were all more or less involved in war.

Such were the times in which George Fife Angas
was born; now let us turn to the place where the
early years of his life were spent.

Newcastle, at the end of last century, was a very
different place to the Newcastle of to-day; its
streets were close and narrow, its general condition
was unsanitary; the spacious streets and squares,
with ranges of elegant buildings that now adorn it,
did not then exist; nor had the philanthropic institutions which now abound been originated; the
great stone bridge connecting Gateshead with
Newcastle had only recently been erected; the
shipping was considerable, but no steam vessel had
as yet been seen on the Tyne.

It was, however, even at that time a very busy place, although its trade was insignificant in comparison with its present state. For several centuries it had been gradually developing its resources, and was giving promise of the important place it was destined to occupy in the commercial history of the country.

Long before the great staple trade of coal export was established, Newcastle was possessed of considerable commerce, and ranked as one of the principal ports of the nation. The first distinct reference to the coal trade on the Tyne is believed to be in the charter of Henry III. in 1239 to the freemen of Newcastle "to dig coals in the Castle fields, and the Forth," but it is probable that coal was shipped in the Tyne before the end of the twelfth century. Certain it is that the coal export trade was in operation at the beginning of the thirteenth century, that it increased rapidly towards its close, and with very slight interruption has continued to increase ever since.

In 1584—the year, it will be remembered, when Alexander Angus took up his abode in Newcastle— the population was estimated at 10,000; in 1801, when George Fife Angas was a boy, it had increased to 33,048; to-day it has a population of 186,345.

During his infancy, George fell a victim to a violent attack of illness, so seriously affecting his nervous system, that, although in after life he enjoyed a fair share of strength, he never wholly recovered from the shock his health then received—and in consequence his nature became highly sensitive.

At the age of six he was sent to an elementary school, and at ten, to one of a more advanced character ; two years later he experienced his first great sorrow in the loss of his mother, and soon after this he was placed in a boarding school at Catterick, under the charge of a clergyman, the Rev. J. Bradley. But George never was a boy—that is to say, he did not enter into the rollicking delights of boyhood; he eschewed its sports and games, and he might have said of himself in the words of Milton—

> When I was yet a child, no childish play
> To me was pleasing ; all my mind was set
> Studious to learn and know, and thence to do
> What might be public good ; myself I thought
> Born to that end—born to promote all truth
> And righteous things.

Although this, as applied to ordinary young mortals, is a distinctly unhealthy utterance, it might have been used, not only by George Angas, but by Lavater, Shelley, Hartley Coleridge, Hans Christian Anderson, and a host of others who never knew, or who knew but little of the joy of boyhood.

It was a distinct loss and disadvantage to George never to experience what it was to revel in and reflect—

> The innocent brightness of life's new-born day,

and in the course of this ¦narrative we shall wish, as we study the developed character of the man, that he had known the buoyant, elastic, airy, volatile spirit of childhood.

Meditative and retiring; indulging in quiet walks, and contemplative musings, forming few attachments, and scarcely ever feeling the delight of rude, robust health, George passed his early years until 1804, when, at the age of fifteen, the choice of a profession had to be made.

It was the wish of his father that he should continue his studies with a view to being called to the Bar, but to this the boy had a well-defined dislike, and begged that he might be allowed to follow his father's business.

Caleb had set his heart on his youngest son entering the legal profession, and on his refusal to qualify himself, sent him to the coach-building, hoping he would soon grow tired of the drudgery of manual labour, and yield to his father's wishes. Accordingly he left school at once, and though, when eventually his place in life became fixed, he sometimes regretted not having gathered in a larger store of learning in his boyhood, he never had reason to reproach himself for not making use of his time and opportunities whilst he remained at school. The foundation of a good sound English education had been laid, and his quiet habits led him to supply deficiencies by carrying on his studies in the intervals of business.

Having determined to become a coach-builder, he resolved to be a good one. To this end he was, at his own request, formally apprenticed to his father for a term of years, and from the first he resolved to go through all the processes essential to a full understanding of the trade; to submit to the long hours of labour, and to take no advantage whatever of his position as a son. After working assiduously for a little over a year, he had made such rapid progress that he was promoted to the " whole carriage and gig-body department." Here, in order to master the various details of the complicated work devolving upon him, he made careful and accurate drawings and diagrams of the parts which require the nicest fitting and adjusting; gave play to his inventive faculty in preparing new designs, and showed himself generally to be an excellent workman. At the end of the third year of his apprenticeship his father, who was no mean judge of good work, pronounced him to be more thoroughly qualified than is usually the case after a seven years' service.

Caleb was naturally proud of his son, and especially admired the dogged determination with which he did everything he had resolved upon doing, and the quiet easy manner in which he surmounted difficulties.

One incident, trifling in itself, occurred in 1807, which illustrates this phase of his character. Visiting London for the first time, during his summer holiday, on his return journey he took passage in a collier bound for Newcastle. When the vessel reached the Yarmouth Roads the captain, on account of contrary winds, brought his ship to anchor, and while she was lying there an embargo was laid upon her which involved her detention for a fortnight. On hearing this, young Angas requested to be put ashore, and turning his face towards York set out on foot to that city, and from thence to Newcastle, walking the whole distance—about two hundred and fifty miles. Whether he had spent all his spare cash, and had nothing left for coach fare, does not appear—the fact only is recorded that when he was left in an awkward position at that distance from home, he promptly settled the difficulty by undertaking this arduous, and no doubt adventurous pedestrian journey.

Young Angas took an interest, not only in his work, but also in his fellow-workmen, and in 1807 he originated an institution for their benefit called, "The Benevolent Society of Coachmakers in Newcastle," the principal object of which was to provide for its sick members, and others needing relief, and to promote economy and temperance. The establishment of this Society—the first of innumerable enterprises in which he was hereafter to be engaged—proved in every respect a success, and with increasing benefits and advantages it continues to this day.

After serving for four years in the manufactory

at Newcastle, George was anxious to put his acquirements to the test, and to see whether his workmanship would be appreciated as much by strangers as it was by his father, and those of his household. To see the necessity for a thing, and then to do it, was the simple practice of the young coach-builder, who now resolved to take up his abode in London, and work at his business as an ordinary journeyman. One day he presented himself at Howe's coach manufactory, found employment, and was soon in the uncongenial society of his fellow-workmen, some of whom were of loose habits and foul tongues. He worked there for over a year with satisfaction to his employers, gained what he sought—an unbiassed opinion favourable to his business qualifications—and in 1809, returned to Newcastle to take the overseership of his father's business.

So little being generally known of the history of the coach-building trade, and of what is involved in a practical mastery of this business, a few words on the subject may not be out of place here.

Britain has always taken an important part in the history of carriage building. Prior to the Roman invasion, a car was in use which Cicero coveted, and, writing to a friend, he says, "There appeared little worth bringing away from Britain except the chariots, of which he wished his friend to bring him one as a pattern."

Although the exact locality of this chariot production cannot be ascertained, there is abundant

proof that Newcastle-on-Tyne was a home of the
carriage-building industry from a very early period.
It was not, however, until towards the end of the
seventeenth century that the heavy old coaches
which took thirteen hours to rumble over the journey
between Oxford and London began to give place to
better contrivances. Even so late as 1760, when
Caleb Angas was a young man of eighteen, a journey
from Edinburgh to London occupied eighteen days
—a part of the road, by the by, being only passable
by pack horses.

In the same year that George went into his father's
business (1804), one Obadiah Elliot, a coach-maker
of Lambeth, patented a plan for hanging vehicles
upon elliptic springs, the first step to a grand revolution in the manufacture of carriages, which was
to affect every variety of vehicle great or small.

At that time, however, the briska, or britchka,
had not been introduced from Austria; gigs, so
largely used by commercial travellers, to whom,
before railways came into fashion, they were let out
at an annual rental, were almost unknown; pony
phaetons and cab phaetons, now known as "Vic-
torias," had not come into existence. Broughams
were unheard of—the first one was built for Lord
Brougham in 1839—Mr. Hansom, the architect of
the Birmingham Town Hall, had not yet invented
his "Hansom Cab," nor had Mr. Shillibeer started
his first omnibus.

The art of the carriage-builder is an intricate

one, but George made himself master of its details,
and it speaks well for his perseverance, that in a
short time he was equally *au fait* in each of the four
great branches of his craft—wood-working, black-
smithing, painting, and trimming; that he was not
only ready to give a competent opinion on the
material used, but was able to show a workman how
to practically apply a principle.

Having glanced thus far at the outward circumstances of the life of George Angas, let us now look
at certain phases of his character which must be
understood at the outset, or we shall fail to appreciate the secret of his successes, and the motive
power of his actions.

He was brought up in a home of the Puritan type,
where all the family traditions were Nonconformist,
and the religious ideals and customs were severely
simple. Old Caleb with his household went to
chapel twice or thrice on Sunday, and the intervals
of the day were occupied in reading the Bible or some
"religious book." Ministers of the gospel, of all
denominations, were the most frequent guests under
that hospitable roof; family prayer was an unfailing
institution morning and evening, and the new spirit
then abroad of liberally supporting the claims of the
gospel was duly inculcated.

George grew up to be a man, the Alpha and
Omega of whose career was religion; from his very
earliest years religion was with him an instinct or
an intuition—that is to say, it was not, at first, the

result of any theory or logical process. As a child
he pondered upon thoughts of God and heaven,
death and eternity. As a boy he set before himself
high ideals of Christian character and Christian
work ; in the days of his youth, when he had
examined the positive claims of religion, and had
been convinced of their " sweet reasonableness," he
gave himself up body, soul, and spirit, to the service
of the Master of his life.

There is nothing remarkable in the story of how
this religious instinct developed itself. No strong
wind rent the mountains, or broke in pieces the
rocks before the Lord; no earthquake or fire appalled
him ; a still small voice lured him, and led him on.
The story of his early religious history is simply that
of the flower unfolding to the sun; of the brooklet
flowing to the river. As a child, home influence
nurtured the good seed ; as a boy of fifteen he was
greatly indebted to the kind counsels and religious
instruction of his Latin tutor, Mr. Sims—services
held, all through life, in the most grateful remembrance; later on the influence of his brother
William Henry, of whom we shall have more to say
hereafter, had much to do with the moulding of his
mind in the same direction. To him George looked
up with reverence and admiration, while at the same
time he could open his mind to him freely. " You
so soar above the crowd," George wrote when he was
seventeen, " as always to raise my thoughts above
the trifling things of this world to brighter and holier

ones; and to contemplate the loving-kindness of our
Blessed Redeemer who gave Himself for us." In
the choice of books, in questions affecting his
position in life, such as whether it would be more
advantageous to study law, as his father wished,
or shorthand as his own inclination suggested, as
well as in all matters concerning religion, George
took advice from his brother William, to whom, in
return, he gave such confidences as these—" I am
now in the slippery paths of youth, and unless I
am on my guard, and am admonished of my faults,
I may fall headlong into destruction. . . . I do not
think I was designed to be a useless member of
society; I hope I have nobler ends in view—the
service of my God and country."

At the age of eighteen George commenced to keep
a journal, and continued the practice almost without
intermission for a period of about sixty years.

During the period of his employment in London as
a "journeyman," he lodged at the house of religious
people in the neighbourhood of Covent Garden, who
he says " were the means of keeping him from many
temptations," and though there was not, he supposed,
" a place in all England where the temptations to
irregular desires were so strong or so numerous as in
the part of London where his lot was cast," though he
was made the butt of his fellow-workmen on account
of his " sanctimoniousness," and was often fearful lest
he should not stand firm against the powers that
assailed him, it was while he was in the midst of this

conflict that he reached what is often regarded as
"*the* crisis" in personal religious experience.

Soon after his return to Newcastle George was
baptized (immersed) by the Rev. R. Pengilly, and
was received into the communion of the Baptist
Church at Tuthill Stairs, Newcastle, of which Mr.
Pengilly was the pastor, and Caleb Angas and the
majority of his family were members.

On the subject of adult baptism George had very
decided opinions, and whatever change of view he
may have had in after years on other points of
doctrine, he ever remained unshaken, and said even
in extreme old age that "he had never seen any
reason to alter his mind in regard to this ordinance."
Strong as this conviction was, however, it never at
any time prevented him in the least degree from
extending his warmest sympathy and support to
other branches of the Christian Church, including
those most opposed to him in this particular.

The visit of George to London was fraught with
other far-reaching consequences. Interesting as was
the society of the "old Christian couple" with
whom he lodged, it did not seem to satisfy all the
longings of his heart, and when a friend of his father's,
Mr. French, of Hutton, invited him to spend a few
days there, George responded without any hesitation.
Much as he was interested in Mr. French, he took
a thousandfold more interest in his daughter Rosetta,
a bright, beautiful girl of sixteen or thereabouts.

It was the ever new yet old, old story. George

fell deeply in love, parents and friends on both sides approved, and on the 8th of April, 1812, George being then in his 23rd year, his marriage to Miss Rosetta French was celebrated in Hutton Church.

CHAPTER II.

HONDURAS AND ELSEWHERE.

Mahogany—First use of the Wood for Furniture—Principles in Business—
William Henry Angas—An Adventurous Career—Wrecked—Death
of Caleb Angas, junr.—Honduras—Indian Slaves—Efforts for their
Liberation—Missionary Agents—Colonel Arthur—Anti-slavery Cham-
pions—Zachary Macaulay—The Legal Right of Indians to Freedom
—Abolition of Slavery in Honduras—The Nicaragua Canal.

CALEB ANGAS was not only a coach manufacturer, he
was also a merchant and shipowner, trading under
the firm of Angas and Co., the " Company " consisting of his four sons, Caleb, John Lindsay, William
Henry, and, in process of time, George Fife, the
youngest of the family.

Apt as George had shown himself for the work ot
a coachbuilder, his interest was even more keenly
excited in the other departments of the extensive
business ; and to these, as we shall see, he eventually
devoted the whole of his energies.

At an early period in the history of his business,
Caleb Angas had opened up an extensive trade in
importing mahogany, dye-woods, and other products
from British Honduras, and had established an
agency at Belize, its chief town. How it originated
it is hardly necessary to inquire ; but mahogany was

largely used by carriage builders, and probably the trade began by supplying the requirements of the Newcastle manufactory.

Sir Walter Raleigh is said to have first discovered the value of the wood, and a Dr. Gibbon, in the end of the seventeenth century, was accidentally the means of bringing it into use as an article of furniture. He had in his possession some junks of mahogany, brought from the West Indies by a brother, and from one of these a candle box was made. Struck by the beauty of the grain he caused the remainder to be worked up into a cabinet. Its fine colour and exquisite polish attracted the attention of the Duchess of Buckingham, who gave to Dr. Gibbon's carpenter—a man named Wollaston —an order for a similar cabinet, and from that time furniture in mahogany became the rage.

It was to log wood that the British Settlement of Honduras, or Belize, owed its existence, although its staple trade has since been in mahogany, and " *Sub umbra flores,*" in allusion to the mahogany tree,* is the motto of the Colony.

* "This magnificent tree is unequalled by any of the forest giants when all its qualities are considered : the height of the trunk to the first crutch, the space of ground covered by its roots, the girth, wide spread of its branches, its umbrageous foliage, coupled with the beauty and durability of its grain and value of its timber. In the present century a tree was cut by a Mr. Charles Craig, of Honduras, the trunk of which yielded a log of fifteen tons. It measured 5,168 superficial feet, squaring 57 inches by 64 inches. The tree takes 200 years to arrive at maturity." ("British Honduras," by Archibald Robinson Gibbs).

Many reasons combined to make George Angas take a deep and growing interest in this important part of his business. In the first place his brothers, for whom he had unbounded admiration and esteem, were actively engaged in it; and in the next place, the aborigines of the settlement were a wild race of Indians kept in cruel slavery, and he panted to give them liberty and devote himself to their moral and spiritual improvement.

George was a born merchant, shrewd, intelligent, far-seeing; but he was " a Christian first, a merchant afterwards," and he had laid it down as a principle not to engage in any business that was not in itself strictly right, and that, whatever his business yielded him—wealth or social position, or influence either over his own countrymen, or the peoples of other lands — he would hold it as a trust from God, to be used not primarily for his own aggrandizement, but for the advancement of the kingdom of God in the world.

He was well supported in carrying out his principle as far as Honduras was concerned, for his father and his brothers were in full sympathy with him.

We must pause here to introduce one of those brothers, William Henry, who exercised a strong influence over George, and whose career was full of marvellous adventure.

William was educated with a view to the legal profession, but when the set time arrived he declined

on the ground that "it was extremely difficult for an
honest man to be a lawyer." So he chose the sea,
and was bound as apprentice to an old friend of his
father. Great trials and hardships ensued, for in the
first year he fell down the ship's hatchway—a depth
of nineteen feet—and was nearly killed. It was
many months before he could walk again, and years
before he could go aloft without pain. At another
time he fell overboard in Shields Harbour on a dark
night, with a strong tide setting out to sea, and as
he could not swim he must have perished had not
an oar floated by, to which he held on until relief
came.

After these escapes he was shipwrecked on the
Flemish coast, and floated to shore on pieces of the
vessel, but no sooner had he reached land than the
French, with whom, as usual, we were then at war,
cast him, cold and almost naked as he was, into
prison, where for twenty months he endured un-
speakable hardships, with straw for his bed in winter,
and horse beans and oil as his only food. While he
was here, without a Bible or book of any kind, or a
single soul like-minded, a French hussar said to him
one evening that he had an English book, and asked
him if he could read it. It was the remains of a
pocket edition of Dr. Watts' hymns, which the
Frenchman had been using for pipe-lights. William
eagerly purchased it, and it was the means of turning
the whole current of his inner life. When almost
sinking under the rigour of his prison discipline, a

Frenchman and a staunch Roman Catholic heard
his name casually mentioned, and remembered that
he had been acquainted with his father in Newcastle,
although the war had long since suspended any
intercourse between them.   This worthy Frenchman
supplied William freely with money, and at length
he was released by an exchange of prisoners.   Just
as he had reached his native shore, and his heart was
full of gladness in the hope of seeing his kith and
kin again, he was seized by a press-gang and forcibly
taken on board a king's ship of war then about to
sail on an engagement against France.   Fortunately
the news reached the ears of Caleb Angas, who was
personally known to the admiral. of the fleet, and
was able to procure the discharge of his son just as
the ship was putting out to sea.   After passing
through many perils, which cannot be enumerated
here, he was placed at the age of nineteen in command of one of his father's vessels, the *Venerable*,
bound for Barbados, where he arrived in safety;
but, on the return voyage, in running down to
Montego Bay, in the island of Jamaica, where he
was to take in cargo, he had to bring to bear all the
tactics of naval war to beat off a French privateer.
This was but a passing incident ; a more abiding one
was that he had on board his brother Caleb, a man
of most exemplary Christian life and conversation,
whose kindly counsels were very helpful to the
spiritual progress of William.

After this he had a narrow escape of losing both

his life and his ship, for the whole of the crew
mutinied, with the exception of one apprentice.
William was, however, equal to the occasion. The
mutineers had resolved to murder the captain, and
pirate the ship' and cargo, but with undaunted
courage William armed himself and the boy, drove
the crew below, worked the ship himself, and kept
the mutineers in durance vile until starvation
brought them to a state of obedience.

His next voyage was to the Gulf of Mexico, and
his brother Caleb again accompanied him as a
passenger. All went well until Caleb, who had
been transacting business affairs at Truxillo, took
passage in a large boat with nine other persons for
Belize. They were overtaken by a heavy gale, the
boat capsized, and everybody and everything was
washed out of her. The boat righted, and the
captain was the first to regain his place on board.
Then Caleb was hauled in, but he was terribly
exhausted in buffeting against the waves. Soon
after he pulled out his watch and, handing it to
the captain, begged him to give it to his brother
William, as he did not expect to live to reach the
shore. Shortly after, with a smile, he kissed the
hand of the captain and expired. Deprived of oars
and of footing in the shattered boat, each of the
survivors was obliged to use one hand as an oar,
while with the other he clung to the wreck. Next
morning they drove upon a dangerous reef, which
they beat over, and were able, after a fashion, to

repair the boat. For the next five days they never tasted food of any kind, and when they arrived at Belize they were at the point of death. William Angas was on the shore to meet them, wrought up to great excitement by long suspense and anxiety, and when the mournful intelligence of the death of Caleb was communicated to him it came as a crushing blow.

The same letter in which he conveyed to his father the sad tidings of the loss of his son, acknowledged one which had borne to him the painful intelligence of the death of his mother.

On his return voyage to England, during a perfect calm, his vessel got into a very strong current in the Bay of Mexico, and carried him with great violence upon a rock where ship and cargo were lost—both, however, being insured. Had it not been that an American vessel hove in sight, and had only escaped destruction by having William's ship as a beacon, they must all have inevitably perished. But captain and crew were taken on board the American, and so escaped with their lives.

Afterwards he took the command of another large vessel belonging to his father, and continued to trade between Britain and the West Indies for several years, during which he had many escapes both by land and sea; twice he was laid prostrate by fever at Jamaica, and once at Honduras.

These attacks, superadded to an extraordinary degree of activity in the discharge of his duties as

captain and managing owner of three ships, proved
so injurious to his health that he at length relin-
quished the sea, and acted as ship's-husband on land.

All these sufferings and trials had their effect in
enlarging and beautifying his Christian character,
and when he and George found themselves working
together as partners in the same business, they
resolved that everything they undertook should be
for the highest good of mankind. William determined to make the moral and spiritual welfare of
seamen his future life-work, while George was bent
not only upon assisting him in this, but also in
endeavouring to secure similar blessings among the
natives of the lands where the trade of the firm was
carried on.

We shall return to follow George in his work
among sailors and others in conjunction with his
brother; meanwhile let us glance at the larger
scheme he had in contemplation.

He began at Honduras. Many evils and abuses
existed there which needed to be swept away. The
settlement was governed by a superintendent and
a "public meeting," consisting of seven magistrates
appointed by the inhabitants; the laws, or rather
regulations, established by the settlers themselves,
were undefined and otherwise defective in their
nature, and by custom and usage were not confirmed
according to the letter, but by what the administrators were pleased to consider the equity of the
case; these administrators, however, being, in nine

cases out of ten, parties directly or indirectly concerned, their decisions were often notoriously and
grossly unjust. The poorer classes were exposed
to fraud and oppression, while the slaves were absolutely unprotected, and no individual could on any
occasion step forward on their behalf without drawing down upon himself very general dissatisfaction.

Many of these slaves were Indians, who it was
alleged by George Angas were kept in illegal bondage.
Whether that was the case or not we shall see hereafter ; certain it was that the most cruel punishments
were inflicted upon them, and that their owners
paid no attention whatever to their spiritual condition, but on the contrary countenanced every
species of immorality. It was needful therefore
that radical alterations should be made with regard
to the political, commercial, religious, and moral
state of the settlement, and that the freedom of the
slaves should be secured.

But the whole question bristled with difficulties.
It was patent that if justice was to be done to the
slave, no slave-owner should be allowed to sit on
the bench, or on the juries in slave-actions, and that
the " powers of ordinary " should be vested in the
officer administering the Government, so that the
slaves who sought their freedom by virtue of the
manumission of their deceased owners might not
be treated with the base injustice they; had been
wont to receive.

The solution of one part of the difficulty would

have been the formation of the settlement into a
colony under the sovereignty of the British Government, but in deploring to a friend his inability to
take action in such a movement George Angas
wrote in Sept., 1822 :—" There can be no doubt of
the Bay merchants opposing the measure to a man
except ourselves, and we are not naturalized, though
probably we have sent as great a quantity of British
goods out during the past year as any of the Bay
merchants, one excepted."

Two courses were, however, plainly open to him
with regard to the slaves of Honduras : the first was
to send among them teachers who should improve
their moral and spiritual condition and prepare
them for an intelligent appreciation of liberty, and
the next to labour for their liberation.

With regard to the traders and others, he conceived
the idea of selecting earnest Christian men as his
business agents, imbued with a missionary spirit
and possessing a knowledge of the Spanish language,
who should encourage and assist all efforts for the
dissemination of the gospel. A practical commencement was made in 1819 by the appointment of
Captain Whittle, a devoted and zealous man, to
the command of the brig *Ocean*, and by the settlement of Messrs. Jeckell and Stevenson in Belize,
as pioneers of the missionary cause.

In the following year another brig, the *Robert*,
was purchased, and made ready, and one Captain
Smith, with a staff of good men, appointed to sail

in her to Honduras. But the vessel was totally wrecked off Margate, the captain and crew being saved as by miracle.

To many men this would have had a very depressing effect, and have damped their ardour for further enterprise, but upon George Angas it acted in a precisely opposite manner. Although his Honduras affairs had in the course of fifteen months involved him in a loss of some thousands of pounds, he saw " an open door for doing good, not only at Belize, but at the Mosquito shore," and he set to work with vigour to avail himself of the opportunity. He at once brought, the matter under the notice of the Church Missionary Society, and other Missionary Societies, but they were not then prepared to take it up, whereupon Mr. Angas gave them a pledge that if at any time they thought well to send out missionaries, he would willingly give them a free passage to Honduras, and otherwise assist them.

With the Baptist Missionary Society he was more successful, and under their auspices, but mainly at his own expense, Mr. and Mrs. Bourne were appointed to the Mission, and were sent out in the brig *Ocean* " to labour in the Mosquito land, or in the neighbouring provinces, or in any other way or place that may appear to the friends of Christianity at Belize most expedient for bringing the natives under the sound of the gospel."

Mr. Angas gave them a letter of introduction to Colonel Arthur, the superintendent of the settlement, commending them to his protection. Colonel Arthur, who, unfortunately for Honduras, was soon afterwards recalled, took a deep interest in everything that concerned the moral and spiritual welfare of the people, and was in full sympathy with the efforts of Mr. Angas. The colonel's successor was a man of an altogether different type, not only opposed to every kind of social and religious reform, but "a persecutor of the Church." This circumstance added to the difficulties of Mr. Angas, who nevertheless persevered, and from time to time for several years sent out fresh agents to circulate freely the Scriptures and other religious books in the Spanish tongue, much to the chagrin of the Roman Catholics, who used every effort to oppose their dissemination.

Meanwhile he put himself in communication with many of the well-known friends of Missions, and gained the co-operation of the Rev. Thomas Knibb, who was soon about to sail on his fatal mission to Jamaica; of Mr. Samuel Hope, of Liverpool, merchant and philanthropist (whose son-in-law, Samuel Morley, was afterwards the equally well-known merchant and philanthropist of London); of the celebrated Mrs. Judson, of Burmah, then on a visit to England; and many others. On the return of Colonel Arthur to this country Mr. Angas considered the time was ripe to call the attention of the British Parliament to the political needs of Honduras. He had hoped that he might induce some energetic member to move that Colonel Arthur should be called to the

Bar of the House upon the subject of the treatment of the slaves, and that this would lead to a full inquiry into the judicial and legislative state of the country. In this he was disappointed, and fresh methods had to be devised.

About this time news reached him that in Honduras placards were being posted up in conspicuous places announcing a motion for consideration at a public meeting, having for its object "the stopping of all religious instructors, except the clergy of the Established Church, from exercising their ministrations."

This roused the righteous indignation of George Angas, and he determined not to rest until a change was wrought. But as there was no power to legislate in civil affairs except by Act of Parliament, which would first have to create the power, and then to invest it in a governor with a council, magistrates, and jury, it was necessary in the first instance to bring in a Bill. This would in any case be a long and tedious affair, and in the meantime he would straightway attack the slave question, more especially as regarded the Indians on the Mosquito coast territory.

Mr. Angas soon became acquainted with Zachary Macaulay, Joseph Butterworth, Fowell Buxton, and other anti-slavery champions, before whom he placed all the ascertainable facts. He laid his scheme before Wilberforce also, and gained from him expressions of the warmest sympathy; but at that time

4

his hands were too full to render any active support.

With Zachary Macaulay, George Angas had many interviews, and much correspondence, and was greatly indebted to him for his aid, while Macaulay was equally under obligation for the information given to him from time to time—all helpful to the great cause he had at heart—of which the following may be taken as a specimen. Mr. Angas wrote :—

NEWCASTLE, *July* 1, 1822.

Very lately I had information that the claim of an Indian family to freedom was laid before the civil court at Belize, and the jury gave a verdict in their favour. The next day a second case, precisely similar, came before the court, which alarmed the magistrates, who are slave-holders, and who saw that unless some means were adopted to check these proceedings, the whole of the Indian slaves would become free, to the serious loss of the owners. (Some slaves have been sold for £500 currency.) The case came on and was referred to the jury, with whom every effort was used to induce them to give a verdict opposite to the one given in the previous case. Three of the jurors were of opinion that as the case was exactly similar to the former one, they would act inconsistently in giving a different opinion, 'and besides,' observed one of them, who is one of our agents in Belize, 'we are under a solemn oath to do justice, and I am determined rather to expire on the jury than violate my solemn oath before God.' This so exasperated one of the jurors, that with great fury he tore the waistcoat from the back of the speaker, who nevertheless continued inflexible, and kept the jury all day and night. Thereupon the court dissolved the jury, and impanelled another, who gave a verdict in favour of the slave-holders.

In consequence of this state of things Mr. Angas

took active measures to procure the establishment
of proper courts of justice in Honduras under the
protection of the king, with power to appeal against
the civil court at Belize.   To this end he presented
a memorial to Earl Bathurst on the subject, in which
also he claimed protection against internal and
external enemies, taking his stand on commercial
ground, and not as making common cause with the
Indians.   It is hardly necessary to say that he had
to be extremely cautious in imparting information
of the kind he had given to Mr. Macaulay, and to ask
that, as far as possible, his name might not be made
prominent, as it was already obnoxious to the
slave-holders and merchants of Belize, who had
combined to injure him in business, and obstruct
every effort of a benevolent nature.   Already, too,
some of the slaves had been punished because
they had shown a willingness to receive religious
instruction.

Although there was no question as to the cruelties
practised upon the slaves, and the disastrous disabilities under which they suffered, there was some
doubt as to any direct evidence in support of the
illegality of their being held in bondage.   Happily,
however, after much investigation an old document
was discovered which inspired fresh hope for the
Indians.   In a record dated 1776 it appeared that
Sir Basil Keith, Governor of Jamaica, sent down to
the Mosquito shore a proclamation declaring that it
was illegal to hold any Indians in slavery.   The then

superintendent of Honduras thought proper to call
together a council, consisting mainly of the proprietors of these poor people, when it was agreed
that all the Indians then in slavery should remain
in that condition, but that they should be registered.
The proclamation was suppressed, and the order of
council adduced.

When this matter came to light, George Angas
resolved to submit the whole question of the right of
the Indians to their freedom, to a legal tribunal in
England, and he called to his aid the law officers of
the Crown, although why any doubt should have
arisen seems unaccountable at this date, as for more
than fifty years there had been no more question as
to the abstract right of all Indians to their freedom,
than there had been that Jamaica was a British
Colony.

It would be tedious to follow the story in detail.
Suffice it to say that, assisted by Sir Matthew
White Ridley, one of the members for Newcastle,
and Colonel Arthur, George Angas left no stone
unturned in furthering the objects he had in view,
and while he worked strenuously, he regularly set
aside one evening in each week " to seek the Lord's
blessing upon the settlement of Belize."

Lord Bathurst took the memorial of Mr. Angas
under his special consideration, and on the 22nd of
December, 1822, wrote to him holding out hopes
"that a legislative measure respecting Honduras
would be submitted to Parliament in the ensuing

session, which would accomplish the specific objects
of the memorial."

Referring to this communication Colonel Arthur
wrote : " This looks as though the matter would
go forward, and it must be highly gratifying to you
to reflect that your efforts have conduced so much to
the benefit of that settlement already, and should
your wishes be accomplished with regard to it, you
will see that you have done very much for the
happiness of that part of the human race."

But a new commercial treaty with Spain was at
that time on the *tapis*, and, until that was concluded,
nothing could be done with regard to Honduras.
When the matter was actively revived, Mr. Angas
received a private intimation that the draft of the
Honduras Bill was prepared, but the question of the
claims of the Indians to freedom was entirely
omitted ! All the machinery of action—the African
Institution, the press, and the pulpit—had to be set
in motion again, with the result that Mr. Angas was
successful in getting an Act of Parliament passed
" for the liberation of the aboriginal slaves who were
kept in unlawful bondage in British Honduras."
" In the year 1824 some two hundred or three hundred Indians were set free as the result of these
labours, and subsequently, during Colonel Mac-
Donald's superintendence, the like justice was extended to some who were held in the same condition
by British subjects on the Mosquito shore. Whatever
odium the oppressor and the enemies of the gospel

may have heaped upon the instruments of these
benefits, there are those in Belize who honour their
faithfulness, and give glory to God for the happy
results." *

The agencies that had been already established for
the welfare of the aborigines were now employed
with excellent effect, and with satisfactory results.

Although the goal that Mr. Angas set before him
was not reached, the following extract from his diary
shows how far in advance he was of the thought of
his time on the subject of Missions :—

I am very anxious to establish on the Mosquito shore a Mission
on an enlightened plan, one to encourage arts and sciences, as well
as to propagate Christianity, and to train up schoolmasters and
native missionaries; and it will not be too much to expect that
eventually the light of the truth will spread over that land and the
Western Provinces of New Spain.

A curious and interesting illustration of the far-
sightedness of Mr. Angas may be given here.

While the Honduras Bill was passing through
Parliament he was much in correspondence with his
friend Colonel Arthur, and in a letter, from which
we quote, he suggested a scheme for cutting a canal
through the Isthmus of Darien, as it was then called
—the first practical suggestion, as far as we are
aware, ever made on the subject.

* " The Gospel in Central America," by the Rev F. Crowe. In
this volume a full account is given of the interest of the House of
Angas and Co., in the welfare of that country, and a cordial acknowledgment of the good they accomplished.

NEWCASTLE, *April* 24, 1823.

The more I read upon the geography of Honduras with the surrounding provinces, and consider the approaching crisis of opening a regular communication between the Atlantic and Pacific Oceans, the more I am convinced of the vast importance of our Government securing a control over the Mosquito land, with its king's consent, and placing all McGregor's attempts under the control of the British Government. According to the present situation of old Spain, do you think it would have any difficulty in conceding her claim to the Mosquito land to our country, and would it not be to the interest of the Government of Guatemala, which is now Republican, to enter into a treaty with Britain to allow her a regular trade through the Mosquito land to the Pacific? And does not the language of Mr. Canning and Lord Liverpool, relating to the recognition of the independency of the new Spanish Government render this the proper moment for arranging these matters, and securing to Britain the advantages of the commerce which would certainly flow through such a channel as the communication between the two seas? Surely such an important measure is worthy the attention of the Government.

At this time there is not on the globe a point which may involve more consequences to British commerce than what nation is to have control of the Isthmus of Darien, or rather, perhaps the Channel between the seas through the Mosquito Land and Lake Nicaragua, &c., to the Pacific.

Directly, at Darien, the British could not have a claim and succeed without infringing upon the rights and laws of nations. The trade from India and the South Seas through that channel would be great, for it is well known what a trade has been carried on between India and Acapulco, and the goods taken many hundreds of miles overland to Vera Cruz. And should Government secure the necessary protection and control, it would be a very easy matter to arrange a plan for raising a Company of British Merchants who would undertake the measure of opening out the communication. There is capital and ability enough in England to accomplish the object upon the principle of shareholders. This great undertaking would, of course, devolve upon other hands, but as it may induce Government to look more seriously at McGregor's measures, would it not be proper for you to suggest this view of the subject to the Ministry? You can judge best of this idea.

In reply Colonel Arthur promised to bring the matter under the notice of the Government, and when recording this in his diary, Mr. Angas writes :— "Now, when I reflect upon it, I am astonished at the idea, and the magnitude of the plan; still there do not appear to be any appalling difficulties in the way."

At that time Mr. R. J. Andrew, formerly a partner in the firm of Angas and Co., was at Guatemala, and he consulted the authorities there with regard to the scheme, and found there was a willingness on their part to grant the necessary concessions. At home Mr. Angas was beset with inquiries, Mr. Butterworth and other influential members of the Government, having taken a strong interest in the matter.

The following extract from the diary of Mr. Angas tells the remainder of the story :—

"*February* 14, 1825.—Spent two hours with Mr. Butterworth in relation to cutting a ship canal through the Isthmus of Darien. I recommended a cut into the Pacific through Lake Nicaragua, but I cannot see my way clear to attend to such a work, from the attention my own business requires of me. In 1823 I gave a great deal of consideration to the subject, but it fell to the ground because

Colonel Arthur * left England, and I did not reside in London at
that time.   It is a great and noble undertaking, and will do more
for the cause of God in that country than any other enterprise, by
giving facility of dispatch to Missionaries, and the circulation of
the Word of God.   But though it may be near the scene of our
business operations, it is a work somewhat out of my line."

The subsequent history of the idea is well known.
Baron de Lesseps, having brought the Suez Canal to
a successful completion, undertook the further great
enterprise of cutting a canal through the Isthmus of
Panama, and declared that " he would make it the
work of the closing years of his life."   But the Canal
has not yet been cut.   Meanwhile an American
Company has undertaken to develope the idea of Mr.
Angas, and Mr. Warner Miller, the President of the
Nicaragua Canal Company, estimates that the " cut
into the Pacific through Lake Nicaragua " will be
opened to the traffic of the world in 1897 or thereabouts.

* Colonel, afterwards Sir George Arthur, Bart., K.C.H., D.C.L.,
was appointed Governor of Van Diemen's Land (Tasmania), and
afterwards of Upper Canada. He remained a true friend and
occasional correspondent of Mr. Angas to the end. He died in
1852, at the age of seventy.

CHAPTER III.

PHILANTHROPY.

Fruits of the Evangelical Revival—Dawn of Popular Education—Sunday Schools—Newcastle Sunday School Union—William Henry Angas and Seamen—Mr. Ward—The Serampore Mission—Sailors and Smuggling—In Ramsgate Harbour—Habits and Haunts of Seamen—The Bethel Mission—British and Foreign Sailors Society—Perils of the Seas—Death of William Henry Angas—The Commercial Society—Business on Christian principles.

FROM 1812, when Mr. Angas married, until 1835, when an extraordinary series of events caused him to plunge into the great work of his life, there is little in his history of a picturesque, or striking nature to record. They were years full of business, rich in Christian zeal, fruitful in influence, and withal, years of rapidly increasing prosperity. But all stories of mere mercantile success have a certain monotony about them; narratives of ordinary, albeit consistent and Christian home-life must of necessity be, to a great extent, commonplace, and the record of public engagements undertaken in the early days of the century, have, as a rule, but a slight interest for the present generation.

We should not, however, understand the character

of Mr. Angas, or be able to appreciate the magnitude of the labours in which he was hereafter to engage if we did not glance, however hastily, at the movements of these intermediate years.

A new spirit was abroad in the second decade of the present century, begotten of the great Evangelical revival. The spiritual life of England was just awakening from a sleep of nearly a hundred years. Between the Established Church and the Dissenting bodies a great gulf had been fixed, and only here and there had any attempts been made to bridge it over. Teaching and preaching the gospel by laymen, except among the followers of Wesley, was rare, and met with virulent opposition. Even Nonconformist ministers were often assailed if they attempted to preach in towns or villages apart from their own gloomy little chapels, while Dissenters generally suffered from social, political, and ecclesiastical disabilities.

Education was at a deplorably low ebb; there were vast areas—miles upon miles of country—round every important centre, where no provision whatever was made for the education of poor children. A spirit of turbulence and lawlessness was abroad; the poor were ground down and oppressed; sanitary science was unknown; the amusements of the people were degrading; crime was rampant, and everywhere, and in almost everything, there was pressing need of reform.

The cleansing wind that was to sweep away the

clouds hanging over the intellectual and spiritual life of England was just rustling among the leaves, and sighing in the branches when, in 1812, George Angas entered upon his married life.

Already the Religious Tract Society, founded in the last year of the eighteenth century, was checking the spread of the pernicious cheap literature of the day, while the British and Foreign Bible Society, founded in 1804, had united Evangelical Churchmen and Dissenters in Christian work, and auxiliary Societies were being established in various parts of the country.

Of all the aggressive religious movements inaugurated about this period, however, there were none that claimed the interest of George Angas more than those which related to education.

The institutions which marked the dawn of popular education in Britain were just beginning to make their impression. The first Sunday School Society, planted in 1785, blossomed into the London Sunday School Union in 1803. In 1808 the British and Foreign School Society, mainly a Nonconformist institution, was founded, and in 1811 the Church party established the National School Society. In that same year the first elementary school for adults was opened at Bala, and in 1815, the first infant school was established at Lanark.

In the formation of Sunday schools Mr. Angas took an absorbing interest, and the fact of his having a home of his own, and new ties to engage his atten-

·tion, did not in any way interfere with his zeal in
·this behalf. To him is justly attributed the foundation of Sunday schools in the North of England.

In January, 1814, an attempt was made to found
" The Northumberland and Durham Sunday School
Union," and to forward this scheme the counties
were divided into districts; committees and visiting
deputies were appointed, and the requisite machinery
got together. But although the machinery was
ready, it was too cumbrous to work; steam was
lacking, the engine stood motionless upon the rails,
and eventually was shunted into oblivion.

During this time George Angas, and a few young
men like-minded were zealously at work in Newcastle,
and all the regions round about, driving out every
Sunday to visit existing schools, or to organize new
ones, with the result that just when the Northumberland and Durham Sunday School Union scheme
had fallen to pieces, a sufficient number of schools
had been formed in the neighbourhood of Newcastle
to warrant a large central organization. In 1816,
therefore, Mr. Angas prepared his plans and submitted them to his friends, by whom, as well as by
some of the supporters of the earlier movement, they
were very favourably received. His idea was to
establish a "Newcastle Sunday School Union," and
it was conceived in the most catholic spirit, its
object, as set forth by him, being to " offer assistance in the establishment and encouragement of
Sunday schools connected with every denomination

of Protestant Christians, without presuming to interfere with the constitution, internal management,
or regulations of any school, much less with the
catechisms and books used by them, or the peculiari-
ties of religious views, discipline, or modes of worship
they maintained."

On this solid basis the Newcastle Sunday School
Union was founded, and George Angas—the head
and front of the institution—became one of its two
secretaries. The task he had undertaken was a
severe one, rendered doubly so by the fact that all
the ordinary business of the Union was for a long
time performed without expense to either officials
or teachers. For many miles round, the country
had to be canvassed, enthusiasm aroused, and plans
devised for forming and sustaining school operations.
It was an understood rule among the visitors appointed to this work that each should find a horse
for himself if he wished to drive, and it was an
equally well understood rule that Mr. Angas should
gratuitously provide from the factory vehicles for all
who required them. Thus even extensive tours of
visitation were taken, at no expense to the Union,
and with comparatively little to the individual
visitors. A principal agent in the journeys of Mr.
Angas was his old gray mare, which for frequent
and valuable services, was jocularly voted a " member
of Committee."

The first annual report showed that extraordinary
success had attended the labours of the committee,

there being 67 schools connected with the Union,
1300 teachers, and above 8000 scholars. Sunday-
school work had become a passion with Mr. Angas;
it holds an important place in his diaries; his
first attempts at public speaking were in addresses
to the children, and in meetings on its behalf; and
his time, influence, and money were ready—not at
this time only but all through his long life—to
advance the cause he had so much at heart.

Eight years after the establishment of the Union
Mr. Angas left Newcastle to take up his abode in
London, and it was with no little regret, that he
was obliged to resign the secretaryship. But he
continued for many years to retain his connection
with the Union by accepting the office of vice-
president, and subsequently of president.*

There were other large classes of the community
for whom, during this period, the sympathies of Mr.
Angas were enlisted, and it was to some extent the
zeal of his brother William that called them into
active exercise.

When William Angas gave up a seafaring life he
settled down, in partnership with his brothers, at

---

* His interest in this organization never ceased. In 1869,
three years after the celebration of its Jubilee, he bore the expense
of publishing a " History of the Newcastle-on-Tyne Sunday School
Union. From its formation to the close of its fiftieth year.
Compiled from documents in the possession of George Fife Angas
Esq., first secretary of the Union. Edited by Rev. W. Walters.
Published in London by Sunday School Union, and in Bristol by
W. Mack, 424 pp. 8vo."

Newcastle. But there had long been burning within him an ardent desire to dedicate himself wholly to the service of God and the needs of man, and he was only waiting until a fitting opportunity presented itself to quit business altogether. He had, however, resolved not to desert his post and leave his brothers, already unduly oppressed with care, to manage a department which he best understood.

In course of time a way was made for him. Two of the largest ships of the firm were lost at sea, one in the Atlantic, and one in the North Sea, and this, with other events, combined to make it comparatively easy for him to retire. From a boy he had been acquainted with sailors and seafaring men in general; he had known their lawless and dissolute habits, and had mourned that although all the world was indebted to them, no man seemed to " care for their souls; " in the intervals of business he had visited their haunts in seaport towns, and had sought to promote the cause of God amongst them, but these efforts had of necessity been only occasional, and his desire was to devote the remainder of his life to ministerial and philanthropic work on their behalf.

He proceeded therefore to the University of Edinburgh, where he studied for two years; then, in order to acquire a thorough knowledge of European languages, for the special purpose of subserving the spiritual interests of seamen on foreign coasts, he travelled far and wide upon the continent, and studied

night and day until he was able to preach with
fluency to sailors in Norway, Sweden, Holland,
Russia, France, and Germany, to every man in his
own tongue! In addition to this he resided for
a whole year in a Moravian settlement to acquire
an experience of their simple missionary habits.

In all these movements of his brother, George
Angas took an intense interest. The two were one
in heart in everything that related to Christian work,
and were wont to take mutual counsel on ways of
doing good.

A quotation from the diary of George Angas will
show something of the relations in which they stood
to one another in this respect :—

The ways of Providence are inscrutable. I do not know the
end that God has in view, by the way in which he is leading my
brother William. He may be preparing him for a great work
abroad, and He may be arranging my concerns in England by every
step that I take to become a helper and coadjutor in the same
great, but at present unknown work—I know not indeed its peculiar
nature, but I know its tendency, which will be the advancement
of the Redeemer's Kingdom.

While George looked to his brother for inspiration,
William looked to him with equal anticipation for
aid and sympathy. Thus when William was studying in Holland, he wrote: "I hope, when I shall
have obtained thoroughly what I am here for, to get
alongside of you, and talk all the nights through
with you upon these great, and truly interesting
things."

One of the first enterprizes in which the brothers actively co-operated was in connection with the Serampore Mission.

In the autumn of 1818, Mr. Ward, the coadjutor of Carey and Marshman, came to England for the two-fold purpose of recruiting his health and of raising funds for the Missionary Training Institution at Serampore, Dr. Carey and his colleagues being convinced that as the spiritual wants of the hundred and fifty millions of people in India could never be adequately supplied by missionary labourers from Europe, the work must rest with native agents.

At that time, too, the Baptist Missionary Society was anxious to establish more intimate relations with their friends of kindred sentiment on the Continent, and Mr. Ward was asked to visit Holland, to lay a petition before the king, to stir up the Churches, and especially "to awaken a missionary spirit in the Mennonite community."

William Angas, who had an intimate knowledge of the country and its language, accompanied Mr. Ward on this expedition and acted as interpreter.

Although the visit, so far as the Baptist Society was concerned, produced little result, it had a marked effect upon the lives of both George and William Angas. In the heart of the latter an interest was kindled on behalf of the Mennonites which led him to devote years of labour to their service, while in George enthusiasm was aroused for the Serampore Mission. He met Mr. Ward on his

return from Holland, and an intimacy sprang up
between them. The sympathies of Mr. Angas were
not only enlisted in the cause, but pen, purse, time,
and influence were forthwith put into active operation.

Mr. Ward was a man worth knowing. He was
the first missionary that had ever returned to England from the East, and his welcome was enthusiastic
in almost every circle. His animated addresses ; his
fine expressive countenance, bright hazel eyes, broad
expanse of forehead, and the novelty of his statements—for people in general knew little more in
those days about the Hindus than they did of the
Eskimos, or the dwellers in Timbuctoo—gave a
peculiar interest to his utterances, and riveted the
attention of popular audiences. George Angas
accompanied him on some of his canvassing expeditions, and when in 1821 he left England for India, a
constant correspondence ensued. But it did not last
long. Mr. Ward resumed his labours with all the
energy of improved health, but a period of only sixteen months elapsed before his life was suddenly
terminated by cholera—the first to fall of the three
great missionary heroes who for twenty-three years
had laboured together, animated by one soul and
purpose.

Although pledged to other branches of Christian
work which were demanding almost all his time, Mr.
Angas did not allow his interest in the Serampore
Mission to die out with the death of his friend ; on

the contrary, he was the more diligent to continue his labours. He had laid it down as a principle very early in life, not to undertake anything that he could not carry on until it should have accomplished its end.

In 1823, the year in which Mr. Ward died, an unprecedented flood swept away the greater part of the Mission premises; financial difficulties, with which they should never have been worried, beset the missionaries, and in order to relieve them, Mr. Angas undertook to assist in raising the sum of £3,000, which, with a grant of £2,000 promised by the Bible Society, would, it was hoped, set them upon their feet again.

The sum was raised, but not long after an unhappy difference arose between the missionaries at Serampore and the Society at home, and in response to an application from Dr. Carey, Mr. Angas issued an appeal for financial help, and succeeded in forming a provisional Committee in London, while Mr. Samuel Hope, of Liverpool, did the same in that city. The appeal of Mr. Angas was instrumental in raising the sum of £2,080 for the Mission.

In 1827 he became one of the treasurers of the Serampore Mission Fund, and this at a time when, as we shall see, he was straining every nerve to keep pace with other engagements, and these extra duties could only be performed at the expense of hours which should have been devoted to home, rest, and recreation. But he was indignant "that the brethren

at Serampore should have to endure ' a great fight of
affliction' from false brethren as well as from the
world," and he spared neither time nor money to
assist them, sometimes travelling to Liverpool solely
for the purpose of conferring with Mr. Hope on the
subject. Eventually, at the suggestion of Mr. Angas,
and also at his expense, a paid agent was employed
to collect and arrange for the transmission of the
funds.

We need not follow Mr. Angas in his manifold
labours on behalf of this Mission further than to give
an extract or two from his diaries to point the course
of his actions.

On the 14th of December, 1833, he wrote:

This day I have written to Miss Jane Cook, of Cheltenham, to
request that she will remit her donation of £1,000 to Glyn and
Co., London, in the name of Mr. Samuel Hope. £500 of this is
for the maintenance and education of the native Christians set
apart to preach the gospel at Serampore, £500 for the support of
the different stations belonging to the Serampore Mission. Thanks
be to God for this noble gift.

Some years later the pecuniary difficulties in the
affairs of the Serampore Mission, which he had been
instrumental in alleviating for a time, returned in
force, and it was a source of great regret to him, that,
" having been already committed to other Christian
objects," before the claims of Serampore were brought
under his notice, he could not again fight the battles
of the missionaries.

· It is indeed a melancholy thought (he wrote in his journal in 1837) ; that these devoted men who have done so much for so many years in India, in translating and printing the Scriptures, besides preaching the blessed gospel, should now be left utterly destitute. It is one of the dark mysteries of God's providence !

We must now return to William Angas to see what was one of the most important of the " other Christian objects " to which George was pledged.

On his return from Holland, William Angas threw himself heart and soul into the great work of his life—the evangelization of seamen ; and in every step he took he always had the sympathy, and generally the active co-operation, of his brother. From the various sea-port towns whither he went, he almost invariably wrote to George to tell him of what progress was being made. Some of these letters are extremely interesting.

In this place we can but quote from one or two. He found that on the coast of Kent " Almost every man, woman, and child you meet are smugglers ; the obstacles to the introduction of anything that would make against their craft are insuperable. Nor are the dissipation and dereliction of principle which this unscrupulous practice brings up in its train along with it, the least among these obstacles. To lift up a voice against this monster, and which I have done more than once, is not a very safe thing, for they are a desperate set."

Writing from Ramsgate one Christmas Day, he says :—" In this work of mine the rough quarter of the year may be considered the harvest, or to keep by the fishing simile, the herring season. For it is in winter that the tempest-tossed are driven, in great numbers, to seek the desired haven as a covert and a hiding place. In this respect, this harbour is a great refuge for ships torn from their anchors in the Downs by south-west gales. Not much more than a week ago it was full of vessels of all sizes and rigs, from the proud tri-master that traverses the vast Atlantic down to the humble cod-smack that dabbles around your coasts. Among these were French, Dutch, German, Russian, and Portuguese, besides British and American. A fresh east wind and fair, swept them all out to sea again in a few hours. Others are collecting again. Judge, then, how precious these opportunities must be which bring me into contact with so many nations, without going out of my own, to do them good."

One of the objects of his tour round the Sussex and Kentish coasts, was to provoke as far as possible all good Christians living within sound of the roar of the sea to do something for the benefit of sailors— either in establishing Marine Libraries, or in more direct spiritual efforts, and nothing struck him more than the almost total indifference of the Churches to their welfare.

Meanwhile, George Angas was commencing a crusade in Newcastle, where the needs of seafaring men were daily brought within his knowledge; for in the stream close at hand there was always a crowd of shipping of every build and flag ready to start to all parts of the world with the black diamonds of the Tyne.

It was a great work in which the brothers were engaged. They felt that there was no limit to the good that sailors might accomplish if only they were imbued with the spirit of Christianity; they would become the pioneers to open the door for missionaries in foreign and heathen lands, a door which unhappily their drunkenness and vice had hitherto done so much to keep permanently closed—to neglect them would be to neglect one of the readiest, cheapest, and mightiest means of converting the world to Christ. Moreover, the brothers knew from a life-long experience the character of seamen, their simplicity and kind-heartedness, their ingenuousness and buoyant spirits, their bravery and generosity— qualities which, undirected, often led them astray, but, influenced by the grace of God and disciplined, would make them the most high-minded, noble, and zealous of Christians, capable of winning affection as well as esteem. But even apart from these higher considerations, a crusade on behalf of seamen was needed on merely humanitarian grounds. Dangers beset them everywhere; their vocation exposed them to eminent hazard; life was always held by a precarious tenure, thirty-five was its average length, while 5,000 per annum was the estimated loss of our seamen at that time by drowning. Nor were the dangers on shore much less than those at sea; land sharks, wily crimps, painted courtezans, insinuating publicans, all made poor Jack their target the moment he set his foot on shore. Oftentimes his chest, bedding, wages —all he had—would vanish as soon as he had yielded to the blandishment of the wretches who plied him with grog, and lured him to ruin.

Having finished his studies, William Angas, in May, 1822, was ordained to the office and work of a Missionary to Seafaring Men, the service being held on board the Floating Chapel at Bristol, and the ordination charge delivered by the well-known Dr. Ryland.

Then and there William Angas pledged himself to devote the remainder of his life to constant and persevering activity to advance the moral and spiritual welfare of seamen, to bear all his own expenses, to labour among mariners in every port he could visit, and to induce individuals and churches to direct attention to this neglected department of Christian evangelization.

It seems almost incredible, but it is nevertheless a fact, that when George Angas joined his brother in this important work, there were only two young and feeble societies in existence for promoting the welfare of seamen. Their origin is interesting.

In 1814 one Captain Wilkins, master of a North Shields collier, held the first so-called "Bethel" meeting in the port of London. He invited the crews of the neighbouring vessels to repair on board his own on Sundays for the purpose of Divine

worship, and in due time a flag was hoisted to
signalize the time of assembling to the other
ships, henceforth designated the Bethel Flag. This
singular effort becoming known to some good
Dissenters in East London, "The Port of London
Society for Promoting the Moral and Religious
Welfare of Seamen" was formed in 1817, and on the
4th of May, 1818, the old sloop of war *Speedy*, of
400 tons, having been fitted and moored in the river,
was opened for Divine service, various ministers
officiating from time to time. Thence arose in 1819,
the "Bethel Mission Society," which appointed
special agents to visit seamen on shipboard, and to
preach to the crews, assembling those from the
neighbouring ships by hoisting the "Bethel Flag."

The operations of these two societies were almost
limited to the river Thames, but Mr. Angas had
larger views. He wished to form a society which
should be useful to all men sailing upon the waters
of the whole globe, a British and Foreign Seamen's
Society, whose pretensions should be as large as
those of the British and Foreign Bible Society—
"the one to be separated from the other by the
margin of a water line."

Years, however, were to elapse before he could see
the accomplishment of this wish, and in the meantime he attended to practical matters within his
reach. Thus in 1820 he took an active part in
meetings which resulted in the formation of the
Bethel Seamen's Union, of which he and his brother

became Honorary Foreign Secretaries. In 1822 he attended the opening of the Sailors' Floating Chapel at Liverpool, and was busily engaged in efforts to effect a union of the existing Seamen's Societies, but the desired end was not attained until some years later. In December, 1822, he became President of the Newcastle Seamen's Society (a large deputation waiting upon him to urge his acceptance of the office), and on his removal to London in 1824, he became an active member of the British and Foreign Seamen's Friend Society, and took a prominent part in its operations.

In 1826 the Port of London Society and the Bethel Seamen's Union were united, and six years later one of the finest philanthropic institutions in the kingdom, the British and Foreign Sailor's Society, was established.

For the seamen in his own employment Mr. Angas made the best possible provision by only engaging Christian men as captains and officers who were in sympathy with his wishes. The perils and dangers of a seafaring life were often brought home to him very vividly. Thus in 1824 he received the distressing intelligence that the *George Angas*, one of the vessels of the firm engaged in the Honduras trade, had been taken by pirates in going from Truxillo to Omao, and after fighting for a long time, Mr. Stephenson, one of the most zealous of his missionary captains, together with the crew, was overpowered. A savage blow from the sword of one

of the pirates cut Mr. Stephenson through the head,
and he perished on the spot. George Angas was
deeply moved. "Here is a young man," he wrote in
his journal, "who was apparently the most valuable
agent we had abroad ; who for industry, courage,
and perseverance, was not to be surpassed in
commercial, civil, and religious affairs, thus cut
off amidst health, youth, and usefulness, at a time
too, when of all others his aid was most needed.
His zealous efforts abroad to redress the grievances
of the poor and oppressed slaves and free blacks, and
to promote the cause of Christ, are considerations
which magnify this loss, and make this providence
the more mysterious."

Yet Captain Stephenson was prepared for death.
"How infinitely more sad to think of men perishing
suddenly, and in horrible circumstances, who had
never known the gospel!" It was this thought that
made Mr. Angas unceasing in his efforts on their
behalf.

Among his ever-increasing duties was the cultivation of a friendly interest, by correspondence and
conversation, with his missionary captains, to whom
he looked for full information as to the welfare of his
crews, and of the influence for good they had exerted
in the ports they visited. Captain Pearson of the
brig *William*, was one of his most reliable men.
He had married a daughter of the heroic Captain
Wilson, who in the ship *Duff* conducted the first
missionaries to the South Sea Islands, and Mr.

Angas was instrumental in persuading her to devote her life to the best interests of sailors' wives.

Captain Pearson wrote long and interesting letters detailing his labours under the Bethel flag, and his intercourse with the negroes in their misery and degradation groaning under the horrible slavery then existing in the West India Islands. Sometimes his stories were good, as when, for example, he recorded ,a conversation with "Old Peggy," a Christian negress, who said:—"My greatest trouble, Massa, am my own wicked heart; even 'pon my bed it wander here and it wander dere; it jump 'pon dis ting, and it jump 'pon dat; and it neber catch any rest, till I fix him 'pon my Maker."

Of all his correspondents, however, there was none whose letters brought such ever fresh inspirations as those of his brother William, who was here, there, and everywhere—now engaging in controversy with Dutch Socinians, or stirring up men to action in foreign universities; now lending the Moravian missionaries a helping hand, or seeking out and supporting at his own expense earnest men studying for the continental ministry.

But the chief burden of his letters was the welfare of seamen. In 1832 he wrote:—"Nothing is more evident to me than that a pious seaman has far more opportunities to promote the work of God among his brother seamen on the stormy element itself, than any one could possibly have on shore. So powerfully convinced am I of this, that I have been more than once tempted to make a long voyage or two for the purpose of making facts speak for themselves. . . . But I still keep on casting the net among my poor perishing brethren of the sea who are found in such shoals on these coasts; with what success another day must declare."

That was one of the last letters he wrote. In September of that year, while at work among the sailors of South Shields where cholera was raging, he was stricken down by that terrible disease and in a few hours passed away.

He was buried in the Westgate Hill Cemetery, Newcastle-on-Tyne, where the following inscription may still be read :—

IN MEMORY
OF THE LATE WILLIAM HENRY ANGAS.

——

Being made early acquainted with the
Saviour of Sinners,
He was deeply impressed with the desire of
Consecrating all the Energies of his life
To the spiritual interests of his fellow-men
The lamentable state of his brethren on the Sea
Engaged his special attention ;
And for their sakes
(After enduring many hardships, in French prisons,
In shipwrecks, in tempests, and in unhealthy climates,
During which
He zealously laboured for their moral
And religious welfare),
He gave up all secular pursuits, and visited
The principal seaports of Great Britain and Jamaica,

And the continent of Europe;
Where he
Successfully laboured to bring sailors under
The sound of the glorious gospel of the blessed God.
In this work
He was engaged at South Shields
When suddenly called to quit his labours
And to enter into the joy of his Lord.
He died, deplored by all,
September 7th, 1832.   Aged 51 years;
And was interred beneath
This memorial of fraternal affection.

———

His record is on high; the stone we raise
Exalts the Saviour—not the servant's praise.
He loved the sons of ocean, and he bore
The sound of heavenly grace from shore to shore.
He fix'd his anchor firm within the vail,
And bless'd the Refuge that could never fail;
The billows rose—he smiled, with Heaven in view,
And dying, proved his living witness true.—E. R.

Although not possessing extraordinary eloquence
he was made the instrument of great good to innumerable persons of all ranks and conditions; Mr.
Tauchnitz, of Leipzic, under his guidance shaped
the career which was fraught with so much blessing
to his countrymen; Pastor Oncken, whose astounding
labours in Hamburg are known in all the churches,
was one of his sons in the faith; while thousands
of sailors at home and abroad blessed God for his
ministry.

The death of his brother was a bitter sorrow and

a severe loss to George Angas. Great enterprises
were looming before him in the near future, and
his friend and counsellor could never more aid him.
But one special object on which the hearts of the
brothers had been set might be accomplished, and
only a few months elapsed before George Angas
was seated in the vestry of the Rev. John Clayton,
with Dr. F. A. Cox and other notable friends of
seamen, discussing the advisability of establishing
a new Sailors' Society. It was resolved to go
forward, and Mr. Angas undertook the heavy task
of "sounding the friends of seamen throughout the
country." A few months later (May 6, 1833), at
a crowded public meeting in the London Tavern,
with the Lord Mayor (Sir Peter Laurie) in the chair,
the new Society was floated. So encouraging were
its prospects that the members of the original
association deemed it advisable to join the new
organization, and in July the amalgamated institution became the famous "British and Foreign Sailors'
Society, for promoting the Moral and Religious
Welfare of Seamen," with Lord Mountsandford as
president, Alderman Pirie and George Fife Angas,
treasurers, the Revs. Dr. Cox and T. Timpson,
secretaries, and a committee of about sixty of the
most influential merchants and ministers in London.

We must not close this chapter on the early
philanthropic labours of Mr. Angas which were
successful without glancing at one attempt in which
he failed.

Having proved that it was possible for a single firm, by sending out Christian men as captains and agents, to effect much good among the natives and others in the lands where such commercial relations had been established, Mr. Angas was naturally anxious that the experiment should be widely extended. From time to time he broached the subject to influential merchants whom he regarded as like-minded, and in 1825 he put forth a prospectus of "The Society for Promoting Christianity and Civilization through the medium of Commercial, Scientific, and Professional Agency." The object of the proposed society was to render the influence of those engaged in these pursuits subservient to the advancement of true religion, and the promotion of civilization throughout the world.

Mr. Angas wrote with reference to the scheme :—

Of all the channels through which the benevolence of the private Christian may be brought into successful operation none bids fairer for extended and varied usefulness than that presented to those who are engaged in mercantile concerns. By means of the correspondence which they maintain with all parts of the world, they have it in their power to elicit and collect accurate information respecting the state of the different tribes of men ; and from the very intercourse necessary to their avocations, they attain that minute and special knowledge of the individual character of those with whom they transact business which must best qualify them for devising the most likely methods to be adopted for conveying the blessings of the gospel, and of civilized life, and for aiding in the selection of the fittest instruments for carrying these methods into effect.

It was further proposed that agents, travelling for the purposes of trade, should be the means of spreading the most recent intelligence relative to the progress of Christianity in other parts of the world, and of pointing out how the salient features of new movements might be adapted to the service of the countries visited.

No one will deny that it was a large and comprehensive scheme—many applauded it. Dr. Chalmers, in a letter to Mr. Angas, said : " There is nothing that delights me more than the impregnation of ordinary business, throughout all its arrangements and details, with the spirit of an expansive and evangelical charity. It is a high walk that you have entered upon, I entreat your perseverance in it—the conception is a most felicitous one." Another correspondent, Dr. Dick, the author of the " Christian Philosopher," considered such a society was " Essentially requisite in order to carry the operations of Bible, missionary, and other philanthropic associations into full effect." The Rev. Dr. Fletcher, of London, Professor Chase, of Columbia College, America, and many more good and eminent men spoke and wrote with enthusiasm of the scheme, while Mr. James Douglas in his work on " The Advancement of Society in Knowledge and Religion," said : " If only ten could be found who were like-minded, we might hail the commencement of their operations as the beginning of better days, and look forward to the merchants of Britain and America as those who shall take an eminent part in the glorious work of evangelizing the world."

But where were the ten ?   They were not at that time to be found in Britain.   That the world would be better if the pioneers of commerce by action and precept would convey the blessings of civilization to the inhabitants of the new countries they trade with, many were ready to concede, but although meetings were held to advance the scheme, and much correspondence ensued, very few were prepared to take any active and practical part in furthering it, and during the great commercial panic of 1825–6, it fell to the ground.

CHAPTER IV.

HOME AND BUSINESS.

DURING the years of which we have written in the
preceding chapter, the domestic life of Mr. Angas
had been enriched by many new ties. His first child
was born in 1813, his last in 1832, the family consisting of three sons and four daughters.

In the welfare of his children, and especially as
regarded their education and spiritual concerns, he
took an intense interest, but he does not appear to
have been a family man in the sense in which that
term is generally understood. His main delights
were not in the midst of quiet home life. Not that
he was destitute in any degree of home love, parental
affection, or capacity for domestic enjoyment; but
simply because the current of life was too swift to
allow him to rest upon its banks. It is a fact that

men who have made success in business an enthusiasm, like those who have made philanthropy and
religious work a business, are not as a rule the best
home companions. Life is too much occupied to
allow sufficient intervals for rest and recreation; its
pauses are not employed so much in enjoyment as in
recovering spent energies; the calm and tranquil
pleasures of home life, if not unknown, are not of
frequent recurrence; the blessedness of leisure is
rarely enjoyed; the stream rushes along at full
tide and rarely meanders in the quiet woods and
meadows.

In those busy years the intellectual faculties of
Mr. Angas were sharpened, the range of his knowledge widened, and his skill in business developed.
He loved commercial enterprise as a literary man
loves literature, or an artist loves art; it was the
main channel he had chosen for his activities, and
they flowed into it fully, naturally, and freely.

Wanting to make the most of life, Mr. Angas was
an early riser. He found it necessary to economize
time, and as one of the easiest methods was to sleep
less, he was in the habit of rising at four or five in
the morning in order to secure time for reading,
meditation, and prayer.

Within ten years of his marriage there rested
upon his shoulders the main burden of the large establishment at Newcastle, with branches at London,
Liverpool, Aberdeen, Dundee, Leith, and Durham,
besides the trade with Spanish America, the West

Indies, and elsewhere, and an overwhelming multiplicity of public and private affairs. This load of care was pressing heavily upon him, and his health, never robust, showed signs of giving way altogether. Of an anxious temperament, and with a sensitive conscience, every fresh business transaction filled him with anxiety. It is well that this should be borne in mind, as by and by we shall find him engaged in undertakings which might have made the most iron-nerved man quail. '

Business pressure is hard enough to bear when the bodily health is robust, but it is exceptionally trying in times of feebleness. It is not surprising, therefore, that in such circumstances Mr. Angas should sometimes take a gloomy view of his case, and, in 1823, we find him, in the language of Scripture, "setting his house in order," so that he "might not have anxieties and perplexities to distract his last hours." The fact was that he had long been carrying heavier burdens than his strength could bear, and had found no time for air and exercise, or for amusement and recreation. It is always an error to work incessantly; the hardest workers have confessed it, and later in life Mr. Angas added his testimony to this general verdict.

In 1824 it became clear that unless he abandoned his large and ever-increasing foreign business, it would be imperative for him to leave Newcastle and reside in or near London, and as a preliminary step he took offices in East India Chambers, Leadenhall

Street. What followed was brought about so gradually and imperceptibly that he had little more to do
than acquiesce in a movement which had become
inevitable.

There ,is sadness in leaving the home of early
married life, in severing old ties and associations, in
quitting " the paternal hearth, that rallying-place of
the affections," and had it not been for the belief that
God " fixes the bounds of our habitation," he would
have shrunk back at last from the step. There was
probably no· other day in his life when he was more
deeply moved than on one Sunday in August when
he took formal leave of the New Court Church at
Newcastle, with which so much of his religious
life had been associated. A farewell sermon was
preached by Mr. Sample, the pastor, and after the
service the church members remained " to specially
commend the family to God "—a good old custom in
vogue when church life was a much more real affair
than it is to-day.

Ilford, in Essex, at that time a charming suburb
of London almost in the heart of the country, was
selected by Mr. Angas as the place of his new
residence, and there he remained for several years.

Scarcely had he commenced business in London
than he was beset by many new and unexpected
anxieties. The years 1825–6 will always be
memorable in the commercial annals of this
country for the great panic which threatened the
overthrow of many, if not most, of the largest

mercantile houses in England. It was a time
of general disquiet, and George Angas was
naturally in a state of painful uneasiness. He
had given liberal credit to his customers, but
the sellers were clamouring for cash payments,
and in the pressing demands made upon him he
sometimes feared lest he should not weather the
storm.

The year 1826 opened disastrously for the
mercantile world. A glimpse of the state of the
times is given in the following extract from his
journal :—

Feb. 16.—For the past few days things have been getting worse
and worse. The 3 per cent. Consols are down to 74, and all foreign
securities from 35 to 45 per cent. less value than the contracting
prices. A multitude of failures have occurred, and confidence
between man and man is nearly destroyed. To add to this gloom,
Government has ordered the withdrawal of all £1 and £2 county
bank notes before three years, and bankers are to give security for
the other notes which they issue ; all tending to make money
scarcer than ever, and to place merchants in awful difficulty and
perplexity. . . . I cannot be too thankful that Providence has thus
far preserved our house through all its difficulties. There is daily
destruction of many mercantile houses, and more would unques-
tionally have stopped payment but for the aid of the Bank of
England, and we must apparently have fallen but for this timely
assistance.

Not when he penned these lines, nor for three
years later, did George Angas know that his good old
father, Caleb, had been shielding him in the midst

of these financial storms.　In 1829, George wrote in his diary :—

When lately at Newcastle my father adverted to the circumstance of his sending a letter to Messrs. Currie and Co., bankers, with an ôffer of bonds and mortgages as security for me for £10,000 during the panic.　My father said that one morning as he was sitting at breakfast thinking of the state of mercantile affairs in London, it was strongly impressed upon his mind that I might be none the worse if he made a demonstration ·of help in my favour at such a crisis.　I had said nothing about it in any of my letters ; indeed I felt so safe and strong as not to need any help.　With that native energy that characterized my father's mind he thought, determined, and acted, and wrote by that day's post.　Now it appears that had he delayed one day longer I must have dishonoured some heavy bills, and probably have become bankrupt, or at least have sought time from my creditors.　Glory to God for thus influencing my father's mind.

This, and similar occurrences, confirmed him in his belief that it was possible " to make God a factor in every business relation."　Some of his notes on Commerce and Christianity, or business in relation to God, may be quoted here.　Thus in October, 1826, the year of panic, he writes :—

The circumstances of a British merchant in London, and in these times, present such singular obligations as to render it difficult to say where, when, and how, he may draw round his affairs a line of circumvallation. . . . It seems that at present the only rule of judgment is the measure of his time, and the measure of his pecuniary capital, and both of these in my case are broken in upon by previous connections and untoward circumstances.

Notwithstanding this, he was not a man to worship principle and wink at practice. In that same year, when every pound was an object, he wrote in his journal :—

I have this day been advised of a sum of insurance money due to me from the loss of the *Aurora*, and I cannot do better than consecrate the whole to the God of Missions. I have been in great want of money, and am at this time, but as this is a God-send in one sense, it shall help the cause of the Redeemer, and may God bless its use when it is placed in His treasury.

On the 4th of November, 1826, George Angas dissolved partnership with his brother, John Lindsay Angas, and thus became released from a share in the management of the coach manufactory at Newcastle —a consummation he had long desired. The mercantile and shipping business was still to be carried on there under the firm of Angas and Co., and in London under that of " G. F. Angas and Co."

All the arrangements were settled in " a perfectly agreeable, honourable, and satisfactory manner to both parties," and considering the varied, complicated, and extensive nature of the transactions, this spoke well for the brothers. Under the new *régime* it was necessary for George Angas to establish a separate place of business at Newcastle, which was placed in charge of Mr. James Grant, an old Sunday-school colleague. A change of offices was also made in London, and Mr. Angas removed to No. 2, Jeffrey Square (St. Mary Axe).

The years spent in London and Ilford were fruitful in many works of usefulness. Among the matters in which he was particularly interested was the British and Foreign School Society, and in the direction of its affairs as one of the Committee he took an active part.

It was at his instigation and expense that Mr. and Mrs. Henry Dunn went out to Guatemala to establish the Lancasterian school system in that country —an enterprise which failed of its purpose; and subsequently he obtained for Mr. Dunn the appointment of Secretary to the Committee of the Society. Referring to this, Mr. Angas says:—

It is delightful to see such a growing spirit of piety infused into the Committee and Council of the British and Foreign School Society; the new secretary, Mr. Scott is, happily, full of zeal. Well will it be if Mr. Dunn should also be associated with Mr. Scott in this Society, to take the oversight of the young men training as schoolmasters. Surely, if the streams are to be fertilizing the fountain ought to be pure. I am glad that the last report attaches due importance to the religious education of the scholars, and thus redeems it from the charge of indifference to that subject.

He watched with pleasure the gradual crumbling away of the middle wall of partition which had so long kept Churchmen and Dissenters apart, and lost no opportunity in helping forward any movement which might accelerate this desired end. On visiting Newcastle, in 1828, he attended the anniversary meeting of the Sick Society, and was much struck to

see "the contrast during the past twenty years.
Churchmen and Dissenters are engaged in visiting
the sick, and supplying the temporal and spiritual
wants of the whole town." Sunday-school work
had always a fascination for him, and now that two
of his daughters were diligent and enthusiastic
teachers, his sympathies were more than ever drawn
out in that direction, and most of his Sundays—or
rather, "the intervals between Divine worship," as
the phrase went—were occupied in active engagements on this behalf.

For more than twenty years he had been almost
continually a sufferer, until, as he says, he had
become "enfeebled in body, soul, and spirit."
Throughout his diaries he makes frequent reference
to this, and also to his "irritable disposition," which
he constantly deplores. Every man has his infirmity,
and there is no gainsaying the fact that Mr. Angas
was not always a good-tempered man. This failing
was partly constitutional, partly the result of his lack
of child-life, partly induced by the strictness of his
religious beliefs, partly caused by over-work and
chronic ill-health, partly by lack of diversity and
amusement.

No one was more conscious of the fact than himself, and he regretted it bitterly. Some of the
confessions in his diary are painful reading.

Thus, in reviewing the year, 1829 :—

Supineness of mind, bodily inertness, irritability of temper,

pride, and self-glorification have been dreadful combatants all
through the year. It is indeed possible, and perhaps probable,
that the state of my health and consequent weakness of nerve may
have been the cause of much that I deplore. I feel that to be consistent I must be more meek and lowly of heart—my peace and
happiness demands it; my usefulness demands it; my family
demands it. Oh how anxiously do I desire it too. The chief
of my unhappiness has arisen from this sole cause. Many a time
have I groaned within me, being weary, tormented, afflicted, and
distressed. . . . And still my progress is so slow, my spirit is so
haughty, and my temper unsubdued. . . .

In the case of many successful merchants, life in
all its varied departments has gone on steadily and
smoothly with them. It was not so with George
Angas, his career was full of fluctuations. Thus,
while he was residing for a time at Cheltenham, the
coach factory at Angas Court, Newcastle, was burnt
to the ground and very few of the books were saved ;
the shipping trade was a much more precarious affair
then than it is now, and there were ebbs and flows
in the tide of business generally, more sudden and
sweeping perhaps than is often experienced by the
commercial world of to-day. In 1830 Mr. Angas
writes :—

A most remarkable and permanent revolution for the worse has
taken place in the foreign commerce of Britain, the effects of
which continue to this day, and are gradually altering the whole
character and employment of the old, true, and real British merchant. Before the year 1825 mercantile business generally yielded
a profit, so also did shipping, but from the time of the panic every
year has been more and more discouraging. Up to the autumn of

1825, we had a profit on every import of mahogany, but since that
period every vessel has left losses from 15 to 65 per cent. on the
invoice cost at Honduras. . . . It has been the hope of better
times and a disinclination to throw any of my people out of employment that has induced me to go on from year to year, until my
capital has been reduced at least one-half, if not more. The crisis
however has now come when necessity compels me to decline all
foreign business. I have been reading in *The Quarterly Review* for
May, 1830, an article on the causes of the national distress, which
accords entirely with my experience on the subject. The writer
attributes the origin of it to the rise in the value of precious metals,
and to the increased demand in Europe for a metallic circulating
medium, together with the decreased supply from America. Of
course as the precious metals rise in value, all goods decrease in the
same ratio. This writer recommends merchants to do no business
until the evils are removed, as the only possible way to save the
little capital left in the hands of any one. These are truly
eventful times both at home and abroad, with 'distress of
nations.'

On his return from a further visit to Cheltenham
in 1831, he found himself at once overwhelmed with
work, and truly he had many things upon his hands:
the three vessels *Ocean*, *William*, and *Caleb Angas*;
the commercial business with Honduras, Buenos
Ayres, and London; the coach factories at Newcastle
and Durham; mahogany trade and copperas works in
the North. To these may be added the care of a
large and growing family, and the inevitable business
that philanthropic work brings with it.

Just when he was feeling the strain of this
accumulation of things, he received a letter from
his father requesting him, in consequence of old age

and failing strength, to take the entire management of his affairs. George could not do otherwise than respond heartily and promptly. But only a few days elapsed before he received the sad intelligence—not altogether unexpected—that his father was seriously ill, and evidently near his end. He proceeded at once to Newcastle, and arrived in time to receive the old man's blessing, and to hear the expression of his last wishes. On the 14th of May, 1831, Caleb Angas sank peacefully to rest at the advanced age of 89.

As in the case of so many other families, death followed death rapidly. Within two months, George Angas had to mourn the loss of a beloved daughter; early in the following year he received the painful news of the death of his partner in Honduras, Mr. R. J. Andrews, whose return in the *Caleb Angas* he was daily expecting—" a faithful and beloved friend, companion, and counsellor; " and a few months later there came the distressing intelligence of the death by cholera of his brother William, with whom he had been more intimately associated in all kinds of Christian and philanthropic work than with any one else in the world. He wrote in his diary on the 10th of September, 1832 :—

Little did I expect when I drove the Rev. John Campbell, of Kingsland, up to London in my chaise this morning, that such melancholy intelligence awaited me at my counting house. . . . According to his talent he was a burning and a shining light, and few men could be found of greater philanthropy, or more noble disinterestedness in the great cause of Jesus. May the mantle of his zeal and devotedness fall on his brethren yet alive, and may I love and serve Thee more than ever I did in my life!

The year 1832 was eventful. In view of the Reform Bill passing, many of the friends of Mr. Angas urged him to stand for the representation of Newcastle in Parliament. The idea was repugnant to him. He wrote, "I have neither time nor talent for such work." But scarcely had he declined the invitation of his friends at Newcastle to become a candidate for that town, than a similar proposal was made by friends at Sunderland. A week later he received a formal application to stand for Pontefract, the electors promising to return him free of all expense. His reflections were as follows :—

My mind has been painfully exercised in spite of every wish to satisfy myself that I am not called upon to take an active part in the civil affairs of the nation. I have an impression that I cannot be absolved from a share of the work in removing the dreadful moral, political, and religious evils which are destroying the bodies and souls of my countrymen. I have endeavoured to entrench myself behind the principle of the non-interference of the disciples of Christ with the affairs of worldly kingdoms, for He said, ' My kingdom is not of this world.' I have tried to excuse myself on the ground of health, limited capacity, lack of the power of elocution. I have thought that my business demands all my time and strength. But these considerations are not weighty enough to counterbalance still more serious ones affecting the country at this awful juncture. It is now certain that vast good or evil will depend upon the character, morals, principles, and the independence of the next House of Commons. All the titles, wealth, and des-

potism of the nation will be ranged against the reformation and
removal of the abuses in Church and State which have too
evidently caused the wickedness, poverty, and misery of the land.
The Reformers and Dissenters have a great duty to perform, which
Providence has called them to discharge with honesty and justice,
but the great difficulty in the way is the want of proper men to
send to Parliament. Such men are really not to be found in the
higher ranks of life; nearly all the aristocracy being Tories, corrupted more or less with riches.

In the early days of Mr. Angas the sentiment was
almost universally prevalent among Dissenters that
" professors of the gospel " ought not to take any
part in public or political affairs.   The Test and Corporation Acts barred every man from office unless he
took the Lord's Supper as a qualification.   And even
when this point was ceded, it was notorious that
Dissenters were almost entirely excluded from every
post of emolument and trust in all civil, military,
ecclesiastical,   and   political   departments   under
Government.   Making a virtue of necessity, many
posed as though principle alone were keeping them
out of office, and to a certain extent this was the
case, their consciences not permitting them to conform to the unjust and bigoted terms imposed upon
them by the State.   But when many of these
obstructions were removed, Dissenters were placed
in quite a different position in relation to public
duties.   They could neither urge necessity, nor
violation of conscience—nothing except the strained
and old-fashioned notion that political office was

7

incompatible with Christian duties.   Mr. Angas had
no sympathy with this view.

Now that Dissenters are admissible to every office of the State
(he wrote), the providence of God appears to call upon them not
to shrink from public duty of any kind.   Their position may be
pregnant with danger, but let them daily pray to Almighty God for
grace to meet the danger ; not to flee from it, but to boldly advance
and grapple with all its difficulties, carrying their religion into the
world, and into public office, but never allowing the office or its
associations to rob them of their religion.

At that particular juncture, however, he did not
see his way clear to accept either of the invitations
he had received to stand for Parliament, but meanwhile he interested himself actively to secure the
return of "Wellesley and Leonard for the county of
Essex," feeling that "the time had come when, as a
Dissenter, he should make a demonstration in favour
of civil and religious liberty."

Of the agitated state of the country at the time of
passing the Reform Bill, when the air was thick with
rumours, and the most conflicting statements were
bandied about, all claiming to be authoritative, a
graphic picture is drawn in the following extracts
from the diary :—

All business is at a stand-still.   No one knows what to do.   No
ministry is yet formed.   The accounts from all parts of the country
express a feeling of the greatest indignation at the King (or rather
the Queen) and his advisers behind the throne, who evidently
possess a greater power than the King himself, which is the true

cause of his failure to keep his promises to Earl Grey, and fulfil his good intentions towards the country. The City of London has sent an address to the House of Commons advising it to withhold supplies until the Reform Bill passes. Every part of the kingdom resolves to pay no taxes in money till Reform passes, and many say no tithes will be paid till then. . . . At this moment the Oligarchy are our rulers proved beyond doubt by Earls Grey and Brougham being forced to resign. It was last week ' the King and People '—it is this week ' the King and nobles ! ' Here commences a conflict of most intense interest to both civil and religious liberty, not only to Britain and her Colonies, but to every country under heaven. . . . The Tories both in and out of office are the decided, uncompromising enemies of civil and religious liberty all over the world, and had it not been for the great and bold spirit and combination of the British people at this moment, we should have been as Russia and Prussia. A conflict of a terrible kind is inevitable unless the Lord in mercy disposes the King's heart to take back his ministers, or by some means to grant the Reform of Parliament. It appears to me to be the perfection of folly for the peers to dare this conflict, and to put the Duke of Wellington at the head of affairs, who is but too disposed to coercive measures against a whole nation. . . . Many fear that the new Government will go to war with France to divert the attention of the people from home affairs.

1832. *May* 18. . . . Some opinion of the intensity of public feeling may be gathered from the report in to-day's *Times* of the spontaneous meeting held at Birmingham by the Political Union to express their congratulations upon receiving intelligence that the Duke of Wellington had failed to form a Ministry, and that the King had sent for Earl Grey again, which the meeting construed into the virtual carrying of the whole unimpaired Reform Bill. The first feeling of the vast multitude was a most affecting expression of gratitude to God for bringing about such a desired end by His providence, and thereby saving the country from a civil war. The chairman desired a clergyman to express the thanks of the people for this mercy, when all took off their hats, and a dead silence ensued, while a prayer of thanksgiving was offered up to the Almighty.

May 19.—The glorious news was laid before the country that Lord Grey was authorized by the King to carry the Reform Bill unimpaired, and that of course the present ministers retain their places. All the country agrees that we were just on the point of a revolution. A few days more, and blood would have been shed, and no man can tell when it would have ended. Thanks be to God for His salvation.

The invitation to stand for Newcastle was made in the first instance by personal friends, but after the passing of the Reform Bill the Baptists, Independents, Methodists, Presbyterians, and Friends, united for the purpose of putting Mr. Angas forward as one of the representatives of that town. A definite answer was necessary, and he gave it in the negative. Two years later a similar appeal was made to him from the same quarter, but at that time he was more reluctant than in 1832. For then his health was in a very precarious state, and he shrank with a feeling of dread from the noise and excitement of parliamentary life. Although strongly urged by such men as Mr. Samuel Hope of Liverpool, Mr. John Fenwick of Newcastle, and Mr. Thos. Harbottle of Manchester—each man a centre of widespreading influence—he came to this conclusion:

I am now decided in my course. I am fully persuaded that it is my duty to retire for a season from active public life, to re-establish my health, nerves, and constitution, hoping that after the country becomes more peaceable and quiet I may then come forward to advance its true interests.

That time never arrived, although in 1835 Mr. J. G. Shaw-Lefevre, then Colonial Secretary, urged him strongly to enter the House of Commons. But he was then in the midst of his great labours in founding the Colony of South Australia, and it would have been madness to add to the burdens already too heavy for him.

From the early age of eighteen, when he established in his father's factory a Savings Bank and Provident Fund for working men, George Angas had shown strong proclivities towards banking and kindred institutions. In 1828 his cousin, Mr. Thomas Joplin, who had made banks and banking a speciality, and had written various pamphlets on the subject, submitted to him a scheme for associating a number of provincial banks together, with a certain amount of local government, but under the general manage-ment of a central establishment in London, such institution to be called " The National Provincial Bank of England."

Singular as it may appear, the probable expense of making the experiment was estimated at the modest sum of £300, which Mr. Angas was asked to advance, and, in the event of success ensuing, he was to be-come a Director. At first he did not respond, but on a renewal of the application in the following year, he promised to find the amount required for necessary expenses, to take a certain number of shares, and to become a Director.

The time, however, was not then ripe, owing to

the disturbed state of the country, and the political
changes consequent upon the passing of the Reform
Bill. It was not, therefore, until April, 1833, that
the scheme was revived, and his opinions upon it are
given in the following extract from his diary :—

April 13.—The plans and principles commend themselves to my
judgment, and I think the present a favourable time to introduce
such a measure; besides, it is likely to decide the great and perplexing dispute raging at this time between the Conservatives and
Whigs, or rather between the Currency Club, who wish to raise
prices by an over-issue of paper, and the Political Economists who
have got the standard of metal in currency established, and wish
to keep it so that all prices may be low—cheap food and cheap
everything. There is also a third party in the dispute, namely,
Dr. Chalmers, who advocates low prices and high wages. The
principle of this bank being an extension of the currency upon
safe and sound principles, only to be limited in its supply by
real security of capital and in its issue by the real and national
demands of the empire, does appear to me to meet the views
of both parties, and it will improve and extend the currency as
much as they will desire. It will afford a limit, and security
quite equal to a metallic currency without the danger, expense,
and inconvenience of it. And as to the other party, if it does
not keep down the price of food, it will assist to raise the wages
of labour, and most certainly it will be a valuable handmaid to
the exertions of the Government to create new channels of trade
and demand for labour, besides affording the means of employing
industry, and producing that quantity of provisions which will
come so near the increased demand as to at least prevent the rise
in the prices of food and goods becoming a serious disadvantage.
Government must create the demand for the employment of
labour, and this bank will afford the means of supplying it. With
respect to my taking a personal interest and active part in the

management of this institution, I had quite given up the thought of it.

It was not to be expected that a large undertaking like this could be started without difficulty, and throughout this year we find constant notes in the diary referring to frequent, protracted, and somewhat stormy meetings, and had it not been for the sake of his cousin Mr. Joplin, he would have retired from the direction. On the 4th of August he records with satisfaction :—

Last night, after some difficulty and discussion, I succeeded in getting Mr. Joplin's name placed in the Deed of Settlement for the new National Bank as one of the Directors, and *as the originator of the Bank*.

This was perfectly true, but it was an unusual instance of disinterestedness as the scheme would probably never have been accomplished but for the persistent labours of Mr. Angas, and for his supply of the sinews of war.

A few weeks later he writes :—

It was desired that my name should be put into the Deed as one of six. . . . I have decided to sit on the Board.

Mr. Angas was not accustomed "to do things by halves," and having seen his way to take an active and prominent part in the affairs of the bank, he entered heartily upon his new duties, and at the end of a year was able to record that nearly every day he had been in attendance.

But in 1836, when resident at Dawlish in Devonshire, he found it impossible to retain a grip upon
the affairs of the bank at that distance from the
scene of operations, and he had laid it down as a
business principle "not to occupy any post, the
duties of which he could not attend to fully." Moreover, he had accomplished the end he had in view;
the bank had overcome all its initial difficulties,
more than fifty branches and agencies had been
established, and were in good working order;
shares had gone up firmly and rapidly; in addition to this Mr. Joplin "with whom," he says, "I
was the chief agent in the establishment of the
concern from the very outset," had left the direction and an entirely new set of men, with whom
Mr. Angas had little or no sympathy, then sat upon
the Board.

But there was one reason which overweighed
all the others. A far vaster matter was claiming
every hour of his time, and all the energy of his
mind, and he sought to avoid everything which
diverted his attention from it. At the end of 1836,
therefore, he resigned his position on the Board
of the National Provincial Bank, which in conjunction with his cousin, he had so successfully
founded.

It was with a perfectly justifiable pride and
pleasure that, many years afterwards, he pasted in
his diary a cutting from the *Economist*, which
ran as follows :—

Next to the Bank of England there is hardly any bank of which the substantial soundness is so important as that of the National Provincial Bank of England. It runs through every part of England; if its credit is good, it strengthens all other credit; if it were not good, it would weaken all other credit; and therefore it is most satisfactory to find that we have such thorough and complete grounds for national reliance upon it.*

The Fifty-Seventh Annual Report of the National Provincial Bank of England, issued the 8th of May, 1890, is an amusing commentary on the correspondence lying before the present writer relating to the matter of "£300, the probable expense of making the experiment" of its foundation.

The Report shows a subscribed capital of £12,037,500; a reserve fund, invested in English Government securities, of £1,450,000; the number of shareholders as 8,921; the profits for the current year, after making all necessary deductions, £515,206 14s. 6d.

It would be impossible to refer in detail to the enormous amount of work that fell to the lot of Mr. Angas in the years 1832–3. In addition to the labours we have already indicated, he was lecturing or addressing crowded meetings on Slavery, the state of Missions in Jamaica, and other religious questions of the day; he was acting as treasurer of the Baptist Continental Society, and had accepted office as deacon of the Baptist Church at Ilford, besides the

* *Economist*, May 11, 1867.

routine of labour in connection with the various philanthropic institutions to which he was already pledged.

In May of this year, 1833, he writes :—

I have been unwell for several days, and during this period of great depression of mind and body, I have been most singularly situated, for I had the *Excellent* in from Honduras to deliver her cargo, refit, and sail again, and all my letters and despatches to prepare and forward by her. I had the *Caleb Angas* to unload, and go through a considerable repair, her outfit to be made, her large shipment of goods to prepare, and get her clear at the Customs. I had last night a public sale of a mahogany cargo to arrange for. I had to attend the provisional committee of the new National Provincial Bank almost daily, and direct my best energies of mind to its affairs. I had also the new Sailors Society to confer upon, form a committee, and attend all the preliminary arrangements under the most perplexing difficulties and obstacles, besides the Slavery agitation and many other matters.

A month later when in Wales with several members of his family, he hired a conveyance to visit some slate quarries. In descending a precipitous hill, part of the harness gave way, and but for his presence of mind in acting on the instant in concert with the driver, a terrible catastrophe would have ensued. " The Lord saved us," he said, " by as marvellous a deliverance as the imagination could paint, from instant and horrible destruction." He could not for some time afterwards think of the subject without a sickening sense of horror.

Towards the end of 1833, he had some thought

of leaving Ilford, and removing to Devonshire. It was not however until March of the following year, that he took up his abode at Park House, Dawlish. Distant as it was from his place of business, he was so accustomed to long journeys, that he thought the disadvantages would be more than counterbalanced by the increase in health of himself and his family. He had no intention of withdrawing from business or public life; on the contrary, he held the reins of all his large concerns with a tighter grip than ever, and was casting about in his mind, as health improved, for more extended spheres of usefulness.

In every fresh session of Parliament, the claims of Nonconformists were coming more and more to the front, and he was often asking himself whether the time had not come for him to take some part in the mighty battle that had yet to be fought before the disabilities of Dissenters would be entirely removed.

The change of life, scene, and air, he found to be highly beneficial, and on the 1st of May, 1834, the forty-sixth anniversary of his birthday, he wrote:—

I have reached my forty-sixth year, the meridian of my late father's life. My health and strength better than in former years, and I think my constitution bids as fair for my future usefulness in the cause of religion, humanity, and charity as ever it did—more so than twenty years ago. . . . For many years I was getting information in manufactures, shipping, and commerce at home and abroad, which led me into a great variety of connections in every branch and class of society, from the nobleman to the pauper. I have weathered many storms, surmounted many obstacles, and overcome many difficulties. I am now in the position of having plenty of time at my command, and the very utmost of my heart's desire of wealth. How shall I apply and improve these talents? . . . My multifarious engagements in so many businesses, and my incessant journeys and correspondence have made me acquainted with many people and places in Britain and abroad, both of Christians of all denominations and worldly men, and as my circumstances are such as to afford me the means of doing much good, I hope the love of Christ will constrain me to do so."

The right use of wealth was a subject on which his thoughts were much exercised about this time, and a few extracts from his diary may be given here in illustration. He begins with a quotation :—

'With respect to the increase of wealth, it seems clear that the accumulation for the mere sake of accumulation cannot be founded on scriptural principles—it is neither advantageous to the individual himself, nor has it any tendency to advance the Divine glory. Having accumulated a sum adequate to the respectable maintenance of our families in that sphere which circumstances and habits seem to indicate as the appointed path, the ultimate of parental solicitude, so far as the same is authorized by spiritual wisdom, seems to have been attained, and the whole surplus capital subsequently realized, as well as redundant annual profits, are, I think, upon true Christian principles, committed to our trust, not for the individual aggrandisement of ourselves, or children, but with a specific design of disposing of the same in the promotion of the Divine glory, by advancing the true interests of the human family at large.'

This advice coincided with his own sentiment,

for he had long been of opinion that, although it is as bewitching as it is ensnaring to the Christian man to accumulate wealth, the wisest course of the rich man is to make comfortable provision for his family, and to regard the surplus as money simply held in trust for charitable and religious purposes.

As a matter of fact his wealth about this time was the source of considerable anxiety to him. He says :—

There has been a very constant conflict going on in my mind for some years as wealth has increased, how to dispose of it, and whether an increased style of living, of house, of furniture, equipage, and company might not be allowed, nay, might it not be really proper and right to expend money in this way, for the sake of affording employment to others, the reward of industry being better than the reward of indolence. Be it so; but these things do, notwithstanding, engender pride, vanity, and self-indulgence, and evidently indispose to a performance of the meaner and more self-denying duties of a Christian. It is clear, then, that it is undesirable for a man to be rich, and, in proportion as he becomes so he will need more grace to save him from the temptations peculiar to his position.

Such considerations have kept me thus far from increasing my style of living in any degree since I married, except a larger house or a larger family, and for such things as may tend to improve the minds and habits of my family.*

Despite the fact that he was over 200 miles from London, the whole of his business operations were

---

* To the close of his life Mr. Angas maintained the greatest simplicity in his style of living.

carried on under his direct control, and he had
worked up his affairs to such a point of nicety that
he could say :—

I am now able to conduct my commercial affairs as I have long
desired to do. I only require to be in London from four to eight
weeks in March and April, and about the same time in October
and November. While there I can find time also to attend almost
daily at the bank, the Sailors Society, and other London Committees. When I leave London all the business absolutely demanding my personal attendance is finished, and neither my clerks
in the city, nor I in the country, have much to attend to of pressing
moment.

The residence of Mr. Angas in Devonshire was
beneficial in every respect. There was looming
before him in the near future, the great work which
was not only to shape his own destiny, and that of
his family, but was to inaugurate a new career for
tens of thousands of his fellow creatures ; exertions
almost superhuman were soon to be put forth, every
nerve would have to be strained to the uttermost ;
and here, in this quiet retreat, he was gaining that
recuperation of bodily and mental power which alone
could fit him for his task.

Perhaps there was no other place in the world
that could so well have afforded him the exact kind
of rest he needed. He was a man of many moods,
and he found satisfaction and inspiration in the
quick, sympathetic responses of nature. Devonshire
is rich in contrasts. There are wild spots which for

ages have defied cultivation, and glory in their wild-
ness now as they did when the first human being
broke their solitudes; peaceful plains studded with
rural homesteads; wildernesses of beauty where wild
flowers bloom; rocky hills standing up clear against
the sky; quiet lanes with hedgerows and bushes;
dense forests where " the green-robed senators, tall
oaks " have stood for centuries in the unbroken calm.
In the openings of the hills the eye rests now on
wild moorland in the distance, now on bright green
strips of meadow lying open to the sunshine, while
along the coast, bold cliffs overhang the pebble-
strewn shore, and the broad blue sea reflects upon
its bosom the image of the Eternal.

Never before had Mr. Angas enjoyed so long a
rest; wood and stream, coast and moorland, sylvan
vale and barren rock, all were visited, and each
had a voice to soothe or stir the heart of the weary
man.

I bless God (he wrote) for His goodness in affording me the
opportunity of retiring into this remote part of the country for a
season, by which I am not tempted to go frequently to London as
I should if I lived within a hundred miles of it. I thank the Lord
also for disposing my mind to improve my retirement by reading
and reflection. May such seeds be planted in my heart as will
spring up into a glorious harvest hereafter to the glory of God.

That prayer, as we shall presently see, was
answered.

CHAPTER V.

SOUTH AUSTRALIA.

A High Ideal—Mr. Robert Gouger—Early Attempts to Colonize South Australia—The Land Company—William Penn—Government Opposition—" The South Australian Association "—Outline of the South Australian Act of 1834—Appointment of Royal Commissioners—Difficulties and Complications—Hard Conditions—A Collateral Association necessary—Sense in which he became a Father and Founder of South Australia—Reduction in Price of Land—" The South Australian Company " established—Its Plans and Principles—Retires from Board of Commissioners—An Impending Crisis averted—Outfit of Pioneer Vessels.

FROM a very early age there had been borne into the mind of George Fife Angas the idea that he was, in some way or other, to leave his mark on the world's history. When quite a youth he wrote in his diary: " I know not what work God has for me to do; but I have an impression on my mind which induces me to think that He will honour me in some way by employing me as an instrument to promote His cause in more parts of the world than one. If He calls me to a great work, I am persuaded He will capacitate me for it."

This may sound like the utterance of a young man's pride, or ambition, or as the high-flown language of mere religious sentiment. But it was not so; it was the refrain of a soul-song learnt in boy-hood, and sung in snatches till he had passed the meridian of life; and it helped to mould his cha-racter, and to shape his career. If he had done no more than to originate and continue the good works at which we have glanced in the preceding chapters, he would, we think, have done enough to earn the gratitude of after generations, but he would not have realized his ideal.

In 1831 the dream of his life began to come true. The depressed and agitated state of the country had made men turn their eyes to other lands, and emigration was one of the main topics of the day.

In 1829 one Mr. Robert Gouger conceived the idea of founding the colony of South Australia on the system propounded by Edward Gibbon Wakefield— that is to say, to sell the land in small lots to attract settlers, and to apply the purchase money to assist further emigration. Mr. Gouger was successful in organizing provisional committees, and in finding some adventurous and enterprizing people ready to colonize, but he was unable to obtain a subscribed capital sufficient for his purpose, or to induce the Government to favour his proposals, and his scheme fell to the ground.

Two years later the suitability of the country west of the Murray for settlement was made known by the discoveries of Captain Sturt, and a party of intending colonists made application to the Govern-ment, through Major Bacon, to sanction the establistment of a chartered colony in Southern Australia. Lord Goderich, the Secretary of State for the Colonies, received a deputation, consisting of Colonel Torrens, Mr. Gouger, Major Bacon, and others, and it was believed that he regarded the scheme with favour, the Government having in that same year applied the principles advocated by the deputation to the waste lands of New South Wales.

The Government, however, required in the first instance a substantial guarantee of the *bona fides* of the applicants. It was therefore determined to form a provisional committee, and to invite names and subscriptions, conditional on the sanction of the Government.

On the 31st of March, 1832, Mr. Angas received a prospectus of " The South Australian Land Company," and regarding the matter as one that might have an important influence upon his future, he at once intimated his wish to take up as many shares as would qualify him to become a Director, and offered his office in Jeffrey Square for the use of the proposed Company. He was nominated accordingly, and went on the provisional committee.

His first steps were to enter a protest against paupers being sent out, to express the hope that the appointment of a governor would be left in the hands of the Company until the population reached 10,000, and secured a Legislative Assembly, and that " Bible truth should be given unfettered and without State aid." In the event of his associates not approving of these views, he begged that his name might be struck out.

The one object he had in view at this time was to show, that though the British Government had shut out Dissenters from its universities and colleges, its places of honour and emolument, there were among them disinterested and patriotic men, who, in spite of prescriptions and exclusions, would assert their rights and pave the way for religious liberty somewhere.

Once plunged into this matter, he went ahead with it, and despite the cold water thrown upon the scheme by Lord Goderich, he felt confident that eventually all that was required of the Government would, in substance, be obtained.

As the colonization scheme shaped itself more clearly in his mind, the platform of Mr. Angas was enlarged, and he stood out for the following distinctive points :—1. The exclusion of convicts. 2. The concentration of the settlers. 3. The taking out of persons of capital and intelligence, and especially men of piety. 4. The emigration of young couples of good character. 5. Free trade, free government, and freedom in matters of religion.

It is probable that most men who take up some great cause, set before themselves an ideal hero, real or imaginary. This was the case with Mr. Angas, and his hero was William Penn.

When I reflect (he says) upon the vast benefit derived from the
influence of one man, William Penn, in consequence of his great.
wisdom and integrity, and the grace of God, I shall not despair
of doing some good with my very inferior talents, if I am faithful
to improve them.

And again :—

The career of William Penn is a remarkable proof of talents,.
knowledge, wisdom, piety, and virtue exhibited with singular con-
sistency through a long life ; meeting in return nothing but reproach, contumely, neglect, and ingratitude. Should the South
Australian colony go forward, and regard be shown for liberal
principles of government, and devotion to the moral welfare of the
community as William Penn exhibited, I shall not feel surprised at
a similar return.

He lost no time in setting forth his views, and
while yet the provisional committee was in its early
work of framing a charter, he succeeded in getting
a resolution carried to the effect " that it is very
important to adopt the most effectual means to
promote the moral and religious instruction of the
youth of the colony, and the Committee strongly call
the attention of future Directors to this point."

In course of time the draft of a charter was submitted to Lord Goderich, and negotiations with the
Government began. The draft of a Bill to give
effect to the acts of the proposed Chartered Land
Company was prepared, in which the locality of the
new settlement was defined, and the operations of
the Company in this country and in the colony

were fully set forth—"a clear and comprehensive
view of the plan in all its bearings," as Lord Goderich
was pleased to remark. But on closer examination
he found that the scheme was altogether too comprehensive, and began to oppose it point by point.
Despite the strenuous advocacy of Colonel Torrens,
and the zealous labours of Mr. Gouger and Mr.
Angas, Lord Goderich eventually declined to entertain the proposal as it stood, or to originate any
scheme in substitution, and so it came to pass that
this second attempt to found a colony in South
Australia ended in failure, and the intending emigrants took their departure for Canada and the
United States.

For a couple of years the negotiations had been
carried on with the Imperial Government without
success, and, disheartened and depressed, Mr. Angas
withdrew from the movement, intending to take no
further part in the proposed settlement.

Meanwhile a third attempt was made in July,
1833, by Mr. W. Woolrych Whitmore, M.P., who
submitted to Mr. E. G. Stanley, successor to Lord
Goderich, a plan for purchasing land in South
Australia by a Joint Stock Company, and by private
individuals, and with the proceeds to send out the
pauper or unemployed population of the United
Kingdom ; the whole expense of establishing the
colony to be defrayed by the Company. To this
proposal the Colonial Secretary replied favourably,
but added so many conditions—among them, " that

the Company must be bound to purchase the whole
of its land by fixed instalments within a limited
period "—that negotiations with the Government
were again broken off.

It was not for long that Mr. Angas was to adhere
to his resolution to have no more to do with South
Australian colonization.   Early in 1834 a number
of influential men formed themselves into a society,
called "The South Australian Association," Mr.
Robert Gouger again coming forward to assist largely
in its organization, and Mr. W. Woolrych Whitmore.
once more acting as Chairman of Committee.*

Although all the members of this committee were
highly in favour of the scheme to obtain from the
Government a charter for founding the new colony,.
the main work devolved upon a few.

It would be foreign to the purpose of the present
biography to incorporate into these pages a history
of South Australia, except in so far as that history

---

* The Association was composed as follows :—W. W. Whitmore,.
M.P., Chairman; George Grote, M.P., Treasurer; Joseph Parkes,
Solicitor ; Robert Gouger, Secretary.   Provisional Committee :—
A. Beauclerk, M.P., Abraham Borradaile, L. Bulwer, M.P., Charles
Buller, M.P., J. W. Childers, M.P., William Clay, M.P., Raikes.
Currie, M.P., Wm. Gowan, Rowland Hill, Matthew D. Hill, M.P.,
William Hutt, M.P., Sir W. Molesworth, Bart., M.P., Jacob
Montefiore, John Melville, Samuel Mills, George Warde Norman,.
H. G. Poulett Scrope, M.P., Dr. Southwood Smith, Edward Strutt,.
M.P., Colonel Torrens, M.P., Daniel Wakefield, junr., Henry
Warburton, M.P., Henry G. Ward, M.P., John Wilkes, M.P.,.
Joseph Wilson, M.P., John Ashton Yates.

forms part of the life of Mr. Angas; but it is necessary in this place to glance at the work effected by
the Association.

After much discussion and correspondence with
the Government as to whether the colony should be
founded by charter or by the Crown, and a hundred
other questions, the South Australian Bill was introduced into the House of Commons by Mr. Whitmore,
with the sanction and approval of Mr. Secretary
Spring-Rice, and in the House of Lords by the
Marquis of Normanby, supported by the Duke of
Wellington.

The leading features of the Bill were, briefly,
these:—The territory to extend from the 132nd to
the 141st degree of east longitude, and from the
South Coast, including the adjacent islands, north-
wards to the tropic of Capricorn; the whole of the
territory within the above limits to be open to
settlement by British subjects; it was not to be
subject to the laws of other colonies, but only to
those expressly enacted for itself; in no case were
convicted felons to be landed on its shores; all
public lands were to be open for purchase by cash,
the minimum price being 12s. per acre; the sale
of such lands to be under the management of a
Board of Commissioners empowered to give a title
in fee simple to each purchaser; the whole of the
money derived from the sale of waste lands to be
employed in conveying labourers, natives of Great
Britain and Ireland, to the colony, the labourers so

conveyed to be an equal number of both sexes, preference being given to young married people without
children, so that purchasers of land might obtain
labour for its cultivation; land to the value of
£35,000 to be disposed of, and a loan of £20,000
raised before the colony could be occupied; the
affairs of the colony to be regulated by the Commissioners until a certain population was reached,
at which time a representative assembly should be
entrusted with the duties of government upon the
condition that it undertook to discharge any existing
colonial debt.

In the passage of the Bill through Parliament,
Mr. Whitmore, Colonel Torrens, and Mr. Shaw-
Lefevre were conspicuous in their labours, and their
toil was rewarded. The Bill passed triumphantly
through both Houses of Parliament, and received
the Royal assent on the 15th of August, 1834.

Owing to a change in the Ministry there was some
delay in appointing the Commissioners, most of
those who had been named declining to act under
the new Government, although it is difficult to see
why the formation of the colony was regarded as a
political affair.

The task of selecting suitable men to act on the
Board, and of submitting their names to Lord Aberdeen for approval, devolved upon Mr. Gouger and
Colonel Torrens, who at once urged Mr. Angas to
allow himself to be' so named.

Mr. Angas says in his journal :—

Under Lord Melbourne's Ministry I had given my promise to Mr. Gouger that I would consent to act, if appointed, provided my six months' residence in London in the year would satisfy the Secretary of State, but not having been called on by Mr. Secretary Spring-Rice, of course I thought I was not required. Now, being asked to act under Sir Robert Peel's Government, and [Lord Aberdeen having pledged himself that no one shall be considered bound to any particular course of politics by taking office in this affair, it being entirely gratuitous, I see no reason to refuse the pledge given to Mr. Gouger under the former Ministry. My sole desire is to promote the success of the new colony under God as [His agent, rather than that of any government on earth, and I pray that my appointment may not take place if it shall not result in His glory, and the amelioration of the condition of the poor and industrious.

Mr. Angas, having thrown all his energy, business tact, and religious enthusiasm into the earlier efforts to found a colony in South Australia, had already won the full confidence of the men who were to compose the Board of Commissioners, and it was no mere complimentary language that Mr. Gouger used when he wrote :—

Nothing will be undertaken in the Commission (at first, certainly) without you. I hope you will be induced to leave Devonshire for the purpose of setting us afloat. Should I have to make this request I shall be able to present to you motives you cannot but appreciate, namely, the alleviation of disappointed emigrants who have been tortured by the embarrassing delay of months.

A new colony was to be founded upon new principles, and everything depended upon the first Commissioners giving their best and most conscien-

tious services to carry the Act of Parliament into
effect. It was a great work, and the thought
perpetually borne into the mind of Mr. Angas was,
that everything doing, or to be done, would affect in
the future thousands of his fellow-creatures, among
whom chiefly were those struggling with poverty.

On the 5th of May, 1835, the names of the Royal
Commissioners were gazetted. They were as follows:
—Colonel Torrens, M.P., Chairman, George Fife
Angas, E. Barnard, William Hutt, M.P., J. G. Shaw-
Lefevre, W. A. McKinnon, M.P., S. Mills, Jacob
Montefiore, G. Palmer, junr., J. Wright, Rowland
Hill, Secretary to the Board.*

The hopes of intending emigrants revived when
the public announcement was made of the appointment of Commissioners to carry the Act into effect;
but these hopes were soon dispelled. Difficulties
and complications arose, and it was found that the
monetary conditions and guarantees required by the
Act seemed likely to wreck the whole scheme, such
conditions being the disposal of land to the value of
£35,000, and the raising of a loan of £20,000 before
the powers conferred upon the Commissioners could
take effect.

At the first meeting of the Board Mr. Angas
pointed out that these conditions stood as an
insuperable barrier to progress, but the other
members of the Board were sanguine that the

---

* Afterwards Sir Rowland Hill, Secretary to the Post Office, and
originator of the Penny Postal System.

stipulated sums would be raised. In May, however, Mr. Rowland Hill wrote to Mr. Angas: "Some objection or other attaches to every arrangement proposed for raising the £35,000; indeed, there is an essential difficulty, namely, the necessity for selling land, or doing that which is equivalent to the sale of land, which no one knows anything about."

To meet the difficulty one course, and one course only, seemed possible to Mr. Angas, and he forthwith proceeded to lay his suggestion before the Board. It was that a Joint Stock Company should be formed to purchase the stipulated £35,000 worth of land, and thus make a way for the Commissioners to begin their work.

But the plan was pooh-poohed by the Board, and the emigrants looked with a jealous eye upon the scheme, fearing that a wealthy and influential Company might obtain exclusive privileges detrimental to the interests of intending settlers. Even Mr. Gouger was opposed to the measure, and for some weeks Mr. Angas allowed the matter to drop.

Meanwhile South Australia was engraven on his heart, and it was the subject of his meditation by night and day. It is the theme of almost every entry in his diary. Here is a specimen:—

June 4, 1835.—For the success of this colony I look to God, and to Him will I look. America was founded on that basis by God's people in a tempest; this colony will, I hope, be raised upon a similar foundation, although in a calm. If I can get pious people sent out to that land, the ground will be blessed for their sake; and if justice be done to the aborigines, as was done by William Penn, then we shall have peace in all our borders, for I reckon that the principles of God's government will apply to South Australia as to elsewhere.

Every day the idea became clearer to his mind that, unless the Board of Commissioners were assisted by some collateral association to relieve them of the financial difficulties which hindered them from taking any practical steps to establish the colony, the whole scheme must inevitably collapse.

The position must be clearly understood, or we shall fail to see in what sense Mr. Angas became Father and Founder of South Australia. As already shown, the Commissioners were required to raise £35,000 by the sale of land, and £20,000 by bonds, such amount to be placed in the hands of trustees, and held as a guarantee or security to the Government, that the public purse should be protected against any expense on account of the colony. And here was the difficulty; the land was an unexplored wilderness, and the colony, the revenue of which was to be the security for the proposed loan, was not yet in existence. To add to the difficulty, the price of land had been raised from 12s. to £1 per acre. Nor was this all. Before an acre of this wilderness land could be sold, or a shilling raised upon the security of revenues yet to be created, it was necessary that considerable expense should be

incurred in providing offices, engaging clerks and
agents, and disseminating information—by means of
pamphlets, printed papers, and advertisements—with
regard to the principles and prospects of the proposed
colony, and towards these preliminaries the Government would lend no aid whatever.

When once an idea took full hold of his mind, Mr.
Angas was not a man to let it slumber there. The
burden of his cry was, " Establish a collateral company to purchase the requisite amount of land, to
employ the emigrants, and to provide the capital
necessary for the working of the Colonial Government, and unless these objects be accomplished,
the project of the colony will assuredly prove a
failure."

The Commissioners, however, continued to entertain a different opinion; nor did they alter it until
events demonstrated to them that they were in error.
The land did not sell, none of their expectations as
to money being forthcoming were realized, and it
became patent to them that they were utterly
powerless to carry the Act into execution.

The alternatives before them were either to seek
the assistance of a collateral Joint Stock Company, in
which case they must reduce the price of land from
20s. to 12s. an acre to make such a Company possible;
to apply to the Government for pecuniary aid—an
application not likely to be successful;—to tender
their resignations to the Government—or to allow
matters to remain indefinitely *in statu quo.*

The first course seemed to offer the only feasible way out of the difficulty, and even that was by no means clear to them until Mr. Angas, who had been absent in Devonshire, again appeared upon the scene. He says in his diary :—

September 8, 1835.—On my arrival in London I found the progress of the new colony paralyzed and at a dead stand, without any hope of making up the £35,000 for months to come, thereby keeping the governor, officers, and emigrants in a state of most painful suspense. As the Act is for the purpose of selling land and establishing the colony, I am convinced that by no other means can it be done than by selling at 12s. per acre, thereby inducing people of capital to come forward and form a company, through which to employ the labour sent out. I have directed my efforts to this point, and having received the opinion of my solicitors (Messrs. Bartlett and Beddome) that such a company could be got up, I this day proposed the reduction of the price from 20s. to 12s., declaring at the same time my belief that the remainder of the £20,000 for the sale of land could be raised within five weeks. After much discussion a resolution to that effect was unanimously agreed to by the Board.

"I can see no possible way for the colony to be founded if the Company is not formed." This summed up Mr. Angas's view of the position, and nerved him for continuous action. He at once set to work, and, assisted by two or three others, subscribed sufficient capital to purchase the whole of the unsold land, to be handed over to the Company, when formed, at cost price, with interest at 5 per cent. This purchase was the basis of the operations of the Company, as the Company was

ipso facto the basis of all future operations of the
Royal Commissioners.

On the 25th of September the price of land was
formally reduced, and Messrs. Bartlett and Beddome,
the solicitors into whose hands the legal negotiations
were entrusted, were informed that the deposit must
be paid by noon of the 30th of September, and the
last instalment of the purchase money on or before
the 3rd of November. This was sharp work, but it
was accomplished. Mr. Angas and two others
(Messrs. Smith and Kingscote) at once put down
£3,000 each, and then proceeded to get the co-
operation of wealthy and influential men as directors
and shareholders of the proposed Company.

The Commissioners held out a bait to capitalists
by announcing that, if the Company succeeded in
raising within the required time a subscribed capital
of £200,000, £50,000 of it paid up, the Board would
sell an additional 20,000 acres at 12s. an acre at any
time before the 1st of March, 1836.

Mr. Angas was well aware that his motives were
open to misconstruction, and that his enemies—for
he had them, as all successful men have—would say
in effect, "This is the man who, while holding the
king's commission to establish the colony, used
his influence at that Board to get great concessions
for himself and his friends, in order to form a Company in which he was to be the leading spirit."

Besides this, South Australia was not considered
the legitimate offspring of the Colonial Office, but was

rather regarded as a dependency adopted into the
already large family of Britain, and whether it would
prove a boon or a bane was a question on which
there was a great variety of opinion.   But none
of these things moved him.   He had " the answer
of a good conscience," and that was enough   He
wrote :—

September 30.—After battling for many months, personally and
by letter, with nearly all the Board, they have at last come to the
very conclusion which I have pressed upon them from the beginning,
viz., that land must be sold at 12s. per acre, and that pasturage
must be raised from 10s. to 40s. per square mile.

A subscribed capital of £200,000 had to · be
obtained before the Company could be considered
as fairly established, and Mr. Angas had to go to
the capitalists of the kingdom and say in effect :
" Gentlemen, lend us your money to carry out this
scheme, notwithstanding there has not yet been an
acre of the land surveyed, or a British harbour
formed.   Advance it to us on the faith of our settled
conviction that the project, notwithstanding its
difficulties, is quite practicable ; that from the
information we possess of the country we believe
it must succeed, and will eventually lead to a rich
reward for your confidence."

Such an appeal would be hazardous at any time,
but it was particularly so then, for public opinion
was adverse to the scheme, partly because a strong
prejudice existed against some of the early projectors.

of what was called the "New Colonization," partly
because the Government was only lukewarm, and
many members of both Houses of Parliament openly
opposed the whole project, while a powerful opposition was made by those who were deeply interested
in the rival colonies of Western Australia, Van
Diemen's Land, and New South Wales.

Despite all opposition, by the morning of the 29th
of September he had in hand the sum of £20,000—
his own subscription and that of four others—to
complete the preliminary sales.

On the 9th of October five men met in a small
room at 19, Bishopsgate Street, Mr. Angas being in
the chair, and proceeded to pass resolutions to form
"The South Australian Company," to issue a prospectus, to insert advertisements in the leading
papers, and to transact all necessary business.

The character of Mr. Angas comes out in an entry
in his diary, in which the proceedings at this small
but important meeting are recorded :—

In order that no time should be lost Mr. Thomas Smith and
I resolved to go on with the business with our own capital to the
amount of £20,000, whether the Company went on or not.

It is needless to say that, with spirit like this at
headquarters, matters went ahead rapidly. On the
11th of October the advertisements appeared, and on
the 14th Mr. Angas wrote :—

October 14, 1835.—This day the number of shares applied for
in the South Australian Company is about 4,000 at £50 each,

making up £200,000, the sum required by the prospectus to justify
the Directors in proceeding. This enables us to apply for the
further purchase of 20,000 more acres of land at 12s. . . . I can
view this in no other light than as a signal instance of the aid of
Divine Providence and a distinct and peculiar answer to prayer. I
pray God not to leave me in this great undertaking, in which is
involved the moral, temporal, and spiritual welfare of multitudes of
our own countrymen for ages to come, and also of the aborigines of
New Holland.

On the following day the South Australian Company was formed Mr. Angas was elected chairman,
and the provisional Board of Directors was appointed.*

The plans and principles of the company were,
briefly, these : 1. They desired no exclusive privileges,
but only to be placed on the same basis as other
private houses. 2. They proposed to raise in shares
a sufficient capital to carry on the business contemplated. 3. The lands they had purchased of the
Commissioners they would let out to farmers on long
leases, with the power of redemption by the tenant
at any time, on fair and equitable terms, and they
might occasionally cultivate a part, in case tenants
were not forthcoming, after the farm-houses, &c.,
were prepared for letting. 4. They would establish

---

* The following constituted the original Board of Directors :—Mr. G.
F. Angas, Chairman, Messrs. Raikes Currie, Charles Hindley, M.P., James
Hyde, Henry Kingscote, John Pirie (Alderman), Christopher Rawson,
John Rundle, M.P., Thomas Smith, James Ruddell Todd, and Henry
Waymouth. Though few of these were ever personally known in the
colony they assisted to establish, the streets of the capital perpetuate the
names of Angas, Currie, Hindley, Pirie, Rundle, and Waymouth.

such trades as would be requisite for founding and
carrying on the colony, and would retire from them
when private tradesmen could be obtained to take
them up on fair conditions. 5. They proposed to
rear stock, until private adventurers should arrive
and be disposed to purchase it at remunerative
prices. 6. They would raise and cure salt provisions
of beef, pork, and fish for exportation as well as
for home consumption. 7. They intended to build
vessels of all sizes for fishing, coasting, and whaling,
and especially to found a new nursery for seamen.
8. They would of necessity build houses on their
town lots and dispose of the same until their whole
sections were worked out and sold.

On these principles the proposed Company was
compared by Mr. Angas to a scaffolding, which is
needful to the erection of a large building, but is
taken down when such building is completed.

The Directors had been selected with great care,
as able, experienced men of business, of high character, and with no inconsiderable share of property.
They were men with whom Mr. Angas found it a
pleasure to work, and they had unbounded confidence
in him, insomuch that they repeatedly and unanimously declared they would only remain on the
Directorate so long as he continued to be the moving
spirit of the Company.

And herein lay a difficulty, foreseen, however,
from the first. His connection with the Company
disqualified him from continuing as one of His

Majesty's Commissioners for the colonization of
South Australia, no member of that Board being
allowed to have any pecuniary interest in the colony
it was appointed to establish. It was hoped by his
colleagues that, in the particular circumstances of the
case, Mr. Angas might be made an exception to
the rule, and Colonel Torrens took this inquiry in
hand.

Oct. 3.—This morning (Mr. Angas wrote in his Journal) Colonel
Torrens, Mr. Lefevre, Captain Hindmarsh, the governor-elect, and
myself had an interview with Lord Glenelg at the Colonial Office
by his special appointment. We reported the sale of £35,000 of
land, and our hope of raising the requisite loan to complete the
conditions required by the Act. Colonel Torrens explained my
position in relation to the Company, and said that the Commissioners wished me to continue at their Board, but that the gentlemen forming the Company declined to go on without me. He
desired leave for me to sit on both Boards, and to be appointed a
Special Commissioner for the civilization of the aborigines of
South Australia.

There was great kindness in this suggestion of
Colonel Torrens. He knew that the one great matter
which made Mr. Angas reluctant to leave the Board
of Commissioners was that, as it gave him access to
the Government, he could best serve the cause of
the poor neglected aborigines in that capacity. The
question of dual office was referred to the Law
Secretary of the Colonial Office, and in process
of time the following answer was received by the
Chairman of the Board from Lord Glenelg :—

Oct. 22, 1835.

. . . The established reputation, both in the commercial world and in private life, of the gentleman in whose person this question has arisen, precluding the possibility that any decision of it could be ascribed to a failure of respect for him, Lord Glenelg finds himself unembarrassed in stating distinctly the grounds on which he thinks it right to proceed.   No case could present to His Majesty's Government stronger inducements than that of Mr. Angas's to sacrifice the general principle involved in this inquiry to the advantage to be drawn from the zeal, ability, and character of the party whose continuance in the public service it affects.   So much importance, however, does Lord Glenelg attach to that principle, that he is prepared to adhere to it, even though at the expense of losing Mr. Angas's assistance in the execution of your Commission. That principle is, that no Commissioner who has acquired any personal interest, whether direct or indirect, whether of great magnitude or trifling amount, in any contract entered into with the Board, can any longer continue to be a member, but must be regarded as henceforth disqualified to act in that capacity, and will be expected to tender an immediate resignation. . . .

Lord Glenelg does not hold himself bound to subject the public to the inconvenience of the immediate retirement of Mr. Angas if it can be avoided.   If that gentleman should be disposed to continue his services as a Commissioner until a successor can be appointed, Lord Glenelg will thankfully accept them, but on the condition that his seat be vacated within three months at farthest from the present time.

It was not without regret that Mr. Angas resigned his seat on the Board of Commissioners, although he saw clearly that the business of founding the colony was virtually transferred from the Commission to the Company.   He availed himself of the permission to retain his seat on the Commission for the present,

and occupied it until the 19th of December, by
which time he had seen all the preliminary measures
required by the Act completed.

On retiring he was courteously allowed to nomi-
nate his successor, and his old friend, Mr. Josiah
Roberts, of Camberwell, a retired American merchant,
and for a long time a member of the British and
Foreign Bible Society, was appointed to the vacant
office.

For many weeks there had been a severe mental
strain on Mr. Angas, and immediately after the
matter of his resignation was settled he went down
to Dawlish to recruit his health. But in his absence
the Directors would not act, and difficulties having
arisen, the Secretary wrote to urge his immediate
return. "All are afraid to stir a step without you,"
he said ; " your presence alone will inspire the
Directors with that confidence which seems entirely
to have forsaken them."

Mr. Angas, therefore, returned to town immediately, and he says :—

Oct. 30.—I feel extremely thankful to God that though the
greatest despondency appears to have seized the Directors, and the
Governor also, I feel confident that God designs to bring something
out of this Company, and therefore, should all the Directors go
away, I will go on with it, trusting in the providence of God.

Early in December he visited Leeds, Manchester,
Liverpool, and other large towns and cities, for the
purpose of interesting influential men of capital in

the South Australian Company. On every road and in every coach, in spots " where merchants most do congregate," on the platforms of Sunday School and other philanthropic Societies, at the social board, in season and out of season, he availed himself of the opportunity of making South Australia known, of removing prejudice and of gaining supporters.

While thus engaged vexatious delays and mis-understandings were occurring in London. The Government would not hurry themselves or be hurried; the Commissioners could not act without the Colonial Office, and the Company could not act without the Commissioners.

Mr. Angas, on the other hand, was as prompt as he was energetic. When he found that there was little prospect of the speedy outfit by the Government of a vessel to convey the Governor and such officers as the Commissioners deemed necessary, he at once fitted up the *Duke of York*, one of the vessels purchased by the Company, and offered her for their service.

Such a proposal was a shock to the Red Tape and Circumlocution Department of the Colonial Office, and when, after a long delay, a reply was received, it was to decline the offer, and therefore, in order to save the whale fishing season, the ship's state rooms were removed, and she was fitted up entirely as a whaler. In the meantime a question of considerable importance to the Company was raised by the issue of some amended regulations for the sale of land

signed by Mr. Rowland Hill, the Secretary to the
Board of Commissioners.

The unauthorized insertion of the word "hereafter" would have deprived the Company of the
right to a special survey of their land.   By the
interposition of Mr. Angas the word was withdrawn,
but he had little doubt that it had been inserted
purposely to deprive the Company of an important
privilege, and his confidence in the Board of Commissioners was thenceforth somewhat shaken.

Matters had improved but little when the new
year, 1836, opened.   The Commissioners either could
not or would not take any decisive action, and meanwhile governor, officers, agents, and emigrants were
all kept in idleness and suspense.

So critical had the position become that Mr. Angas
determined to apply to Lord Glenelg for authority to
settle the agents and servants of the Company at
Kangaroo Island, the ships to sail on or before the
1st of February.   If the Government declined to
afford facilities for this, then, either the ships were to
proceed to the South Seas for shipping purposes
and the agents to be settled in the Swan River
(Western Australia) or some other colony, or, the
Company would dissolve, return the land into the
hands of the Commissioners, and apply to Parliament for compensation, the three ships purchased
and paid for from the private resources of Mr. Angas
being retained in his business.

Meanwhile the shares moved slowly; nobody felt

inclined to invest heavily, for, as one of the largest
shareholders wrote to the founder, "I see clearly
that in case of your death or incapacity from ill-
health or other cause to take the part you now
do, the Company will inevitably be swamped, and
therefore I do not like to take any greater risk or
responsibility."

Notwithstanding all drawbacks and discouragements, by persevering effort the impending crisis
was averted, and on the 26th of January, 1836, Mr.
Angas wrote :—

> I am now deeply engaged in the outfit of the three ships, and in
> the onerous duty of appointing captains, officers, and crews. As
> far as is in my power in the appointment of managers, officers, and
> men for the Company, I have sought out and engaged those who
> fear God, and when I could not do this I took the next best I
> could find. The whole of the thoughts, plans, and arrangements
> have fallen mainly upon me, and, with the exception of Alderman
> Pirie, I have had little assistance from the Directors.
>
> I trust the present movement will lay the foundation of a new
> kingdom in truth and righteousness, and I pray that the power and
> influence put into my hands may be used for His glory and for the
> good of the people of South Australia.

For many weeks he was working from eight in the
morning till midnight, and sometimes till two in the
morning, and his labours were crowned with success.
On the 22nd of February—one month to the day
from the legal formation of the Company—the *John
Pirie* set sail with emigrants, provisions, and live
stock, and two days later the *Duke of York* followed,

with Mr. S. Stephens, the colonial manager of the
Company, together with other of the Company's
officers and servants on board.

The South Australian Company had already more
than justified its existence. It had been the direct
means of enabling the Commissioners to surmount
their chief difficulty and make the foundation of the
new colony possible. The remaining obstacle—the
raising a loan of £20,000 to be vested in Trustees
—was removed by Mr. Wright, one of the Commissioners, undertaking to negotiate in the matter,
but as he was to receive a commission on the transaction it involved his retirement from the Board.

Indirectly this loan was contingent upon the
establishment of the Company, as no sane man would
have advanced money on the security of lands situate
12,000 miles away if the Company had not first
guaranteed to introduce into the proposed colony
the capital, stock, and labour of British merchants,
shipowners, and artizans.

CHAPTER VI.

Genius for Business—Arrival of Pioneer Vessels at Kangaroo Island—South Australia created a British Colony — The South Australian Bank established—Its Success—On the Horns of a Dilemma—Mr. Oakden —Foundation of the Union Bank of Australia—Its subsequent History — Ill-requited Labours — The Aborigines of South Australia— Their Rights and Privileges—Efforts for their Civilization—German Missionaries sent out—Native Reserves—Establishment of Schools— "The South Australian School Society"—Rev. T. Q. Stow—How the Wesleyans received their Minister — A proposed National Labour College.

No better proof of the genius of Mr. Angas for business could be furnished than the Letters of Instruction given by him to the heads of the various departments of the Company who had proceeded to South Australia.

But they would fill half a volume. It will be sufficient to refer to one of them, addressed to the officer sent out to take the general management of the Company's affairs. It contained minute instructions on the following among other subjects:— Banks and banking; ship and boat-building operations; the commercial and financial affairs of the Company generally; shipping and chartering of

ships ; sperm and black whale fisheries ; the white
fishery; salting of fish, beef, and pork; erection of
houses, warehouses, wharves, and dockyards; the
charge of stores; buying and selling produce and
manufactured goods; working of mines and quarries; flour, saw, and other mills, and a multitude of
minor matters.   In addition to this it fell to the lot
of Mr. Angas to arrange in minute detail, not only
for everything considered necessary for the successful
issue of an undertaking of such great magnitude and
capable of such splendid results, but to provide
against every conceivable contingency that might
arise.

Of course some mistakes were made, but most
of these arose from circumstances beyond human
control.   For instance, the destination of the first
settlers was a mistake.   Kangaroo Island, the site
fixed upon by the Company, had been formally
reported upon by Captain Flinders, by whalers, and
others who had visited it ; it was the only port of
the new province where there were any European
settlers, and the eastern shore of the Gulf of St.
Vincent, which afterwards became the great centre
of population, was comparatively unknown.   It was
never anticipated that the capital of the colony
would rise on the shores of Nepean Bay.   But the
first settlers must have a means of livelihood, and
as the whale fishery was the only branch of business
the Company could enter upon in the first instance,
Kangaroo Island was considered more suitable as a

station than any other part of the coast then known. Eventually the island was abandoned, and the majority of the Company's staff removed to the mainland. The fishing operations, commenced on an extensive scale, with stations at Encounter Bay and Thistle Island, led to disastrous results. Four of the Company's vessels were wrecked and one stranded on the dangerous coast, and, ceasing to be a profitable pursuit, the whale fishery was abandoned.

The *Duke of York* was the first of the Company's vessels to reach the new colony. She arrived in Nepean Bay on the 27th July, 1836, and Mr. Samuel Stephens was the first settler to land upon its shores. Tents were immediately reared, and a little band of adventurers set out to explore the surrounding country, and, losing themselves in the bush, did not return from their perilous adventure for three days, when they found the *Lady Mary Pelham* safely anchored in the Bay. The *John Pirie* arrived a fortnight later, and the *Rapid* (the first vessel sent out by the Commissioners) on the 20th of August, 1836.

On the 28th of December, 1836, just five months after the first of the South Australian Company's vessels had anchored at Kangaroo Island, Governor Hindmarsh and his party landed at Holdfast Bay, and in the name of King William IV. took possession of the land by reading, under a venerable blue gum-tree near the shore, the Order in Council creating South Australia a British colony. His way had been prepared mainly by the operations of the South Australian Company.

The first letters from the colony received by Mr. Angas were full of encouragement. "I hope you will see that the Commissioners," said Mr. S. Stephens, "are not tardy in sending out emigrants. We cannot have too many of them, nor have them too fast. All who are willing to work may here be happy and comfortable, and, beyond all doubt, tens of thousands who are at this moment, by hard and long-continued labour barely earning a scanty subsistence, might here, with less toil, live in peace and plenty."

As this is not a history of South Australia we must leave the settlers, and turn back to see what was being done for the colony by the Company and also by the Commissioners.

It was patent from the first that a banking establishment would be an imperative necessity in the new colony, and the prospectus of the South Australian Company stated as one of its objects :—

The Establishment of a bank or banks in or connected with the New Colony of South Australia, making loans on land or produce in the Colony, and the conducting of such banking operations as the directors may think expedient.

But it was equally clear that it should not form a branch of a commercial company, and therefore, with great wisdom and foresight, it was omitted from the original plan submitted by Mr. Angas to intending shareholders.

Almost immediately after the formation of the Company negotiations were commenced with the Bank of Australasia to transact its monetary affairs in the colony, but as no satisfactory arrangements could be concluded, and applications were being made by intending emigrants to the Company to receive deposits of money for transmission to the colony, Mr. Angas at once submitted a plan to the shareholders to meet the difficulty. He proposed to divide the original £50 shares in the South Australian Company into two of £25 each, and to issue an additional number of shares at a premium of £1, to afford sufficient capital for the commencement of a bank, or banks, in the colony. The proposal gave satisfaction all round ; a supply of specie and small notes was sent out in one of the first vessels despatched by the Company, and Mr. Edward Stephens, as cashier and accountant, soon followed with a framed banking house, iron chests, and the entire plant of the Bank, together with bank notes, engraved in London, varying in value from 10s. to £10, and representing in the aggregate the sum of £10,000.

Mr. Stephens was instructed that the Bank was to be one of issue, discount, deposit, and loan ; that it would undertake, upon commission, the collection of debts and receipt of moneys, exchange its own notes for bills on England, and open up, as circumstances might require, a system of exchange between the colony and the mother country. Subsequently these instructions were widened, and in time of need the Bank gave assistance to the Governor and the Colonial Resident Commissioner, and an arrangement was made with the Board of Commissioners that the notes of the Bank should be received in the colony, not only in payment for land, but also for any taxes that were to be levied for the support of the Government.

It may be well in this place to take a glance at the subsequent history of the Bank.

Although it was very advantageous to the colonists to have banking facilities supplied from the very commencement, and to the colony itself to open up relations with other colonies, and although it was a praiseworthy action on the part of Mr. Angas, and reflected great credit upon his judgment for working out successfully the whole scheme, nevertheless neither the South Australian Company nor its Bank were regarded with favour by the authorities in the colony.

As a matter of fact grievous dissensions arose in process of time between the Governor's party and the Resident Commissioner's party, and both sets of persons continued to regard the South Australian Company as a third and interloping faction acting in rivalry to both.

These jealousies and animosities eventually led to the recall of the first Governor (Hindmarsh), while the Bank outlived all the opposition that had been directed against it, and became a permanent and useful institution.

At a meeting of the South Australian Company, held only eighteen months after the colony had been proclaimed, it was shown that money had been lodged at the London office for repayment by the Bank in South Australia amounting to upwards of £15,000, while the drafts drawn in the colony on England amounted to nearly £7,000. When the land was more fully surveyed, the business of the Bank increased so rapidly that it became the most popular of the Company's departments. As Mr. Angas had long foreseen might be the case, its prosperity became an obstacle in the way of the Company obtaining a charter of incorporation, and the directors were on the horns of a dilemma : either the Company must abandon its hope of obtaining a charter, or abandon its Bank, which in 1840 had increased its business to nearly a quarter of a million, and was yielding the Company a profit of 15 per cent.

Mr. Angas was always fertile in expedients, and as soon as he was fully persuaded that the Government would not grant a charter while the Bank formed part of the Commercial Company, he drew up a scheme for placing the Bank under a separate Board, but composed of the same men who were Directors of the Company.

Early in 1841 he submitted his plan to the

Directors, and it was accepted almost in its entirety.
The leading features were: To divide the capital of
the Company into equal halves of 10,000 shares of
£25 each, and, on condition that the shareholders
of the Company would give up their Bank and its
business—so far as to regard the latter as a distinct
establishment—each holder of two shares in the stock
of the South Australian Company was to have the
privilege of holding one share in the stock of the new
banking Company, and so on *pro rata* according to
the number of their shares.   To meet the case of
non-shareholders in the original Company who might
be desirous of taking up shares in the new Bank, he
proposed that such persons should either go into the
share market and purchase two shares in the original
Company to entitle them to one in the new Bank, or
else that the Directors should issue 2,500 shares at a
premium of 30s., the capital to go. into the stock
of the new Bank and the premium to be handed
over to the original Company as goodwill for the
transfer of the business of the Bank.

Mr. Angas never for a moment entertained the
slightest doubt as to the success of his plan, and
this inspired confidence in his fellow-directors.   He
wrote in his diary :—

June 19, 1841.—At last every shareholder of the Company has
consented to the separation of the Bank.   It has been so difficult
an operation, and so obstinate have been some of the shareholders
in resisting it, and in refusing all concessions, that I have reason
to believe that it has ultimately been accomplished by the over-

ruling providence of God. . . . I have also had to combat with
the Directors for two years before they would introduce it.   After
they at length consented to the plan, I worked out the scheme
before the Committee of the House of Commons, and had private
interviews with the Government with the view of obtaining a
charter for it.

The charter was obtained, the separation affected,
and " The South Australian Banking Company "
(as for some inscrutable reason it was called) was
established, the following being the original
directors and officers :—

*Henry Kingscote (Chairman).

*George Fife Angas.	J. K. Mills.
George Davenport.	*Sir John Pirie, Bart, Alderman.
*Edward Divitt, M.P.	*Christopher Rawson.
*John Fussell.	*John Rundle, M.P.
J. H. Leckie.	*James Ruddell Todd.

Manager—*Edmund John Wheeler.

Manager in South Australia—Edward Stephens.

It would not be interesting to the general reader
to give in detail any further account of the labours
involved in starting the South Australian Banking
Company.   It commenced its independent career
just when the colony was recovering from the
great crisis in its history consequent on the dishonouring in England of the bills drawn by Governor Gawler, of which we shall have more to say

---

* Those against whose names an asterisk is placed were also
Directors of the Land Company.

hereafter. This untoward event shook the infant settlement to its very foundation and brought about a state of almost universal bankruptcy and ruin. The increase of capital and the greater facilities which the Bank was able to offer to merchants and tradesmen were therefore as opportune as they were important to the improvement of the monetary con- dition of the community.

When Mr. McLaren, the General Colonial Manager of the Company's affairs, returned to England in 1841, he was able to say of the first Bank: " I do not hesitate to state that the progress of the Colony and the success of the individual colonists has been more owing to the Bank of South Australia than to any other cause whatever—perhaps I might say than to all other causes put together."

The subsequent history of the Bank is practically the history of South Australia. In this place it will be enough to say that in 1844 heavy losses were incurred which necessitated the suspension of dividends, but that since 1846 good dividends have been received by the shareholders varying in value with the depression or prosperity of the Colony, as influenced by droughts or rain, the discovery of gold, metals, and so forth. In 1852 the capital was increased, and again in 1857, while in 1862 it was raised to £500,000, and again in 1879 to £800,000. From the foundation of the Bank to the end of 1888 profits to the extent of about two millions sterling were realized. In 1867, upon

renewing the Company's charter, the name of the
Bank was altered back to its original designation,
"The Bank of South Australia," and in 1884 the
word "Limited" was added to the title. At the
present time there are sixteen branches of the Bank
in the Colony, and thirteen agencies or sub-branches,
and a local directorate in Australia.   There is also a
branch in Melbourne, opened, with gratifying results,
in 1888. "It may be said of the Bank of South
Australia that the institution brings more money
into the Colony than any other Bank, and that its
advances are the largest in the Colony. In this
way, apart from its historical interest, it has
proved a mainstay of the Colony in times of great
depression, and will revive with its revival." *

Banking had become a passion with Mr. Angas.
He had assisted in founding the National Provincial
Bank of England, and, later, this South Australian
Bank. Let us now, while upon the subject, tell the
story of the Union Bank of Australia—one of the
most successful banks ever established in connection
with the Australian colonies, and which owes its
origin to his labours. It is the simple narrative of
a rill expanding into a river, or an acorn developing
into an oak.

In the year 1837 Mr. Philip Oakden, one of the
Directors of the Tamar Bank in Tasmania, came to
England to negotiate for the sale of that Bank to an

---

* "The Banking Institutions of Australasia." By R. L. Nash.

English Company in order that its capital might be increased and its operations extended. He obtained an introduction to Mr. Angas, who found in his visitor not only a man of business, but a man after a godly sort, and an old friend of the late W. H. Angas. It had been on the mind of Mr. Angas whether it would not be well to establish a bank to transact in neighbouring colonies the business of the South Australian Company's Bank, and regarding this visit as favourable to his plans, he set the matter before the Company, with the result that, as the Deed of Settlement confined the operations of their Bank exclusively to South Australia, the idea was abandoned so far as the Company was concerned.

Then Mr. Oakden urged him to form an independent Company, and Mr. Angas writes in his diary:—

We walked together for an hour or two on Southwark Bridge, and considered how far it was proper for me to add to my present engagements. . . . If, without injury to the other affairs I have in hand, I can lay the foundation of this projected Company on such principles and with such men as will glorify God and promote the weal of man, and at the same time tend to benefit South Australia, then indeed it might be my duty to do so.

He was at that time overwhelmed with the affairs of the South Australian Company, and was longing to be at Dawlish, " especially," he says, " as my dear boys have been at home some weeks for their holidays and I shall have very little of their company." But the positive good that the formation of such

an institution would do to the Company and to
his beloved South Australia overcame every other
consideration, and he resolved to make the attempt.

Within a fortnight from the day he arrived at this
conclusion, " The Union Bank of Australia " was
formed, directors, trustees, and officers were appointed and operations had commenced.

The story, unique in the annals of banks and
banking, may best be told in the words of Mr.
Angas.

July 5, 1837.—This morning I earnestly sought direction in the
difficult task of selecting proper men as directors of the new bank.
I have applied to Mr. Cummins and he has consented to act, and
will invite others to join us.

July 7, 1837.—I have induced the directors of this bank, which
was only formed this day, to place the following on its minutes:—
' That the Union Bank now formed shall not establish any bank in
South Australia without the consent of the directors of the South
Australian Company.' Without this I could not agree to go on
with the measure.

July 13, 1837.—I feel grateful to God, who ordered all things in
so great mercy towards me, in enabling me to lay the foundation of
a new Joint Stock Company during the past fortnight. The Union
Bank of Australia is actually formed, the prospectus is printed, the
directors appointed, the office taken, the clerks at work, and many
shares actually applied for. Every essential principle of the Company
is agreed upon, the proposition of the Tamar Bank to join us has
been accepted, and Mr. Oakden proposes to leave London next Monday for Manchester and Liverpool, after the question of the bankers
is decided, to complete the bank arrangements there preparatory to
our appropriating the shares in London. Thus, by the manifest
working of the hand of a gracious Providence, has this Company
been formed in a couple of weeks, and the directors, solicitors,

secretary, and accountant are now acting. There were two grand
objects I had to gain in getting up this great Company. First, the
protection of the Bank of the South Australian Company from
competition. Second, the appointment of such a body of directors
as would select and appoint pious men to places of trust at home
and abroad and carry on all their operations on the principles of
justice, integrity, and morality; and especially with a view to the
best interests and moral welfare of colonists. I do consider that
both these objects are permanently secured, so far as human foresight can effect it.

The original prospectus was dated, 38, Old Broad
Street, September 1st, 1837, and the names of the
first directors were as follows:—

DIRECTORS.

George Fife Angas.	Charles Edward Mangles.
Robert Brooks.	Philip Oakden.
James John Cummins.	Christopher Rawson.
Robert Gardner.	Thomas Sands.
John Gore.	James Bogle Smith.
Charles Hindley, M.P.	James Ruddell Todd.

TRUSTEES.

George Carr Glyn.   James John Cummins.   John Gore.

BANKERS.

Glyn, Hallifax, Mills, & Co.

The attendance of Mr. Angas at the Board of the
Union Bank was of necessity irregular. A thousand
other things were claiming his attention, and every
day he was struggling against a threatened attack of
prolonged and serious illness. This tended to lessen

the influence he would otherwise have had on the directorate, but, as the business of the bank made satisfactory progress, and the ends he had in view were accomplished, he was content.

One of the most remarkable features in the establishment of the Union Bank was the small cost of the preliminary expenses. Up to the 31st of December, 1837, nearly six months from its formation, the total expenditure on this account only amounted to £859 2s. in which sum was included £167 2s. for law expenses in preparing the Trust Deeds, &c., and £210 for passage money of clerks sent to the colonies, the remainder being for rent, salaries, stationery, engraving notes, and so forth. Mr. Angas hated extravagance, and it was to his good management and active exertions that the expenses were kept down to so small an amount. It was he who drew up and presented to the proprietors the sound and practical plan on which the Bank was founded, it was he who superintended the economical details of its initiation, and it was his influence that, without much trouble and without any expense, secured the original shareholders.

When the first general meeting of the proprietors was held on the 26th of June, 1839, at which Mr. Angas presided, it was reported that the assets of the Company to the 31st of December of the previous year were £150,136 and the net profit £4,711 17s. In the following year the profits had risen to £44,404 9s. 6d.

A year later and Mr. Angas, from causes which will
be explained elsewhere, was called upon to tax every
financial resource to meet demands unexpectedly
made upon] him, and it became absolutely necessary
not only to withdraw the capital he had invested in
the Union Bank, but to free himself as much as
possible from other undertakings he had established
and fostered.

It was a painful step, as the sale of so many of his
shares necessitated the resignation of his seat on
the Board. On the day when the deed was done
he wrote in his diary with a trembling hand:—

Dec. 20, 1841.—I have received a letter informing me that the
Board have, with much regret, accepted my resignation. Thus has
terminated my connection with a Company which cost me much
labour and anxiety to form, but which has already profited to the
extent of from £150,000 to £200,000 on the premiums on shares
alone. This Company was dear to me from having been its
founder, and having selected all the first directors and chief officers;
also because it was the most successful of all my labours in public
companies and gave me great influence at home and in the colonies.
It was, in fact, like plucking out a right eye.

Unlike most monetary institutions the Union
Bank owed its existence to pure philanthropy.
There was nothing that Mr. Angas would not do to
further the interests of South Australia; he had
glorious visions of its being a haven of rest, a new
starting point in life, for myriads of his fellows
trodden down by competition, persecuted for conscience' sake, or struggling to be honest, and as the

formation of a Bank would help forward this larger scheme, he formed it, and for no other reason.

The shareholders, when he retired from the directorate, either did not know, or did not care to know, to whom they were indebted—nor, in all probability, has one in a thousand ever known since. When he resigned, a letter of thanks and regret was the only recognition of his services, and there is just the echo of a sigh in the words he wrote to a friend on the day of its receipt :—

"As to public business I confess to you that I have always been ill requited for the labours I have given in that way."

Our interest in the Union Bank of Australia ceases here. But it will enhance the appreciation of Mr. Angas's labours in its foundation, and his self-sacrifice in abandoning his connection with it—from causes for which, as we shall see, he was in no way responsible—if we just glance at a stage or two in its subsequent history.

In 1887 the Bank completed the first half-century of its existence, and up to that time it had made net profits exceeding eight millions sterling. No other Australasian undertaking can show such enormous profits, due to a great extent to the large amount of capital embarked in it from its very commencement. But that capital "has received dividends without a single interruption since they were started in 1839, and dividends that have reflected the condition of commerce in the Colonies more perhaps than those

of any other Australian institution.* The directors
have always pursued the policy of dividing, with
certain allowances, nearly what was earned in the
period covered by the accounts; and when Australia
passed in 1844 from inflation to depression, or ran
wild with excitement in 1852–53, the dividends
equally with the net profits recorded the state of
the country." †

Including a considerable reserve of securities in
London and cash in hand and at call to the extent
of over three and a half millions sterling, the Board
of Directors had, according to their balance-sheet
given in the Fifty-Second Report (July 1890), the
management of assets amounting to £19,174,584.
And the business is rapidly increasing. With
branches in all the Colonies, and large supplies of
home money, it will probably continue to increase
and play an important part in the almost illimitable
future of Australasian Banking.

Of the original Directors there are none now to be
found amongst the governing body, the last of them,
Mr. Robert Brooks, having retired in 1876.

Having digressed so far in order to complete the
history of Mr. Angas's labours in connection with the

---

* Thus in 1844 the dividends were 6 per cent. per share; in
1854 they were 86 per cent. per share; in 1860–61, a period of
reaction, 15 and 12 per cent. respectively, and so on.

† "The Banking Institutions of Australasia." By Robert Lucas
Nash.

banking affairs of South Australia, we must now go
back to gather up some connecting links in the narrative of his early relations with the colony.

How to do justice to the aborigines of lands
occupied by colonists has always been a difficult
question, and it proved to be so in the case of South
Australia. Mr. Angas set before himself the model
of William Penn and his treaty with the North
American Indians for establishing friendly and
equitable relations with the Europeans. But even
Penn's well-devised plans to a great extent failed,
because the treaty was not binding upon future
colonists.

In the case of South Australia the Act of Parliament for establishing the colony virtually ignored
the existence of the aborigines, but this did not
prevent the Colonization Commissioners from making special provision for their welfare, and Mr. Angas
from the first hour he entered on his duties did not
cease to do everything in his power on their behalf.

The Austral negroes, the original possessors of the
enormous continent of Australia, represented the
lowest members of the great human family. Practically coverless they were altogether homeless. The
women were porters to the tribe when on tramp,
which was almost always, and the poor creatures
wandered after their lords bowed down beneath the
load of food and kangaroo skins constituting their
whole supplies and stores.

Their religious ideas were confined to faith in an

Evil Spirit who pursued and harassed them. Death was the result of sorcery. They had certain customs by which, among themselves, they regulated their wanderings, their fightings, their marriages, and the ceremonies of life from the day of birth till the day of burial. Of a Supreme Being they appeared to have no knowledge whatever.

One of the first acts of Mr. Angas in his capacity as Commissioner was to bring before the Board the question of the treatment of these aborigines, and to secure for them certain rights and privileges necessary for their sustenance and protection. In the first annual report of the Commissioners the following liberal measures were put forward as objects to be aimed at in dealing with the natives. "To guard them against personal outrage and violence; to protect them in the undisturbed enjoyment of their proprietary right to the soil, wherever such right may be found to exist; to make it an invariable and cardinal condition in all bargains and treaties made with natives for the cession of lands possessed by them, in occupation or enjoyment, that permanent subsistence shall be supplied to them from some other source, and to promote amongst them the spread of civilization, and the peaceful and voluntary reception of the Christian religion."

An admirable programme, but, like William Penn's, difficult to carry out from circumstances which could not have been provided against by human foresight.

Lord Glenelg reserved to himself the power of

appointing an officer as "Protector of the Aborigines," and Mr. Angas used every endeavour to urge
upon him the importance of selecting some one who
would be solicitous for the spiritual as well as the
material well-being of the natives.

If that appointment (he wrote in his diary) falls into the hands
of any but a Christian man, it will be sure to fail in its object.
O ! that the Lord would direct the Government to adopt such
measures as will be perfectly effectual to the civilizing and
Christianizing of the natives.

At a banquet given to Captain Hindmarsh in
London, in September, 1835, prior to his departure
for the new colony, Mr. Angas, in proposing the
toast, " The welfare of the Aborigines of South
Australia, and the gentlemen who are forming
societies for their protection and benefit," gave a
sketch of the principles and plans which he thought
should be adopted to secure the end in view.

Let us send out persons among them (he said), to learn their
language, if no one can be obtained already acquainted with it ;
to treat with them for the purchase of those lands which they
claim as belonging to their tribes ; to make them acquainted with
the habits and views of the white people ; to construct a written
language for them ; to publish the Gospels and New Testament in
it ; to teach them to read ; to make them acquainted with the art
of raising food from the ground ; to instruct them in the mode of
fishing in the sea, of which they are quite ignorant, having no
canoes ; the method of making necessary utensils, raising huts,
the use of clothing, and in time they may be induced by sufficient
reward and kind treatment to allow the settlers to take their youths
and teach them to work as labourers.

In order to carry out these views he had many
interviews with Mr. Fowell Buxton, and other
friends of the Aborigines Protection Society, and
a parliamentary committee was appointed to obtain
information on the subject. But Mr. Angas had
greater faith in individual action than in parliamentary committees, and having conceived the idea
that the best way to proceed would be to establish
at the influx of the River Murray into Lake
Alexandrina, where the natives were wont to assemble
in large numbers, a kind of missionary station with
store and farm where the arts of civilization could
be taught and the gospel preached, he proceeded to
offer a princely contribution to any Missionary
Society that would undertake the work. He gave
preference to the principles employed in the
Moravian Missions, where, in addition to religious
instruction, labour schools would be formed, so
that, while making ample provision for Christian
education, the natives would, at the same time,
acquire correct and industrious habits, and a
knowledge of agriculture and simple trades which
would enable them to raise food and decent habi-
tations.

About this time, as we shall presently see more
fully, Mr. Angas was brought much into contact
with many excellent German Lutherans who were
suffering persecution in their own country. Through
them he opened up communications with the Evangelical Lutheran Missionary Society in Dresden,

and almost entirely at his own expense succeeded in sending out two devoted men, Messrs. Teichelmann and Schürmann, to labour exclusively among the aborigines of South Australia and carry out his views.

The missionaries set sail on the 21st of May, 1838, in the same ship which conveyed the new governor, Colonel Gawler, appointed to succeed Captain Hindmarsh, and were kindly and formally received by Mr. William Wyatt, acting Protector of the Aborigines, who shortly before their arrival had reported as follows :—

I am impressed with the thorough conviction that the only means which can be permanently successful is first to teach the natives the simple and sublime doctrines of Christianity, and that to begin by any other method is truly to commence at the wrong end. The success of such an undertaking appears to be the more certain in that the aborigines do not appear to be attached to any superstitions of whose influence it would be previously necessary and perhaps difficult to divest them. Their minds rather seem to be in that unoccupied condition which capacitates them for receiving impressions of whatever may be presented to them in a sufficiently interesting form. Entertaining this opinion I cannot but believe that the arrival of special missionaries for the aborigines would be the greatest benefit which could be bestowed upon them, and there can be little doubt, that, aided as they would be by the co-operation of the Protector and immediately put in possession of as much of the difficult dialect as is now known without having to overcome the first difficulties of acquiring an unwritten, and, therefore, variable language, their progress would be commensurate with the wishes of those who look upon the aborigines of South Australia as fellow members of the great human family.

11

Henceforth a fresh interest was given to all the communications of Mr. Angas with the new colony. Almost every mail brought him letters from the missionaries detailing the progress of their work, in which they were mainly guided by him, of their difficulties in acquiring the language, of their excursions with the natives, and other matters interesting in themselves, but not calling for description here. The Governor testified to their labours from time to time, and wrote to Mr. Angas in July, 1840 :—

I have very great reason to believe them to be sincere, intelligent, persevering Christian men, and if their efforts had not at all succeeded, they, I think, would have been blameless. The change of the aborigines in any moderate time even to mere civilization would be an especial effect of the power of God. The deep-rooted prejudices of a very ancient people, agreeing universally throughout the whole island in the leading points of a very ancient system, are not to be overcome in a few years. The protector and missionaries have done much to shake it, but the progress will be slow, and not very discernible to indifferent spectators.

Two other missionaries, Messrs. Meyer and Klose, were sent out by Mr. Angas under the auspices of the Dresden Society in the spring of 1840, and they were enabled through the exertions of the two who had preceded them to fall at once into places ready for their reception.

It was not only in these direct efforts that Mr. Angas showed his zeal for the welfare of the Aborigines of South Australia. In 1841 he gave evidence

before a Select Committee of the House of Commons,
and went thoroughly into the whole subject, repeating
once again the old story, so often told in relation to
the treatment of native tribes, how the British
Government had secured for themselves the oysters,
and given to the original possessors of the land the
shells :—

With respect to the Act (said Mr. Angas), I conceive that those
words in the preamble which declare that South Australia consists
of waste and unoccupied lands, clearly exclude the aborigines from
any advantage whatever arising from the land; it does not even
recognize their existence.   They have no existence in a legal
point of view, therefore no provision could be made for them by
the Commissioners.   The natives cannot purchase and hold land.
The Commissioners are to declare, according to the Act, that all
the lands of the said province are public lands, open to purchase
by British subjects, consequently the natives can hold no property.
In the next place, no grant of land can be legally made to the
aborigines, because in the sixth section of the Act it is stated that
all lands are public lands open to purchase, and that the said
public lands shall be sold in public for ready-money. . . . Hence,
it follows, if I am right in my construction of the Act, that the
selection or grant of lands made by Governor Gawler on behalf
of the aborigines at Adelaide and Encounter Bay, of which we
have had recent advice, is positively illegal, and, should the
aborigines settle upon them and improve them, it will end in their
disappointment, unless there shall be an alteration in the Act
hereafter.   I think, too, that positive injustice has been done to
the natives by the Act itself, inasmuch as a portion of land was
occupied by them at the time the Act was framed, whereas it
declares that there was no land occupied.   The missionaries
inform me that every adult native possesses a district of land
which he calls ‘his country,’ and which he inherited from his

father. Some of them indeed say that they gave their land to the whites, and that they have received in payment for it a little rice, biscuit, and sugar. . . .

To repair as far as possible these wrongs, he suggested that certain lands should be appropriated to the use of the natives; that each tribe should have its own location, on which there should be a village, on the Moravian or other useful system, where a missionary and a few families of Christian people should reside permanently. These suggestions commended themselves to the Committee, and the following resolution was passed: "That it is expedient that Her Majesty should be authorized to reserve and set apart within the said province, for the use of the aboriginal inhabitants thereof, any lands which it may be found necessary so to reserve and set apart for the occupation and subsistence of such aboriginal inhabitants."

Although to the end of his life the interest of Mr. Angas in the welfare of the Austral negroes never abated, the same circumstances which made him recall so many of his subscriptions, and curtail business and philanthropic operations, caused him for a time to suspend active efforts on behalf of these poor people.

It was found that they would not avail themselves of the Native Reserves set apart for their use, and the South Australian Government therefore leased the Reserves, and contributed something annually out of the general revenue for their support and protection. For the twenty-five years dating from 1840 to 1865 the aggregate sum so expended amounted to £30,160 9s. 4d.

In three instances native villages and institutions were formed at Poonindie in the Port Lincoln District, Point Macleay on Lake Alexandrina, and on Yorke's Peninsula, on the plan suggested by Mr. Angas, and they proved more successful than any that had previously been tried.

The promotion of religion and education among the colonists was another of the chief concerns of Mr. Angas, in his labours for the welfare of South Australia. His first endeavours were directed, as we have seen, to the appointment of persons of pronounced religious character to become officers and agents of the Company, and next to secure Christian families as the first settlers in the colony, and godly captains and surgeons to sail in the ships of the Company.

In more direct efforts the establishment of schools took the first place.* The system, elaborately drawn

---

* An interesting incident in this connection is recorded by Mr. John Howard Angas. At one of the first meetings of the South Australian Company, Mr. Angas as chairman said to his fellow-directors that he considered it a first duty, even before a tent was set up in the colony, to provide for Christian education there, and he put down on the table a sum of money to commence a fund for that purpose, and invited his fellow-directors to do the same. This they did, and most of them lived to see the wonderful effects of this early movement. Mr. Angas then asked his solicitor, who was also the solicitor of the Company, being present, if he could not invite some friends to contribute towards the fund. In pursuance of this request the solicitor obtained among other

up by Mr. Angas, was to include Lancasterian
schools until the age of twelve was attained, when
the children were to proceed to higher schools where
half their time would be spent in labour at such
trades as might be selected for them to learn. This
was called the Labour School, and here they would
remain until they were sixteen years of age, after
which they would be apprenticed to the Company, or
to respectable settlers. When the population increased sufficiently to warrant it, infant schools were
to be established.

In arranging educational and missionary matters
Mr. Angas was much indebted to the sagacious
advice of the ready-witted and enthusiastic John
Williams of the South Sea Islands, who was at that
time in England.

The first practical step to this, and a number of
closely allied schemes, was the sending out of Mr.
B. Shepherdson to superintend the arrangements in
the colony. He had for some time been visiting
various parts of England to make himself acquainted
with the different school systems, and especially
those which allied themselves to technical education.

subscriptions two five pound notes from two Christian sisters, and both
these ladies lived for that solicitor to place in their hands twenty-five
years afterwards a statistical account of the colony, in which it appeared
as a result of that early educational fund that there were then eight hundred
schools in which more than ten thousand children were receiving a
scriptural education, besides all the ordinary courses of tuition ! Other
colonies unfortunately left education as one of the last things to be
thought of, and only wakened to its importance when ignorance and
vice were working the ruin of the rising generation.

Meanwhile, in order to create and sustain an interest in this country in what was going on in the far-distant colony, Mr. Angas organized an association called "The South Australian School Society," and took the lion's share of responsibility in supplying funds. The School Society met with considerable encouragement. Hitherto, unhappily, colonization had been viewed in no other light than as a source of commercial profit or military strength, and the moral condition of many of our British possessions had sunk to a lower level than when they were inhabited simply by the native savages.

To each Governor in succession for many years, Mr. Angas commended his school system for support and encouragement, at the same time pledging himself to foster it financially from this country, and he begged the first Governor to enact as one of the laws of his council, that certain degrees of honour and privilege should attach to the well-educated and industrious children of the poor.

In Mr. D. McLaren, the chief commercial manager of the Company in South Australia, Mr. Angas found a man able and willing to carry out all his philanthropic designs, while in religious matters he had the co-operation of Mr. William Giles, who held an important position in the affairs of the Company. Mr. Giles was a staunch and back-bone advocate of the abolition of State aid to religion, and of the establishment of civil and religious equality, and his indefatigable labours to this end have caused his name to be held in grateful memory by the colonists.

The pioneer missionary of the Colonial Missionary Society, the Rev. T. Q. Stow, who was sent out through the influence of Mr. Angas, and mainly at his expense, also rendered important services to the colony. He warmly co-operated with Mr. Giles in resisting State aid to religion—a subject on which, as we have seen, Mr. Angas had held strong views all his life long.

In a letter to one of the early Governors of South Australia, he wrote this characteristic passage :—

Above all things avoid the establishment of any particular sect in religion. Let every man who is a Christian, and honestly worships God according to his conscience, not be degraded on that account. Confusion, disputes, and every evil work will follow. The Episcopalian system of the Church of England will best flourish when it sets the brightest and noblest example of piety, humility, and benevolence. It is sound in doctrine, and needs not the puny arm of man to prop it up. If it looks to and depends only upon God, it must prosper ; but if it resorts to earthly power, confiscation, taxation, and constraint of men's conscience, or punishment of any kind for nonconformity, then its glory has departed, and it will infallibly decline by a slow, but sure process.

Shortly after the arrival of Mr. Shepherdson in Adelaide he formed a colonial branch of the School Society, and the first Governor presided over the inaugural meeting. That Society exercised a very powerful influence for good at a time when the thoughts of most persons were occupied with almost every other matter than those of an educational and religious character.

The schools founded under the auspices of this English and Colonial School Society flourished; no denominational creeds or catechisms were used in them, but a sound, practical, and religious education was given.

Mr. Angas established, at great expense, one or two newspapers, but they failed, mainly, it is to be feared, from the introduction of religious topics into them. He wanted its pages to be useful in promoting in every way moral and religious truth, and the improvement of the colony in everything good and useful — a laudable design, but fatal to the commercial value of the undertaking.

Mr. Angas was in no sense a sectarian, and therefore we are not surprised to find that among those ministers of the gospel he was instrumental in sending out, various denominations were represented.

The manner in which the Wesleyans received their minister is so curious a story that it deserves insertion here.

Among the early settlers were about sixty devout Wesleyans who grieved that they had no minister among them. They were wont to pray that one might be "raised up," and their prayer was answered in an extraordinary manner. The Rev. W. Longbottom, sailing with his wife and child from Hobart Town for Western Australia, fell in with a gale

which increased in fury until at midnight the vessel
struck on an unknown coast and they were landed,
through the surf, by means of a rope. They suffered
for want of a fire till on the second day of their
escape some friendly natives ventured near them.
After a fortnight spent in a forlorn condition, and
not knowing whither to turn, a crew of shipwrecked
mariners found them. By means of a chart they
had saved they had come a hundred miles, and
were going fifty more in search of a whaling station.
The two companies made common cause, and for
forty-five days they wandered through the bush,
and reaching the station they were taken by sea
to Adelaide, where the pastorless society of sixty
members welcomed the minister, and would not let
him go. From the outset, Wesleyan Methodism
had been an immense evangelical power in every
part of the Australian continent, and it took root
and flourished in Adelaide, and "all the regions
round about," through the faithful ministrations of
the man who, in this extraordinary way, was "raised
up" for the work.

Among the institutions that Mr. Angas was
desirous of establishing was a National Labour
College, and he elaborated a scheme for carrying it
into effect—a scheme far in advance of that time
and identical in principle with some of the technical
colleges of to-day.

A paragraph or two from the prospectus he drew
up will not be uninteresting :—

If our colonists are to receive an education which shall fit them for the high vocation to which they are called of raising cities in the wilderness, of breaking up the soil of waste but fertile regions, of sowing in far distant lands the seeds of British institutions, arts, and sciences, and above all, of diffusing far and wide the principles of that Divine religion which has raised the mother country to the elevated station of queen among the nations, it can only be by the adoption of a system suited in every respect to the position in which they are placed—a system which, while fostering the highest degree of intellectual improvement and literary acquisition, will at the same time develop and mature the bodily energies, promote habits of industry, and by making labour honourable, secure that community of interest, apart from which neither genuine social happiness nor permanent national prosperity can be enjoyed.

Unfortunately, the scheme proved a failure; its one fault was that it was in advance of the time.

Of the untiring labours of Mr. Angas in promoting emigration, some details will be given later on. Meanwhile, we must devote a separate chapter to one particularly interesting phase of the subject.

CHAPTER VII.

PERSECUTION, AND WHAT CAME OF IT.

ONE day early in 1836 two German gentlemen called at the office of Mr. Angas, having heard of his philanthropy through merchants in Hamburg with whom he had trading connections. One of the visitors was the Rev. D. Shrievogel, a missionary on the point of starting for India; the other, the Rev. Augustus Kavel, formerly Evangelical Lutheran pastor of Klemzig, Harthe, and Golgin in Prussia, who was sent over to this country as a deputation on behalf of his people, having been compelled, from conscientious motives, to resign his spiritual oversight of them, and to secede from the United Evangelical Church after eleven years of service.

Mr. Angas was engaged; Mr. Shrievogel was pressed for time, and could not wait; and Mr. Kavel remained therefore alone. When the time for an interview arrived, it was found that Mr. Kavel spoke very little English, and that little most imperfectly, while Mr. Angas knew nothing whatever of German. Fortunately, his confidential clerk, Mr. Charles Flaxman, was an excellent German scholar, and he acted as interpreter. A simple and natural train of circumstances—in itself not worth recording; but that interview was to have far-reaching consequences, and to affect the destiny of thousands of persons, while those two men, Messrs. Kavel and Flaxman, were to play a part in the near future which should influence the whole of the after life of Mr. Angas.

The story Mr. Kavel had to tell was to this effect :—

In 1817, the union between the Reformed and Lutheran Churches in Prussia had nearly everywhere been adopted; but the Church ritual being different in various places, it was thought desirable to substitute a regulation for uniform worship over the whole of the evangelical part of the Monarchy.

Accordingly in 1822, King Frederick William III. himself issued a new liturgy, introduced it by Cabinet Order, caused it to be used in the Royal Chapel and the military or garrison churches, and recommended its adoption by all Protestant communities in the State.

It was compiled partly from the old Lutheran

liturgy, and partly from that of the Reformed
Church (with some, though only a few, additions from
the prayer book of the Church of England).

But the views of the two great Protestant communities in Germany differed in regard to Baptism
and the Lord's Supper. The Reformed Church, moreover, held the doctrine of Reprobation, while the
Lutherans rejected it entirely, although acknowledging the doctrine of Election.

There were other "minor" points, as they may
appear to us, which, however, they regarded as
"error," and when these were incorporated with the
new liturgy, the Lutherans, whose ancestors had
for centuries opposed them, felt it to be their religious duty to stand out against the innovation at
all costs.

The opposition was increased in consequence of
those who accepted the reform being favoured with
State approval and preferment, while those who conscientiously disapproved and refused to adopt it,
incurred the displeasure of the Government. So
long, however, as the Government confined itself
to a simple recommendation, the objections raised
against it were not of great importance, but when,
in 1825, steps were taken to make it compulsory, the
gauntlet was thrown down which led to battle.

National federation and religious union had been
for many generations the policy of Germany as tending to the consolidation of the various kingdoms,
principalities, and duchies into one great Germanic

Empire. But the Lutheran Church had never recognized kings and princes as having any authority to rule in Church matters, and this new liturgy, drawn up, it was alleged, by the King himself—whose ancestors had for two centuries been members of the Reformed Church—they utterly rejected.

The Church party, with Schleiermacher at its head, fought bravely against Auguste, Marheineche, and others for the freedom and independence of the Church, and against the "Agenda," as being the work of the Government without the consent of the respective Church communities.

The quarrel lasted until 1829, when the Government sought to end it by issuing a new edition of the liturgy, in which certain concessions were made, and promulgated a formal order fixing the 25th of June, 1830—the third centenary of the presentation to the Emperor Charles of the statement by the early reformers, since known as the Augsburg Confession—as the day for its universal introduction.

But the order was not universally obeyed. The "original" Lutheran Churches were in deadly opposition to the new liturgy, their contention being that it contained statements at variance with the Augsburg Confession, and was a violation of the Treaty of Westphalia, which had constituted that Confession the standard of appeal for all purposes of the reformed religion.

Dr. Scheiber, professor in the University of Breslau, who was one of the first to incur the royal displeasure by refusing on conscientious grounds to adopt the new formula, was suspended from office. Coercion, amounting to persecution, followed; pastors declining to use the liturgy were dismissed from their churches, and forbidden to attend private meetings of their parishioners for the purpose of instructing them, or of administering the Lord's Supper.

On appeal to the constituted authorities they were characterized as "obstinate and self-willed people," who needlessly incurred the royal displeasure by not submitting. Nevertheless they stood firm, and in proportion as they did so the violence of the persecution increased. Forcible possession was taken of places of worship when the pastors refused to conduct the service according to the new form; several obnoxious ministers were banished or imprisoned; fines were levied, police supervision was enforced, and a system of petty tyranny was established.

Matters went on from bad to worse until, seeing no chance of enjoying religious freedom and toleration in their own country, many determined, as the Pilgrim Fathers had done before them, to seek some part of the globe where they might worship God according to their judgment and the dictates of conscience.

It was to acquaint Mr. Angas with the state of affairs in Prussia, and to ask his advice as to South Australia being a good field to which his persecuted countrymen might emigrate, that Mr. Kavel made his visit to the office of the London merchant on the 12th of April, 1836.

The sympathies of Mr. Angas were immediately aroused, and he determined then and there, on verification of the statements, to lend all the aid in his power to assist the persecuted Lutherans to find some place where they might be free to worship God after their own manner.

When Mr. Kavel resigned his pastorate to plead the cause of his countrymen in England, the following curious testimonial was given him by the superintendent of the District of Züllichau in which his church was situate :—

January 6, 1836.

It is hereby officially certified, to serve him for the future, that the Rev. A. Kavel, who was minister of the Evangelical Lutheran Church at Klemzig, in the circle of Züllichau, from Christmas, 1826, till Easter, 1835, and who then, on account of a change in his convictions, voluntarily resigned that situation, and was released from his ministry by the Royal Prussian Consistory of the province of Brandenburg, conducted himself irreproachably during the period of his ministry, and strove to fulfil the duties of his pastoral charge with conscientious fidelity according to the measure of his knowledge and ability. May the Divine Lord and Master of our Evangelical Church guide him in the way of peace and preserve him in His grace.

South Australia, to which Mr. Angas had just despatched the pioneer vessels of the South Australian Company, at once suggested itself to him

12

as a suitable place for the Prussians. He broached
the subject to Mr. Kavel, and ascertained that the
large majority of those anxious to emigrate had not
the funds to pay for their outfit and passage.

Another difficulty was in the way. Information
was received from the pastors of churches that,
although the Government gave orders to the provincial authorities at Züllichau to ascertain and send
to the Ministry at Berlin the number of persons
wishing to emigrate, with particulars of age, family,
and so forth, some time must elapse before the
necessary permission to leave would be given. How
long a time they little knew then!

When once the emigration movement was promulgated in Prussia, twenty-five congregations, com-
prising 727 individuals, immediately decided to avail
themselves of it, although electing to go to the
United States, and to this end it was agreed by all,
whatever their resources might be, to put their
possessions into one common fund, and share and
share alike. The total fund amounted to between
£5,000 and £6,000.

In various parts of Germany the movement was set
on foot, in some instances among persons too poor
to think of emigrating at their own expense, and
these were the ones Mr. Angas was most anxious to
assist.

Yet another difficulty arose. The people whom
Pastor Kavel specially represented, thinking that
there would be no hindrance to their departure, sold

all their little property, and engaged vessels for
their conveyance to Hamburg, the negotiations
made with the Prussian Government being of such
a character as to lead to the conclusion that no
opposition would be offered. Meanwhile, Mr. Angas,
backed by the Company, fitted up a vessel, the
Sarah, to proceed to Hamburg and embark 370
Lutherans for South Australia. But the Prussian
Government refused to furnish them with their
passports, and for months the poor people were kept
in a state of uncertainty, their scanty resources
daily diminishing.

By the Treaty of Westphalia free emigration was
granted to every subject of Germany and Prussia,
provided he could not enjoy the unfettered exercise
of his faith in his own country. Such being the
case the Government could not honourably give
a direct refusal to the intending emigrants, but, by
raising petty and vexatious obstacles, contrived to
keep them in painful suspense.

To bring matters to a crisis, Mr. Angas, at great
personal inconvenience, for he was in the midst of
most bewildering business in connection with the
new colony, sent his chief clerk, Mr. Flaxman, to
Hamburg, with instructions to proceed to Berlin,
if necessary, in order to remove any difficulties in
the way of the departure of the Prussians. He was
armed with a certificate from the Colonization Commissioners, attested by the Colonial and Foreign
officers and the Prussian ambassador.

Meanwhile Mr. Kavel remained in England, where
he speedily acquired a thorough knowledge of the
English language, and, at the instigation of Mr.
Angas, commenced a missionary crusade among
Germans in London. It was little thought when
he first commenced this work that two years would ·
elapse before he would be able to sail with his former
congregation to South Australia. But in some
respects the delay was advantageous. He laboured
successfully among his sailor-countrymen on the
Thames ; conducted regular Sunday services in
various parts of London ; largely assisted the German
Sunday School—the first and only institution of
the kind in London, founded a few months before
his arrival by three German tailors ; preached
under the Bethel Flag at the London Docks ;
established in London a Lutheran auxiliary to the
Dresden Missionary Society ; organized a committee
of English and German gentlemen who founded
" The London German Sunday School Society," an
institution which was the means of doing incal-
culable good, and rendered important service in
assisting Mr. Angas to send out missionaries from
Dresden for the evangelization of the aborigines of
South Australia. So that out of apparent evil came
real good. Nevertheless it would be unjust to give
the credit solely to Mr. Kavel. He laboured honestly
and well, and his efforts were singularly successful ;
but he was absolutely penniless, and all his personal
expenses, as well as the expenses inevitable in under-

taking new and high enterprises, were borne entirely
by Mr. Angas, who also supported him with what
was better than money—his time and influence.

Mr. Flaxman returned with the melancholy
tidings that his mission had been unsuccessful, and
that the people, having disposed of their farms and
effects, were rapidly exhausting their little capital.
The bright side of the picture was that they were
bearing persecution in the spirit of meekness, and
in not one single instance had they offered resistance
to the police, who had closed their places of worship
and watched them to prevent their assembling in
private houses.

In these circumstances the *Sarah*, chartered at
great expense, was told off for other service, and
nothing remained on either side but to wait patiently
the issue of events.

It soon became apparent that the Prussian
Government was in an embarrassed position, and
did not quite know what course to take. The
detention of the people, and the cause of the re-
strictions put upon their liberty, was becoming
known in Britain and elsewhere, and was leading
to severe comments and censures. So far coercion
had proved fruitless, but to let the people go was to
proclaim the fact far and wide, as well as the cause
of their voluntary exile.

A year passed away, and still the Lutherans were
detained. The whole of Mr. Kavel's late congregation in Klemzig had determined to emigrate with

their former pastor to South Australia, and aided
by his energy, and the influence of Mr. Angas, they
were taking active steps to obtain a solution of their
difficulties. They presented a petition to the King,
with the result that he instructed Dr. Strauss, a
councillor of the Consistory in Berlin, to proceed to
Klemzig, and use his best endeavours to bring the
people back to the Established Church ! His mission
totally failed, the people remaining stedfast and
immovable.

Many of the ministers and philanthropists of
London joined together to expedite matters, and
proposed to call a meeting to ventilate the whole
question. But Mr. Kavel declined to be present,
or to accept the well-meant intervention, on the
ground that claiming the political interference of
a foreign power was contrary to the Lutheran belief
in the teaching of Scripture, although it was not
inconsistent for them to leave a country where their
religious freedom was endangered. " If they per-
secute you in one city, flee into another " was the
letter and spirit of their warrant. The proposed
meeting was therefore abandoned.

On the 20th of November, 1837, Pastor Kavel
wrote to Mr. Angas :—

I have received a letter from home, but matters are still as they
were. No reply to the last petition for passports. My poor flock
enjoys some rest at present, and they have not been disturbed for
the last eight weeks by the police during their meetings. All the
Lutheran ministers, however, are still in prison. The room where

the Lutheran congregation at Berlin used to meet was locked up by order of the police some time ago. The congregation then assembled in two adjoining rooms, and when the policeman came to lock them up also, the people declared that they would rather allow themselves to be beheaded than leave off their meetings. Some of the deputies sent by the United Lutheran congregations to request an audience with the King are still imprisoned. . . .

In a subsequent letter it was stated by Mr. Kavel :—

All the Lutherans of the district of Züllichau were ordered to appear before the sheriff, when a document was read to them the substance of which was that if they would not join the United Church, or allow the sacraments to be administered to them by the clergymen of the Establishment, after the form of the Lutheran liturgy, or, if they wanted to have a church of their own, they were ordered and permitted to leave the country, and might go to Russia if they could prove that they had money enough to pay their way. If they refused either course they would be punished according to the severity of the laws.

In consequence of this order a fresh complication arose ; everything seeming to be against their going to South Australia, many of the people expressed their wish to emigrate to Russia, lured by the promise of large quantities of land to be given them by the Emperor, and as they were for the most part ignorant of the respective merits of a residence in the wilds of Russia and in the newly settled colony of South Australia, they chose the former—the fact that they could reach it by land, instead of by a long sea-voyage, telling strongly in its favour.

In acknowledging these letters of Mr. Kavel, Mr. Angas, who was then at Dawlish, wrote :—

I pray God to guide you and them to the adoption of such measures as will be for His glory, and your welfare. As the people of your charge appear inclined to direct their steps to Russia instead of South Australia, I am quite willing to absolve them, and do now absolve them, from all obligation to proceed to the new colony. . . . If, however, you still wish to go there, I will do all in my power to facilitate it, only I think the time has come when I should know your decision positively one way or another. So I leave it with you to inform me what course you will pursue, while I do earnestly pray God to direct and bless you, and deliver you from perplexity.

This stirred up Mr. Kavel to renewed action, and in very forcible letters he urged his old congregation to come to a decision. " I want you to tell me as soon as possible who, and how many of you, are determined, under God, to proceed to South Australia. If any of you are so prepared, I will go with you."

In response to his appeal, nearly every family belonging to his congregation agreed to emigrate to South Australia ; but with every movement of the Lutherans some fresh coercive measure was put forth by the Government, and it was now intimated that only those who were of full age, and had served their time as soldiers, would obtain their passports. The object of this was to cause separation in families, and to keep back the young men whose services were most required in the colony.

Nor was this all : fines, imprisonments, seizure of

cattle, household furniture, and implements of husbandry followed; deputations to the King were forbidden, persons assembling for worship were dragged away from their conventicles by the police " even during the reading of the sermon ; if the door chanced to be locked it was broken through with an axe, and all the persons arrested were subjected to fines and penalties."

In an address of Deputies from Silesia, cases are cited of which the following is a specimen—

Fathers of families and widows have been thrown into long imprisonment, have been robbed of their property, clothing, house utensils, of their cattle, nay, even of their ploughs . . . solely because baptism and confirmation were performed by Lutheran pastors. The child of Cattert at Dunkawe, baptized by a Lutheran Pastor, was brought by the policeman Berg to the United Minister, Butzki, at Suhlaw in order to be re-baptized. . . . Children are torn from us by the police and with violence brought into their schools in order to be educated there according to their own views. Some who have even passed their fourteenth year, and have been confirmed by Lutheran pastors, are taken by the police to the United Schools, or to the State Minister for examination, in order that by the semblance of right they might be incorporated with their church, or be made subject to it. Every father or widow who omitted to send such children to school as had·been confirmed by a Lutheran pastor, were fined five dollars per month or adequate imprisonment. We can no longer live with a quiet conscience under such violent dominancy. Our distress is aggravated when we consider the present state of our Lutheran Church. Roused from its lethargy by the attempted Union, it has begun a new life and a new epoch, in which, like a tender babe, it will pine and perish without the nourishment of faithful doctrines.

At the end of January, 1838, Pastor Kavel was able to inform Mr. Angas that 165 persons, belonging to four different districts, were ready to emigrate, provided the South Australian Company would furnish certificates that they were prepared to receive them, and state under what circumstances the directors would embark the emigrants, advance the passage money, and employ them in the colony.

It seemed that at last, having tried every means of exhausting the patience of the Lutherans, the Prussian Government was prepared to grant passports. At all events there was an alteration in its attitude, but unfortunately a great change had also taken place in the affairs of the South Australian Company, and it was not now in the same favourable position to promote the emigration of the Lutherans. The Company had already incurred heavy expenses, and still heavier risks, on their behalf, a ship having been chartered at the outset at a cost of £2,300. Moreover, when the subject was first mooted, only a handful of pioneer colonists had set off to the new colony, now a large number of English emigrants had proceeded, and were proceeding thither, and it was, of course, the policy of the Company to care first for their British emigrants.

While the sympathies of Mr. Angas remained personally unaltered, as Chairman of the Company he could not in these circumstances hold out the same hopes of assistance, and we find him casting about in his mind for new sources of help. Among other

plans which he devised was an application to Lord
Glenelg, Secretary of State for the Colonies, for
permission to settle the Lutherans upon some portion
of the new territory, where they might form a
distinct community—an application which was not
favourably received.

Writing to Mr. Kavel from Dawlish, in February,
he says :—

How the affair is to terminate I really cannot at present conjecture, for at this moment, to my apprehension, clouds and darkness
are round about it. In the meantime patience and hope in the
kindness of the Lord is our duty. In due time He will bring it to
pass, although we cannot now see how. I do not think the proposition can again be brought before the South Australian directors.

Later on he says :—

All thoughts of the directors of the South Australian Company
taking the case of your people in hand must be given up. I am
certain they will not again interfere, and, indeed, as they are only
stewards of the shareholders, I could not conscientiously recommend
it, especially as they could not by any means engage to employ the
people after their arrival in the colony, as their attention and
capital have, in consequence of the former disappointment in their
behalf, been directed to other objects. As it respects myself, I feel
the same towards them as before, only my own means of capital
have also been diverted into other channels since that project was
started.

This seemed at first like a death-blow to the whole
scheme. But Mr. Angas was fertile in expedients,
and the letter closed with a hint that if he could

bring certain matters to pass he might be able to command capital enough of his own, with what the Lutherans might have left of the wreck of their properties, to establish them in the colony.

Poor Mr. Kavel was the victim of alternating hope and fear, of gratitude and despondency. Just when the way seemed open, just when the Prussians almost unanimously abandoned the idea of proceeding to Russia, and pronounced in favour of South Australia, it was found that the Company could not give the certificates required by the Prussian Government, and Mr. Kavel was in the unenviable position of fearing he would be charged with " a sort of high treason " for having held out false hopes of finding a place of refuge for hundreds of his fellow-countrymen.

To add to his distress fresh applications to share the exile of the Lutherans were coming in from all quarters. Let one illustration suffice. Baron Von Koszutski, the proprietor of an estate in Silesia, was heavily fined for holding prayer-meetings in his house ; his state-coach, oxen, and cows were seized and sold, and he was cast into prison for many months. He wrote to say that if the South Australian Company would send a declaration that his people—the inhabitants of Great Tschunkarve near Trühan in Silesia, and the Lutherans of the districts Militsch, Trebnitz, Oels, Wartenberg, and Krotoszyn, would be received as settlers in the colony, he would immediately apply for passports.

In like manner applications were received from congregations in Breslau, the capital of Silesia, in Berlin, Magdeburg, and elsewhere.

The ball had been set rolling, and no one could tell where it would stop.

It was a critical time in the history of Mr. Angas. All through life he had set before himself the ideal that business as only to be regarded as stewardship for God—that time, money, influence, were only lawfully used when employed for the good of men and the glory of God. Now there was another opportunity for putting these principles to a practical test, although it came at a time when, if he chose, he could bring forth a hundred arguments for not doing so. But the case of the persecuted Lutherans was borne in upon his heart, and formed the subject of his hourly thoughts and prayers. He could not and would not desert them in the time of their great need, and the following extract from his diary records the resolution at which he arrived.

Feb. 23, 1838.—Whatever the directors of the South Australian Company may do, I have told Mr. Flaxman that I intend to send out the hundred and sixty-six persons of Mr. Kavel's congregation. I will advance the money for their passage, to be repaid with interest, and also employ them for a time in the colony, and, with my land, £4,000 or £5,000 will do. May the Lord direct all my efforts to relieve His poor persecuted servants. Inasmuch as I do it to them I do it to Him—were *He* in such a case then how should I act ? If this gentleman (Von Koszutski) suffered loss by fine, may I sacrifice my money freely for their liberty. He gave up his coach from necessity, I have resolved to give up my carriage voluntarily.

and also by living plainly and economically I may make the property which God has graciously given me the means of refreshing many a barren soil and cheering many a thirsty soul.

Feb. 24th.—This day I wrote to Mr. Ward, the coach-maker of Exeter, to dispose of my carriage, only retaining my little phaeton for the use of my wife and for conveyance in journeying. . . . These are not times for needless expense when the people of God are in a state of persecution.

Mr. Angas at once applied for a list of the names, ages, sex, and relationships of the members of Mr. Kavel's congregation, and the amount of goods, stock, tools, or other property of each person, to enable him to arrange for their employment in the colony, and also requested that a deputation of two of the leaders of that congregation, and three of the chief men of the sixteen hundred other persons anxious to go to South Australia should wait on him ; holding out hope at the same time that some arrangements might be made with regard to the whole number.

The money which I shall advance to your people (he wrote to Mr. Kavel) will be to a few as Trustees for the whole, to be repaid in the colony when able, with usual interest should I require it. Possibly I may see it proper to appropriate the interest to providing instruction for the people.

In due course the deputies arrived, when it was found that two hundred instead of one hundred and sixty-six of Mr. Kavel's people were anxious to go, and had obtained their passports, but their money, which at first was £1,800, was reduced to £400 !

Hundreds of other applicants were clamouring to share the privileges offered to their more fortunate countrymen and co-religionists. It was stated by the deputies that the King, who for two years had put every obstacle in the way of emigration, was now literally thrusting the people out of the land, allowing them only two months for preparation and departure.

That night—the 19th of April, 1838—was memorable. The responsiblility of sending two hundred foreigners to a British Colony 15,000 miles away, at his own sole risk and cost, pressed heavily upon Mr. Angas. But this was not all. He had asked the deputation to inform him on what principle they wished to settle in South Australia, whether as large farmers, or as small ones on the allotment system, namely, for each two families to have about twenty acres of land. The latter was the unanimous choice, and this increased his perplexity, as the state of the colony and his own means rendered it impossible.

My mind was greatly perplexed (he wrote), I could not see my way at all; there was the conflict of mind between duty, fear, and loss. So I threw myself upon God, and then went to rest.

Next morning he dictated off-hand to Mr. Flaxman an elaborate scheme, which, when read to the deputies in German, met with their hearty approval, although it differed widely from the plan they had

suggested. A translation was made and signed by
the deputies and Mr. Angas for transmission to the
Prussian authorities. But before dispatching it, Mr.
Angas said to Mr. Flaxman, "This scheme involves
in it the absolute necessity of your going out and
taking the charge of these people immediately." It
was a great sacrifice to make, for Mr. Angas was in a
bad state of health, and it would be impossible for
him to have leisure to recruit it if he parted with his
right-hand man. But he was willing to make the
sacrifice, and Mr. Flaxman was willing to undertake
the responsible task, saying, "he felt so great an
interest in the welfare of these people that he had
fully made up his mind to go with them."

Thus, in two hours, the scheme had been prepared,
considered, and adopted by all the parties concerned.
Almost immediately afterwards an old friend offered
Mr. Angas a vessel, the *Prince George*, on such
advantageous terms that he determined in his mind
to accept them.

The deputation left London a few days later, but
before doing so the vessel was inspected, approved,
and chartered to sail on the 1st of June for Hamburg, whither Mr. Flaxman would go in the meantime to buy everything necessary for the voyage, and
prepare for the reception of the two hundred
emigrants who would leave Hamburg for South
Australia on the 1st of July, 1838.

Every part of the scheme seemed now to dovetail,
and despite the anxiety and arduous labour involved,

it is doubtful whether Mr. Angas, in the whole
course of his life, ever spent happier weeks than
those which immediately followed the settlement of
these arrangements. In the extensive series of his
voluminous diaries there is perhaps no one passage
that unconsciously but more sharply and distinctly
brings out the whole character of the man in his
deep religious earnestness, his keen business capa-
bilities, his wide and all-embracing charity, and his
broad catholicity than the following :—

It is a very happy circumstance that Mr. Flaxman is able to
speak and write German and English so well, and is in every way
fitted for the office of superintending the emigration of these two
hundred souls. This people will be able coadjutors with the two
German missionaries * in the colony in their inland settlement
among the aborigines. May the Lord in great mercy to these poor
blacks cause this mission to prosper. Happily for the two missionaries, they got a passage in the same·ship in which the new
Governor, Lieutenant-Colonel Gawler, goes out. I took the opportunity of introducing the Rev. A. Kavel and the two missionaries
to the new Governor, when he promised to take them under his
special protection. The Governor being a Christian man, as also
his private secretary, some good results may flow from this newly-
formed acquaintance. I also introduced these Germans to the
Committee of the Society for the Protection of Aborigines. As
Mr. Kavel and the German missionaries are Lutherans, and hold
the doctrine of consubstantiation in the Lord's Supper, and baptismal regeneration as a sort of mysterious and indescribable
change, which they do not pretend to explain or account for in any

---

* Sent out under the auspices of Mr. Angas, see page 145.
They came to London *en route* for South Australia, just before the
Prussian deputation arrived.

satisfactory manner, I felt at one time great difficulty in taking up
their cause, but believing them to be the true friends of and
believers in the Lord Jesus Christ, I conferred not with flesh and
blood, but gave them the right hand of fellowship. I shall see
henceforth how far I have been right in breaking down the petty
barriers which have kept apart many from joining in the common
defence of the gospel. My duty, I apprehend, is to love all who
love the Lord Jesus Christ, of every age, kingdom, colour, language,
and sect. Men, who for His sake have suffered the loss of all
things, may be supposed to be sincere in their professed love for
Him.

The *Prince George* left London early in June, and
on her arrival at Hamburg it was found that she
could not afford sufficient accommodation for the
first part-instalment of emigrants, more persons than
were included in the list given in by the deputies
having resolved to leave Silesia with their friends
and neighbours. A ship for the conveyance of the
stores of the South Australian Company was on the
point of sailing, and Mr. Flaxman wrote to the
Company to see if some arrangement could not be
made. But the Company, as such, had ceased to
take any interest in the persecuted Lutherans, and
the reply was that they could only be sent out at the
usual passenger rates. These were prohibitive, and
the prospect of a number of persons being left
behind who had sold all their little possessions, and
had arrived in a strange city with the most scanty
means and totally unable to pay their way to the new
colony, was very distressing.

On a representation of the case to Mr. Angas, he

made short work of the difficulty by undertaking to
send the surplus number at his own expense in
the *Bengalee*, a vessel of the South Australian
Company.

It was a curious sight that many thousands of
persons witnessed in July in the year of grace 1838—
large loads of poor emigrants bearing with them all
their earthly possessions, leaving home and Fatherland in search of liberty of conscience! Smoothly
but swiftly they glided along the Oder, crowds of
people in the villages and upon the bridges pressing
to see them, and to listen to the hymns they sang
with fervour. Some of the spectators ridiculed, some
looked on in idle curiosity, while others uttered a sympathetic "God-speed." At some of the halting-places
"like-minded brethren" came down to join with
them in prayer, and then took leave with tears and
lamentations. Past Frankfort-on-the-Oder, through
the many bridges of Berlin, amid the pleasure-seekers
and the gay and fashionable throngs of Charlotten-
burg, Spandau, and Potsdam, the pilgrim exiles
sailed, spending their hours in singing and prayer,
until they reached Wittenburg, the last Prussian
town upon their route. Then they glided down the
Elbe to Hamburg, and went on board the *Prince
George*, bound for Plymouth, to take up Pastor Kavel
and Mr. Flaxman.

Mr. Angas was at that time living at Dawlish, and
he went across to Plymouth Sound to see the first
band of emigrants depart. We say the *first* band,

for only a few days previously he had noted in his
diary :—

July 14.—Provided the means of deliverance for another three-
hundred souls in addition to the two hundred of Mr. Kavel's
people. In this affair the hand of the Lord has been singularly
manifested. Glory be to His grace vouchsafed to them and to me
for so far honouring me in being an instrument in any way to aid
them.

It was with no little emotion that he went on
board the *Prince George.* He was about to see the
people for whom he had been labouring for over two
years, and for whose sake he was risking, or about
to risk, so large a proportion of his fortune. No
sooner was it known that he was on board than every
man, woman, and child came up by the 'tween deck
ladder like bees out of a hive ; a forest of hands was
held out for him to shake, while his were kissed in
return ; tears streamed down the faces of strong,
rugged men, while murmurs equivalent to " God
bless you," were uttered and repeated by all. When
the people assembled on deck, the men for the most
part took the larboard side, and the women the star-
board. The first to come forward and express their
gratitude were old Mr. and Mrs. Kavel, who had both
reached their three-score years and ten, but were
taking their lot with their son in seeking the
Land of Promise. Then men, women, and
children, with broken voices and tearful eyes, poured
out with one accord such a burst of thanks that
Mr. Angas was glad to make his escape, on the

plea of inspecting the ship, but really to hide his own emotion.

Later on he addressed them in English—the speech being interpreted by Mr. Kavel. He spoke of the leadings of Providence on their behalf; the favourable prospects before them, the singular fact that they were in the very harbour from which the Pilgrim Fathers set sail to lay the foundation of the great Western Republic, leaving their homes as these people were doing, on account of religious persecution, and going forth that they might worship God according to the dictates of conscience. He then advised them as to their conduct on board ship, and in the new colony; told them of the plans he had in his mind for their future welfare, and urged them to submit to the superintendence of Mr. Flaxman. Then, commending them to the care and blessing of God through all the future of their lives, the whole company knelt down upon the deck and prayed.

The following simple lines on the visit of Mr. Angas to the *Prince George* were written by Miss Rundle, daughter of one of the directors of the South Australian Company, better known by her married name of Mrs. Charles, author of the "Schönberg Cotta Family."

> From depths of far Silesia,
>   Across the ocean bound,
>   A little band of exile men
>   Lay in the Plymouth Sound.

No dreams of gold or conquest
  Had lured them thus to roam ;
No pressure of hard poverty
  Had urged them from their home.

The fields that fed their fathers,
  Enough for them had grown,
And they no longings for the world
  Beyond their homes had known.

They did but seek for freedom
  To pour their prayers to heaven,
To hearken to the voice of God ;—
  That freedom was not given.

Then, as one man, the people
  Followed their pastor forth,
Dearer one atom of God's truth,
  Than all most dear on earth.

In the same spot where long ago
  The Pilgrim Fathers lay,
These stood for God and conscience' sake,
  As resolute as they.

For the first time beholding him
  Whose toils for them had won
Freedom to serve their God in peace,
  Beneath the southern sun.

Strangers in land and language,
  What claimed they of his care ?
Christians, and for Christ's sake oppressed,
  What labours could he spare ?

He knew that they had suffered
　He knew they would be free,
" And what ye do to these the least
　Ye do it unto Me."

They stood with hearts o'erflowing,
　That little rescued band,
Strong men, and grey-haired sires, and babes,
　Thronging to kiss his hand.

And tears from young and aged,
　Fell thick as summer rain,
And eyes wept sore with thankfulness,
　That had not wept for pain.

May those soft drops be heralds
　Of a most blessed spring,
Whose toils shall harvests of rich fruit
　For Heaven's own garners bring.

His eyes, who ne'er forgetteth
　A single sigh or tear
Poured forth in faith and for His sake—
　His gracious eyes were there.

Faith never missed her triumph,
　The rainbow lights her now,
And clouds that shroud the noon, shall weave
　A crown for evening's brow.

Behind the storm is sunshine,
　As though no storm were near,
In God's good time, He knows how soon,
　That sunshine shall appear.

A few days later and the *Prince George* was on her
voyage to South Australia, where she arrived on the
16th of November. The Germans strongly objected
to be scattered over the country, and wished to
settle down together as a body of agriculturists, but
owing to delays having taken place in the survey of
the country lands, many who were already in the
colony were prevented from engaging in agricultural
pursuits, and in consequence agricultural labourers
were at that time largely in excess of the demand.
In these circumstances Mr. Flaxman took upon
himself the responsibility of settling them upon
some land belonging to Mr. Angas on the river
Torrens, a short distance from Adelaide, to which
they gave the name of Klemzig, after their native
town in Prussia.

The further history of these excellent people
belongs to the history of South Australia. It will be
sufficient in this place to say that they were soon
recognized as a power in the land, and that the
following description, given in an Adelaide newspaper a few months after their arrival, was not only
true at the time, but was a fair basis on which to
calculate their future prosperity :—

All our readers are probably aware that there exists about three
miles from North Adelaide a German village called Klemzig, but
we have reason to think that this interesting little settlement is not
so well known among us as it deserves to be. Klemzig is situated
on the northern side of the Torrens, on the estate of Mr. George
Fife Angas. Like Adelaide, it is surrounded with noble trees, and

from many points commands near views of our magnificent range
of mountains. The river winds past it, and contains for the season
a considerable depth of water. An air of serenity pervades the
spot, which is exactly such a one as the imagination would portray
as the retreat of persecuted piety. The industry and quiet perseverance of the German character have been fully developed at
Klemzig. Four or five months only have elapsed since the hand
of man began there to efface the features of the wilderness, yet
nearly thirty houses have been erected, and good and spacious
houses some of them are. All are neat, clean, and comfortable.
They are built mostly of pisé, or of unburnt bricks which have
been hardened by the sun. The more humble cottages consist of
brushwood and thatch. The sloping bank of the river is covered
with gardens. These consist of small unfenced plots of ground,
separated by narrow paths. Considering that the season most
favourable for gardening has not yet commenced, the number of
vegetables which the Germans have at the present moment under
culture affords strong proof of their industry. . . . The inhabitants
themselves are interesting. The visitor will find them one and all
as busy and cheerful as English bees in the spring-time. Out of
doors they are weeding, watering, building, fishing, milking, washing, cutting wood, or carrying water. Within doors the housewife
plies her domestic toil with equal assiduity. Not a soul is idle.
Even the children who are too small to work, yet large enough to
learn, will be found in ordinary school hours receiving the tuition
of their excellent and indefatigable pastor. The visitor will be
struck by the obliging dispositions and courteous manner of the
people. The male peasant raises his hat as he passes you, and
bows with an air equally removed from boorishness and servility.
The female, although perhaps bending under a load of wood, has a
smile, and some other expression of respectful courtesy to offer the
passing stranger. Even the few natives who assist them in some
of their labours appear to have imbibed their spirit, being retiring
and unobtrusive. . . . Our neighbours are entitled to much consideration from us. Driven from their native country because they

would not yield to that worst form of tyranny which seeks to rivet chains on men's minds and dictate to them their faith, they came here, erected their altar among us, and are now presenting us with a model of practical colonization well worthy of our individual imitation.

Let us now turn back to glance at the further efforts of Mr. Angas on behalf of the Lutherans still suffering persecution.

Soon after the first batches had been despatched a number of Lutherans flocked to Hamburg in the hope that they might find the same assistance that their fortunate countrymen had received. Mr. Angas was of course appealed to, but it was impossible for him to provide for them all, especially as circumstances had arisen, to which we shall refer more particularly later on, which made it necessary for him to husband his financial resources. He wrote to Sir George Grey, Under Secretary of State for the Colonies, and to many others for assistance, hoping that the Government or private individuals would come to the aid of the Germans waiting at Hamburg. But all these efforts failed. Then we find this entry in his journal :—

I have already gone so deep into obligations on behalf of the *Prince George*, *Bengalee*, and *Zebra*, that I am afraid to do more, and yet if no one else will help that does not discharge me if by any means I can do it. . . . Now I see it my duty, in the fear of God, to make an offer to Mr. Swaine * that if he can buy the pro-

---

* Mr. Swaine was a Hamburg merchant, a Christian friend, and a man deeply interested in the German movement.

visions at six months' credit, I will accept for £1,000, being the sum he wants, and by that time I hope, by the blessing of God upon my affairs, to be able to get in as much money from those indebted to me in this country.

The third vessel to sail was the *Zebra*, with 199 Lutheran emigrants on board, under the command of Captain Hahn, a somewhat remarkable man. On arriving in South Australia Mr. F. H. Dutton, who had taken a special survey of 4,000 acres in the Mount Barker district, and had come down to the coast to sell cattle, met Captain Hahn, and invited him to visit the spot. The worthy captain went and was enchanted with the beauty and fertility of the land. He was a warm supporter of the Lutherans, and was extremely anxious to help them. Arrived at the end of the journey, he was asked by the owners of the district what he thought of it. " It seems to me as if nature had lavished her choicest gifts on South Australia," answered the Captain, " I should like to end my days here, and never return to the busy world." Then, turning to the wealthy owners, he said, " Now I ask you, do you think it is the will of God that this beautiful land, on which so many hundred individuals could find an ample maintenance, should be destined merely for grazing cattle ? In such a boundless tract of land you could scarcely miss it were you to grant my emigrants from fifty to one hundred acres in some corner where they might raise a settlement. Would not the consciousness of having made so many

people happy repay you a hundredfold for your bit
of land ? and do you not think the land would be
rendered doubly valuable if it were cultivated by my
industrious countrymen ? ''

Then the good captain took higher ground and
pleaded the religious aspect of the case, describing
the heroism of his countrymen in their fight for
liberty and truth.

The result was that the people were invited to
come up bag and baggage, one hundred and fifty
acres were to be appropriated to their use, a year's
provision in advance was guaranteed to them, and
other highly advantageous arrangements were made.

The agreement thus provisionally made was, with
the assistance of Mr. Flaxman, ratified and confirmed, and thus the still flourishing settlement of
Hahndorf had its origin.

It may be noted here that in 1839, at the celebration of the Queen's birthday, a large number of the
German emigrants, to testify their loyalty, and also
to improve their position, took the oath of allegiance,
and subsequently letters of naturalization were
granted to them. This enabled them to become
purchasers and possessors of land in their own right,
and entitled them to various other privileges of
which they were only too glad to avail themselves.

We do not propose to give details of the sailing of
other batches of Lutheran emigrants, but seeing that
all of them were sent out under the immediate

auspices of Mr. Angas, and almost entirely at his
expense, some idea of the magnitude of the undertaking in which he was involved may be gathered
from the following summary.

On the 26th of September, 1838, the *Catherine·*
sailed from Hamburg with a party of one hundred
and twenty. This brought up the total number of
Germans who had arrived in the colony to over
five hundred, or one-tenth of the entire population.

In 1839 large numbers of Lutherans elected to go·
to the United States, mainly on the ground of the
shorter distance, and consequently the cheaper rates·
for passage-money. Mr. Angas, being unable to·
charter ships for the conveyance of all who were·
anxious to proceed to South Australia, rendered
substantial assistance in time, money, influence, and
personal exertions to those who, as a *dernier ressort,*
had resolved to cross the Atlantic.

On the 28th of June, 1839, the following entry
occurs in his journal :—

Letters from Mr. Flaxman appear to represent Mr. Kavel's people·
as in much perplexity. They cannot get employment, and he has
been obliged to let them, on seven years' lease, one hundred and
thirty-four acres of my land, and to agree to advance them £1,200·
of money as outfit. Also, he thinks of doing something of a
similar kind for those who were expected to arrive in the colony.
This is a terrible pull upon my funds when I have so many engagements to help others forward.

A characteristic incident occurred about this time.

Among the Lutherans to whom Mr. Angas had
agreed, through Mr. Swaine, to advance the sum of
£1,000 for their passage, some differences of opinion
arose, and they determined to break up the contract
that had bound them together. To Mr. Angas,
who from first to last never turned aside in his
advocacy of their cause, this was inexcusable, and
he wrote :—

As they have dissolved the bonds which bound them together I
must consider my obligation to lend the £1,000 at an end, and I
cannot but reflect upon it as a fortunate circumstance that I had
not finally concluded the chartering of a ship for the two hundred
souls, for in that case the loss of the passage-money would have
fallen upon my hands. Men who suffer themselves to be governed
by their feelings instead of by their faith and judgment ought
never to have left Silesia.

Some of these seceders went to the United States,
and Mr. Angas did much to establish them there.
They went to New York, and eventually settled in
Buffalo, where they were joined by large numbers
of their countrymen, and their flourishing German
towns continue to this day.

In 1840 the flow of German emigrants received a
check. In May of that year Mr. Angas received
information that some thousands were ready to leave
their homes, and that all difficulty with regard to
passports had been removed. But a new set of
hindrances had arisen on the other side of the
question. The emigrants to the United States

were sending home glowing accounts of their state
and prospects while South Australia was under a
cloud in consequence of the British Government
dishonouring the bills drawn upon it by Governor
Gawler. Moreover, the circumstances of Mr. Angas,
as we have said, had materially altered, and though
he was as willing as ever to assist the Lutherans
financially, it was now out of his power to do so.
But his influence was exercised as readily as heretofore on their behalf, and we find him interviewing
Mrs. Elizabeth Fry—who wrote to the King of
Prussia to do justice to the Lutherans—and many
other philanthropists and capitalists, with a view
to the advancement of their welfare.

So long as Mr. Angas could provide the funds
and facilitate the arrangements for the outfit and
embarkation of the Lutherans all went well, but
when it was sought to raise funds from other sources
many discouragements and disappointments were
experienced. A spirited appeal was made to British
Christians, and especially to Nonconformists, but
although meetings were held and fluent addresses
delivered there were no tangible results. No one
made it a matter of deep personal interest.

The sequel to the story of Mr. Angas's untiring
labours is disappointing. He had to suffer the most
perplexing difficulties and inconvenience in consequence of the advances he had made to the German
emigrants; and he was straitened and cramped

because these advances were not refunded in the
time agreed upon. But though these things only
worried him, it was a source of positive grief that he
was unable to continue his assistance to intending
emigrants.

As time went on his consolation was to know that
there was not the same need for exertion. The
king, seeing that coercion had failed, as it generally
does, became much more tolerant. Pastors were
released, fines ceased to be exacted, public worship,
with sacramental rites, was re-established in places
that had been arbitrarily closed.

The necessity for immediate and active personal
efforts being now removed, Mr. Angas, from the
circumstances we have named, left it to others to
carry on the work of assisting emigration, and this
was successfully done by Mr. Swaine, the Hamburg
merchant to whom we have already referred, and
by Mr. Delius, the son of a wealthy retired merchant in Bremen, to whom Mr. Angas gave the
benefit of his information and counsel.

Vessel after vessel was sent out under the auspices
of these gentlemen, and for several years there were
regular sailings from Hamburg of German emigrants,
until about 8,000 had settled in the colony. They
became nearly all prosperous men, but those who
laboured so hard for their welfare in sending them
out were losers to the extent of several thousands of
pounds in consequence of some of the emigrants
failing to repay the balance of their passage-money.

In the early days of several of our Colonies it was
unhappily proverbial that many of the religious
customs of the old country ceased to be observed.
Everybody was intent on labour and making haste
to be rich, and with the removal of social and
religious restraints there set in laxity with regard
to religious observances, or a putting aside of professed Christianity altogether.

The Lutherans were not an exception to the
general rule. They were eager to make their settlements models of prosperity, but in doing so they
omitted to make corresponding efforts to discharge
their pecuniary obligations to Mr. Angas, who was
placed in a most difficult position in consequence.
Good Pastor Kavel was sorely grieved at the scandal
of having under his care a congregation who had
emigrated for conscience' sake, showing so little
regard to their conscientious duty, and he adopted
the stringent measure of refusing to administer the
Lord's Supper to any who were failing to make
faithful efforts to pay their debts. For a time he
was a pastor almost without a flock, but the lesson
he taught his people resulted in their honourably
fulfilling their engagements. and expressing their
gratitude to Mr. Angas for his generous and timely
aid.

How much they owed to him few, if any of them,
ever knew. But, as will be shown in a subsequent
chapter, his labours on their behalf, their dilatoriness
in repaying their debts, and other circumstances

which arose out of his kindness to them, brought
him to the verge of ruin.

Of the Germans who had proceeded to the United
States, and who were largely assisted by Mr. Angas,
a friend wrote in 1850 :—

I never visit Buffalo without thinking of your German friends in
that city. Indeed it has almost become a city of Germans. They
are as prosperous, if not more so, in Buffalo than in any portion of
the United States that I am acquainted with, and, generally speaking, they are good citizens.

We cannot close this chapter without referring
again to Pastor Kavel, who occupies such a prominent place in the early history of the German
emigration movement. He continued his ministerial labours faithfully and well until the 8th of
December, 1859, when he was seized with an
apoplectic fit, and died a few days afterwards, loved
and respected by the whole community before whom
his light had always consistently shone.

Little did he or Mr. Angas think, when they
met for the first time in a London counting-house,
that the destiny of thousands hung upon the issues
of their interview, or that for both of them so long,
toilsome, and thorny a pathway would have to be
trodden before the end they had in view could be
reached. But both were willing to confess that the
toil was worth the trouble, and the visitor to South
Australia to-day may see the fruits that trouble
yielded.

There are now upwards of 9,000 Germans in the
colony, the townships in which they are principally located being Angaston, Blumberg, Greenock,
Grünthal, Hahndorf, Lobethal, Lyndoch, Nairne,
Nuriootpa, Rosenthal, and Tanunda. The majority
of them are engaged in agriculture, gardening,
and vine-growing, although there is a fair comple-
ment of artizans and tradesmen. They maintain
their character for thrift, industry, and honesty,
and are generally allowed to be very good settlers,
keeping themselves apart from Trades and Labour
Unions, and seldom appearing among the ranks of
the unemployed and useless classes in the courts
of justice.

Since the days of which we have written in this
chapter, many thousands of Germans — a large
proportion of them naturalized, as they cannot hold
land unless they become British subjects — have
become scattered thoughout South Australia and the
neighbouring Colonies, and there is no doubt that
they were for the most part drawn to their new
homes through the influence of the pioneers, the
persecuted Lutherans, sent out by Mr. Angas.

CHAPTER VIII.

HOW NEW ZEALAND BECAME A BRITISH COLONY.

Tasman—Captain Cook—M. Marion du Fresne—Whalers—Rev. Samuel Marsden—Land purchases from Natives—The New Zealand Association—Baron de Thierry reveals a Secret—Letter to Lord Glenelg—Proposals to the British Government—The New Zealand Land Company—Captain Hobson sent out—The Treaty of Waitangi—New Zealand proclaimed a British Colony—Arrival and chagrin of the French—M. Guizot's version of the affair—Offer of a Baronetcy.

WE have to relate in this chapter a strange episode in colonial history, and as it will come as a surprise to many who, as they suppose, are well acquainted with the full details of the colonization of New Zealand, we shall, as far as possible, confine ourselves to "documentary evidence" in confirmation of the statements made.

In order to make the matter clear to those who may not be familiar with the early history of New Zealand, a brief account must be given here of the state of affairs prior to the date of the remarkable episode in which Mr. Angas played a most important though not a conspicuous part. New Zealand, discovered by Tasman in 1642, remained a *terra incognita* until 1769, when Captain Cook visited

the islands, discovered the strait which divides them
and still bears his name, and explored the coast.
He landed on different parts of the islands, left
pigs and other animals as evidence of his having
been there, and took, it has been alleged, formal
possession of the islands on behalf of King George
III. The war with America and the subsequent
revolution in France would seem to have completely diverted the attention of the British Government from the idea of planting a colony in New
Zealand, and no claim was ever made to the islands
on the ground of Cook's discovery.

His description of the islands appears to have
been received in France with greater interest than
elsewhere, and New Zealand was at once looked
upon as suitable for the establishment of a French
colony. Accordingly, in October, 1771, two ships
were despatched under the command of M. Marion
du Fresne, who was instructed to thoroughly acquaint
himself with the character and resources of the
islands. The expedition ended most disastrously.
Placing too much confidence in the friendliness of
the natives, M. Marion landed with a party of
sixteen, including four officers, all of whom, apparently without provocation, were killed and eaten
by the savages. Another party of twelve, who
landed shortly afterwards to procure wood and water,
unconscious of what had befallen the commander
and his party, shared their fate. One only escaped,
and " when the melancholy facts became known on

board the two ships, a strong armed force was at once sent on shore which inflicted a summary and terrible punishment upon the natives, many of whom were shot down without offering any resistance, apparently paralysed at the fatal effects of the firearms. This sad catastrophe led to the abandonment of the object of the expedition, and probably gave the French an unfavourable opinion of New Zealand as a suitable locality for a colony."

The particulars of this terrible massacre were conveyed to the French Government by M. Crozet, first lieutenant of one of the ships.

Early in the present century New Zealand was occasionally visited by whalers from the South Seas, and by small craft from the infant settlement of New South Wales. These vessels sometimes left behind a hand or two who were either "sea-sick or sick of the sea," or more often a convict refugee possessing a strong desire for freedom. Being colonized in the first instance by characters of this description, it is not at all likely that the natives would derive much benefit from the intercourse thus established, nor is it to be supposed that the European population who sought a home among savages would improve themselves in the scale of social life.

As a matter of fact there sprung up a population of desperate, reckless, and dissolute men, who corrupted the natives and added to their original

savagery the detestable vices of the off-scouring of
Europeans.

The Rev. Samuel Marsden, Senior Chaplain of
the colony of New South Wales, was the first to
realize the position of affairs, and to take steps to
remedy it. He communicated with the Church
Missionary Society, and represented the case. He
was the first to discover the latent superiority of the
Maories over all other savage tribes. Mr. George
French Angas, a son of Mr. Angas, in an admirable
book he wrote on New Zealand,* says, of the
natives : " The countenances of some of the chiefs
indicate a great degree of mind, and are totally
divested of anything approaching a savage, while
the nobleness of their appearance and bearing pro-
claims at once their superiority over most of the
uncivilized races of men. It is only in moments of
excitement and passion that their countenances are
lighted up with savage ferocity, at other times they
display a combination of dignity and mildness which
is sure to win the confidence of the stranger."

Christian missionaries, sent out by the Committee
of the Church Missionary Society, and working
under the direction of Mr. Marsden, were the first
to proceed with good intent to New Zealand as
settlers—a handful of brave, noble men who were
willing to hazard their lives for the sake of spreading
the gospel amongst the natives. In 1814 they
settled in the Bay of Islands, and soon afterwards

* " New Zealand Illustrated," by G. French Angas.

an Act of Parliament was passed by the Imperial Legislature extending the jurisdiction of the Governor of New South Wales to New Zealand and other islands in the Pacific. Governor Macquarie thereupon appointed Mr. Thomas Kendal to be Resident Magistrate or British Consul in the Bay of Islands, not only to protect the missionaries from the natives, but also to protect the natives from the lawless Europeans who imposed upon them and treated them with basest cruelty and injustice.

We need not follow the history in detail, but will merely indicate certain landmarks to show the course of events.

In 1833 Mr. Busby was appointed British Consul or Resident Magistrate in the Bay of Islands. He was well received by Europeans and natives, whose joint interests he was appointed to protect. In course of time, however, dissensions arose ; the missionaries having been first in the field desired to keep the leading position, and the evils generally attendant upon divided authority were experienced.

One of the earliest and most fruitful sources of trouble in the infant settlement was the purchase of lands from the natives, who were acknowledged on all hands as the rightful owners of the soil. They, as a rule, acted honourably in these matters, although they could not give proper title to the land, while the European adventurers, in the large majority of instances, cruelly defrauded the natives.

With a view to enable the chiefs to protect themselves against the ill-treatment they and many of their countrymen received from the lawless and unscrupulous people who either called at or settled in the island, Captain Lambert, of H.M.S. *Alligator*, in 1835 formed the chiefs into a confederation and presented them with a national flag, which was recognized by British vessels. This was on many grounds an unwise step, but it must be borne in mind that throughout all this period the only real redress for injuries was obtained through the intervention of British men-of-war which occasionally called at the principal settlements to give a semblance of protection to those who needed it, whether natives or Europeans.

In 1837, in consequence of a war which was raging between some of the leading chiefs, Sir R. Bourke, Governor of New South Wales, requested Captain Hobson, commanding H.M.S. *Rattlesnake*, to repair to New Zealand in order to afford protection in case of need to British subjects and to British shipping.

Captain Hobson was somewhat alarmed at the aspect of affairs. He reported : " With British subjects fast accumulating, and every day acquiring considerable possessions of land, it must become a subject of deep solicitude with the British Government to devise some practicable mode of protecting them from violence and of restraining them from oppression. Heretofore the great and powerful moral influence of the missionaries has done much to check the turbulence of the native population,

but the dissolute conduct of the lower orders of our
countrymen not only tends to diminish that holy
influence, but to provoke the resentment of the
natives, which, if once excited, would produce the
most disastrous consequences.   It becomes, therefore, a solemn duty, both in justice to the better
classes of our fellow-subjects and to the natives
themselves, to apply a remedy for the growing evil."

Captain Hobson proposed a temporary measure
which, in his opinion, would meet the difficulty, but
it does not appear to have been carried into effect.

In 1837, about a year after the first ship had
sailed for the new colony of South Australia, which
had come into existence through the instrumentality
of Mr. Angas and the South Australian Company, a
number of gentlemen in England turned their attention to New Zealand, in the hope that they might
add yet another colony to the British Crown by
operating on somewhat similar lines.

Accordingly the " New Zealand Association " was
formed, the Committee consisting, among others, of
the Hon. Francis Baring, M.P. (Chairman), the
Earl of Durham, Lord Petre, Sir W. Molesworth,
M.P., Sir G. Sinclair, Sir W. Symonds, R.N., Mr.
W. Hutt, Mr. W. W. J. Whitmore.   One or two of
these had taken part in the colonization of South
Australia.

An elaborate scheme was drawn up by the Association and submitted to the Imperial Parliament.
It recognized the sovereignty and independence of

the New Zealanders; foresaw that cession of the
whole territory to the British Crown could only be
a very gradual process; recommended the establishment of British settlements; and proposed measures
for obtaining and disposing of land. The work of
forming and regulating settlements was "to be
confided, without regard to any private interest, to
a few persons of station and character selected from
among the originators and most zealous patrons of
the undertaking."   These, under the name of
"Founders of Settlements in New Zealand," were
to be appointed by Act of Parliament after approval
by the Crown, and vacancies in their body were to
be filled up by the Crown. It was proposed that
they should form a corporation, make treaties with
the native tribes for cessions of territory, administer
upon lands ceded to the Crown the whole system of
colonization, including the receipt and expenditure
of colonial funds, establish courts in the settlements
for the administration of British law, make regulations for the government of the natives, provide for
the defence and good order of the settlements by
means of a militia and a colonial military and marine
force, and appoint and remove at pleasure all such
officers as they might require for carrying the whole
measure into effect.   It was also proposed "to give
encouragement to religion by an allowance from the
public funds to all denominations, and to appoint a
bishop of the Church of England for the whole of
the settlements."

Such were the leading features of the plan. The
draft Bill was submitted to Lord Melbourne, who
gave it but little encouragement, and Parliament
finally rejected it.

Prior to its rejection the Committee of the Association fairly besieged the Colonial Office, and at one
of their interviews Lord Glenelg, the Chief Secretary
for the Colonies, pointed out one serious difficulty
in the way of their plans.

" There were diplomatic reasons," he said, " against
colonizing New Zealand in particular : the Russians,
the Americans, and the French would object to it.
In South Australia the case was different, both as
regarded the natives and as regarded foreign Powers.
The sovereignty of England in that quarter was
universally recognized, and there were no complicated aboriginal claims on the soil. Moreover, the
Crown was then nominally represented by the Commissioners appointed under the Act of Parliament
for founding the colony. The South Australian
Company, though practically the mainstay of the
colony, was theoretically a mere commercial association."

Opposition to the scheme came from all quarters,
and notably from the Church Missionary Society,
whose plea was—" Only let New Zealand be spared
from colonization, and the Mission have its free and
unrestricted course for one half-century more, and
the great political and moral problem will be solved
of a people passing from a barbarous to a civilized

state through the agency of Europeans, with the complete preservation of the aboriginal race and of their national independence and sovereignty."

The Wesleyan Mission also opposed the plan of the New Zealand Association, or rather they objected to its agent, Mr. E. G. Wakefield, who, having failed in his efforts to obtain a foremost place in colonizing South Australia, was now turning his attention eagerly to New Zealand.

In June, 1838, a further unsuccessful attempt was made to pass a Bill through Parliament for the establishment of a colony and British authority in New Zealand.

Although not taking any prominent part in the public discussion of New Zealand affairs, Mr. Angas watched every movement with great interest, and when this second attempt to pass a Bill was unsuccessful, backed as it was by Mr. Baring, who had been Chairman of the "New Zealand Association," he gave the matter still more earnest attention. It was so much upon his mind, that entries with reference to it are frequent in his diary, especially as to the state of the natives. Thus, after recording some details of a tribal war, he says :—

Surely something ought to be done, and if the government of the chiefs is unable to protect Europeans or their property, and if the tendency of it is to lead to a total extermination of the present natives, surely humanity and Christianity as well as sound policy demand the interference of the British Government.

Again :—

My thoughts have been long turned to New Zealand and its miserable condition. When the Rev. John Williams, of the South Seas, was here, I often spoke with him about it, but nothing came of it; he seemed unable to devise any scheme of rescue. I have read all the books and pamphlets written by the New Zealand Association, and watched the Bills for colonizing it that were attempted to be brought into Parliament, and which I am persuaded, if passed, never could have been carried into effect, at least by the parties who formed the Association and were to be the Commissioners. I have brought the matter before the Aborigines Protection Society, and have written to Mr. Fowell Buxton, Sir George Arthur, and others, and only on Saturday last to Mr. Hume, of the Board of Trade. Still, I cannot see my call to engage in this work, nor can I yet see any plan that will meet the difficulties of the case.

Not more than a week after these words were written, the "call" came in a manner as strange as it was unexpected. One day two gentlemen waited upon Mr. Angas, and stated that having failed in securing from the New Zealand Association the co-operation they needed, they had come to him, on the ground of his successful efforts on behalf of South Australia, to enlist his sympathy and counsel in the case of New Zealand. One of the visitors was a Mr. McDonnell, who claimed to be the possessor of not less than four hundred square miles of land on the Hokianga river; the other visitor was Baron de Thierry, a Frenchman, whose brother, also a Baron, had, it was affirmed, attained to the rank of "a chief," or "the sovereign chief," by reason of the purchase he had made of a large tract of land in the northern island.

This eccentric Baron de Thierry sailed· for New
Zealand in 1837, and as he intended calling at
Sydney, Lord Glenelg mentioned the circumstance
in a despatch to Sir Richard Bourke, then Governor
of New South Wales, in reply to which Sir Richard
wrote :—

"I take the present opportunity of stating that
the Baron de Thierry, who was mentioned in your
lordship's despatch of the 26th of August last, is at
present in Sydney, where he has arrived on his way
to New Zealand to take possession of a large tract of
country which he claims to have acquired by purchase. I have not considered it my duty to interpose any obstacle to his proceeding to New Zealand,
of which country he claims to be a chief by right of
his purchases. He denies all intention of preju-
dicing the interests of Great Britain, and professes
a reliance upon moral influence alone for the
authority he expects to acquire among the New
Zealanders."*

* The Rev. James Buller, in his "Forty Years in New Zealand" says,
"Early in November, 1837, a strange character arrived in the *Nimrod*.
This was the Baron de Thierry, an Englishman with a French title. He
was by birth and education a gentleman, but a visionary. He proclaimed
himself as the 'Sovereign Chief of New Zealand.' He had met with
Hongi (a native who visited England) at Cambridge in 1820, and Mr.
Kendall received from him thirty-six axes, wherewith to buy land for
him, on his return to New Zealand. In virtue of those axes, the Baron
claimed an estate of forty thousand acres. He brought with him ninety-
three persons, including his secretary, master of stores, and other officers.
I was present at a conference he had with the native chiefs at Otararau.
They smiled at his demands. It ended in the cession of about three
hundred acres of good forest land to him, on the part of Tomati Waka, and
Taonui. They said they were sorry they had not a good house to offer

It was the brother of this eccentric Baron who
sought the aid of Mr. Angas, to whom he represented
the necessity there was for the British Government
to assume at once the sovereignty of New Zealand.
Mr. Angas was not prepared to take the matter up,.
but was willing to give the benefit of his counsel tc
the Baron. This became the occasion of several
subsequent visits, at one of which the Baron inadver--
tently let drop some information which Mr. Angas
considered of far too serious a character to be kept.
from the Secretary of State for the Colonies. It
was to this effect : Finding that the British Govern--
ment was somewhat indifferent in the matter, he had
turned to the Government of his own country, which
had long looked upon New Zealand as a possible
place for a French colony. The description given of
the country by the Baron, and his account of the
apathy of the British Government, appear to have
revived the old desire to form a settlement there, and
the information the Baron inadvertently let slip was,.
"that the French Government was actually engaged
in fitting out an expedition for planting a French
colony in New Zealand, and the vessels were expected to be ready for sea in the course of two or
three weeks."

for the accommodation of himself, the Baroness, and their retinue. . . .
Ere long the poor Baron was deserted by all his followers. He afterwards
took up his abode at Auckland, where he obtained scant living as a teacher
of music, and died in great poverty in 1864, at the age of seventy-one.
Airy as his scheme was, his claims were recognized by the French.
Government. Their ships of war that touched at Auckland had orders to
pay him great respect."

This was startling intelligence, and Mr. Angas communicated it to Lord Glenelg in the following terms :—

LONDON, *Dec.* 20, 1838.

MY LORD,—The present state of New Zealand is so intimately connected with the moral improvement of the southern hemisphere —with the security of the British interests embarked in the Sperm Whale Fishery, and the peace and safety of Her Majesty's Australian colonies, that I venture to call the special attention of your lordship to the injurious consequences which in all probability will ensue, unless a remedy be speedily applied to the evils which afflict that portion of the globe.

The failure of the attempt, made about twelve years ago by the New Zealand Land Company, to establish a settlement there ; the more recent abortive efforts of the New Zealand Association, and the unsuccessful endeavours to obtain an Act of Parliament, establishing a British settlement in that country, have not passed unobserved, and might be considered sufficiently discouraging to deter any one, however sanguine, from undertaking to ameliorate the social condition of the inhabitants of those islands.

When, however, the path of duty is plain, and the welfare of one's fellow-men the object, no difficulties can be insurmountable, because the benevolent purposes of Divine Providence cannot finally be frustrated. In the case to which I refer, it appears to me that the way is open for the accomplishment of great good, and the averting of impending calamities, should Her Majesty's Government feel disposed to patronize such measures as may be adopted for the attainment of those objects. The imperative necessity of immediate attention to this matter is most apparent to my mind, from a long interview I had on the 10th instant with the Baron de Thierry, brother of the gentleman of that name, who is at present settled at Hokianga, as well as from a fact which has subsequently transpired, namely, that the Count De Mole, the President of the Council of France, has expressed his determination to appoint

Baron de Thierry to the office of French Consul in New Zealand, which appointment he is in daily expectation of receiving.

For the last year and a half it seems this gentleman has been exerting himself to induce the French Government and the merchants and manufacturers of that country to direct their attention to New Zealand. His and his people's sympathies are clearly French. By the aid of an ingenious piece of machinery they have produced a most beautiful flax of silken texture and appearance, and specimens of common and fine white paper, manufactured from the *Phormium tenax*, so highly spoken of by Dr. Murray in his account of that indigenous plant, printed on paper made from its leaves, besides specimens of rope, sailcloth, flax dyed in several colours, and waterproof linen cloth, without being subjected to any chemical process. These specimens, all of which I have carefully examined, have excited great attention in France, and rendered the acquisition of New Zealand exceedingly desirable as a French colony.

Your lordship is well aware of the great increase of late years of French vessels of war now traversing the South Seas, doubtless with other objects in view than such as are of a merely scientific nature, as well as that the Baron de Thierry and his brother have represented to the French Government the practicability of subjugating the islands of New Zealand with a force of from five hundred to six hundred organized settlers. Should New Zealand fall into the hands of a foreign Power, the possession of our colonies in the South Seas would become very insecure, not one of them being in a condition to offer any successful resistance from within, and all of them being entirely destitute of external defences. I need not here remind your lordship that two French vessels easily took possession of and destroyed the English settlement at Sierra Leone, soon after its establishment.

Your lordship is likewise aware that New Zealand is at present nominally an independent nation in which British interests are represented by a Consul, &c., and that in its present position and relation to this country the French may establish a settlement

there with as much propriety as the British, providing the Baron
de Thierry possesses sufficient influence with the leading chiefs to
obtain their concurrence—a point to which he appears to be
directing all his efforts, merely because Her Majesty's Government
has declined to avail itself of the predilection known to exist
amongst the New Zealanders in favour of this country.

There is reason to believe that at the present moment it would
not be difficult to connect Baron de Thierry's influence with the
commercial interests of this country, and thereby terminate the
connection which now subsists between that nobleman and France.

It would be superfluous to represent to your lordship the deplor-
able consequences that must inevitably ensue from the establishment of French settlements on the shores of New Zealand, where
the harbours are excellent, and naval stores of every description
are ready at hand; and whence at any time, should hostilities
unhappily be provoked, an instant stop would be put to the
intercourse between the British colonies and New Zealand, Van
Diemen's Land, Port Phillip, South Australia, and Swan River—
not to mention the ease with which the British whaling trade
might be obstructed, and the certain destruction of our infant
commerce with the islands of Australasia and the South Seas—a
commerce which, from the gradual civilization of the South Sea
Islanders, is likely, in a few years, to become of great importance to
this nation. Permit me, however, to suggest that at present considerable supplies of grain and naval stores are obtained by the
Australian colonies from New Zealand ; and that as those colonies
are more suitable for the growth of wool than for the production of
grain (but for which New Zealand appears admirably adapted), any
interruption between those places would be disastrous to our
southern colonies.

If it be not too late, Her Majesty's Government have it in their
power to prevent these threatened calamities by granting a charter
to a commercial company to be formed for the establishment of a
British Factory, with the guarantee of protection from the Government. Such a measure might be preparatory to a permanent

connection between Great Britain and the New Zealand islands,. which the chiefs are already prepared to consummate; or, what would be still better, did not the claims of international law present obstacles to it, a contract could be entered into with the chiefs, through the agency of a special officer, appointed for that purpose,. to incorporate their native country with the British Empire—a measure which, in all probability, the French nation will soon adopt, should the British Government decline or neglect it.

I now feel that I have discharged my duty in bringing this matter under your lordship's consideration, not doubting that it. will receive that attention which its importance demands.

I have the honour to remain, my lord,

Your lordship's most obedient servant,

GEORGE FIFE ANGAS.

A few days later, in response to the request of Lord Glenelg, Mr. Angas appeared at the Colonial Office in Downing Street.

What took place at that interview is recorded in his journal thus :—

For my letter on the present condition of New Zealand, Lord Glenelg thanked me. After a conversation of an hour and a half I left him with the understanding that he would bring this *important business before the Cabinet.* The first proposition that I submitted was that the British Government should immediately claim New Zealand as belonging to Britain by virtue of first discovery.. Second, that if this were objected to, then let it be an independent Government in amity with, and under the protection of, Great Britain, so as to keep away the power and claims of the United States, and of France. Third, that in either case a charter might be given to a Company of British merchants in London to found a Factory there under British protection, and with the support of men friendly to the Missionary Societies, Church and Wesleyan, of this country. Fourth, that delay or neglect would.

throw this fine country into the hands of France or America.
Fifth, that it would be better managed by the Colonial Office than
by any body of Commissioners like South Australia. Sixth, that
if proper means were used the Missionary Societies here, their
representatives abroad, and the chiefs, might all be brought in to
agree to some such measure as British rule over the three islands.
After expressing his satisfaction at this interview, Lord Glenelg
said he quite saw the case, which was a very difficult and perplexing one. I told him I should always be ready at his command
if required.

Mr. Angas knew enough of the Colonial Office to
be sure that there would be no over-intense and
immediate activity, and he knew equally well the
importance of conciliating the missionary societies,
and removing, if possible, their objection to
colonizing New Zealand and establishing British
authority there. He therefore set to work
vigorously, and had frequent interviews with the
Rev. Mr. Coates, the Secretary of the Church Missionary Society, and Dr. Beecham, representing the
Wesleyan Missionary Society. He also wrote to the
Rev. John Williams, the famous South Sea missionary, who was then in England, and received the
following reply :—

With reference to the New Zealand Association, I look upon it
as a dangerous experiment, but I do not see how the missionaries
at New Zealand can oppose it, since they have purchased thousands
of acres of land from the natives. Now at Tahiti we have ever
advised the people not to part with any of their land, and there is
no missionary who possesses a single inch of land in any of the
islands. No portion has ever been alienated from the natives. As

it is not probable that the New Zealand Association can be stopped
in its progress, the best way appears to me for such as yourself to
be on the Board of Commissioners and infuse as much good as
possible into their proceedings.

Mr. Angas was not disposed to follow this advice;
he saw the extreme danger of the British position as
probably no one else saw it; to him the rumour of
a French consul being sent there, and the fact of
French Roman Catholic missionaries having recently
settled in the islands, were significant circumstances,
and it was impressed upon his mind that whatever
was done the first thing was to see that no time was
lost.

His efforts with the two great Missionary Societies
were successful, as will be seen from the following
extract from his journal :—

January 14, 1839.—Went up to the office of the Chief Secretary
for the Colonies, and placed in his hands a copy of the Church
Missionary Register for June, 1838, containing the distressing
account of the fighting in New Zealand, the burning down of the
Church Mission premises, and the threatening of the lives of the
missionaries themselves. I told his lordship that I had seen the
Secretaries of the Church and Wesleyan Missionary Societies, also
the Committee of the Aborigines Protection Society, and had
induced them not to oppose any measure for the settlement of
New Zealand which the Government might adopt on its own
responsibility, but that great opposition would be given to the
scheme of the Association, or to political power being given to any
commercial company. His lordship inquired as to the objects of
these Societies, and I replied that it was the moral and spiritual
welfare of the aborigines and the inhabitants of the islands.
Should any Commission be appointed I submitted the propriety of

not more than three being selected, for if more, as in the case of the Commissioners for South Australia, it would work badly.

In the emergency Lord Glenelg suggested the formation of a Joint Stock Company, but Mr. Angas declined to take any active or responsible part in an undertaking of this kind. "If it were possible to get a hundred pious persons to advance £1000 each," he wrote in his journal, "I think Lord Glenelg would give them a charter, and commit the direction of the sale of land and the selection of emigrants to its Board as an agency."

About this time, that is to say, in the spring of 1839, some of the members of the original New Zealand Association formed themselves, with others, into a Joint Stock Company called "The New Zealand Land Company," with the Earl of Durham at the head, and several members of Parliament among the directors. The object of the Company was stated to be the employment of capital in the purchase and re-sale of lands in New Zealand and the promotion of emigration, and in these respects it was similar to the South Australian Company. In the case of South Australia, however, there was this difference—there was no probability of any dispute about the proprietorship of the soil, the Commissioners having been invested with authority by the Imperial Parliament to give a valid title to all land sold, whereas the title proposed by the New Zealand Land Company rested upon negotiations made with the natives in 1825.

Of the hot haste with which the New Zealand
Land Company dispatched Colonel Wakefield to the
colony as their agent, before a satisfactory settlement had been made with the British Government,
and of the varying successes and disasters that befell
him and the Company, it is not necessary that we
should particularize here. Mr. Angas watched their
proceedings with interest and anxiety, and wrote in
his journal about this time :—

I am under great apprehension that serious difficulties and
perplexities await the New Zealand Land Company, of which we
shall hear before this time next year, but eventually the Government must take up the case, and New Zealand will be colonized,
and few, if any, will thank the Company for its risks, losses, and
expenditure.

It so happened that while the Company were
actively engaged in fitting out their first expedition,
the Government, acting upon the information given
them by Mr. Angas, and being now well aware of
the intentions of France, were taking steps to secure
the sovereignty of the islands, and to this end
Captain Hobson, R.N., was appointed to proceed
to New Zealand as " Her Majesty's Consul, and as
eventual Lieutenant-Governor of such territory as
may be ceded to Her Majesty in the New Zealand
Islands." The instructions given him by the
Marquis of Normanby were clear and emphatic.
" You will point out to the natives or their chiefs
the dangers to which they may be exposed by the

residence among them of settlers amenable to no
laws or tribunals of their own, and the impossibility
of Her Majesty's extending to them any effectual
protection unless the Queen be acknowledged as the
sovereign of their country. . . . The chiefs should be
induced, if possible, to contract with you, as representing Her Majesty, that henceforward no lands
shall be ceded either gratuitously or otherwise except
to the Crown of Great Britain. . . ."

Colonel Wakefield, the agent of the New Zealand
Company, arrived at Cook's Straits in September,
1839, a few days after Captain Hobson left England,
and at once proceeded to purchase land from the
natives, paying for it by bartering muskets, cart-
ridges, and gunpowder! Truly the time had come
for the intervention of the British Government.

On the 29th of January, 1840, Captain Hobson
and his staff arrived in the Bay of Islands, and on
the following day made proclamation of his commission in due form. Some portions of that proclamation sent dismay into the hearts of those who
were adherents of the New Zealand Company—such,
for example, as the following passage : " All purchases of land in any part of New Zealand, which
may henceforth be made by any of Her Majesty's
subjects from any of the native chiefs or tribes of
these islands, will be absolutely null and void, and
neither confirmed nor in any way recognized by Her
Majesty."

Shortly afterwards Hobson assembled the chiefs of

the Native Confederation and other chiefs, and in the presence of the missionaries and the principal European inhabitants the document known in New Zealand annals as the Treaty of Waitangi was read, agreed to, and signed. It ceded to the Queen of England " absolutely, and without reservation, all the rights and powers of sovereignty which the said confederation, or individual chiefs respectively exercise or possess over their respective territories as the sole sovereigns thereof."

This related only to the Northern Island. The authority of Her Majesty over the Southern Island was proclaimed on the ground of discovery. Then Captain Hobson proceeded to deal with the New Zealand Company, whose agent, Colonel Wakefield, had laid out the town of Wellington in the harbour of Port Nicholson as the chief town of the Company; had established a "constitution," and appointed magistrates. Here, as elsewhere, the authority of the Queen was proclaimed, and the fiction of "independent functions" swept away; the Company's flag was hauled down, and the British ensign officially hoisted.

This happened in June. Two months later Captain Hobson had to turn his attention to another matter —the anticipated arrival of a French expedition to claim possession of the Islands. The truth of the information given by Mr. Angas to Lord Glenelg was about to be verified. Not only had Captain Hobson been apprized of the probable time when the French ships might be expected, but the port to which they were bound had been named.

He therefore instructed Captain Stanley, of H.M.S. *Britomart*, to be on the watch for the approach of the French, and to inform the commander of the expedition that the sovereignty of Her Britannic Majesty had been proclaimed over all the New Zealand islands.

How Captain Stanley fulfilled his mission may best be told in his own words.

Captain Stanley, R.N., to His Excellency Captain Hobson, R.N.

September 17, 1840.

I have the honour to inform your Excellency that I proceeded in Her Majesty's sloop under my command to the Port of Akaroa, in Banks' Peninsula, where I arrived on the 10th of August. The French frigate *L'Aube* had not arrived when I anchored, nor had any French emigrants been landed. I landed on the 11th of August, accompanied by Messrs. Murphy and Robinson, police magistrates, and visited the only two parts of the bay where there were houses. At both places the flag was hoisted, and a court, of which notice had been given the day before, was held by the magistrates. Having received information that there were three whaling stations on the southern side of the peninsula, the exposed positions of which afforded no anchorage for the *Britomart*, I sent Messrs. Murphy and Robinson to visit them in a whale boat. At each station the flag was hoisted and a court held. On the 15th of August the French frigate *L'Aube* arrived, having been four days off the port. On the 16th of August the French whaler *Comte de Paris*, having on board fifty-seven French emigrants, arrived. With the exception of M. Bellegni from the Jardin des Plantes, who is sent out to look after the emigrants, and who is a good botanist and mineralogist, the emigrants are all of the lower order,

and include carpenters, gardeners, stonemasons, labourers, a baker
and a miner—in all thirty men, eleven women, and the rest
children.

Captain Lavaud, on the arrival of the French emigrants, assured
me, on his word of honour, that he would maintain the strictest
neutrality between the British residents and the emigrants, and
that should any difference arise between them he would settle
matters impartially. Captain Lavaud also informed me that as
the *Comte de Paris* had to proceed to sea, whaling, he would
cause the emigrants to be landed in some unoccupied part of the
bay, where he pledged himself they would do nothing which could
be considered as hostile to our Government, and that until fresh
instructions should be received from our respective Governments
the emigrants should merely build themselves houses for shelter,
and clear away what little land they might require for gardens.

Upon visiting the *Comte de Paris* I found that she had on board,
besides agricultural tools for the settlers, *six long 24-pounders
mounted on field-carriages.* I immediately called upon Captain
Lavaud to protest against the guns being landed. Captain Lavaud
assured me that he had been much surprised at finding that guns
had been sent out in the *Comte de Paris*, and that he had already
given the most positive orders that they should not be landed.
On the 19th of August the French having landed in a sheltered,
well-chosen part of the Bay, where they could not interfere with
any one, I handed on to Messrs. Murphy and Robinson the
instructions intrusted to me by your Excellency to meet such a
contingency.

Having shown how the timely information acquired
by Mr. Angas in his interviews with Baron de
Thierry, and communicated to Lord Glenelg, bore
its fruit in stimulating the Colonial Office to take
prompt and decisive measures for securing the
sovereignty over New Zealand, let us now turn to

French testimony to see the light in which this *tour de force* was regarded by that nation.

The version given by M. Guizot in his famous work in vindication of Louis Philippe's Government, entitled "France under Louis Philippe," although discreetly silent on some parts of the narrative, not only confirms the general account we have given, but adds some fresh particulars of this race between two nations for a colony. He says :—

The convenience of securing to our navy a place of rest and refreshment in the South Pacific began to be felt more and more. Public interest took the initiative. Towards the end of 1839, a Company formed itself at Nantes and Bordeaux, to attempt in New Zealand a French colony. It asked and obtained from the Cabinet of that epoch a certain extent of adhesion and co-operation; but when the time for execution arrived, it was ascertained that the English had forestalled us in those large islands ; that since 1815 they had formed private establishments there, which, step by step, were assuming a national character ; that in August, 1839, an English officer, Captain Hobson, had sailed for New Zealand with instructions from his Government ; and that in the first months of 1840, before the arrival of the French ships, the sovereignty of the Queen of England had been proclaimed there. The enterprise, supposing that on our part contest had a basis, became thus singularly grave and difficult. The demands which the Nanto-Bordelaise Company then addressed to the King's Government in virtue of promises made to them became an object of serious inquiry, which left us convinced that if that Company had for private interests titles to our support, we could not set up, against the anterior possession of the English Government, any legitimate claims embracing the slightest chance of success. The reports of Captain Lavaud, a mariner equally intellectual and brave, who was sent at that time to those seas in command of the corvette *L'Aube,*

confirmed us in this conviction. It became necessary to seek elsewhere than in New Zealand the establishment we wanted in the
Pacific Ocean. Captain Dupetit Thouars, having returned in 1840
from his voyage round the world in the frigate *Venus*, was the last
of our sailors who had visited those regions, and on him we could
rely for recent and certain information. He presented to the
Minister of Marine a report on the Marquesas Islands, which he
had recently examined with that object. We had a double end in
view. At the same time that we wished to procure for our navy
and for French commerce in those seas a good maritime station,
we had before us an important question, long inserted in the penal
code—the establishment of a place of transportation beyond the
continental territory of the kingdom. Repeatedly examined with
this view, our various colonial possessions had presented serious
objections on the score of health, security, political or commercial
interests, and moral propriety. Studied with care by the Ministries
of Marine, Justice, and Foreign Affairs, the proposition of Captain
Dupetit Thouars seemed to meet the various exigencies we were
bound to consider. The Marquesas Islands were perfectly salu-
brious, situated in a fine climate, limited in extent, and easy to
watch or defend. They offered a good harbour to our navigation ;
the tribes which inhabited them were few in number, and could be
easily won over or subdued. Since the commencement of the seventeenth century, when Quiros discovered and gave them the name of
Marquesas, in honour of the Marchioness de Mendoza, wife to the
Viceroy of Peru, his patron, no European power had acquired any
right over them, no foreign colonists had established themselves
there. If the distance of the place was a cause of delay and
expense, it had, in the penal point of view, the advantage of acting
on imagination without shocking humanity. Our establishment,
therefore, at this point combined at home all the political and
moral conditions of the double end we proposed to ourselves, and
could not lead abroad to any embarrassment. The proposition of
Captain Dupetit Thouars was accepted, and he took his departure
in August, 1841, in the frigate *Queen Blanche*, invested with the

rank of Rear-Admiral, with the command of our naval station in the South Seas, and furnished with formal instructions to take possession of the Marquesas Islands in the name of the King's Government.

The course pursued by the French Government at this critical juncture was a matter of congratulation not only to the British Government but to the British colonies in Australasia, and it is evident that a few months' delay in sending out Captain Hobson might have led to serious complications, if not to an open rupture, with France.

The French Government proved the intensity of its ambition for empire in the Southern Seas by seizing the Marquesas Islands, and subsequently by taking possession of Tahiti and New Caledonia, but it was a poor compensation to them for the loss of New Zealand.

On May 3, 1841, New Zealand, which at first had been annexed as a dependency to New South Wales, was proclaimed an independent British colony, and Captain Hobson received his appointment as Governor and Commander-in-chief.

We need not concern ourselves here with the troubles of the New Zealand Land Company, or of the means taken to solve the vexed question of their claims; but it may interest the general reader to know that in 1843, being unable to give any good title to their lands, the Company suspended their land sales, and as these sales were their sole source of income, they were obliged to discontinue their

colonizing operations altogether. Up to that time
they had formed three settlements — Wellington,
Nelson, and New Plymouth, and had conveyed to
those places nine thousand emigrants.

It is almost impossible to exaggerate the
importance of the services rendered by Mr. Angas,
both to this country and to the Australian Colonies,
in assisting to secure New Zealand as a British
possession, when it is remembered how serious
have been the difficulties in dealing with the French,
not only with regard to the Marquesas Islands and
Tahiti, but even to the insignificant colony in New
Caledonia, which, with its penal settlement, has been
a source of constant trouble and annoyance.

A French colony in New Zealand—a country
large and fertile, with abundant coalfields, and good
harbours for a fleet—might have endangered British
influence in the Pacific.

The Government of this country was not unmind-
ful of the invaluable assistance of Mr. Angas in
saving New Zealand from the French, and he was
offered, in consideration of his services, first a
knighthood and then a baronetcy, but both offers
he promptly declined.

To him the highest reward was the knowledge
that he had been enabled to render permanent benefit
to his country.

CHAPTER IX.

The Pioneer Fleet—An Offer to the Government—Governor Hindmarsh
—For Conscience' Sake—Success of the " Company "—Abolition of
Slavery—Bad News from South Australia—A Sore Trouble—Colonel
Gawler—A Journey on Horseback—Removal from Dawlish—Mr.
Flaxman and the Great Land Purchase—In perplexity—An Arbitra-
tion Case—The Valley of Humiliation.

WE must now go back in the narrative to the year
1836 * in order to follow the fortunes of the South
Australian Company, and ·to trace Mr. Angas's connection with it from the time when the pioneer fleet
set sail for the new colony.

After resigning his seat on the Board of Commissioners, all the officers and servants of the
Company constituting the pioneer party of
colonists, were selected and sent out under his
immediate superintendence, while his office, in
which the business of the Company was entirely
carried on, became the recognized place of call for
intending emigrants, and all who wished to obtain
reliable information about the colony.

Those were busy days. From the outset of his

* See p. 123.

connection with South Australia he had made it one
of his chief concerns to select suitable agents to
advocate emigration, and more particularly to find
the right kind of persons to send out to the
colony, not only among capitalists and professional
men, but also among the industrious poor. To this
end he frequently made extensive tours—sometimes
driving and at others on horseback—throughout the
length and breadth of the land, holding meetings,
visiting ministers of religion and philanthropists,
scattering printed information, forming county associations and local committees, and otherwise
popularizing the subject.

When the *John Pirie*, and the other vessels
forming the pioneer fleet of the South Australian
Company, set sail in March, the weather was very
stormy off the coast, and this occasioned Mr. Angas
some anxiety. He wrote in his journal :—

My earnest prayers to God have been that He will protect these
vessels and all on board, and carry them safely to their destination
at Kangaroo Island. The whole colony has been launched upon
the sea of faith, so far as I have had to do with it, for the difficulties
which rose against it, first in the Board of Commissioners, and
after that in the Company, seemed insurmountable.

It was characteristic of him that in his anxiety
for the safety of the fleet he should seek the prayers
of the people with whom he worshipped, and in
doing so he pointed out to them "the example of
the first expedition that went out from Plymouth to

America, who departed, continued their course,
landed, and prospered under the influence of the
prayers of the churches."

The *John Pirie* only got a hundred miles beyond
Scilly when she met with a terrible storm, and after
beating about many days was obliged to return to
Falmouth, with the loss, however, of only six or eight
sheep. Then followed fair winds, and " the prayers
were answered."

Some idea of the promptitude and energy of Mr.
Angas and of his abhorrence of the lack of these
qualities in others, may be gathered from the following extract from a letter to Mr. Shaw-Lefevre written
only a little more than a month after the pioneer
fleet had sailed :—

April 14, 1836.

The South Australian Company has sent away long ago two
South Sea whale ships, and a vessel for the coasting trade all full
of stores, provisions, &c., and about 120 people. A fourth vessel
of about 180 tons is nearly ready to sail full of stores, &c., and
about forty-five to fifty people. I expect her departure next week.
The Company has expended above £25,000 since the 22nd of
January last, when it was formed.

I must say our Directors have supported me nobly, and fully
justified the high opinion for talent and judgment which I had
formed of them.

While I am grateful to these generous men, we have all beheld
with deep sorrow of heart that the Commissioners have only
chartered and sent out one vessel besides the *Rapid*, about to sail,
but no emigrants who can be employed by the purchasers of land
in the colony ! Besides, has it ever been known in a colony of
this or any other country, that so large a body of settlers as the

Company has sent and is sending out has proceeded to a colony established by Act of Parliament, without any Governor or Government officers to keep the peace ? Should any mischief arise, some one will have to account for it.

Determined not to leave any stone unturned which might aid his plans, Mr. Angas was hither and thither, now travelling in search of suitable men for the different departments of the Company's service, now laying before the Commissioners plans and estimates for erecting 150 rough cottages in the new colony at a cost of from £5,000 to £6,000, now urging the Colonial Office to at least a show of activity.

At length, in July of this year, he was rejoicing in the fact that Captain Hindmarsh, the first Governor elect, was ready to depart for the new colony, and Mr. Angas hurried down to Portsmouth to take leave of him, to hand him papers for perusal relating to suitable laws for the Government of South Australia, and to give him words of fatherly advice on the difficult position he was about to assume.

It is not surprising to find that soon after this there came a reaction, and a significant entry in the diary relates :—

Aug. 27, 1836.—Here am I laid up, as it were, in ordinary like a ship-of-war dismantled, my physical strength much reduced, and my nervous system shattered to pieces.

Days of enforced leisure in the life of a busy man are rarely wasted days ; certainly they were not so

in the case of Mr. Angas. Writing did not appear
to exhaust him; as a matter of fact it was a recreation, and among his papers there are copies of
voluminous letters to Governor Hindmarsh on
almost every subject that touched the best interests
of the new colony. On the question of education
he begged the assistance of the Governor to the
scheme he had set afloat, and which we have
described elsewhere, adding : " In the accomplishment of this great design nothing is more likely to
realize it than your enacting a law of your Council
attaching certain degrees of honour and privilege to
the well-educated and industrious poor."

Although, as we have stated, writing did not
appear to exhaust him, he was greatly aided in the
manual labour by two of his daughters, who acted
as his private secretaries. For hours together he
would pace the room with his hands behind his back,
dictating important documents which they would
write simultaneously, so as to obtain two copies, and
with long practice they not only learned to write
with great rapidity, but at exactly the same pace,
and so much alike that the two documents would be
almost facsimiles. When pressed for time, if the
correspondence was not such as to require very
careful thought, he would dictate two separate
letters simultaneously, giving first a sentence of one
and then of the other. His daughters were also
accustomed to read books on colonization, and make
abstracts and summaries of the contents, and also to

make lists of every necessary article for domestic or personal use, garden implements, seeds, and so forth, so that small but important articles, such as pins, needles, tapes, shoe-laces, brushes, rolling-pins, pens, or ink, might not be forgotten in sending out supplies to the young colony.

About this time Mr. Angas became acquainted with Dr. J. Murray, of Hull, well known in scientific and literary circles, who had recently written a pamphlet on New Zealand flax (*Phormium tenax*), and was interesting himself in the introduction of British plants into British colonies. Another friend at this period was Dr. Dick, the astronomer, author of " Siderial Heavens," " Celestial Scenery," and the " Christian Philosopher," a quasi-scientific work which obtained great popularity. With both these gentlemen he kept up a correspondence, and eventually enlisted their active services, the former to visit Jersey, Normandy, and elsewhere, to make selection of all kinds of seeds for the use of the colony, the latter to draw up plans for a South Australian College.

In his leisure at Dawlish it is refreshing to turn to an entry in his journal in which he records some relaxation from the strain of business :—

Jan. 22, 1837.—I regularly devote from two to three hours a day to the reading of history with my daughters.

The year opened well, and from time to time good

news reached him both from London and Australia. When Captain Hindmarsh left England the sub- scribed capital of the Company was £200,000; in November of the same year there was added to it £100,000 by the issue of 4,000 additional shares of £25 each, at a premium of £1, which almost at once went up 5s. per share, and promised a steady increase. From Australia the welcome intelligence arrived in April that Mr. D. McLaren had landed safely at Nepean Bay, and had at once assumed the general management of the Company's affairs. By his firmness and judgment he succeeded in evolving order out of chaos, and having more ample resources at his command than either the Governor or the Residential Commissioner, he took the lead, as the Company he represented had already done, in the great work of colonization.

The site of the capital having been decided upon, he fixed his quarters there, and at once commenced the erection of some substantial buildings upon the Company's town acres, of which they possessed, in all, 162 : 114 in South Adelaide, and 48 in North Adelaide, besides six acres at Port Adelaide.

Under his administration the affairs of the Com- pany prospered. The Bank became a flourishing institution, and transacted business, not only with England, but with various other parts of the world. The sheep and cattle department was largely extended; the country lands were surveyed, and farmers, sent out under the auspices of the Company, settled upon them ; brickfields were opened up in the neighbourhood of Adelaide, for which excellent clay was found, and a reign of prosperity appeared to have set in.

It was with no little satisfaction, therefore, that Mr. Angas drew up the report to present to the first annual general meeting of the share-holders, and it was quite pardonable, in the flush of early triumph, to conclude it in the following terms :—" The proprietary of this Company will have the satisfaction of perceiving that they have essentially aided the British Government in carrying into execution one of the noblest experiments in colonization which has ever been attempted — the planting of a nation in the region of a desert, on the soundest principles, under the sanction of an Act of the Imperial Parliament, with a Government secur-ing to its people the enjoyment of the inestimable blessings of civil and religious liberty, where the climate, soil, and waters bid fair at some future time to place it in a commanding position in the Southern Hemisphere."

There was only one drawback to his satisfaction, and it is naïvely told in the following extract from the journal :—

June 26, 1887.—This afternoon I had to fight a battle with the Board on the subject of those passages in my report which dis-tinctly acknowledge the hand and protection of Providence, which parts they wished to be omitted ; at least, two of the Directors thought that in matters of business religion ought to be kept out.

I persisted, however, and declared that I would protest against such a course, and would rather resign my chair than be a party to such a neglect of the Divine Being.

When the annual meeting was held, the obnoxious passages were read, and were well received, " the remarks made by the shareholders being of a decidedly benevolent and religious character."

After the annual meeting there was again a brief respite to the business activities and anxieties of Mr. Angas. But it was impossible for him to enjoy repose for any length of time. " Quiet to quick bosoms is a hell," and to no man more so than to him. We find him, therefore, indulging the bent of his inclination by making a tour of all the chapels within a reasonable distance of his house in Dawlish, assisting in working off debts upon them in some instances, and in temporarily plunging them into debt in others by erecting new chapels. Almost every Sunday he was engaged in preaching, sometimes under very trying circumstances, as the following incident will show :—

Feb. 25, 1838.—Last night, or rather this morning, there was a frightful storm of wind and rain, and the tides being spring, much damage has been done. Walked to Kenton this morning with great difficulty and preached. Part of the road was so flooded that I was obliged to get on a man's back who had on fisherman's boots. . . . This afternoon preached at Eastwood in a room that had three feet of water in it this morning. It was very damp, but full of people, who were very serious and attentive.

It was only to be expected that having been instrumental in emancipating slaves in Honduras and the Mosquito coast, he should throw himself with enthusiasm into the great slave question at that time agitating the whole of Britain. His interest took many practical forms, and throughout the year we find him attending public meetings, journeying up to London to form a part of deputations to Ministers of the Crown, and stirring up enthusiasm in neglected quarters by correspondence. At last he had the intense satisfaction of writing in his diary :—

Aug. 1, 1838.—This is a memorable day—the abolition of the apprenticeships system in the British Colonies. Blessed be God for bringing this matter about at a time and in a manner so different to the expectations of the friends of the negro. We all felt that the late rejection of the measure of abolition by the House of Commons, and the consequent passing of the Bill by Lord Glenelg to force the planters to do the labourers justice for the two years of their term, was a death-blow to all our hopes, but the Lord has designed it otherwise, and now we learn that the Colonial Legislature has adopted Lord Glenelg's advice, and passed the measure of abolition from among themselves. . . . This is a day long to be remembered by every friend to liberty. The world never exhibited a more remarkable instance of the true nature and effects of Christian benevolence. This great moral conflict required no less than sixty-six years to obtain a victory, during which time the hearts of the leaders have remained true and unshaken by all their defeats, year after year, notwithstanding the mighty power against them. Is not this the 'faith and patience of the saints' ?

The period of comparative rest and ease was not

to last long.   Intelligence was received from South
Australia that affairs were in a somewhat unsettled
state there, and hardly any question of importance
arose that the Governor did not submit to Mr. Angas
for instructions.   In like manner the agents of the
South Australian Company brought before him in
voluminous correspondence   not only their own
grievances but those which were more immediately
proper for the consideration of the Commissioners,
while Mr. McLaren, the general manager, wrote :
" I do seriously and sincerely consider that your
authority and influence will be required here, and
that unless you come and see with your own eyes,
and judge with your own judgment, you must find it
difficult, if not impossible, to decide accurately, either
as to character, persons, or circumstances."

It is a curious fact that up to this time the
thought of going out to Australia had scarcely ever
entered the mind of Mr. Angas, as he considered
that his position in this country, both as regarded his
family, his property, and his public engagements,
was clearly opposed to it.   There was now, however,
an "incipient inclination," as he calls it, on the
part of several members of his family to go to
South Australia, and his own feelings were far from
being distinctly against it.   But, as we shall see,
many weary and eventful years were to elapse before
that came to pass.

It is not always advantageous to a successful man,
holding in his hands considerable power, to have his

own way in everything, nor is it well for him to continue his activities without check. Early in 1838
Mr. Angas succeeded in escaping the " woe " pronounced upon those of whom " all men speak well."

After the first flush of success, some reverses in
the affairs of the South Australian Company caused
the confidence of the directors to be shaken, and a
prejudice was created in their minds against Mr.
Angas, whose only fault would appear to have been
that he was not omnipotent. Some of them went
so far as to force a number of shares into the market,
which brought them down to par after standing at
a fair premium. Notwithstanding this, Mr. Angas
kept the whole of his 1,300 £25 shares, thus showing
his confidence in the undertaking.

For all his labour, expenditure of time and money,
and loss of health, he was placed by ballot as one of
the first two directors to retire ! It was a heavy
blow, and a sore trouble. But, feeling that it was
undeserved, it had no permanent ill effect.

His sky was clear again in June, for although he
had contemplated the annual meeting with some
anxiety, it turned out better than he could have
possibly anticipated. The shareholders expressed
their unabated confidence, the directors acknowledged his valuable services, and he was requested,
without a dissentient voice, to resume the chair.

Much of the uneasiness felt by the directors and
shareholders of the Company was due to the fact
that from time to time reports had been received

from the new colony of the unpopularity of Governor
Hindmarsh, who was, unfortunately, not a peace-
maker. During his rule there was a dual government
vested in himself on the one hand, and in the Resident Commissioner on the other, and, instead of
striving to work together amicably and for the
general prosperity, they became two noisy and
quarrelsome factions, engaging in endless disputes,
which for a time put a stop to all progress.

This state of things led to the recall of Governor
Hindmarsh, after he had been in office only about
fourteen months.

It was a source of pain and regret to Mr. Angas,
but, as a sensible man, he set to work to repair the
mischief, as far as might be, by endeavouring to
secure the appointment of a new and a better
Governor. It was largely due to his persistent
efforts in interviewing all the leading members of
Parliament personally interested in Colonial questions, that Colonel Gawler was appointed Governor
in succession to Captain Hindmarsh.

Colonel Gawler was a man after Mr. Angas's heart;
deeply interested in all questions relating to the
moral and spiritual welfare of the people ; calm,
determined, and vigorous, and bent on one object—
the inauguration of a system of progress in the new
colony. Both before and after his departure a great
many interesting letters passed between him and
Mr. Angas. We can only refer to a few. In one Mr.
Angas regrets that " so many, who stood well in

Christian estimation in this country, act inconsistently after emigration," and that his efforts "to induce Christian men and families of good principles to proceed to the new colony are not always successful." In another he urges him to "promote religious peace among the different bodies of Christians who agree in the essential doctrines and precepts of Christianity," and is especially anxious for him to "look after the German Lutheran emigrants, 600 of whom have probably reached Australia before this." He deplores the constant conflicts with the natives "which no human prudence can prevent," and referring to certain murders treacherously committed by the natives, he asks :—

"How is this to be met but by missionaries without arms going amongst them and living as part of each tribe far away from the white traders? By the Gospel they will be taught the unlawfulness of revenge, and by the missionaries how to raise food for themselves, especially potatoes, on a few acres of land, and hence will not feel much jealousy at the intrusion of white men."

Unhappily there were at this time many feuds, discords, and litigations, not only among the powers that be, but also among the powers and the colonists, and these form the subject of many letters in the correspondence—great matters then, but the interest in them is now past.

Colonel Gawler arrived in South Australia on the 12th of October, 1838. Throughout that year almost every letter from the colony received by Mr. Angas was depressing, "full of woes, lamentations, and predictions of woe," all tending to "waste his nervous energy, depress his mind, and wear down his spirits."

But for all his persistent labours there was a strong inspiring cause.

My great object (he says) was, in the first instance, to provide a place of refuge for pious Dissenters of Great Britain, who could in their new home discharge their consciences before God in civil and religious duties without any disabilities. Then, in the next place, to provide a place where the children of pious farmers might have farms on which to settle, and provide bread for their families : and lastly, that I might be the humble instrument of laying the foundation of a good system of education and religious instruction for the poorer settlers.

The sword was wearing out the scabbard, and from time to time failing health made drastic measures for recovery imperative. In August of this year, therefore, he resolved to take a long journey on horseback, and leaving Dawlish on August the 6th, he visited Exeter, Wells, Bristol, Bath, Hungerford, Oxford, Stratford-on-Avon, Liverpool, Manchester, Halifax, Durham, Newcastle, Leeds, Birmingham, and London. Everywhere along the route he scattered information about South Australia, putting before all classes its advantages as a field for emigration—to the farmers dilating upon the excellence of its soil, to the religious people upon its liberty of worship.

In September he was back again in Dawlish, and with the enormous strain upon his energies in so many other directions, it is curious to read in his diary such entries as the following :—

Sept. 23, 1838.—Commenced a course of familiar lectures to the Sunday school children at Mr. Collet's chapel.

Feb., 1839.—Last Sunday I preached twice to the people at Kenton.

March 31, 1839.—For several weeks I have had strength sufficient to take the morning service at Kenton. To-day I was able to walk to Kenton, nearly six miles, preach there, and walk back in a streaming rain.

As the years went on, Mr. Angas found that Dawlish was not a good place of residence for "a business man of London city." The wear and tear of frequent journeys to London, and occasional ones to Newcastle, tended to undo the good effected by the pure air of Devonshire ; and as for home life, he knew less of it there than he would have done in a London suburb. In the summer of 1839, therefore, after a residence of nearly six years in Dawlish, he took up his abode at Park-place Villas, Paddington.

It was with no little regret that he left his pleasant country-house. Much good had been wrought during his sojourn there. Mainly through his instrumentality several chapels had been built, restored, enlarged, or their debts removed. Sunday schools and libraries had been established, and the poor had been systematically visited and helped by Mrs. Angas and her family. And, curious to relate, it was during that same period that Mr. Angas had served on the South Australian Commission, had founded the Company and devised innumerable measures for the welfare of the colony, had assisted multitudes of persecuted Lutherans to emigrate, had formed the Banking Company of South Australia and the Union Bank of Australia, and had induced the British Government to establish sovereignty in New Zealand—a startling catalogue of successful enterprises.

But the stream of success was not to flow on without interruption, and in this same year there came the beginning of troubles such as he had never before experienced. It will be remembered that when the first batch of Lutherans left Hamburg, Mr. Angas parted with his chief clerk, Mr. Flaxman, to overlook them, and at the same time entrusted to him certain monetary matters, not only on their account, but also on his own. The confidence reposed in him was based upon faithful service for over nine years in a responsible capacity, and upon Christian character and trustworthiness.

Wherever Mr. Angas could confide he did so implicitly, and he entrusted Mr. Flaxman with a general power of attorney, guarded of course by such limitations as an experienced and far-sighted man would think it prudent to impose, although in the

somewhat chaotic condition of affairs in the colony
at that time, his instructions were obliged to be to a
certain extent elastic and indefinite.

Instead of confining himself to the mission he
was sent out exclusively to perform—of collecting
moneys advanced to the Germans, looking after the
improvement of their settlements, and so forth—
Mr. Flaxman went into business on his own account,
and established or joined the mercantile firm of
Flaxman & Rowlands at Adelaide.

At that time a mania for land purchases was
prevailing in the colony, and Mr. Flaxman soon
became infected with the Land Fever. Studying his
own interests in a somewhat marked manner, and
at the same time not losing sight of those of his
employer, he conceived the audacious idea of bringing by one bold stroke a fortune to himself and to
Mr. Angas.

Without any authority whatever, and in opposition
to the often expressed wishes of his employer not
to be a party to any speculations in the new colony,
Mr. Flaxman bought seven special surveys of 4,000
acres each in the sources of the Rhine and Gawler
Rivers, secured the titles in his own name, and
coolly sent drafts, amounting to £28,000, on account
of purchase money, for Mr. Angas to meet at once,
and wrote, " You must not be surprised if I draw on
you for £100,000 " !

This happened at a time when, from several causes
in combination, he was less able than he would have

been in many preceding years to meet the exigencies
of the case, and he wrote in his diary:—

My position is such that I cannot advance any part of the money
for Mr. Flaxman's drafts of £28,000; the South Australian Company will not do it, and the times are such that there is not the
least probability of my selling much, if any, of the land. With
man it is utterly impossible to escape the ruin that is coming upon
both Flaxman and me ; with God, however, nothing is impossible,
and I yet have hope in Him. Perhaps He will have mercy upon
us and remember our kindness to His persecuted servants from
Silesia. The Lord knows that I have not looked for any profits
from these Germans, nor would I desire to be enriched by such
unjustifiable means. Flaxman and I were nearly the sole
instruments in carrying them out to South Australia, and none
seem now disposed to help us. Truly the ways of God are
mysterious, and what can I do ? O Lord, often my extremity
has been the hour of Thy help, and may it be so now.

That "cry from the depths" was apparently
unheard, and years of darkness and distress were
to follow.

Of course Mr. Angas was not legally bound to
accept Flaxman's purchases, but unfortunately the
drafts had, without authority, been discounted by the
Company's Bank Manager, Mr. Edward Stephens.
Of this bank Mr. Angas was, as we have seen, the
founder, and he still retained the post of Chairman
of the London Board of Directors. To have repu-
diated the drafts would have been to bring about the
ruin of the South Australian Company and its Bank.

As soon as he recovered from the blow, which at
first had staggered him, he determined upon his

course of action. Happen what might and cost what
it would, he felt bound to honour the drafts as they
came to hand, making what arrangements he could
with the Board of Directors.

Meanwhile Mr. Flaxman, who was still his paid
agent, was recalled, and Mr. Anthony Forster—
whose name is to this day greatly honoured in the
colony—was appointed his successor.

It was not to be expected that the statement
Mr. Angas had to make to the Board of Directors
would be allowed to pass unchallenged, and he had
to defend himself against an imputation to the effect
that it was incredible the purchase would have been
made without distinct authority from him.

I positively denied (he wrote in his diary) that I had given Mr.
Flaxman orders to buy any land whatever, and I further explained
to the Board the policy I had all along pursued in respect to the
colony, and in relation to the Company, namely, that I had
uniformly neglected my own business in favour of that of the
Company.

But philanthropy such as that was not understood
by ordinary business men, and the terms proposed
to him were hard. The Board would allow him four
months to pay £25,000 of the amount, the balance
to be raised in as short a time as possible.

Mr. Angas was sorely perplexed and distressed.
Although compliance with these terms would greatly
inconvenience him — and subsequently it almost
caused his ruin—he proposed to accept them rather

than bring trouble on those who had discounted the bills in the colony, upon the Company at home, or upon any of the parties concerned in the transaction. His ample capital was locked up, and he had to become a borrower on a large scale when money was scarcer and dearer than he had ever known it to be before. But borrowing, even upon the best security, was a difficult matter, and it became imperative to withdraw the capital he had invested, with such splendid financial results, in the Union Bank of Australia, and in other companies and institutions he had founded and fostered.

The Union Bank shares were among the first to go, although at a time when it was most undesirable to part with them,* and solely because he " had determined not to damage the South Australian Company by selling his shares in it."

Referring to the surrender of his shares in the Union Bank, and the resignation of his seat on the Board in consequence, he wrote in his diary :—

May God graciously accept of this painful sacrifice to a sense of duty in my extremity, that I may do justice to all men.

In the religious aspect of his trouble the mind of Mr. Angas was much exercised, and in self-communings in his diary he raises curious questions, such as " whether these calamities are the work of Satan to frustrate the accomplishment of benevolent

* See Chap. vi. p. 188.

plans," or "whether they are the work of God to
cause him to withdraw from worldly occupations,
and devote himself exclusively to preaching the
Gospel, not as a pastor, but simply as an evangelist
to the poor of the flock."

Sometimes his faith became clouded, and like Job
he took to argument. In the confessional of his
diary he asked himself:—

What lesson is this to teach me? Is it that the principle
which I have been so long contending for, namely, to make commercial business instrumental in promoting religion, is a fallacy?
that the Lord will not spread His cause by such means, but by
the pure preaching of the Gospel alone, by His own ministers
set apart for this very work, and that the commerce and trade of
the world is not to be so honoured? If so, I must have mistaken
my way and still do so, and henceforth my course should be to
follow the example of my brother, W. H. Angas, and give up
secular business in order to become a lay preacher of the Gospel.

This was but a thought which came to him at
recurring intervals. The main idea of his life was
expressed in his reply to an invitation to become the
Treasurer of "The Society for securing Religious
Liberty for Nonconformists." "I consider," he
said, "that colonization and emigration are topics
that imperatively demand my personal attention by
a special call of Providence as my proper and
legitimate business."

The financial position of Mr. Angas at this time
will perhaps hardly be understood by those who have
not to deal with large sums of money. When sorely

pressed to meet the drafts constantly arriving from
South Australia, he made a calculation of the value
of his worldly estate, and found that it stood at
about £180,000 ; yet instead of this fact affording
him any consolation, he says, and says truly, " What
vanity attends earthly possessions. With the substance in my hands of this large amount, I am as
poor as if I were only solvent, and have as little
enjoyment from it."

· In May, 1840, Mr. Flaxman arrived in England,
and for several weeks Mr. Angas was engaged in
negotiations with him for the settlement of the
unauthorized purchases. A more harassing and
complicated matter it is difficult to conceive.
Although the land had been bought with the money
of Mr. Angas, the land-grant for the 28,000 acres
had been made out in the name of Mr. Flaxman for
the reason, it was alleged, that it should be an
available collateral security for the South Australian
Bank in the event of Mr. Angas refusing to accept
the drafts, which would then have been returned to
the colony with a re-exchange charge of twenty per
cent. This land-grant, the title deed to the whole
property, was held by Mr. Flaxman, who resolutely
declined to give it up until such terms as he might
dictate were acceded to by Mr. Angas, the position of
Flaxman being that he had rendered his employer a
most important service, that the lands would turn
out to be a principality, and that the purchaser
should share in the benefit !

The audacity of this proceeding was astounding, and Mr. Angas naturally felt deeply indignant at the proposal, seeing that Flaxman had not advanced one penny towards the payment of the land purchase, and had thrown upon him an almost ruinous responsibility. But no amount of indignation would settle the matter; the deeds were made out in the name of Flaxman ; *prima facie* he was the absolute legal owner, and he declined to convey an inch of the ground to Mr. Angas unless he allowed him to retain over 4,000 acres of the best of the land in the Barossa district !

The demand was preposterous, and at first Mr. Angas stoutly resisted it ; but having determined to accept the purchase, it became all-important that he should obtain possession of the title-deeds, and he was advised not to run the risk of an expensive and uncertain lawsuit in which Flaxman could lose nothing, as, of course, no fraudulent intent could be proved. It was necessary, therefore, to open up negotiations.

After many protracted and painful discussions and many months of disquietude, during the whole of which time Flaxman posed as the great benefactor of his employer in securing for him one of the finest prizes in the South Australian land market, the matter was at last brought to a conclusion by the cession of over 4,000 acres of land to Flaxman, for 2,000 of which, as a matter of form, Mr. Anthony Forster took his acceptances.

In conveying the remainder to Mr. Angas, Flaxman

resolutely declined to give up the original grant, merely giving the usual covenant to produce, and, as far as is known, the original deed never passed into the possession of Mr. Angas. This was a source of annoyance, not to say of danger, for many years to come, as, if so important a document had been in the hands of a dishonest person there was nothing to have prevented him from going to India or elsewhere and exhibiting a clear title to 28,000 acres of most valuable land, and of raising say £15,000 or £20,000 upon it. The Real Property Act of Mr. (afterwards Sir) Robert Torrens, to which reference will be more particularly made later on, and which was carried through the Legislative Council of South Australia by Mr. Anthony Forster, and has long been the law of the land in all the Australian Colonies, including New Zealand and Tasmania, has happily rendered such a proceeding impossible now, but under the old law of conveyancing there was nothing to prevent it, and for many years it hung as a drawn sword over the head of Mr. Angas.

The settlement with Mr. Flaxman did not in any degree alter the financial position of Mr. Angas. Drafts to the amount of £40,000 had to be met; interest upon borrowed money was accumulating, lucrative sources of income were cut off, and a cloud, "no bigger than a man's hand" when the reckless purchase was announced, was now threatening to break in storm. He compared himself to a man sick and giddy crossing a rapid river on

horseback. " If he looks at the opposite bank, or at
the sky, all is steady ; if he looks around, he is
almost sure to lose his balance. My only hope of a
safe crossing of this ' sea of trouble,' is to look
upward."

While in the Valley of Humiliation, "stripped,"
as he said, " of that imaginary importance attaching
to men who are supposed to have property," he was
not bereft of consolations. He had the satisfaction
of feeling that as he had never exceeded in his
domestic life the plainest living, and the simplest
society, he had not far to fall in that respect. Nor
did his altered circumstances alienate from him one
true friend, although he was exposed to the jibes of
some with whom he had been associated—and this
was one of the main ingredients in his cup of
bitterness—that he had largely speculated in land
in Australia with a view to the eventual feathering
of his own nest.

It is curious how many public men who have lived
for the service of others have, in the time of their
own personal trials, lacked any acknowledgment of the
good they have wrought. This was, to some extent,
the case with Mr. Angas. He had healed the distress of thousands : only one here and there turned
back to give thanks. A hundred wrote to him
to complain, or to harass ; only one, occasionally,
gave him encouragement. But at this time, when
sorely perplexed and cast down, one who had known
him well in former years—the Rev. E. Baines—wrote

to him a letter which brought refreshment and strength. In the course of it he said :—

I have thought for years, before our friendship was revived some two years ago, that God intended you for distinguished honour in connection with His dear Son and His cause in the earth. You say, How? I reply, in founding and being instrumental in peopling a colony with good people, where millions are to be brought to Christ, and where most probably the lamp of evangelical truth shall shine and blaze with splendour when it shall nearly have become extinct in this our beloved land. Your name will be mentioned in connection with South Australia years, perhaps ages, after you are dead. Such being my impression, I do not wonder at your trials. Had all things been according to your wishes and succeeded without difficulty to your desires, it might have been your undoing.

CHAPTER X.

HARASSED and beset as Mr. Angas was with personal
troubles, he did not relax his hold upon the public
movements in which he had taken so much interest.
Although in moments of depression he threatened to
abstract himself from business, and even went so far
as to make a long list of things he proposed to
give up, it was not in his nature to carry out the
plan. He scented business as the war-horse does the
battle, and soon after he had examined into the
extent of his liabilities he was again, to use his own
words, "devoting himself to work more closely
than for many years past."

Among other matters claiming much of his time
and attention was a proposal made to him to become
Chairman of the "East Coast of Central America
Land Company," for establishing a colony upon

lands offered by the Republic for that purpose. The
thorough way in which he entered into everything
brought before him of this kind is shown in the fact
that before he declined the offer, he made exhaustive
inquiries into the suitability of the climate, the resources of the promoters, the state and prospects of
the Central American Government, and a dozen
kindred matters, which other men would probably
have deferred until they had decided upon the course
they would take. He had such a mastery over the
details of colonial affairs, and these were occupying
much of the public thought at this period, that,
within a few months of his declining to interfere in
Central American colonization, several other companies for the promotion of emigration solicited his
aid, among them being the North American Association for Ireland, the committee of which he joined,
the Devonport Company for promoting emigration to
New Zealand, and a company for colonizing the
Falkland Islands.

Without referring to his action in these matters
specifically, let us cull from his diary the details of
one day's work :—

Rose at 7; private and family devotions, breakfast at 8; programme of day's duties dictated by me, and written by my dear
daughter Rosetta while preparing for a start; met cartload of
goods for our new house, and saw them all stowed away in my
library; rode to Chancery Lane, called on Mr. George Morphett,
Secretary to the South Australian Society, about the affairs of that
colony; walked to *Patriot* office and saw Mr. Boykitt about shares

and colonial affairs; went to see Mr. J. Stephens at his house in
Blackfriars, was out, went to his printers in Warwick Lane, and
made an appointment for the afternoon; walked a mile, took some
refreshment, and read the papers for the day; thence to Mr.
Thomas Joplin's, who wanted me to join the new Loan Company;
thence to the North American Association Board Meeting at Bank
Buildings and discussed the law as to stamps, transfers, &c.;
walked with Mr. Beddome, solicitor, to his office, and consulted
him on various matters; walked to my office and perused letters
from Mr. Hughlings, from an emigrant at Cheltenham, from Mr.
Wermelskirch, of Dresden, and several others per post; wrote to
Messrs. Bartlett and Beddome for legal advice, and wrote in
accordance therewith to an applicant for same; prepared articles
for *The South Australian Colonist;* wrote to Mr. Stephens with
reference to them and the paper; read and corrected the circular to Dissenting ministers; wrote to Mr. Hughlings, to Barry,
King, and others; arranged with Mr. Miller for two Lutheran
missionaries to go to Adelaide in the *Caleb Angas;* called on
Chalmers and Simpson, half a mile off, about shares, dividends, &c.;
on returning to my office had a long talk about a disputed freight;
examined and decided on the general circular about *The South
Australian Colonist;* late home for dinner; wrote another letter to
Messrs. Bartlett and Beddome about agreement for the new house,
and despatched all the letters.

Such is a specimen of one day's work in the life of a
city merchant.   It touched upon, and in some degree
affected, the commercial, civil, moral or religious
affairs of London, Cheltenham, Cork, South Australia, Port Phillip, Hobart Town, Sydney, Honduras,
Africa, and North America!

In reply to a question put by Mr. Angas whether
the tide of emigration was not flowing into South

Australia too rapidly, Colonel Gawler reported in 1840 that land had been surveyed capable of bearing 100,000 persons, and that in one sense emigration was not rapid enough ; while in another sense it was far too rapid, inasmuch as the whole body of colonists clung with desperate tenacity to the immediate vicinity of Adelaide. Another difficulty was the excessive and disproportionate number of men of general education with little capital, experience, or aptitude for colonial life, so that there was an immense consumption going on and comparatively little production.

In giving a nomenclature to the new districts surveyed, it was only right that the name of Mr. Angas, one of the Fathers and Founders of the colony, should be honoured. It was, however, very much against his wish that this should be done, for although he had no hesitation in naming vessels after his honoured father and brother, *Caleb Angas* and *W. H. Angas*, he did not approve of *lands* bearing the names of the owners.

As it may be a matter of surprise to some that the name of one who took so important a part in the formation of the colony should not have been perpetuated more widely in the designation of places, we insert an extract from a letter written by him to Governor Gawler :—

In the early settlement of the colony, and in the first maps of it, my name appeared in the Inlet at the port, and also to a part of

the district around it.   The one was called ' Angas Inlet,' and the
other was named ' Fife-Angas,' both of which I am pleased to see
have been removed and others substituted.   For this I feel a great
obligation to the individual who has done me this real service.

When the town at Nepean Bay was first named, our Directors
called it ' Angas,' and the Bank notes were sent to be engraved
with that heading, but I so disliked it that I took upon me to order
' Kingscote ' to be put in its place, and the Bank notes were thus
presented to the Board of Directors, and of course approved. . . .
Allow me, therefore, to beg of you, as a particular favour, that the
foolish plan adopted at the Barossa Range by Mengé,* of applying
the name ' Angas ' to the parks and valleys of that district may be
set aside, and some title more appropriate adopted.

When Colonel Gawler arrived in South Australia
he found affairs in anything but a satisfactory state.
While grievous dissensions were rife among those in
offices of authority, many of the settlers were in a
state bordering on destitution.   It was imperative, if
South Australia was to become a rich and prosperous
country, that its latent resources should be developed,
and unless it were content to accept the penalties
which cling to either place, or person, having a bad
name, the distress of the settlers must be immediately
relieved.

Without delay, therefore, he proceeded to inaugurate a number of Government works so as to
give employment to the colonists ; and, among other
things, constructed the present Government House
at a cost of £20,000, and made a fine road between
Adelaide and Port Adelaide.

* A German geologist who was employed by Mr. Angas.

In a letter to Mr. Angas, he said :—

The most heavy and incessant press of business has led me to neglect almost all private correspondence. I have been obliged to a great extent to take, as my rule in the discharge of my public commission, ' Salute no man by the way.' The immense land sales, the regulating of public offices, incessant calculation of public expenses, and the general getting into order of the mixed masses which were so rapidly thrown into the province, have demanded every temporal thought.

Everything now appeared to be progressing in the new colony. On behalf of the " Company " Mr. McLaren was constructing the wharf, which still bears his name, and forming a good macadamised road across a swamp between the wharf and the shipping lying in the stream and the Government road on the solid ground or mainland.

At home, Mr. Angas was disseminating reliable printed information concerning the new colony, and, to encourage emigration, had set on foot, at his own charges, a weekly newspaper, *The South Australian Colonist*, with Dr. Dick, Dr. Murray, and Mrs. Sigourney among the contributors. His pen was unusually busy at this time in defending the colony from the attacks of the Tory and High Church press, which was naturally opposed to the Dissenting element prevailing amongst its staunchest friends.

But "all is not gold that glitters," and the reign of seeming prosperity was soon to come to an end. Unfortunately for Colonel Gawler he was not supplied with the necessary wherewithal to meet the heavy expenditure rendered inevitable by the too rapid increase of the population. To benefit the colony he had spent his own private fortune in paying the wages of those employed, and for the rest he could only pay by means of drafts on the British Treasury amounting to about £300,000.

To the astonishment and horror of all concerned these drafts were dishonoured by the Government, and the new colony was insolvent! Ruin, irretrievable ruin as it seemed, stared it in the face, and Commissioners and Company were alike terror-stricken. To no one, however, did the blow come with more sudden and startling force than to Mr. Angas, and it came at a time when he was staggering under the weight of care placed upon him by the reckless conduct of Mr. Flaxman.

But he was a man of iron will, and while others were wondering and lamenting, he was alert and active. One of his first strokes was to write to Lord John Russell, at that time Secretary of State for the Colonies, and the following extract from the letter shows the white-heat of his feeling:—

Oct. 24, 1840.

. . . It is impossible for me to feel otherwise than greatly alarmed at the present dangerous position of the new colony and the destruction that awaits it when the dishonoured drafts of the Governor, now under protest for non-acceptance, shall reach Adelaide in utter disgrace with 20 per cent. damages for non-payment. From whatever causes, that colony is at this moment in a state of advancement and completeness in the fourth year of its existence without a parallel in the history of the Empire, and if it should not continue to progress, the cause of its obstruction cannot be chargeable upon its inhabitants, or upon the professed friends of the colony in this country who have nobly done their duty in the furtherance of this important experiment in coloniza- tion.   Neither in the measures of the Government nor in the application of the finances have they had any power whatever, and they cannot understand how it is, that with an unappropriated emigration fund of about £80,000, and the power given to Her Majesty's Commissioners by the South Australian Act to raise a loan of £200,000, of which £120,000 remain untouched, that the Governor's drafts should have been refused acceptance.   Thus, in an instant, the public credit of the colony has been destroyed, and if not restored by a timely interposition of the Government, must end in anarchy, confusion, and ruin.

Most happily the interval between the first presentation of the drafts, and their maturity, will afford time for your lordship's intervention, and the awful consequences of a general bankruptcy may yet be averted.   Here is a colony, raised up within four years without trouble or expense to the mother country, with a population of 16,000 persons, whose sea-ports have during the past few years admitted about 200 merchant ships, and where more than a million British capital has been embarked, even at a distance of 14,000 miles.   The celebrated colony of Pennsylvania, at one-third the distance, could not in seven years number half this population, or a fourth of its commerce.

The appeal was not in vain.   The Government decided to guarantee a loan, and to recommend its adoption by Parliament, and gave orders to the Commissioners to pay the dishonoured drafts forthwith.   A Parliamentary inquiry upon the whole of the affairs of South Australia was to follow.

Thankful as he was for this relief, it did not

materially affect his own immediate position, now
rendered doubly painful. For more than seven
years he had laboured night and day for South
Australia without compensation of any kind, nor
had he reaped even the usual 5 per cent. for sunk
capital. Now, at the critical moment, when it was
imperative for him to raise money, he found every
avenue closed, while all the branches of his own
private business were brought to the verge of ruin
for want of the capital he had advanced to the
colony.

From the days of Job downwards men have
sneered (and they will sneer yet more) at those
who in the midst of great trial cling to the good
old-fashioned belief in prayer, and in the immediate
intervention of Divine Providence. " Only one
thing," wrote Mr. Angas, " preserves me from
hopeless depression, and perhaps utter despair; it
is the belief that all my troubles are ordered and
overruled by God for my good, and for His glory."
And he was as sincere as the Patriarch Job was
when he cried, " Though He slay me, yet will I
trust Him."

The following characteristic entry in his journal,
written while the decision of the Government was
pending, shows at once the agitated state of his
mind, and the sincerity of his religious belief :—

Oct. 31, 1840.—Wrote to Revs. E. Baines, Stratton, and J.
Thornton entreating their prayers, that God would bless an appeal

to Lord John on behalf of South Australia, having to meet his
lordship next Tuesday to beg aid from Her Majesty's Treasury to
save the colony from the ruin that threatens it.   On that occasion
its fate will be decided by the British Government for good or evil.
What awful results thus hang upon the decision of one man,
involving the fate of thousands.   Besides, what is more serious
than the temporal ruin of 16,000 persons, this decision involves
the public verdict of good or evil attending the experiment of the
system of colonization that has been so substantially made at
the expense of so much labour and treasure in founding South
Australia.

But he did not believe in prayer apart from works,
and he adds:

> I am of necessity shut up to incessant worldly occupation—public
> and commercial—which must have ' all my might.'   The present
> financial crisis in South Australia, the Parliamentary Committee to
> be appointed by Lord John Russell, the circulation of informa-
> tion throughout the kingdom relating to South Australia (now
> indispensable), daily attention to the South Australian Company,
> the separation of the Bank from that Company, and the increase of
> its capital fourfold, also the sale of my own lands in order to meet
> my debts—all are imperative upon me, and leave me no alternative
> but to fag—fag—fag.

In due course a Select Committee of the House
of Commons was appointed to inquire into the
affairs of South Australia generally, and Mr. Angas
was called upon to give evidence. The matters
upon which he was particularly examined were:
1. As to the consequences likely to result from
delay or refusal of aid by the Government to the
colony. 2. As to the resources of South Australia,

and its capability of guaranteeing the repayment of loans. 3. As to the amount of assistance required. 4. Whether it was then too late to come to its assistance.

It was a searching examination, with cross-questioning on all sides by different members, and as it was the first time in his life he had ever given evidence before any "tribunal," and the examination lasted on several occasions for four or five hours at a stretch, it was no slight tax upon his nervous resources.

The result, however, well repaid him for his labours. A vote, recommending an immediate application to Parliament for a loan, was passed by the Committee, and a few days later Lord John Russell brought forward his motion in a Committee of the whole House, to guarantee a loan of £210,000 to South Australia.

In the course of the debate, which lasted for four and a half hours, Lord Stanley opened out one of the most bitter attacks ever levied upon the South Australian scheme generally, and the South Australian Company particularly.

A curious incident in connection with this speech is recorded by Mr. Angas in his journal. He says :—

I prepared some questions to elicit facts from myself that would open the eyes of the Committee on the points raised in Lord Stanley's speech, and enclosed them in a letter to Sir George Grey. While waiting in the lobby, a gentleman came up and said, ' Mr. Angas, are you going again before the Committee?' I said, 'Yes, I wish to state some important facts.' I then went into the calculations I had made in proof of the resources of the colony, and also mentioned the news I had just heard from there of three ships being laid on to sail for London on the 1st of January with 4,000 bales of wool, &c., and made some very strong remarks upon the speech delivered by Lord Stanley, adding that the colony was not to be put down by misrepresentation. After a long and animated conversation, the gentleman left me, and to my astonishment I was told that my questioner was Lord Stanley himself!

A good impression had been made upon him, and when, two days later, the question again came before the House, the motion for a loan of £154,000 was passed at once—the question of the £56,000 taken from the Emigration Fund to be considered at a future date.

In addition to the evidence given before the Parliamentary Committee, Mr. Angas brought the claims of the new colony before every member of Parliament to whom he could gain access, with a view to obtaining their support to the recommendations of the Committee.

In a letter to a friend he stated : " The colony never would have got Colonel Gawler's drafts paid if I had not so laboured as to obtain a majority of the House to support the recommendation of the Committee on South Australia."

His voluminous correspondence with the Colonial Office, and with men of position likely to bring influence to bear on Downing Street, is a startling testimony to his unceasing labours on behalf of the

colony, but it would not now interest the general
reader.

A serious check to emigration occurred when the
financial crisis in South Australia exhausted the
resources of the Emigration Fund. Labour was
deficient in the colony, and capitalists could not be
induced to go out unless they were accompanied by
labourers, and the Government declined to send out
any more free of expense.

To remove this check was the continuous work of
Mr. Angas in 1842 and onwards, and he petitioned,
memorialised, and visited the Colonial Office from
time to time with the object of regaining the
£56,000 * which had been borrowed from the
Emigration Fund for general purposes and, despite
the recommendation of the Select Committee of the
House of Commons, had not been restored.

The applications were unsuccessful, and Lord
Stanley wrote finally to say that " on the part of
Her Majesty's Government he could hold out no expectations of assistance for the purposes of emigration
to the colony of South Australia, which was equally
desired by, but could not be afforded to, the other
colonies of Australia," the argument upon which
this decision was based being that " it was unnecessary that sums due from one branch of the
service to another should be paid."

Other means, therefore, had to be devised, and
none were more successful than the lecturing tours

* Or rather £87,000, £31,000 having been added since 1841.

of Mr. Angas, and the distribution of reliable
information through the press. Among those who
greatly assisted him in this latter department of
work was Mr. John Cassell, the eminent publisher,
at that time the proprietor of the *Standard of Freedom*, which circulated largely among the working
classes.

Notwithstanding the loss of about £1,200 by the
issue of the *South Australian Colonist* in 1839, Mr.
Angas was mainly instrumental in starting another
periodical called the *South Australian News*, to be
published monthly at a cheap rate, with a view to
circulate reliable information about the colony.

One of the best things done in emigration literature was the preparation of a little pamphlet written
by Mr. Angas and entitled " Facts Illustrative of
South Australia," which was sent to every member
of Parliament, to ministers of all denominations, and
to the press, where it was most favourably reviewed.

In all the principal towns of England he lectured
on South Australia. Night after night he was
engaged in this exhausting work, the lecture generally occupying an hour and a half in delivery, and
this was followed by at least an hour more in
answering questions addressed to him by the
audience.

These lectures were often reported incorrectly ;
articles in the daily London press were sometimes
grossly and mischievously incorrect, and *The Times*
was uniformly unfriendly. But it was nobody's special

business to reply to these, and yet if allowed to pass unnoticed without any effort to neutralise their effects, they could not be otherwise than injurious; and this censorship of the press constituted not the least of the many labours of Mr. Angas.

Throughout his diaries ample evidence is given that there was not a movement occurring in the colony that was not regulated in some measure by his action at home. Here are two or three instances, selected almost at random.

May 12, 1842.—Went to the Colonial Office with Messrs. Rundle and Divett (M.P.'s), and spent an hour with Lord Stanley on the new Land Sales Bill. Happily my efforts to modify the powers given to the Governors were not in vain. Lord Stanley agreed to return the extra price of land sales raised by the Governor (if disallowed by the Queen in Council) to the buyers in the colonies, and the half of the gross proceeds of land sales, and not of the net proceeds, was to be applied to emigration. . . . He said the new Bill for South Australia was prepared, and only waited the items from the Treasury.

July 12, 1842.—Got a sight of Lord Stanley's new Bill. The clauses prohibiting convicts and all allusion to the aborigines are left out. Wrote to Sir George Grey, Lord Elliot, Messrs. Ward, Hope, Lefevre, and others on these subjects to-day. May God bless these efforts. . . . Joseph Hume, M.P., I regret to see is against us, for although Lord Stanley is willing to give us the £155,000, Hume wants to make the colony repay it, which it cannot do.

July 13, 1842.—Spent two hours this morning with Joseph Hume at his house, and the result was that he said he did not wish to do anything to obstruct the new colony; in fact he would clear off the whole debt if the colony had a General Assembly, and had the entire control of the expenditure. He severely and justly blamed the Government, Whig and Tory, for their bad conduct towards us from the first onset, and now wished to remedy the evil. He acknowledged that the colonists had done nobly. I pray God that the man who threatened us with much evil may be the instrument of good to us in his proposed address to the House on Lord Stanley's Bill.

Sometimes in very weariness Mr. Angas would ask himself, " Why do I so constantly prosecute this one subject, which is equally the duty of others ? " And the answer was invariably the same, " Because I believe that God has called me to the work." He had heard, or thought he had heard, the Divine Voice speak to him unmistakably to " go forward." He had never been conscious of that Voice calling him to halt, and therefore, through misrepresentation and calumny, at the cost of health, time, and property, of personal, domestic, and social comfort, sometimes in almost total darkness, and sometimes in doubtful and unsteady light, he staggered on from step to step, often cast down and dispirited, but not less often rejoicing that his labour had not been in vain.

CHAPTER XI.

Success and Failure—In a Dilemma—Opinions upon the Great Land Purchase—Use of a Diary—Changes in Family Life—Instruction and Counsel—Mr. J. H. Angas Sails for South Australia—The Barossa Range—Description of the " Special Surveys "—At Milton, Gravesend—Father and Daughter—Correspondence on Marriage—Habits —A Steamboat Collision—A Gathering Storm—Mr. R. B. Beddome —Wrecks—In Despair—A Tour on Horseback—Resigns Chairmanship of South Australian Company—Eulogies—Correspondence with Mr. J. H. Angas—A Physician's Advice—Farewell to Old England.

At the close of 1840 the South Australian Company was in a very prosperous condition; its country lands had increased to 36,068 acres, its flocks to 14,422, and the estimated value of its property in the colony amounted to £303,680; the Bank was yielding a large revenue, its profits for the year amounting to over £19,000; arrangements were being made to abandon some of the branches of the Company's business, such as the sale of stores and the rearing of cattle, and thus carry out the idea of Mr. Angas, that " as the building rose the scaffolding must disappear," or in other words, that having accomplished its purpose in any given direction, the Company would not compete with private and individual capitalists.

Then followed the rush of emigration, the promotion of public works to save the people from starvation, and after that came the crash.   The South Australian Bank had made advances to the Colonial Government for a very considerable amount, to preserve the colony from absolute ruin.   When the Lords of the Treasury returned the Bills to the Governor dishonoured—and it must be borne in mind that one of the fundamental principles on which the colony was founded was that it should not be a burden to the extent of one penny on the mother country—the Bank had to wait through all the long and tedious period of a parliamentary enquiry in England, and until a loan could be raised there to pay the colonial debt.

This was not all. In 1841 it had been deemed desirable to separate the Bank from the South Australian Company, and in order to effect this an amount of capital, considerably larger than the sum then appropriated to the banking operations of the Company, was ordered to be transferred.   The excess of the former amount over the latter constituted a debt due by the Company to the Banking Company, which took several years to clear off.

Nor was even this all.   The colony was in the midst of financial embarrassments which threatened the complete destruction of the settlement.   The Company's property had greatly depreciated; the tenants on their farms were totally unable to pay their rents, other sources of revenue were cut off, and—a total collapse of the Company seemed inevitable.

On the 15th of October, 1841, Mr. Angas wrote in his journal :—

The proceedings of the Board of the Company this day presented a very distressing position of affairs. . . . If all our capital were actually paid up we have not enough money to' pay off our obligations. Such is the dreadful dilemma into which we are brought by the heavy expenditure abroad. So far as I can form a judgment, the Company must stop payment sooner or later unless God shall in mercy interpose to save us from ruin.

The year 1841 closed drearily for him. Evil tidings came from all quarters, insomuch that he feared to open a letter lest it should tell of the threatened calamity—and this state of feverish apprehension continued for long weary years.

The gloomy state of his mind is shown in much of his private correspondence at this time. His beloved daughter Sarah (Mrs. Henry Evans, at that time of Exeter, but now of Evandale, near Angaston) was mourning the loss of a child, and wondering why her father did not write. A letter was on its way :—

LONDON, *June* 10, 1841.

. . . Perhaps you may think I ought to have written you of late, but, my dear child, I have been myself in a deep sea of trouble, and even now I can see before me nothing but storms and tempests. I may exclaim with Luther, 'How dreadful is this world, and how weak is my faith in God !' So that my own frame of mind was ill adapted to pour out the balm of consolation to others in a state of trial and affliction. God only can help !

Some men are placed in such a position in life as that others look to them for advice and assistance, and by common consent of mankind their province seems only to give and not to receive! All the time our fellow mortals forget that it is the perogative of God only to give and not to receive. All men are made dependent more or less on others, and cannot dispense with their aid, prayers, advice, and sympathy. Thanks be to God, it is a promise of His word that when men forsake us the Lord will take us up!

Then, forgetting his own trouble, he enters fully into hers, and referring to the little one early gathered into the fold, he adds :—

Its soul is safe in Christ. That is certain to our faith. Enjoy, therefore, all the comfort inspired by this blessed knowledge. Soon, and we shall see its face again, more lovely, more happy than its sweet life was on earth!

Notwithstanding the obloquy that had, in certain quarters, been cast upon Governor Gawler, Mr. Angas never wavered in the belief that his motives were pure, and that his devoted efforts to serve the colony had been most unjustly rewarded.

Upon his return to this country Colonel Gawler frequently corresponded with Mr. Angas, and brought to him the only ray of hope that shone in the midst of the gloom—the property so recklessly purchased by Mr. Flaxman might yet be the means of retrieving his fortunes.

Although I am truly grieved for your difficulties and for Mr. Flaxman's conduct (wrote the Colonel), there are blessings in store for you for all this. . . . You have a beautiful property in South

Australia, one in the improvement of which you might find happiness for life—as far as it is to be found.

And again :—

As far as one can judge for another, I really think it would be to your happiness and advantage to settle in South Australia. Such a property as you have there—a most beautiful and valuable tract of country—can scarcely be turned to due advantage by agents. . . . I would also say that I think you would do well for the property and for the colony to sell off large portions of it at moderate prices—the cost price and fair interest, and to make public exertions to let out to lease, on moderate terms, pretty large farms. Farms on too small a scale would be burdensome to you and dangerous for the tenant. The Barossa Range, it appears to me, is capable of immediate settlement.

Owing to the state of the colony it was impossible to act upon this advice, but Mr. Angas was grateful for the hope inspired by this letter, written by a practical man well acquainted with the country and holding an undaunted belief in its ultimate prosperity.

Mitigations to the hardness of his lot, and compensations for his losses, came to Mr. Angas as they come to all men. Early in 1842, when bills to the amount of some thousands of pounds became due, and he had no prospect whatever of being able to meet them, a wealthy man, whose proffer of assistance was wholly unexpected, came forward and " offered to join in any security to the extent of the whole of his property."

At another time in the same year, when driven up

into a corner, hoping against hope, he was able, by
friendly intervention, to negotiate forthwith a loan
of £10,000 on the most easy and advantageous
terms.

But the highest satisfaction of all was that the
troubles in which he was involved were not only not
the result of any fault of his own, but had sprung
almost entirely from his philanthropy. What
comfort was to be derived from this was probably
emphasised in August of this year. He had
just dissolved partnership with Mr. George Miller *
in order that he might the more readily dispose
of his mercantile business altogether when the
critical moment should come ; the net of mis-
fortune was gradually enclosing him, and he was
almost at his wits' end when he was impanelled on
the Grand Jury of the Central Criminal Court, and
had to take part in deciding 491 cases. " Such a
development of vice and iniquity I never knew
before," he says, and he reflects upon what might
have been his own career, "but for the grace of
God."

All through this period of his great depression he
was true to his diary, never allowing a day to pass
without some record of its history. In conversation
he was by nature reticent and somewhat reserved,
although one who knew him more intimately and
for a longer period than any one else has borne this
testimony, that " his conversational powers were of

* Junior partner in the firm of G. F. Angas & Co.

a very high order. He was a most intelligent and
well-read man, and his judgment was more mature
and reliable than that of any other man I ever met
with."   But he could not speak to any human being
as he wrote in his diary, and he says :—

In these records, quiet and simple, I feel my heart relieved from
an almost insupportable burden. It seems as if I thereby threw off
the pressure from the mind and conveyed it from the memory to
the chronicles of another world.

It must be confessed that the entries in the diary
are sometimes wearisome reading. If published
they would fill a dozen or so of large volumes.
They are interesting chiefly as showing the texture
of his mind.

Like most ultra-religious men, he suffered in having
his motives questioned, and the diary is specially
valuable for this—that, making every allowance for
ex parte statements, it is consistent throughout.
The following may be taken as a specimen :—

Nov. 24, 1842.—This is a work that God has given me a command to perform, and in no outlay or purchase relating to South
Australia or the South Australian Company have I entered upon it
with a view to profit. God is my witness in this.

It was this " answer of a good conscience towards
God " that sustained him in the presence of all
calumniators. The barb that rankled in his bosom
most as a public man was the downfall of his hopes
with regard to the prosperity of South Australia,
and, in his private capacity, that he, on the high

road to an enormous fortune, should have been
suddenly confronted with poverty, the foe he least
expected to meet.   And it wounded him to the
heart to be treated with neglect by men who, in
the days of prosperity, he had been wont to help.

The early part of 1843 brought no solution to his
difficulties, and there is a kind of wild cry in some
of the heart-breathings of his diary at this time.
Thus :—

Feb. 7.—I know not what to do. My affairs are drifting before
the wind without rudder or compass.   I am at my wits' end, while
the rocks of destruction are ahead and near at hand. The cold,
damp, gloomy weather, with occasional blasts of the hurricane
and showers of sleet, is a perfect emblem of my mind. O God,
help me while walking in this darkness to trust in Thee.

If there was monotony during this year in the
trials of Mr. Angas, there was endless variety in the
changes which were wrought in his family life—
changes which brought with them mingled joy and
sorrow.

In April his eldest daughter Rosetta was married
to Mr. James Johnson, a solicitor at Manchester.
Ten days later (Good Friday, April 15th) his son,
Mr. John Howard Angas, and Mr. and Mrs. Henry
Evans, of Exeter (his daughter Sarah and her
husband), with their infant son, sailed for South
Australia in the barque *Madras*.

Mr. J. H. Angas was commissioned to look after
the affairs of his father in the new colony, to examine
and develop the large tract of country purchased by

Mr. Flaxman, and to undertake such measures as would tend to retrieve the fallen fortunes of the family. This was a most important mission, and all the future welfare of his father hung upon it. The remarkable business ability of Mr. Angas was shown in every transaction, and his judgment was reliable to a marked degree. He always acted with promptness and decision, and was greatly pleased to see these qualities in others.

The first word he ever spoke to his son, Mr. J. H. Angas, with regard to his going to South Australia, was in 1841, when he said, somewhat abruptly, "I wish you to go to South Australia."

John replied, "I am quite willing; when do you want me to go?"

"As soon as you can be ready."

"What am I to do when I get there?" asked the son.

"You must do what you see requires to be done," was the laconic reply.

Those few words embodied positive instructions on an infinite variety of subjects—some to be dealt with on the very day of his arrival, and others from time to time, but continually increasing so long as he was to have the control of his father's affairs there.

"Had he written a book of instructions," said his son many years afterwards, "he could not have given fuller or more detailed information than the single sentence which comprised the whole."

"Before you start," Mr. Angas added, "you must make yourself acquainted with the German language in order that you may look after the seven hundred German immigrants by settling them upon my lands and collecting the advances which I made for their passage-money; and you must spend six months in studying land-surveying, mapping, and so forth."

Mr. J. H. Angas was at that time only a youth of eighteen. Great responsibilities were to be laid upon him, the weight of which not one in ten thousand at his age could have borne.

Mr. Angas, whose faith had been shaken in many men in whom he had reposed confidence in relation to his Australian affairs, had the most unbounded belief not only in the capability of his son but in his absolute impeccability. Everything in the colony as regarded the affairs of Mr. Angas was in hopeless confusion; certain men with evil intent had created difficulties which required the greatest tact and the clearest understanding to adjust; but he had no doubt whatever that his son would overcome them all.

Although the instructions given him may seem to have been very arbitrary, they were only seemingly so. The heart of the father was full of tender solicitude, and soon after his son had gone from home into lodgings in order to be under the tuition of a competent land-surveyor, Mr. Angas wrote :—

May 13, 1841.

I perceive you have commenced your business in a true working style. That is well. Nothing good is given to man without labour.

Every pursuit and business of life must be followed with industry
and application, or there can arise from it neither pleasure nor
profit. . . . It will add greatly to my comfort and satisfaction to
hear a good report of you at the termination of your engagement.

Should you have any spare time in the evenings, improve it by
reading or writing on some useful subject, for at no period of your
life can time be more valuable to you than at your present age. Be
sure to have at all times two or more useful books 'in reading,' to
resort to at leisure moments. It was in that way that I, when at
your age, read through ten volumes of Rollins' 'Ancient History'
during my half-hour allowed for breakfast, and I have continued
the habit more or less all through life. Under God I owe much of
my success to the improvement of minutes. Let the study of the
Word of God be a most prominent object with you.

After urging him to keep early hours, and to be
regular in attendance at a place of worship, he
adds :—

Visit Mr. Baynes (the minister). He is very kind and is my
personal friend. Respect him for his great piety and talents, and
for my sake. His friendship is well worth your best cultivation.
' He that walketh with wise men shall be wise.'

When the set time came for Mr. J. H. Angas to
leave home and country, and bid farewell to many
relations and friends whom he would probably see no
more in this world, his father wrote :—

For weeks past my mind has been tossed with such conflicting
emotions between affection and duty that I have not been able to
collect sufficient calmness to offer you a few suggestions which,
under God, may be of some benefit to you in a distant land, when
you shall reflect that they have come fresh from the heart and soul

of an affectionate father, and are corroborated by the approval of your mother's love to you.

After giving many wise counsels on conduct generally, Mr. Angas proceeds :—

In forming your religious opinions stick to the *Bible ;* admit of nothing essential save what it confirms, and as for such theological points as are non-essential, maintain the liberty of holding your own opinions, but let them always be open to reason and common sense ; and be sure to allow other people to think as they like, and do not respect them less because they differ from you. Attach yourself from conviction to that body of Christians which hold opinions and doctrines nearest to the Word of God, but exercise love and Christian intercourse with every denomination of Christians which holds fast the Gospel of Salvation through Jesus Christ. . . .

I warn you against forming any association or intimate acquaintance with any one in the colony whose principles or conduct would be likely to weaken the moral power of your own principles and habits. 'Evil communications corrupt good manners.' . . .

In going to South Australia you have two grand objects in view as matters of business. (1) The promotion of good in all proper ways. Be fervent in spirit, serving the Lord in the acquisition of knowledge for this purpose, and in practically applying it. (2) The advancement of my worldly interests. Be diligent in business. I have laboured hard for many years to support and educate my children, and it is reason and religion that my sons should now come to my aid when my energies are decreasing. I commend you for the cheerfulness with· which you have sought to render me assistance in my business here, and as the fruits of my many years of labour—and which I designed in due proportion for you—have been wasted so greatly by the treachery and baseness of men, it will afford you the opportunity of exhibiting your filial piety in diligently using the means, under God's blessing, of repairing my ruined fortune. . . .

After urging that there shall be the fullest and freest confidence between them, not only in matters of business but on every subject dealing with personal, moral, religious, and intellectual life, the letter concludes :—

I can scarcely conceive of a finer field for the application of your talents and energies than in developing the property of which God has made me steward in the Barossa Range. Try and make it a moral and terrestrial paradise.

Now, my dear John, with every sentiment of pure and holy affection which it is possible for a father to feel for his son, I commend you to God's gracious care, direction, grace, and protection, to the end of this enterprise and of your whole life. . . . Your mother joins me in every feeling of love to you that is herein expressed.

It will be well in this place to give some account of the property purchased by Mr. Flaxman on behalf of his employer, consisting of seven special surveys of 4,000 acres each in the Barossa Range, sometimes called in those days New Silesia.

It must be understood that by a "special survey" it is meant that when 4,000 acres were purchased at once, great advantages were connected with the purchase. The parties applied for the surveys, in blocks of 80 acres, of a tract of 15,000 acres in any locality they liked. From the lands surveyed the purchasers could select the 4,000 acres they thought best, culling the choicest lands and the finest situations. In those early days the purchaser virtually, therefore, could sometimes obtain, for pasture only, until it was bought by others, the occupation of 11,000 acres in every 15,000 more than he paid for—an extreme but a possible supposition, and as such set forth in the prospectuses of the time. At all events, these were the important advantages obtained in the selection of the special surveys of the Barossa Range, and some of the finest and best watered land was thereby secured.

The Barossa Range is situated about forty English miles to the north-east of Adelaide, and comprises some miles of the best land in South Australia. It is watered partly by the Gawler River, and partly by the Rhine, with splendid " parks " and valleys between picturesque ranges of hills. The soil is fertile, light, and easy to be worked ; there are considerable tracts of pasture land for sheep and cattle, and it retains a large body of fresh water all the year round. The whole district abounds in useful materials, such as large timber trees, gum, wattle-bark, asbestos, marble, iron, limestone, granite, and building stone.

In the most fertile tracts of this country are situated Angas Park, surrounded by as picturesque scenery as is to be found in the whole colony, and Salem, or Flaxman Valley, separated from Angas Park by the hills of the Barossa Range.

The whole property was studded with several varieties of the largest gum-trees (*eucalyptæ*) to be found in the colony, well adapted for many purposes in building, fencing, and for firewood, while on the north of Angas Park rises the Carara

Hill, yielding in abundance the white Italian marble for building and decoration. A remarkable feature of the district is the circuitous course of the River Gawler, which runs through it, and is fed in winter by numerous mountain streams. In a distance of twelve miles the river frontage is nearly doubled in length, not only affording a good supply of water but adding greatly to the beautiful and romantic appearance of the whole district. Last, and not least, the land was freehold, the title secured by Act of Parliament, and the property surveyed, mapped, and registered by the Government, while an almost entirely level road stretched from the western side of the Barossa Range, where the surveys commenced, to the capital, affording the greatest facilities for conveying wool and other produce to the port.

But beautiful and valuable as the property was, it was a white elephant to Mr. Angas. He wanted cash, and they gave him land at a time when £10,000 would have been far more valuable to him than the 28,000 acres of which he had unintentionally become the possessor. He at once arranged for 10,000 acres of the land to be laid down for sale in 80 acre sections, and offered them on the most moderate terms, or he was willing to grant long leases with or without the right of pre-emption.

There was but a poor response. Many difficulties arose of an unexpected kind, and to set matters

right and to develop the estate was the work
assigned to Mr. J. H. Angas.

A few extracts from the letters of Mr. Angas to
his son will, we think, be read with interest, and
will point the course of events. Soon after his
departure Mr. Angas wrote :—

Jan. 24, 1844.

You deeply sympathize in all my troubles and afflictions, and
will do everything in your power to emancipate my estate from
the hands of these men. . . . It is essentially to *you*, as an instrument under God, that I must look to aid me, and as you will
become of age this year, you will be able to act for me then with
efficiency.

Many a time his fatherly heart misgave him as he
thought of the strain and stress he had placed upon
his son, and the letters of advice and counsel which
he sent out to him, no less than the entries in the
diary, written with evident emotion, are beautiful
and touching. He urges him to keep his mind
" close, compact, adhesive," and, above all things,
to avoid rashness :—

Rashness (he says) is everywhere dangerous, but nowhere more
so than in a colony of sharp men of much experience and knowledge of the world, while you are young and know little of it.
My best advice to you is this : confine yourself to the business
marked out for you. On no account attempt to speculate in anything. . . . Never make pretensions to any consequence because
you have important trusts committed to you. Set Joseph in Egypt
before you as your example of prudence and wisdom. Do not
gratify the pride of your heart by ' doing exploits,' by great out-
of-the-way adventures, but let moderation in all things be your

motto.   Be thankful for any advice given to you by friends or
foes, young or old.   Despise nothing and nobody and no danger.
Hear all and choose what is good.   And above all keep close to
God.   Stand by His house at Angas Town and the Sunday School
there.   Seek to do all that you know will please Him, and avoid
what will cause His displeasure.

When Mr. J. H. Angas attained his majority his
father wrote him a long letter, from which the following is an extract :—

Oct. 28, 1844.

Now that you have reached the years of discretion and manhood
I desire rather to cultivate the feelings of friendship with you, my
dear John, than to enforce parental authority.   I am well assured
you will find none on earth who will so naturally care for your
present and eternal interest as your parents must ever do.   We
watch over you continually in our thoughts and prayers, . . . and
follow you in all your pursuits with the deepest interest, constantly
praying God to keep you from evil and to guide you with His
counsel.

In 1844 Mr. Angas received intelligence that a
copper mine had been discovered on the estate of
his son-in-law, Mr. Henry Evans, who had very
generously offered Mr. Angas half interest in its
proceeds.

I duly appreciate this token of Henry's thoughtfulness and
generosity (Mr. Angas wrote to his son John), which will not lose
its reward ; still I feel very far from being at ease in respect to
that discovery.   It has proved the ruin of multitudes to discover
a mine of that sort ; it excites in the mind the feeling of covetous-
ness, and too often ends in the ruin of the proprietor, of his soul
or his fortune.   If successful his affections become chained to

earthly things, and if adverse he is pierced through with many
sorrows.

It was with an instinctive feeling of dread Mr.
Angas ever heard of mines and mining, and would
never encourage any kind of speculation in them.
He wrote to his son :—

I charge you solemnly not to expend money in working mines,
but if worth anything let them remain untouched until others see
their way to work them beneficially and with judgment, and pay
to us a fair and reasonable rent out of the produce for the privilege
of working them.

Later in life, as we shall see, when fortunes were
being made and lost on the Victorian gold-fields,
and there was a prospect of finding gold in South
Australia, Mr. Angas would not so much as lift his
finger to assist in the matter, but on the contrary,
when the Government proposed to offer a reward of
£5,000 for the discovery, he said he would willingly
give £5,000 to prevent it.

How Mr. J. H. Angas performed the mission with
which he was entrusted we shall see hereafter.
Meanwhile the affairs of his father at home were
growing more and more complicated.

Only a few months after the departure of his son
and other members of his family to South Australia
it seemed as if the crisis in his affairs had come.

There appeared to be the glimmer of a chance that
relief might be at hand.   He wrote :—

July 2.—It seems to me that in all probability the next week or two will decide my fate. It looks like the crisis of my temporal ruin or deliverance.

It was *a* crisis only, and it ended in hope being deferred, with the threatened ruin becoming more imminent.

At the end of August he left Park Place Villas, Paddington, for a humble retreat in Milton, Gravesend. There is great pathos in the record of this event in his diary :—

The Lord has called me to leave this beautiful and convenient habitation, where I thought, when I took a lease of it, we were likely long to remain. While we have been reduced in our circumstances and our family, riches have taken wings and flown away, and a sweeping desolation has gone over all my affairs at home and abroad. . . . However, all is not lost. I have my God and Saviour left.

Before they had fairly settled down in their new abode Mr. and Mrs. Angas were called to part with other members of their family. Early in September their daughter Emma was married to Mr. William Johnson, a Manchester manufacturer; and a week later their eldest son, George French Angas, who had chosen art for his life-work, set sail for South Australia. Only the youngest son was left in England, and he was at school.

In family life where all are mutually interdependent and equally loved, it is difficult to say whose loss is the most felt. But it is probable that among the keenest sorrows of Mr. Angas's life was

the parting with his son John Howard, who had
been "the man of his right hand," and with his
daughter Emma, who for many years had been his
devoted amanuensis, and had given up to him the
best of her early life with its peculiar talents and
unflagging energies. It was she who accompanied
her father in the long lecturing tours he took in his
phaeton from north to south and west to east of
England, and sometimes up through the lakes to
Scotland, beguiling the time by reading aloud to
him in the carriage. It was she who had the
happy art of unobstrusively furthering his plans by
wise suggestions, patient labour, and affectionate
forethought. It was to her, probably more than to
any other living soul, he opened out his heart
in freest confidence in all matters — spiritual,
domestic, social, and commercial ; it was to her,
when any great event was pending, that he always
appealed for aid in prayer, and as the trials of his
life multiplied it was to her that, without reserve,
he poured out the whole burden that oppressed
him.

There lies before the present writer a mass of
correspondence between father and daughter relating
to every conceivable subject, and compassing a
period long before and long after that of which we
now write. To information in this correspondence
we shall be much indebted in future chapters of this
work, but it will be well in this place to give the
reader just a glimpse of the correspondence, confining

ourselves only to passages which bring out the characteristics of Mr. Angas.

He always insisted in the family that everything begun, if worth beginning, should be finished, and this principle he carried forward to the highest things. Thus when his daughter had disclosed the state of her mind to him on religious matters, he wrote to her :—

April, 1837.

Nothing can be more certain than this truth, ' He who perseveres to the end shall be saved.' Indeed, it would be unreasonable to expect it to be otherwise. Suppose this letter (written in London) were to be carried only to Kenton instead of Dawlish whither it was bound, would the postage be paid if it never reached you ? It mattered little how far it advanced on the road if it never reached its destination. If, however, the mail guard proceeded to the end as he commenced his course, then he or his master would get his reward. In case of neglect, his urging the plea of having carried the letter 150 or 160 miles would avail nothing if it never reached your hands. Indeed, in all human affairs the sole merit of an action depends upon its completion, and the reward upon a perseverance unto the end of the work.

One of the first letters he wrote to her after her marriage is so rich in the beauty of fatherliness, that we quote several passages from it :—

Milton, *Oct.* 22, 1843.

My beloved Daughter,—Ever since the events of Divine providence called upon me freely to give you up to the charge and affection of another, I have laboured greatly to place my mind and will in the posture of acquiescence, and not only so, but to exhibit the heroism of a Christian philosopher ! As you were the last of my private secretaries, the last of my social co-operators, the last moving exhibition of filial sympathy and affection, continually passing before me, that I should ever see again in this world ; in short, the remnant of a family broken to pieces by the storms of time, I have felt a strong repugnance to the writing of a letter to you that was likely to portray but too vividly to my heart and imagination the painful recollection of the scenes that have passed away now for ever. . . .

But I have had left to me another of your mementoes, although not of so gratifying a kind, which is, the ever-recurring demands of my letters for copying and endorsation, bundles of foreign and home newspapers, composition of MSS., and hosts of other little matters lying at my elbow, which only tried to impress my mind the more sensibly of the value of what has been taken from me by the want of it. Then there was the advantage of your recollection, which so often aided me in seasons of dulness and depression, with the numerous well-timed suggestions, hints, consolations, and counsels that are no longer to sound in my ears and refresh me by the way, now the more necessary from increase of years, infirmities, and afflictions. Yet it is well. . . .

It is not in my power to tell you how much I owe you, my beloved child, for all the assistance you have rendered me in works of business and benevolence for several years past, and for the dutiful affection and respect you have manifested. . . .

There is but one thing that embitters the recollection of it to my mind, and that is my inability to render you that justice which under more favourable temporal circumstances I should have been able to have performed. . . .

But it is not temporal prosperity that constitutes human happiness. Outward comfort and conveniences are valuable in their place, but you must look to the frame and condition of the heart for happiness. Next to that peace which arises from reconciliation with God through faith in the atonement and merits of Jesus Christ and the consolations of the Holy Ghost, domestic peace is the great source of comfort and earthly happiness.

Shall I say, my dear Emma, that you have the peace of your family and the domestic happiness of your dear husband in your own keeping? Yes, under God, it is really so. Meditate upon your serious responsibility in this respect. Bless God that you have a husband whose amiable and affectionate disposition will make the discharge of your duties in this matter comparatively easy; still, you will find that the great adversary the devil, who hates peace, and goes into every family—into Christian families especially—to promote strife, confusion, and every evil work, will not let yours alone.

My advice to you, therefore, is to ' Watch '—watch against the beginning of strife of any kind. Never trifle with peace or feeling on any account. Excellent as is your beloved husband, he is but human nature; so, just in proportion to his sincere affection for you will be his chagrin and disappointment if he should find you ever deficient in marks and tokens of affection and attention to him. Let it consist of a mild, submissive deportment; a dignified and natural manifestation of affection towards him at all times.

You must never allow yourself to believe *in the possibility* of any change taking place in your husband's love to you. Therefore, if through indisposition of body, depression of mind, or the excitement of feeling produced by the ills of life, and necessary association with the business of the world, he should ever appear on his return to his home distant or cold in his deportment towards you, attribute it to its real cause, and never suffer yourself to think it arose from diminished affection for you. Then is the time for you to put forth all your powers of female excellence on Christian principles, and you will surely succeed, with God's help, in strengthening your position in your husband's heart.

You also are subject to infirmities. Times will arise when you cannot be always happy, when excitement will cease and exhaustion commence, when the flow of spirits will come to an ebb, and you will feel dull and unhappy. In that case carry your trouble to God, and He will give you grace to bear it in peace and quietness. That your husband may not mistake your disposition, confide in him ever, and tell him freely, and he will sympathise with you, and embrace the occasion to testify his love to you. . . .

When his daughter was settled in her new home, many of the letters relate to domestic matters, treated in the frankest manner on either side, and some to the principles upon which he had ruled his own household. Thus:—

> You know, my dear child, it is no part of the advice I have endeavoured to instil into the minds of my children to despise the day of small things, even to the saving of a thread, for small and large are equal terms in God's dispensations—
>
>   ' Who sees with equal eye, as God of all,
>   A hero perish or a sparrow fall.'

This brings out one of the strongly marked traits in the character of Mr. Angas—the method and exactitude he brought to bear on his daily work. This was the great secret which enabled him to get through an amount of labour impossible to the large majority of men. His papers and documents were always kept in such scrupulous order that he could lay his hand on any of them at a moment's notice, and almost in the dark. He never wasted anything —half-sheets of unused paper were carefully preserved, and whenever he received a parcel he would not cut but untie the string and put it away for future use in a drawer reserved for the purpose.

We do not propose to linger over the details of

the various misfortunes of Mr. Angas, but merely to
note in passing a few landmarks in the history of
these sorrowful years.

In October, 1844, he succeeded in disposing of his
copperas works and mahogany business at Newcastle, which afforded him some relief and put him in
possession of additional capital. " Thus," he says,
" my mind and time will be free for carrying on my
Honduras and South Australian concerns, and my
energies will be concentrated on fewer objects."

On the 13th of December, 1845, he had a narrow
escape of his life. He was on his passage in the
steamer from London to Gravesend when a double
collision occurred, first with a large Hamburg
steamer, afterwards with a brig. It was at night,
and in a fog. He says, " What a mercy that I had
not to *seek* religion at such a moment."

In a letter to his daughter, Mrs. William Johnson,
he alludes to the event thus :—

Milton, *Dec.* 25, 1845.

Although certainly I expected to have finished my course on the
moment of the steamboat's collision, it was to me a very interesting
circumstance, although awful indeed. I stood at the companion,
and never moved until I started off and took refuge in the brig. My
mind was calm and peaceful, nothing painful in my feelings except
the idea of cold water. I saw everything from first to last that
took place, and heard everything, sad as it was. I was employed in
intently watching all that was going on.*

---

* This story reminds us of the great lion story in Livingstone's Life.
When on the ground, with the lion over him, and being shaken as a
terrier does a rat, ' the shock,' he says, ' produced a stupor similar to that.

The spring of 1846 brought gladness with it. In March, his son, George French Angas, returned to England from an art tour in Australia and New Zealand, bringing with him a large collection of native costumes and implements, besides many portraits of natives which he had taken as well as sketches of the places he had visited. These he had the honour of showing to Her Majesty and the Prince Consort, who became patrons of some of the illustrated volumes he subsequently published.*

The return of this son, and the frequent letters from his family still in South Australia, brought the question of his own settlement in that colony vividly before Mr. Angas, and there are many entries in his diary referring to the subject.

With respect to my personal feelings (he says) I have no peculiar desire to leave England, rather the contrary, but if it is God's will for

---

which seems to be felt by a mouse after the first shake of a cat. It caused a sort of dreaminess in which there was no sense of pain, nor feeling of terror, though quite conscious of all that was happening. It was like what patients partially under the influence of chloroform describe, who see all the operation but feel not the knife. . . . The shake annihilated fear, and allowed no sense of horror in looking round at the beast. This peculiar state is probably produced in all animals killed by the carnivora ; and if so, it is a merciful provision made by our benevolent Creator for lessening the pain of death.'

It will be remembered that when Livingstone returned to England he was asked what he was thinking of when in the lion's grasp, and he answered quietly, ' I was thinking with a feeling of disinterested curiosity which part of me the lion would eat first ! '

* " South Australia Illustrated," " The New Zealanders Illustrated," " The Kaffirs Illustrated." Mr. George French Angas was also the author of " A Ramble in Malta and Sicily " and of " Savage Life and Scenes in Australia and New Zealand," 2 vols. 8vo.

me to go—and I shall be fully persuaded of it in my judgment, from
the advice of my friends and the concurrence of the events and circumstances of Providence—*I will go.* ' The path of duty is the path
of safety.' It matters little where I go to on earth ; it is the Lord's,
and any part of it will be equally near to heaven when my Master
calls me up to it.

But the year 1846, which opened in sunshine, was
to close in the blackness of darkness. Cloud after
cloud arose in all quarters, and, in the autumn, the
storm burst. One of his most intimate friends, to
whom he could open his heart unreservedly in
correspondence, feeling sure that his business difficulties as well as his spiritual struggles would be
understood and appreciated, was his solicitor, Mr.
Richard B. Beddome, of Nicholas Lane (a de-
scendant of Benjamin Beddome, the well-known
hymn writer). Mr. Angas wrote to him in October
as follows :—

82, Parrack Street, Gravesend,
Oct. 8, 1846.

My case is so peculiar, that few of even Christian persons can
enter into it at all, much less understand the mysteries of Divine
Providence in His conduct of my affairs. You, however, can do so,
and with grateful praise to God and warm thanks to you, I believe
that but for your sympathy and generous efforts on my behalf I
should most likely have sunk under my burdens.

The benefit of such kindness may be estimated in some measure
when you are made aware that the worst features of my calamities
have been a constant morbid sense of fear and apprehension of
coming evils, an extraordinary weakness of memory and great in-
decision and irresolution of mind, with great sensitiveness and
irritability. These baleful influences have been kept in constant.

operation during the past seven years by real occurrences, almost daily, of a trying and sorrowful nature, some of which you have been acquainted with.

Almost every effort of body and mind which I have put forth in business has been unprofitable, almost every transaction has been vexatious in all parts of the world, whether in relation to my private affairs or partnerships or trusteeships. Yet amidst all these accumulated evils I have had to go forward, because I have felt convinced that such a course was my proper duty.

In the same letter he mentions his determination "to close his contract for ship mahogany, to sell all his house property in the North, at Newcastle and Gateshead, also the Copperas Works and the Durham property, paying off the mortgages, &c., which will relieve him of much profitless anxiety."

Within a week of writing this letter he noted in his journal :—

Oct. 15.—The sad news came to hand this evening that the *Helen Jane* foundered in a dreadful hurricane on the 10th September, and six of the crew were lost. Our cargo unfortunately was not insured, as we had not received any invoice, nor had she sailed when our last letter came from Belize. This wreck will entail a loss of £1,500, if not more, at a time when every hundred pounds is in danger of foundering my credit.

Only four days later, on reaching his office, he was informed that another of his vessels, the *Caleb Angas*, was a total wreck upon the rocks off Barbados. Every soul on board had been rescued, but nothing was insured except some of the goods going to Honduras. About £1,400 had been spent in repairing the vessel for her voyage.

It was in vain to struggle on longer. Stroke upon stroke, loss upon loss, came as death-blows to his hopes of ever working through his pecuniary troubles. His health was shattered, his nerves unstrung, and there was nothing left to him but to accept the urgent advice of his medical man, to leave everything and go right away.

On the 13th of November he wrote in his diary :—

Closed my business at my counting-house. Melancholy was the feeling with which I turned my back upon Jeffery Square, and I could not even take leave of the clerks. . . . I leave my home in the greatest extremity I was ever plunged into.

He left home, and for the first time since his youth left his diary behind him. It was too painful to continue and no further entry was made in it until the 30th of May, 1847.

In the midst of his anxieties his medical man (Dr. George Moore, of Hastings) wrote to him, urging rest : " You cannot get into the habit of rest that you require in two or three months. A little change will not change your great disorder. You must free yourself altogether from your daily torments in the city ; seek the agreeable, avoid business talk, simply enjoy the sunshine and fresh air in the most natural manner you can, leaving all thought of business. A thousand miles on horse-back will do you no good if Care rides behind with her arms around you."

Excellent advice ! but, as Mr. Angas wrote to his

son John : "Thus an earthly physician may pre-
scribe, but it is only the Heavenly one who can
render it possible for me to adopt such advice. How
can I get well when so much oppressed on all sides
and in all places ? "

There was one resource in time of settled gloom
and depression of mind that had never failed to
bring back strength and spirits—exercise on horseback. Mr. Angas left Gravesend on horseback, and
day after day, for five months, journeyed north,
south, east, and west—through towns and cities,
over plains and moors, in foul weather and fair, now
in regions north of Newcastle, and now on downs
and sea-coast south of London, until the nervous
system was restored, and health, appetite, and spirits
returned.

During that interval he had ceased to be a shipowner. The whole of the Honduras business, " out
of which so many thousands have been drawn to
enable me to meet the enormous demands from
South Australia made upon my finances," had been
taken off his hands, and Mr. Beddome had been
actively employed in winding up his affairs.

This, however, could not be accomplished for the
present. He must first dispose of what property he
had left in London, and all efforts in this direction
proved vain. The year 1847 was memorable in the
commercial annals of this country as the year of
panic, when the resources of most men were taxed
to the utmost, the year of famine and disquiet

ushering in the stormiest year in : European history.

In a letter to Pastor Kavel he says :—

I pray God to move the hearts of the Germans in my debt to pay me what they owe me ; this would help to extricate me out of my perplexities, which all originated in my labours to serve them and their families.

But no help came from that quarter. There was no one in England who would advance money on mortgage of land in a British colony at 5 per cent., and general perplexity became again the order of the day.

We must not lose sight of the South Australian Company, but as it would not interest the general reader to narrate in detail its struggles through the weary years in which it was fighting for existence, a few brief notes from the journal of Mr. Angas will sufficiently tell the story for our present purpose.

March, 1843.—The Company's affairs seem in a condition of hopeless adversity, vastly worse than I ever could have conjectured.

June 2, 1843.—No profits for the past year, but very serious loss. The Board decided not to offer the shareholders any dividend for this year.

No dividend was declared for 1844. In June, 1845, he writes :—

The annual meeting was long, rather stormy, and very perplexing. . . . My mind was much depressed, for not only had I

the reflections of the proprietors to bear and answers to give to all
the difficult questions put, but to feel that there was no dividend
for them or for me, although my stake was so large and I so much
needed the money. Besides this, there was the uncomfortable feeling
about next year !

June 30, 1847.—No dividend !

Then came the tide in the affairs of the Company
which led on to fortune. On the 28th of June,
1848, at the Annual General Meeting a dividend of
4 per cent. was declared !

No one rejoiced more than Mr. Angas, and yet
his was the saddest heart in all that meeting. He
had held on to the Company until it should have
weathered the storm that threatened its existence,
and now, when the clouds were drifting away, cir
cumstances made it necessary for him to tender his
resignation of the office of Chairman, and also his
seat at the Board of Directors.

For twelve and a half years he had stood at the
helm of the whole concern, and it could not be
otherwise than that he should leave it with deep
feeling, or that he should receive overwhelming
expressions of regret from all with whom he had
laboured.

The following formal resolution was passed at the
last Board meeting over which he presided :—" That
the Board in accepting Mr. Angas' resignation as
Chairman and Director cannot fail to record their
regret and to express their unanimous opinion of
the eminent services he has rendered to Great

Britain and to colonial interests in the establishment
of the flourishing colony of South Australia, as well
as their sense of his successful efforts in the formation of the South Australian Company, and of his
exertions for its prosperity."

In acknowledging this resolution, Mr. Angas
said :—

I am not aware that any other Company has been formed for the
purpose of establishing colonies that has not totally failed. I could
point to four or five such instances or more in which they have not
only failed entirely in their undertaking, but have lost their capital
into the bargain. Take, for example, the Western Australian
Company, established fifteen years before the South Australian
Company was contemplated. That colony at this moment does not
possess a population of more than 4,000 or 5,000, and is still a
burthen to the finances of the country to the extent of some
£8,000 a year. The colony of South Australia, on the other
hand, which has existed only ten or twelve years, has a population
of 83,000, is no burthen on the finances of this country, and has a
surplus of £15,000. . . . An attempt was made to establish
Australind by a Company having very considerable capital, and
what was the result? Australind does not exist at all. The whole
of the capital has been lost, every shilling of it, and there is not a
house or a man left to tell the tale. If your capital had been at
Australind it would have gone in the same way, whereas you have
abundant remuneration for it. In New Zealand, too, an experiment was tried with one of the largest and most influential Companies that ever existed in London, and what is the present result?
They began at the very moment when we were relapsing into
difficulties. They seized that opportunity to make the experiment,
and what is the result? After eight or ten years of labour they
have expended £400,000, and they have not a shilling left of their
capital except that which is lodged in the land. . . . ·

This would not be the place to chronicle the many flattering things that were said of Mr. Angas when his resignation was announced, nor would it be worth while to record here the testimonies borne on all hands to his great ability and the important services he had rendered to the British Government and the colonies.

The language of Colonel Torrens in a letter to Lord John Russell tersely expresses what many others said in perhaps less emphatic terms :—

"Without the noble and disinterested aid of Mr. Angas the colony could not have been planted, and his information regarding its state and prospects is probably more accurate and extensive than that of any other individual in the country."

"Whenever the history of South Australia is written," says Mr. Harcus in his admirable work on that colony,* "the name of George Fife Angas must occupy a prominent position in its records."

Towards the end of 1847 he had the idea of future life in South Australia borne very distinctly into his mind, and he even went so far as to elaborate details of his plans. How vividly he realized the needs of the colony and of his property there may be gathered from letters to his son, Mr. J. H. Angas. Thus :—

GRAVESEND, *Dec.* 21, 1847.

I want to call your particular attention to the following points :—
1. That you would find it useful to form a committee of three or

* "South Australia : Its History, Resources, and Productions." Edited by William Harcus, Esq., J.P. (London : Sampson Low and Co.)

four chief persons resident in Angaston, with yourself as chairman, to watch over the improvement of Angaston, its buildings, roads, pavements, common sewers, supplies of water, &c. ; and you would do well to keep one or two acres free for town use as a green—not to give it to the town, but to let the inhabitants have the free use of it. 2 and 3. See to its sanitary arrangements ; each house must have proper offices ; also for baking, washing, gardens, &c., &c. 4. Discourage by every means spirit shops and public-houses. Encourage the growth of vineyards and the use of wine made therefrom. 5. You might employ many children and young people to collect gum off the land at per cwt. It is always worth bringing home. To save expense it might be packed in skins dried in the sun, as indigo, cocoa, and cochineal are from Honduras. 6. Tallow might be packed in like manner, if needful. 7. Look sharp after trespassers on our runs. 8. There will soon be a want of runs near Adelaide. Your object will be to keep your lands for fatting cattle and sheep for sale, and to that end you must keep down your increase. I know no other way than boiling down for export if a means of curing to perfection can be provided. I think that is practicable ! Therefore let me hear your mind fully on this subject, that when I leave England I may take all needful implements with me. 9. A good style of buildings in our villages and farmsteads, with gardens and so on, is worthy of our attention ; as well as proper regard to roads, places for relaxation, &c. 10. It also strikes me that if houses in South Australia were built more upon the Italian plan, to keep out *heat* as well as cold, it would be good. 11. Take care, above all things, to have schoolrooms and libraries everywhere ; *give* ground to any good people, for schools, more especially Sunday Schools, and invest it in trustees.

Not a bad programme for one letter !

On many practical questions Mr. Angas was vastly in advance of his time. Thus, in relation to the question of transporting meat to this country from Australia, he writes :—

July 5, 1848.

I think it will be worth your while to try Warrington's curing patent, by making up half a dozen barrels, in such barrels as are used for salt meat for ship's use, upon the recipe I enclose in this letter. The point is to have the cask full up to the brim with hot tallow, 800°, and when cool fix in the top, well pressed down to keep out the air, and ship to my consignment in London, and this will fully test the plan. Strong gravy that forms a thick jelly will answer as well as tallow to preserve the meat.

He was as full of eyes as Argus, and everything, from greatest to smallest, attracted not only his attention but his investigation. He appears to have ransacked the Patent Office to discover the last new things that could bring welfare in any shape or way to the South Australians, and in voluminous letters he kept his son John " posted " on the points. His letters are full of such sentences as the following, with the addition of elaborate details :—

I have seen a capital machine for making tiles, bricks, and pipes for draining land. (Then follows description.) Also a hydraulic ram, that cost only about £8 or £10, and threw up water from a pond a quarter of a mile distant from the house to the top storey of Sir W. Blackett's place.

I send you a few black mulberry seeds, which we have been obliged to get from the Mediterranean.

Everything, everywhere, and at all times was henceforth seen in relation to its practical bearing upon his future residence in the colony. There was scarcely a question of any kind that could conduce to the welfare of South Australia generally, and Adelaide and Angaston in particular, that did not claim his careful consideration. He seemed to see the place and its requirements in his mind's eye as distinctly as if he had lived in it for years.

With respect to cutting timber for fuel upon my property great caution will be necessary. When timber is removed from any country situated like South Australia, Judea, Cape of Good Hope, and so on, from the tops of the hills, it is sure to produce barrenness and want of water. It has been so in New South Wales and in the Cape of Good Hope colony in some places. All English trees will grow upon the hills of our surveys, and ought to be planted. For the hilltops the trees now there should be retained.

It will have been seen that during the long period of depression under which Mr. Angas had suffered, his old love of "doing good" had not in any way decreased. When he was crippled in cash he was bountiful in gifts of land, and running through all his correspondence in connection with affairs in South Australia there are instances of his broad philanthropy. Thus, when the question of a Labour College was mooted, he proposed to invest 160 acres of his land in the hands of trustees for the purposes of that institution; but the public did not support his efforts. Therefore, when, in 1845, the Rev. G. Stonehouse went out, Mr. Angas was desirous of founding a Baptist College in Australia, and wrote to his son:—

I request that you will grant a lease for seven years of 160 acres to the Rev. G. Stonehouse, at a peppercorn rent.

(reserving the minerals), of such sections on the surveys as you and he shall agree to be most suitable for the site of a future college, within a few miles of Angaston, so as to be available for the chapel, and so on. The lease must be to Mr. Stonehouse alone, and he may apply the produce of it to the support of himself . and family, on the understanding that he does what he can to found a college thereon.

But that time never came. A Baptist College was ultimately founded in Adelaide, and Mr. Stonehouse became its first president; but it was not established on Mr. Angas's land.

Thorough Baptist as Mr. Angas was from conviction, his liberality of sentiment was conspicuous on all occasions when he took part in any matter concerning the spiritual interests of the community. Thus, in a letter written in 1848 to his son, Mr. J. H. Angas, he says :—

I have told Mr. Stonehouse that I can see no reason why those Christians of all sects who have believed the Gospel and do now receive the Lord's Supper from his hands at Angaston, should not all unite and form a Christian Church. Let them agree to sink their differences in non-essentials and accord in all essential points. I hope he will try this plan; it is the principle upon which our pastor, Mr. Pryce, has formed the Baptist Church at Gravesend, and it succeeds and prospers well.

In 1849, in consequence of failing health and alarming symptoms, Mr. Angas was compelled to place his case again in the hands of a physician, who wrote to him in these strong terms :—

Tell Mrs. Angas to use her utmost exertion to keep you from

21

taxing your brain with any kind of business whatever, and under any pretence whatever. If you are wise and stop now you may recover a sufficient amount of health and strength to enable you to enjoy yourself both mentally and physically, and still be useful to others, not as an acting assistant, but an adviser, and so finally you may go down to the grave full of years, free from pain and disease, rejoicing in the pleasant reminiscences of a well-spent life, with all your faculties about you. But if you will not stop now, . . . then the strong possibility is that disease and imbecility will overtake you, embittering your old age with sickness and suffering, making you useless either to yourself or others, and what is worse than all, you will deserve it.

These were wise and excellent words, but a better restorative than physician's advice, and a better tonic than physician's medicine was in store for him.   In 1850 the commercial depression was passing away in England, and he had the prospect of speedily and advantageously selling his property in the north, which had hitherto been an incubus on all his plans ; the Germans were paying back the money that had been owing so many years, and the letters from his son, Mr. J. H. Angas, were full of good cheer, urging his immediate departure for the colony he had founded, and holding up golden prospects in the future from the very sources which had proved his temporary ruin.

Every labour now became a pleasure.   The hand of Providence, in which, through life, he had trusted, was, unmistakably to his faith, pointing to Australia ; every circumstance continued to make the path of duty the path of his own choice also ; there was

still energy, capacity, and enterprise for beginning a
new life in a new land, even though sixty summers
had passed over his head, and on the 3rd of October,
1850, he bade farewell to Old England, and with
Mrs. Angas and his youngest son set sail from Plymouth in the good ship *Ascendant*, bound for South
Australia.

CHAPTER XII.

SOUTHWARD HO !

FOR several years prior to leaving England Mr.
Angas was actively engaged, first in assisting to
obtain a new Constitution for South Australia, and
next in shaping it to meet the requirements of the
colony.

He was strenuously opposed to the introduction
into the "Australian Colonies Government Bill"
of any provision for a Federal Assembly, and
emphatically protested against the proposal to
place the sale of waste lands in the hands of an
Assembly, meeting, it might be, many hundreds of
miles away from the spot in which such lands were
situated. He pointed out the injustice of such a
course by comparing the prices paid for land in
different parts of the colony. He, the largest pro-

prietor of land in South Australia, had paid thirty
shillings per acre, whereas most of the land in New
South Wales had been obtained from the Crown at
less than five shillings per acre, besides the advantage of receiving a large amount of convict labour
at the expense of the Imperial Government.

On these points he sent many letters and petitions
to Earl Grey, the Secretary of State for the Colonies,
and to Lord John Russell, at that time First Lord
of the Treasury, besides working hard to create
public opinion among friends of the colony throughout the country.

Another matter in which he took an absorbing
interest was the recognition in the New Constitution
of the principle that no aid whatever from the State
should be given to religion. It was upon that principle the colony was originally founded, but a large
number of the colonists, and an overwhelming
number of partizans at home, were opposed to it.
The battle of State aid and voluntaryism had, therefore, to be fought out, and while the advocates of
religious liberty were doing their best in the colony,
Mr. Angas was using all his influence in England,
not only with the acknowledged friends of the
voluntary principle, but also with the Colonial
Office to establish that principle by constitutional
means.

The burden of his letters to South Australia was
to urge his correspondents to deluge the Home
Government with petition after petition, and thus

aid him in obtaining support in the House of
Commons.

Ever since 1831, when his attention was first
directed to colonization, the one great object he
always had in view was the establishment of civil
and religious liberty, and the separation of Church
and State.

It was no new experience for him to engage in
that time-honoured controversy. Twenty years
before he had fought a desperate battle, almost
single-handed, with the Government of Honduras,
when the Governor, his officers, and the Council,
were all hostile, and had resolved to banish every
dissenting missionary Mr. Angas had been instrumental in establishing there. An outbreak of fever
threatened to aid the opposition, as some of the
missionaries fell ill, and others went to the United
States to escape. Then the Government resolved
to shut up every chapel as soon as the last missionary had left the shore, and not to grant any more
licenses to preachers other than those of the Church
of England. But when the last preacher left, the
manager of the business of Angas and Co. took
possession of the pulpit, and despite of threats and
attempted arrest, occupied it until the missionaries
returned. Then Mr. Angas brought his influence
to bear with the Colonial Office, and thenceforth
there was only a chaplain, but no State Church in
Honduras.

How far he was successful in assisting to obtain

an application of the same principle to South
Australia we shall presently see; meanwhile he left
no stone unturned to benefit the cause which lay so
near his heart.   He wrote in his diary :—

June 29, 1850.—I had made up my mind to remain in England
a year longer in case the Australian Colonies Bill had been cast
out by the change of Ministry as was expected, but the Ministers
got a majority of forty-six, and the Lords have agreed upon the report.

July 6, 1850.—Last night the Australian Colonies Bill was read
a third time in the House of Lords, and passed in a state free
from many imperfections contained in it on its first introduction.
For this mercy I praise and bless God, whose hand has been visible
in all its movements and progress.

Now that the Bill has passed I feel that my work is done here, at
least as regards South Australia.

It was not in his nature to linger anywhere when
his work in that place was done, and almost immediately after the passing of the Bill, he commenced his preparations for leaving England.
Thenceforth his mind was set on this one thing,
and nothing turned him aside from his purpose,
not even the flattering proposal of a number of
influential members of Parliament who wished to
entertain him at a public farewell banquet.

It could not have been otherwise than a satisfaction to know that his services to the Empire had
been appreciated, and the letters giving expression
to. this feeling were abundant.   We quote from one
only, written by his old friend and coadjutor, Colonel
Torrens :—

I see by the *South Australian News* that you depart in the course of the [present month for the country of your adoption, or more correctly for the colony of your creation. . . . May you meet in South Australia an ample recompense for your arduous labours and noble sacrifices, and a full realization of all your hopes. While deeply regretting your departure for the Antipodes I feel consoled by the reflection that your presence in South Australia will have a beneficial influence on all the most important interests of the rising province.

There was only one keen regret in leaving England, and that was the bidding farewell to his daughter, Mrs. William Johnson, who, in an especial manner, had entwined her love around him. Just a few days before his departure he wrote her a long and tender letter of farewell, in the course of which he said :—

Now, my dear child, may God bless and keep you and yours in all your ways, night and day, from all evil, and reward you for the sympathy, kindness, and prayers on our behalf in our time of trouble. You are now the representative in England of all my family, with your beloved husband, so that you will hear more of us and know more about us than any other people, and to you we must look for all news. I know not what we should have done in preparing for our voyage but for your kindness and assistance. I pray God to reward you abundantly.

On October 3, 1850, Mr. and Mrs. Angas, with their youngest son, set sail, as we have said, from Plymouth on board the *Ascendant* bound for South Australia, the ship that carried out on that same voyage the New Constitution for the administration of the affairs of the colony !

There was nothing unusual in the voyage except that a somewhat serious disturbance broke out amongst the crew, almost amounting to a mutiny, and Mr. Angas rendered seasonable and successful assistance to the captain on the occasion by using his influence to restore peace between him and his refractory men.

On January 14, 1851, he noted in his diary, which had been his constant companion on the voyage :—

To-day we first sighted Kangaroo Island, happily in broad daylight, for the reckoning of the captain was from twenty to thirty miles out.

It is impossible to describe the intense interest he took in every part of the land over which, for so many years, he had yearned with a fatherly solicitude almost unparalleled, and it is amusing to cull from his diary, not only at this first moment when "faith was lost in sight," but in all subsequent voyagings and journeyings how keenly alive he was to everything that could benefit the colony and its settlers. The very first entry in the journal after sighting the land is a case in point :—

Jan. 15.—Rose at 4 a.m. Had just passed Point Marsden when the sun arose above the mountains, near Cape Jervis, with extreme beauty, and our eyes were feasted all the way up the gulf with the very beautiful range of hills on the east side, with Mount Lofty at the top, extending into the interior far out of sight. . . . A lighthouse is needed at the north-west end of Kangaroo Island, also on Troubridge Shoal, and one on Point Marsden would be useful.

Emphasis was given to this observation almost immediately after, when the hull of a ship (the *Grecian*, Captain Hyde) was seen on her beam ends.

So well did Mr. Angas know the country through the " clairvoyance of the imagination," as Lord Lytton calls it, that although the captain of the *Ascendant* knew the coast well, as he thought, Mr. Angas was the first to point out Mount Lofty and other landmarks to him.

Every one who has made a long voyage to some far distant land of promise—and especially in the days when luxury on board ship was almost unknown —will recall the thrilling moment when the pilot comes on board to take the ship into the desired haven. It was an intense moment in the experience of Mr. Angas, only surpassed by another, when his two sons, John and George, and his eldest daughter, Rosetta, stepped on board, bearing news of the health and prosperity of all his family, and of the wonderful good fortune that had attended the arduous labours of Mr. John Howard Angas in the development and management of his father's affairs.

Quite apart from his own family and connections, Mr. Angas felt at once that he was among friends. Not a man, woman, or child in the colony but knew how much they were indebted to his labours. The very pilot who took him ashore was one whom he had selected in 1836 to go out with the *South*

Australian, the ship that conveyed Mr. McLaren as manager of the South Australian Company.

A few days after landing a public dinner was given in his honour to testify respect for him personally, and to express the feeling of the people for the active part he had taken in the formation of the colony, to introduce him to many whom he had not previously known, and to give him an early opportunity of uniting with old friends, amongst whom was Mr. William Giles, the manager of the South Australian Company.

There were wonderful things to talk about that night. Gathered around him were some who had gone out in the pioneer vessel and had dwelt in the canvas town on Kangaroo Island, now leading men in the colony, and it was no mean compliment that the Chairman paid him, when, in describing the early attempts to found the colony, he said that "after the first efforts were made the machine stuck fast, and but for George Fife Angas would have stuck there till the present moment," a saying that was greeted with loud and continued cheering.

It had been an ambition of his to be the personal bearer of the official copy of the New Constitution Act to the colony, and application had been made to the Colonial Office to this end, but it was found to be contrary to precedent, and red-tape triumphed, the important document being sent from the Colonial Office in charge of a clerk, who was instructed to

take it on board the *Ascendant* and deliver it into
the hands of the captain. But he had gone ashore,
and as the ship was on the point of sailing, the
clerk, either through negligence or from not understanding the importance of the papers with which
he was entrusted, gave the package to a steward,
who, being very busy, thrust it into the nearest place
of safety. The ship sailed, and if the captain gave
a thought to the matter at all, he merely supposed
that there had been some delay or fresh arrangements had been made. On arrival in Adelaide the
proper authorities came on board to demand their
Constitution and receive it with due honour, for
advices from England had informed them that it
would arrive in the *Ascendant*. The captain, of
course, protested that he had seen nothing of it,
and there was a great hue and cry for the lost
Constitution, until one day shortly after, in turning
out the captain's soiled linen for the laundress, it
was found, to the great amusement of every one, at
the bottom of the bag, the place in which the
steward had hurriedly placed it for security!

After spending a few days in Adelaide while
luggage was leaving the ship, Mr. Angas and his
family party drove in a carriage and four to Lindsay
Park, Angaston, a distance of fifty-five miles, only
changing horses at Gawler Town, about half-way.

Those were proud and happy days for Mr. Angas
when he first became personally acquainted with the

country he had so largely assisted to create. This
was what he found : Fifteen years before, the land
was an uninhabited wilderness ; the nearest human
beings, except a few miserable savages, were many
hundreds of miles away ; the country was but little
known, had never been properly explored, and had
probably never been inhabited by a white man.
Now, there was a population of 63,700 souls,
exclusive of 3,730 aborigines.   There were 102
places of worship and 115 schools, 174,000 acres of
land were enclosed, and 15,000 square miles de-
pastured by cattle and sheep.   Seven years before
the colony was in a state of bankruptcy, but now
it produced a revenue of £280,000 per annum, with
a surplus over expenditure of £40,000, applicable
to general purposes, and of £20,000, applicable to
the reduction of debt.   Its import trade was
£887,000, and its export trade £571,000, employing
a tonnage, inwards and outwards, of 168,500 tons.
So rapidly had her flocks multiplied, that in the
previous year 3,289,000 lbs. of wool had been exported, while her mineral resources had so developed
that in the same period 44,594 cwts. of metal and
8,784 tons of copper ore had also been exported.

Nowhere in South Australia had greater changes
and improvements been effected than in the Barossa
District, and upon the extensive lands possessed by
Mr. Angas.   Through the judicious and far-seeing
management of his son, Mr. J. H. Angas, the
wilderness had been made to blossom as the rose,

order had been evolved out of chaos, and the lands that had been acquired under such peculiar circumstances, and had been the cause of years of poverty and anxiety, gave promise of yielding to their possessor a more than ample fortune.

Mr. Angas wrote in his diary soon after his arrival in the colony :—

Truly I have around me as extensive and as beautiful an estate as falls to the lot of man. When it shall be better with me as regards my income from it, I pray God to dispose my heart to greater liberality, and never allow my worldly possessions to attach my heart to them, but to use them for God's glory as His faithful steward and for the good of my fellow men.

It was no part of his plan or policy to settle down quietly on his estate and enjoy himself while there was work which he conceived it to be his duty to perform. He barely had time to look round before he found himself in the midst of a new life with fresh and responsible duties. He was, almost immediately upon arrival, invited to stand as a candidate for the Legislative Council, under the New Constitution, and in response to a requisition signed by two hundred influential electors, he consented to come forward as a candidate to represent the Barossa District.

The following notes from his diary show how thick and fast new public engagements came upon him.

March 20th.—Gazetted a Member of the Board of Education and a J.P.

March 23rd.—Gave address in chapel at Truro, on " What is truth ? "

„   25th.—Dined with a number of Pastor Kavel's people at Tanunda.   .

„   26th.—Election business.

,,   27th.—Old colonists' festival.   Gave toast in absence of Governor.

From letters written to his daughter in England we insert a few extracts giving his early colonial " impressions."

LINDSAY HOUSE, *March* 24, 1851.

Every day and hour has its occupation ; besides, I feel it requires much more sleep or rest to recruit the waste of the day than it does at home—at least, in the summer.

April 2, 1851.

Public matters, travelling, attending John's business, and obtaining information needful to enable me to carry my points, attending house arrangements, building rooms, getting up goods, unpacking, &c., &c., may well excuse me for writing much home. The new Assembly is to meet in June it is said, and I shall lodge in Adelaide during its sittings (about three months) if I get all comfortable in the country.   I shall then have leisure and time to study the laws.

July 8, 1851.

I feel the most extraordinary confusion of mind from this (July) being winter and all the movements of life and business being reversed.   All my life time I have been accustomed to write from England to the colonies, now it is from this colony to England ; then there are so many new scenes, new occupations, new trains of thought, new sympathies, associations, and influences, that these confusions materially affect my memory.   That local memory which I established in England with no little trouble, and those associations of ideas which tended so much to strengthen that faculty, are in this colony dissipated and lost. . . .

There was only one thing at this time that appeared to give him anxiety. He did not find the moral and social condition of the people all that he had anticipated, and he feared that the various Christian Societies were not in a healthy state.

In politics, too, judging from the speeches of candidates for the Legislature, he perceived a great deal of truckling to the democratic element, whose cry was: " The ballot and universal suffrage ! " and he feared that if true to their promises to the people they would be a strong opposition to Government, unless " after their election, instead of being dictated to, they became the dictators."

On the 19th of August the first Council under the New Constitution was gazetted, and on the 20th it met in the then new Court House in Victoria. Square, and Mr. Angas, who had the honour of being returned for the Barossa District unopposed, took his seat.

Important improvements in the government of the colony had taken place from time to time. The attempt to govern the new settlement by a Board 16,000 miles away having proved a decided failure, the Commissioners were dispensed with, and at the time when Captain (afterwards Sir George) Grey became Governor, the Home Government undertook the direct management of the colony. Later, the affairs of the colony were administered by a Council,.

consisting of three official and four non-official members, with the Governor as President.

By the New Constitution now coming into force it was provided that there should be a Legislative Council consisting of twenty-four members, one-third of whom were to be nominated by the Governor, and two-thirds to be elected by the people. Of the nominated members one-half were to be official and the other half non-official. The Act admitted of such alterations and amendments being made as the Colonial Legislature might deem desirable.

On the 29th of August the first reading was moved of a Bill to continue "An Ordinance to Promote the Building of Churches and Chapels for Christian Worship, and to Provide for the Maintenance of Ministers of the Christian Religion." This was the signal for the great battle of the Session to commence, and it deserves more than a passing notice here.

It will be remembered that the foundations of the colony were laid on the principle of the entire separateness between Church and State. It was determined that no form of religion should be pre-eminently recognized by the State, but that all Churches should be on the same footing of equality, none being specially honoured or subsidized, and none being placed under any civil disabilities.

Notwithstanding this, while Colonel Robe was Governor (1845-1848), he initiated the granting of

State aid to religious bodies — an innovation that aroused great opposition and grew in intensity until the time of which we now write.

Colonel Robe was a Tory of the old school, and disregarding the " Liberal tendencies of the handful of people he had been sent to govern in the Queen's name," and backed by a small clique of men in authority, he determined to put down the modern notions of religious equality, and to re-establish the old relations between Church and State. Circumstances were favourable to the innovation.

The Baroness (then Miss) Burdett-Coutts had offered an endowment of £800 a year each for the foundation of four colonial dioceses, that of Adelaide being among the number. The preferment to the latter see fell to the Rev. Augustus Short, D.D., who, with the three other bishops, was consecrated in Westminster Abbey on June 29, 1847, the occasion being one of unusual solemnity, the ceremony lasting over four hours. In December of that year he arrived in Adelaide, and was formally inducted at Trinity Church, when Her Majesty's Letters Patent were read, constituting South Australia a diocese, and "appointing Dr. Short to be the Bishop thereof, under the style and title of Lord Bishop of Adelaide." By the Act of the Local Legislature, the Church of England was aided with support from Government to the extent of from £1,500 to £2,000 per annum, and this, as we have said, aroused a strong and indignant feeling among all classes of the community. Before it was in any degree allayed, the Bishop, acting upon advice given to him before leaving England, and furnished with a formal land grant under the hand and seal of the Governor, proceeded to claim an acre of ground in Victoria Square as a site for a cathedral. But he had reckoned without his host; the local authorities declared that the document was *ultra vires*, and legal proceedings were commenced. During their continuance popular feeling was again excited in consequence of his meeting the other colonial prelates and attaching his signature to a Minute affirming the doctrine of baptismal regeneration which the Bishop of Melbourne had refused to sign.

Shortly afterwards a large meeting of members of the Church of England was held at Adelaide, when the course pursued by Bishop Short was almost unanimously condemned in the strongest language. This was in 1850, and before the storm had blown over the question of continuing State aid to religion was brought before the Local Legislature under the New Constitution. It was the leading question in the election. The Governor and his Executive Council, the Church of England, Wesleyan Methodists, Roman Catholics, and Presbyterians, were in favour of it. The great body of the people, the Independents, Baptists, Lutherans, and Methodists—not Wesleyans—were against it.

The standpoint of Mr. Angas was that " Religion is a matter with which no Government has a right to interfere "—a very open platform and easily adapted to assault, but in his election addresses he confined his remarks mainly to the political aspect of the question and regarded it as a violation of the principle on which the colony was founded. His views on liberty of worship are embodied in a declaration which he wished to be entered upon the minutes of the House, namely :—

That all mankind have a natural and indefeasible right to worship Almighty God according to the dictates of their own consciences, and no man can, of right, be compelled to attend, erect, or support any place of worship, or to maintain any ministry against his consent ; that no human authority can, in any case whatever, control or interfere with the rights of conscience ; that no preference shall ever be given by law to any religious establishment or modes of worship; that no part of the revenue of the colony of South Australia, from whatever source it may arise, and that no part of the Land and Emigration Funds, can be made applicable to the support of ministers or teachers of any religion or to the erection or repairing of any place of worship.

In the Council the opponents of the grant determined to make the contest as brief and decisive as possible, and an amendment was moved " That the Bill be read that day six months." After warm expressions of opinion this was carried by a majority of three, there being thirteen for the amendment and ten against it, the votes of all the members, with one exception, having been recorded on this important question.

The voluntary principle was adopted, and with this result : amazing progress was made by all denominations to supply the religious wants of their respective communities ; the colony became remarkable for the number of its places of worship in proportion to the population; the Church of England, which, of all other churches, deprecated the voluntary principle, found, on giving it a fair trial, that sufficient funds could be raised from private sources to build churches and pay ministers.

So decisive was the blow struck in that Parliament of 1851 that no attempt has ever again been made to introduce State aid to religion. And the voluntary system has worked so well that it is a thousand pities it has not been introduced into every British colony.

Even Bishop Short did not suffer in the end. His unfortunate law-suit dragged on until 1855, when the Supreme Court of the Province declared that he could not enforce his claims, as, although the Governor could grant *waste* lands, he could not interfere with the public reserves, of which Victoria Square was one. But a far more important decision was in store. On appeal to the Privy Council the whole question of the colonial episcopates was fully discussed, and the startling revelation was made " that letters patent from the English Crown to colonial bishops carried no territorial jurisdiction with them, and were, in truth, of little, if of any, practical effect."

So the good Bishop made the best of circumstances, and laboured on until the year 1882, when,
well stricken in years, he left the colony. During
the time of his residence there he had witnessed the
establishment in the colony of no fewer than ninety-
one churches, and the erection of a handsome cathedral; he saw the Episcopalians heading the list,
numerically, of all the denominations; he found a
wide and influential sphere for his activity, and he
won for himself universal respect.

With the discontinuance of the Government grant
in aid of religion came a measure for the promotion
of education. The Bill provided that religious
liberty should be secured, and religious controversy
prohibited in the schools receiving aid from Government; that instruction and books should not be
given gratuitously, except to orphans and other
destitute scholars; that there should be a Central
Board of Education possessing certain well-defined
powers, and a Normal School imparting a specified
course of instruction; that the District Councils
might be Local Boards of Education, or, in the
absence of a District Council, two Justices of the
Peace might take the necessary powers. The Act
also provided for the appointment of an Inspector
of Schools, for a depôt for school books, and for the
salaries of teachers.

On the subject of education Mr. Angas was an
authority. He it was who had been the first to
introduce any school system whatever into the

colony, and in the old country as in the new, his views had always embraced two leading principles, the first being that schools supported by the State should be entirely unsectarian, the second that the Bible should not be excluded.   His idea of the nearest approach to a perfect system was that embodied in the Lancasterian and Irish schools, and his strongest contention was that no instruction should be given in religious doctrine.   The Bill originally provided for the teaching and maintenance of " the Christian religion," and to this he was strenuously opposed, inasmuch as it would have opened the door to Roman Catholics for teaching the dogmas of their Church, and much sectarian strife and bitterness would have ensued.   Eventually the words " Holy Scripture " were substituted, greatly to his satisfaction.

One clause of the Bill provided that no minister of religion should be a member of the Board.   Of this the Governor greatly disapproved, and forwarded a message urging upon the Council that it should be rescinded, but the Council refused to comply, and carried the Bill with the original clause by a majority of six.

This first Session of Parliament under the New Constitution was perhaps the most important in the whole history of the colony, and it was meet that Mr. Angas should have a voice in it.   It settled for ever, so far as South Australia was concerned, the principle for which he had been contending from his boyhood, of separation of Church and State, and it inaugurated a system of public education, which, with necessary modifications to suit the exigencies of the times, has continued to the present day.

CHAPTER XIII.

LIFE IN ADELAIDE.

A Review of the Year—Discovery of Gold in Victoria—Exodus of South Australians—The Bullion Act—State of Affairs in Adelaide—Return of Gold Diggers—High Price of Labour and Increased Cost of Living—The German Settlers and their Villages—Visit to Southern Districts—Influence of Climate—Arrival of English Mails—Postal Irregularities—Mr. John Howard Angas—Depression in Trade—Overstocking the Labour Market—Dr. Dean—A Colonial Mystery.

AT the close of the year 1851, Mr. Angas, according to custom, entered in his journal a review of its chief events in his personal history. Many years had elapsed since he had been able to write with so much satisfaction and hope, mingled with thanksgiving. He had disentangled himself from all the business that held him to the old country, and had prosperously voyaged to the land of his adoption; his health was better than it had been for many years; he had been marvellously preserved, twice having been thrown from his horse, and once upset from his gig; he had found in the colony all that his most sanguine expectations had promised him; his new duties, legislative and magisterial, yielded him a fair share of pleasure, as well as his position as a member of the Education and Road Boards.

Like Job it seemed that his latter end was to be more than a recompense for the past, ample proof being forthcoming that his property was second to none in the colony for value and beauty. Before another year had passed it had so greatly improved that he was able to clear off all his liabilities in England, and he gratefully recorded " the complete fulfilment of God's promises in his complete deliverance."

But the year which ended so satisfactorily opened under circumstances that caused him considerable anxiety. Gold had been discovered in Victoria, and the colonists of South Australia started off by hundreds to join the " rush " that was setting in from all quarters. Some returned in an incredibly short time laden with spoils only to go back accompanied by friends and neighbours.

The most thoughtful and sober-minded persons in the community could no longer view the extraordinary circumstances in which the colony was placed with composure or confidence. An abundant harvest had been gathered in with some difficulty in consequence of the scarcity of labour, and hence there was no fear of famine. But hundreds of gold diggers had returned with their rich gains and findings, and this created a surfeit of wealth, which could not, however, be put into circulation. The banks had been drained of coin by the numbers who had left the colony.

With the absorption of a medium of circulation

came a stagnation of trade, and consequently the discharge of nearly all those employed, who had not voluntarily left their occupations and pursuits to proceed to the diggings. Business was nearly at a standstill, shops were closed, a great part of the police force resigned, public officers forsook their posts—everything for the time was revolutionized.

The conviction soon forced itself upon the minds of far-seeing men, foremost among whom were Mr. George Tinline, manager of the Bank of South Australia, and Mr. Angas, that the assay of gold into stamped ingots of a fixed value was the only immediate and effectual remedy for the evils arising from the want of a circulating medium.

The Chamber of Commerce earnestly memorialized the Governor on the subject, but without any practical result. Meanwhile, as trade and commerce were paralysed, and disastrous consequences were pending, a further pressing memorial was sent again urging that the gold received into the country should have an exchangeable value imparted to it by establishing an assay office under the superintendence of the Government, and by proclaiming the bullion, which should be there prepared and stamped, a legal tender.

On the 28th of January the Legislative Council was called together to discuss the question, and at once proceeded with the important business of the Bullion Bill, which was read a first, second, and third time, passed, and assented to on the same day !

The Government Assay Office was opened on the 10th of February, and during the day gold to the value of £10,000 was deposited. The scheme surpassed the expectations of the most sanguine, and completely vindicated the prudence and sagacity of its promoters. During the year, gold to the value of over two millions sterling was introduced into South Australia from Victoria!

A graphic description of the state of affairs in Adelaide at this period is given in the following extracts from letters written by Mrs. Evans, a daughter of Mr. Angas, to her sister in England.

Jan. 26, 1852.

Already eight thousand persons have left for Melbourne. . . . The passing of the Bullion Act has tended to raise the drooping spirits of the labourers who remain, and will, I doubt not, be the saving of the colony with the Divine blessing. Gold is to be assayed, stamped, and made a legal tender at the rate of 71s. per ounce—a higher price than they give in the neighbouring colonies, and therefore we may hope that the successful gold seekers will ere long return again and spend amongst us the money they obtain elsewhere.

Feb. 25, 1852.

What changes have taken place in this colony since Christmas. The discovery of gold has turned our little world upside down; thousands have left the settlement for the diggings. . . . In Adelaide windows are bricked up, and outside is written, 'Gone to the diggings.' Vessels are crowded with passengers to Melbourne, and the road to the port is like a fair—ministers, shopkeepers, policemen, masons, carpenters, clerks, councillors, labourers, farmers, doctors, lawyers, boys, and even some women have gone either by sea or land to try their fortunes at the diggings. . . . Somewhere about £16,000 worth of gold has in less than two weeks found its way to the assay office. Many have done uncommonly well, earning £200, perhaps, or more in a week, while some have not earned enough to pay for their food. . . . It is quite ludicrous to see how these labourers spend their gold. One man bought six silk dresses and six bonnets for his ' missus.'

It was a matter of regret to many South Australians that gold had been found in Victoria and not in their own colony. This was not the view of Mr. Angas, who from the first rejoiced that the discovery had been made at a distance. He wrote :—

> It will be ultimately found that it has been good for us that gold has not been discovered here, as the morals of the people will be better preserved ; besides, they will become the producers of food for the gold diggers. Then, again, all the gold above expenses obtained by the labour of South Australians will come back to us, and is now coming in quickly, which will increase the working capital of our people. The disappointed ones will find their way back here the better for their trials and sufferings.

As early as the month of March the unsuccessful South Australian gold diggers returned in hundreds, and the vacant offices in the various departments of the public service began to be filled up.

In many respects this was a very critical time in the history of the colony ; the increased cost of obtaining the necessaries and comforts of life was 150 per cent. in excess of previous years, and it seemed at one time as if the most important interests of the colony were upon the verge of utter ruin. Labour was so scarce that those who had embarked their capital in stock, farming and agriculture were in dismay. Mr. Angas was one of the largest proprietors, and the brilliant future that had at one time presented itself to him became overclouded. Not, however, for long. There was hardly a German in South Australia who was not, directly or indirectly, indebted to him. His own estates were teeming with them, and now the time had come when he was to reap some return for his anxiety, perplexity, and losses on their behalf.

While the gold diggings in Victoria were draining away the greater part of the working classes, nearly all the Germans remained, and with reference to them he says :—

I suffer less, perhaps, than any employer of labour, in consequence of the aid the Germans render me as farmers, shepherds, sheepshearers, &c. Few of them have left the colony, and as the farmers who rent land from me have the right of pre-emption, they hope to buy their farms in time, and therefore stick to the soil with tenacity ; while their strong regard for their religion, and attention to its ordinances, tends to depress the desire for gold digging. So in my present need I am being repaid for my patience towards them in waiting so long, and not pressing them by any appeal to law.

In March, 1852, Mr. Angas took a trip to the southern districts of the colony, visiting Port Elliot, Goolwa, and other places, mainly with a view to examine the public works being carried forward there. He travelled on horseback and alone about

three hundred miles in eight days. "Many parts
were dangerous and difficult to find," he says.
"Many places where I called and hoped to get
directions were shut up—'gone to the diggings.'
My pocket-compass I found invaluable in the glens
where the sun did not shine." He was then nearly
sixty-three years old, as hale and vigorous as a man
could be. "I have not had such good health," he
wrote to his daughter, "for the last fifty years." The
life he was leading suited him exactly; there was
more than enough to keep his mind occupied in local
politics; the improvement of his estate became a
hobby, and the climate, which he considered "far
superior to that of England," agreed with his constitution. In a letter to a friend in which he makes
this statement he indirectly attributes the low state
of religion in the colony to climatic influences.

The tendency of the climate (he says) is to produce nervous
excitement. The novelty of everything around you, and the
multitude of things requiring personal attention, has a very
dissipating influence adverse to spirituality and holiness of heart.
As far as I can judge, religion is at a low ebb in the colony, and
there are more adverse influences to piety here than in England.

It was a great pleasure to him to watch the
progress being made in all directions, and especially
among his German neighbours, who were now
grouped in townships, the chief of which were
Klemzig, Bethany, Langmeil, Tanunda, Lobethal,
and Hahndorf—exceedingly pleasant and picturesque

places, where the quaint gable-roofed houses, similar
to those in old villages of the Fatherland, was an
attractive feature.

Mr. Angas being an excellent whip, and fond of
riding exercise, was able to gratify his taste for
travelling in the colony. Moreover, he could use
his gun, and one of his daughters wrote :—

> He has become quite a sporting character, and a very good shot.
> Being short-sighted, he shoots with spectacles on, and considers
> all birds that are good for food, or noxious to gardens, fit subjects
> for his gun ; the rest he spares.

One of his chief sources of pleasure was the
arrival of the English mails. Thus in 1853 the
same correspondent says :—

> He has just been in and hugged off his English mail letters
> with as much eagerness as a miser would his gold.

Any irregularity in the mails was a sore point
with him, and from time to time he brought the
question of postal communication before the attention of the Legislative Council. In writing to his
old friend and solicitor, Mr. R. B. Beddome, he
says :—

Sept. 20, 1853.

Since I arrived here I have taken some trouble to ascertain the
cause of the miscarriage of so many letters and newspapers on
their way from England, and the result has been undoubted
evidence that it has mainly arisen from the letter bags being sent
on board of merchant ships unsealed and unprotected. In our
Legislative Council we are preparing a new Bill for improving

the post-office regulations by adopting stamps instead of money payments, so I considered it a good opportunity to propose a clause rendering it imperative upon all brokers and merchants who make up letter bags to seal ·and properly fasten them when delivered to masters of ships with their own despatches, and to forward a certificate of the same to the Postmasters-General at every place, under a penalty of £100. We cannot enforce such a law in England, but our Government here will recommend it to Mr. Rowland Hill in London, and we can apply the law at Adelaide in case the seal should be broken, and can withhold from the master his penny or twopence upon each letter to which he is entitled.

In 1854 Mr. John Howard Angas, who for over ten years had been resident in South Australia, devoting himself exclusively to his father's interests, had the satisfaction of finding his labours crowned with exceptional success—continuous prosperity had set in, and everything the hand of his father touched seemed to turn to gold. Mr. J. H. Angas found himself free, therefore, to take a rest, and sailed in the P. and O. steamer *Madras* for a visit to the old country, where he arrived on Good Friday, April 15th, having been absent eleven years to a day. It was a curious coincidence that he left England on Good Friday, April 15, 1843, in a ship named the *Madras*, and arrived again in London on Good Friday, April 15, 1854, having left Adelaide in a steamer named the *Madras*. While in England he married Miss Susanne Collins, of Bowden, Cheshire, and in 1855 returned to South Australia to settle at Collingrove, a beautiful estate near Angaston, leased from his father.

"His attention was now more particularly directed to stock farming, and the purchase of high-class Merino sheep, cattle, and horses. . . . The experience of former years, and his partiality for country pursuits favoured his success, and by careful selection and frequent importations of stud stock from Great Britain and elsewhere, he acquired a position as a breeder which not only proved lucrative to himself, but beneficial to the colony at large." *

The year 1855 was characterized by great depression in trade, consequent upon the dry seasons that prevailed during the former and present year, causing a very deficient harvest, which re-acted upon all branches of industry, and gave a decided check to the rapid progress the colony had been making ever since Mr. Angas had been a resident there.

In combination with these circumstances there was another drawback to prosperity—the impetus given to trade by the large quantities of gold sent and brought from Victoria during the years 1852 and 1853 had raised the price of almost everything. Land had reached a fictitious value both in town and country; wages had increased to such an extent as to render it impossible to employ labour except for indispensable and very remunerative undertakings, and as provisions were still high in price there was a strong disinclination to lower them, every one

* " Representative Men of South Australia." By George E. Loyau. Adelaide, 1883.

being slow to believe that, as the extraordinary influx
of gold had ceased, prices must approximate to what
they were prior to the gold discoveries in Victoria
before the colony could again be in a stable, healthy,
and prosperous condition.

Mr. Angas was a political economist, and he did
not cease to urge that the extravagant habits induced
by sudden prosperity must be broken off and re-
trenchment made in public matters no less than in
private.

In that same year, while the colony only consisted
of about 80,000 inhabitants, the land fund had
proved most prolific, and the emigration agents in
England sent out in one year 12,000 emigrants—of
whom a third were unmarried women. Of course
the great want of all new colonies is people—people
settled on the land and working the land; but when
sent out in such numbers there is neither time nor
opportunity to settle them. In a speech delivered
at the Royal Colonial Institute some years later,
Sir R. G. MacDonnell, who was Governor of
South Australia at the time of which we write,
said that his hearers " might fancy how much
the difficulty of the position was augmented when
he told them that of the above number no
fewer than 4,004 were able-bodied, single ladies.
He questioned whether any other man than he ever
had previously such a number of single women
thrust upon him. He confessed that he had never
been so embarrassed. He did what he could for

them, built them barracks, offered to pay their fare
and all expenses to any employers willing to take
them off his hands, for, he was sorry to have to add
that they were occasionally very unruly. Now, as
women in a state of rebellion are not so easily dealt
with as men, he might mention that by a happy
thought they were on one occasion reduced to
obedience by the cooling effects of water from a fire
engine ! " *

In critical times of over-population, like those now
referred to, the only solution of the difficulty was
for every individual colonist to do his best, and
Mr. Angas undoubtedly did his. His diary is noted
thus :—

LINDSAY PARK, *June 25th.* — In consequence of there being
so many emigrants out of work I felt it my duty to make work
for upwards of twenty families. To get them lodged I had to
devise all sorts of schemes, and to provide them with food,
wages, and materials of stone, brick, lime, timber, &c., is not a
trifling affair. I am building a new bridge with stone piers over
the Gawler, nearly opposite my house. One of the stones is
about a ton and a half, and all others a good size. Both piers
are founded on rocks, one is many feet below water.

In addition to this we find entries recording the
erection of " two stone cottages, coachhouse, and
harness-room. Stone shed and water tank hewn out
of the rock. A cottage in the glen. Brick-making
to a considerable extent across the river," &c., &c.

* " Proceedings of the Royal Colonial Institute, 1875–6," vol. xii.
p. 203.

Of the domestic life of Mr. Angas, of his labours in the sphere of religion and philanthropy, and of his work in the Legislative Council, we shall write in separate chapters. An episode of the elections of 1857, throwing some light on his character and surroundings, may be narrated here.

A vacancy in the House of Assembly was created by the Court of Disputed Returns declaring the election of a certain Dr. Horace Dean for the district of Barossa null and void.

The case of the so-called Dr. Dean was one of the most novel and mysterious that had hitherto been met with in the colony. Professing to be a subject of the United States he had been naturalized as Horace Dean, and Sir Henry Young, the late Governor, had conferred upon him the important appointment of Special Magistrate at Angaston. Circumstances arose which made Mr. Angas suspicious as to the real name of his neighbour, and also as to the truthfulness of his alleged previous history, which was to the effect that he had occupied the position of Captain of a Company of Missouri Volunteers, and also the post of Regimental Surgeon. To prove his statement the doctor exhibited what purported to be duly authenticated documents signed by the Major-General of the Regiment and by the Secretary of War of the United States. These documents, however, were made out in the name of William Thomas Haskell, and his reason for taking an assumed name was stated to be an engagement in

a duel with an individual who had dishonoured his
sister, and which necessitated his departure from
the country. All this seemed plausible enough, but
Mr. Angas, having put himself into communication
with the United States Government, found that the
whole story was a fabrication, and that the doctor
was unknown to the. authorities by either his professed real or assumed name.

While this investigation was in progress Mr.
Angas, no less than the supposed Dr. Dean, was
placed in an unfavourable position both in the eyes
of the public and of the Government. Sir R. G.
MacDonnell, however, considered the matter of
sufficient importance for special inquiry, and accordingly he referred the matter to the United States
Secretary of War, with the result that the charges
made by Mr. Angas were fully confirmed, and the
so-called Dr. Dean was immediately dismissed from
the office of Stipendiary Magistrate and Justice of
the Peace. Sir Richard also addressed a letter
to Mr. Angas, informing him of the steps taken,
which were satisfactory as far as they went, although
the "mystery" of Dr. Dean, Dr. Williams, or
William Thomas Haskell was left unsolved.

Having been a second time returned to the House
of Assembly as member for the district of Barossa,
the Court again declared his election invalid, the
certificate of naturalization having been obtained,
according to the doctor's own admission, under an
assumed name.

Some time after this Dr. Dean left the colony, and the unpleasant and thankless task undertaken for the public good by Mr. Angas, at much personal discomfort, came to an end.

In a letter to a friend, to whom from time to time he had narrated the different stages of the controversy, he gave the conclusion of the whole matter, and we insert the following extract, as it shows how strongly he was still under the influence of the life of his ideal hero, William Penn, and how keenly alive he was to any analogy between the history of that illustrious pioneer of civilization and his own :—

August 24, 1857.

You will see by my correspondence with the Governor in Chief and His Executive Council that I have had my character absolved from all imputations; I remembered Macaulay's history and his libel upon my favourite, William Penn, two hundred years after his decease. So I resolved, if God prospered me, to get every injurious minute upon the records of our Privy Council made in Sir H. Young's time, erased or neutralized. In this I am thankful to say I have entirely succeeded. I did not feel comfortable at the thought that my children might be dishonoured after my decease by the malice of any one who might cull out of the Minutes of the Governor's Executive Council paragraphs to my disadvantage, like W. Penn's, when it might have been utterly out of the power of any of my friends to meet the imputations. If 'the memory of the just is blessed' it becomes the duty of every public man to watch over the malice of his enemies, especially if the wicked bear rule.

CHAPTER XIV.

IN THE LEGISLATIVE COUNCIL.

Dr. Arnold and Colonial Commonwealths—The Basis of Legislation—Advanced Liberalism—Faults of Manner—Captain Sturt, Explorer—Pensions in the Public Service—A Railway Mania—Road-making—Loans for Railways—Search for Gold—Waste Lands and Pastoral Leases—Emigration—A Select Committee thereon—Compulsory Oaths—Amending the New Constitution—The Ballot and Universal Suffrage—The Title of "Honourable"—First South Australian Parliament—Order of Parliament—Federation—A Memorable Year.

In his " Life of Dr. Arnold," Dean Stanley says :— " The growth of rising commonwealths in the Australian colonies, where from time to time he entertained an ardent desire to pass the close of his life in the hope of influencing, if possible, what he conceived to be the germs of the future destinies of England and of the world, came before him with a vividness which seemed to belong rather to a citizen of Greece or Rome, than to the comparative apathy and retirement of the members of modern states."

These words might have been written of Mr. Angas with equal propriety. Over and over again, as we have seen in earlier chapters of this work, he might have been returned a member of the

British Parliament, but his ambition did not lie in that direction; his heart was in South Australia, and for many years it had been a kind of day-dream with him that he should at some time take his part in the deliberations of the Colonial Legislature, and so influence the destiny of all future generations of dwellers in the land of which he was a Father and Founder.

If we have not failed in our portraiture of the man, it will be taken for granted by every reader that Mr. Angas set before himself a very high ideal as to his duties in council. In a pocket-book in which he pasted cuttings from the local journals recording his votes and speeches in the House, there is inscribed on the first page :—" To the Bible we owe all the best laws in our best civil institutions. To the Bible Europe is indebted for much of the liberty which it now enjoys; and, little as we may think of it, the Bible too was the means of preserving the small share of learning which was cultivated during the dark ages."

This was the key to all his words and actions in the Colonial Parliament—the Bible, the basis of all good legislation. With this high standard in view he entered upon his duties in the most rigidly conscientious manner. It was his custom, with such clerical assistance as was at his command, to prepare very carefully all accessible materials bearing upon the subject under consideration, and he never went to the Council without a store of facts and figures at his fingers' ends testifying to the thoroughness of his investigations.

In the Imperial Parliament he would have ranked as a Radical, but in the Colonial Parliament, with its democratic tendencies, he was a decided Conservative. He could not keep pace—or rather he did not wish to keep pace—with the advanced Liberalism which was, in his opinion, developing too rapidly, and he felt it to be his duty to put a drag on the wheels of state. In one of his early speeches, when an amendment of the New Constitution was being discussed, he said :—" He had always admired the wisdom of the Town Clerk at Ephesus, who had recommended a very excited assembly to do nothing rashly, and the same advice he would earnestly give to that House. There were men who would always agree that a change would be for the better, but he was not one of these."

On another occasion, in defining his political position he said: "He was one of the few members of that House who had not been pledged at his election to any particular course, his constituents having so entirely honoured him with their confidence as to leave him to his own judgment. Still, he thought it his duty to consult them on every question of importance."

Although every one acknowledged the motives of Mr. Angas to be excellent, and respect was universally paid to his unflinching steadfastness in everything that was in his opinion for the public

good; although his constituents knew exactly where
to find him in any political need, and could always
rely upon his vote when a principle was at stake;
although it was admitted on all hands that no one
had the best interests of the colony more thoroughly
at heart, it was nevertheless true that Mr. Angas
was not popular as a politician. Certain faults of
manner had much to do with this on the one hand,
and a rigid adherence to hard and fast lines of
action on the other; while his extensive knowledge
and experience in colonization led him to assume
in Parliament an air of seeming superiority or a
confidence of manner, sometimes dictatorial, which
had the effect of raising up opposition and frustra-
ting the end he had in view.

In his first speech in the Legislative Council he
expressed himself as deeply disappointed when he
saw the state of the public roads, the police, and
various works and institutions supervised by the
Government, and soon afterwards he announced
his intention to advocate economy and deprecate
extravagance whether in public works or official
salaries. An occasion arose during the first session
to put his principle into practice. Captain (afterwards Sir Charles) Sturt, the famous explorer, and at
that time Colonial Secretary, wished to retire from
public life, and a motion was introduced "That an
address be presented to His Excellency praying him
to place on the estimates a sum of money which
may be deemed a suitable testimonial to the Honour-

able Captain Sturt for the very important services
he has rendered to us by the discovery of this
Colony, and to provide for his comfortable retirement from public life."

It was a difficult and delicate task for any one
to undertake to oppose such a motion in favour
of such a man, and it was especially so for one of
the founders of the colony to take in hand, but Mr.
Angas always lost sight of circumstances and persons
when dealing with principles, and he moved the
following amendment : " That a respectful address
be presented to His Excellency the Governor requesting him to introduce a Bill into this House
for the purpose of granting an annuity for life to
the Honourable Captain Sturt, and that the proposed Bill have a clause inserted in it declaring that
it is not to be considered a precedent for retiring
pensions to official persons in South Australia."
The motion was carried by a majority of ten to
six ; the sum of £600 per annum was secured to
the gallant explorer, and the Legislature was safe-
guarded against the adoption of an established
system of pensions in the public service—a system
which was declared to be "servile in itself, and
calculated to induce imprudence."

There were many sanguine men in those days who
thought that the royal road to rapid prosperity was in
opening up lines of railway throughout the province ;
others advocated the adornment of the city as a
means of drawing capitalists to the colony and

giving prestige to it among the sister provinces.
To both schemes Mr. Angas was strongly opposed,
and he determined that so long as the public roads
were in the lamentable state in which he found
them he would continue his opposition. He considered that railways, as a general rule, were too
expensive for a country in its infancy; but means
of communication with the capital and with the
sea-board he saw to be absolutely necessary, and
good roads seemed to him to be the best way of
accomplishing the object.

A comprehensive and efficient system of road-
making throughout the colony was his policy from
the first, and for any such work his favourable vote
was certain—as certain as an adverse vote was for
any expensive work of mere ornament, or of doubtful
utility. "Open up the country by means of good
main lines of road and enable settlers to convey
their produce to market," was the constant burden
of his cry.

But his was only one voice; the large majority
were in favour of a general system of railways, the
first to be from the City to the Port. It was in
vain that he protested—he was in the unpopular
minority, and there he was to remain on many
questions involving large expenditure which, in
the then state of affairs, he did not consider the
colony was justified in contracting.

Two instances of his caution in dealing with
public moneys may be given. In 1852, the year

of the gold fever, Bills were brought in for raising loans of £60,000 for a railway from the City to the Port, and £40,000 for a tramway from Port Adelaide to Gawler Town. He opposed both on the ground of principle and of expediency. "If a contract were entered into by persons in England," he urged, " how could they prevent the workmen from leaving for the Victorian or other gold fields?" Nevertheless the Bill was passed, but it was found that the works could not be constructed in the then existing state of things, and from the causes predicted by Mr. Angas. Next year, owing to the unprecedented advance in the price of materials and labour, an increased sum was applied for. This he opposed, not only on the ground of extravagance, but that it would absorb all available labour at a time when it was difficult in the extreme to find artizans who could put up houses for new colonists. But the Bill passed. In 1855 a further sum of £10,000 was asked for, and again he set his face like a flint against the demand. The spirit of prophecy being upon him, he predicted that before the City and Port Railway was completed it would have cost £200,000; and as a matter of fact the total cost, including rolling stock, amounted to £206,105, or £21,695 per mile! It did not pay for years, and many had cause to regret that his warnings had been disregarded.

In like manner a projected railway to connect Port Elliot with the Goolwa was opposed on the ground that it was not a practical scheme, that it was too costly, and that it was uncalled for at that time. " I have no notion of patchwork," he said, " whether in an old country or a new one, and in a young colony like this, particularly in the present state of the revenue, such expenses should be especially censured."

This style did not suit the go-ahead colonists, and the scheme was persevered in. But it never paid interest on the outlay and working expenses.

Many people thought that the constant opposition of Mr. Angas to popular measures was the result of prejudice or pique. It was nothing of the kind. In the case in point he doubted the suitability of Port Elliot as a shipping place, and deprecated large expenditure until this was approximately assured. Only a few years elapsed before it was condemned as a seaport, and after thousands of pounds had been expended upon it in constructing a breakwater, making a jetty, and so forth, the whole thing was abandoned, and a fresh expenditure incurred to make Port Victor the shipping port of the Murray, by extending the tramway thither.

While consistently voting against expensive railways, he as consistently harped upon the question of public roads, as we have seen. The shafts of ridicule, the clamour of majorities, were nothing to him; he stuck to his point until he carried it, and when at last the Government undertook the construction and maintenance of a comprehensive

system of main lines of road, they found in him a
warm and influential supporter.

When almost everybody in the Legislature and
the colony was in favour of instituting in South
Australia a search for gold in order that good luck
might come to them as it had come to Victoria,
Mr. Angas sedulously opposed the voting of any
money for that purpose. He stated it as his belief
that no greater curse could befall South Australia
than the discovery of gold.

Away would go the high credit of the colonists as the growers of
corn for the other colonies; it would have the effect of throwing
land out of cultivation, and seriously damaging the agricultural
and pastoral interests. It was true that gold had raised the price
of lands and houses in Victoria, but it was well known that when
the value of property reached its natural summit a reaction would
follow before long, and such reaction would be serious and fatal.
There was not one single feature of what had happened in Victoria
that he would wish to see realised in South Australia. Its effects
had been demoralizing and destructive. He could not see any
prospect of the discovery of gold being a permanent aid to the
colony from either a social, commercial, or a religious point of
view. . . . For his own part he would rather give £5,000 (the
amount required for initiating the search for gold) out of his own
pocket that gold should *not* be discovered in the colony.

On the points we have cited, as on several others
to which we shall refer in the course of this narrative, the views of Mr. Angas were found in the
main to be the correct ones; and as human nature
is the same all the world over, it is not uncharitable

to say that this very fact added to his unpopularity. No set of men ever yet lived who liked to have the proof brought before them that they were in the wrong. It was not, however, so much in the matter as in the manner that fault was found with Mr. Angas. No one could gainsay his facts or his figures, but many took exception to the way in which he introduced them. There was often a dictatorial or lecturing tone in his speeches joined to a bearing of conscious superiority, and it militated against his personal, as well as his political, influence.

Forcible utterances were marred by such expressions as—"I am no novice in political economy or in colonization, and I make this statement as the result of my experience. If honourable members knew as much of colonization as I do, they would have expressed more liberal opinions than they have done." "I have spent the best years of my life in connection with the colony," he said on one occasion, "and I have never shrunk from the belief that it was and will be a model to the world and a great reward to those who assisted in its foundation."

Egotism was his besetting sin at this time, and it revealed itself in his parliamentary career more than in any other arena. But his errors, such as they were, all lay on the surface, and were of the head rather than of the heart, and we should not have dwelt upon them but for the reason that those who have followed the narrative thus far might wonder how it came to pass that the man who had exercised so powerful an influence over the colony in its earlier days did not occupy a wider sphere when he came personally in contact with its local Government.

It would be foreign to our purpose to enter largely into colonial politics, and we shall confine ourselves, therefore, to the mere mention of the subjects in which Mr. Angas took an active interest.

On the question of waste lands and pastoral leases, while disposed to afford every encouragement to those engaged in pastoral pursuits, he did not consider it conducive to the best interests of the colony to dispose of the Crown lands in fee simple at a very low price, as it was from the proceeds of this fund that emigration and road-making were to be carried on. He deprecated every attempt to reduce the price of Crown lands; at the same time he was strongly in favour of liberal concessions being made to squatters, believing them to be a most useful class of pioneers for opening up the country and preparing it for population, and he advocated offering them public lands at such a price as would enable them to hold them in perpetuity.

Any motion having for its object the supply of efficient labour he cordially supported, and lost no opportunity of censuring the Emigration Commissioners at home for the obstacles they threw in the way of desirable persons emigrating, and for the disproportionate number of unsuitable Irish female

emigrants sent out—notably between the years 1853
and 1855.

In November, 1855, he moved for a return of the
number and description of persons forwarded to the
colony, and urged that they should be proportionately
supplied from all parts of the United Kingdom.
But it was proverbial in those days that the Commissioners paid very little regard to remonstrances
from the colony, and Irish female immigrants continued to pour in. His action, however, was warmly
supported by the Council, and the motion for the
returns was carried unanimously. The evil com-
plained of had assumed a serious aspect, and
threatened to demoralize and pauperize the community.

Not long after, upwards of 3,000 single female
immigrants were landed, and information was
received that more were on the way. A Select
Committee, on which Mr. Angas acted vigorously,
was appointed to deal with the matter. It was a
singular fact that while there were hundreds of
women out of employment, there was the greatest
difficulty in obtaining a really good domestic servant.

Ultimately an agent, with a salary of £500, was
specially employed by the Colonial Legislature to
assist the Commissioners in the selection of suitable
emigrants.

The Report of the Select Committee on Excessive
Female Immigration was interesting and suggestive.
The total excess of females over males in 1853 was

679; in 1854, 1,604; in 1855, 2,829. Of the 4,049 adult single females arriving in 1855, 851 were English, 217 were Scotch, and 2,981 were Irish!

In his private journal Mr. Angas was wont to record his line of action, and his votes on questions of special interest. Thus, under date of September 19, 1853, he writes :—

I tried to throw out of the new Parliament the Compulsory Oaths Bill, except for Quakers and others named in the English Act, and stated a case at Honduras where Baptists refused to take oaths, but were ready to make affirmations, yet were cast into prison for six months. The case was sent to me in London, and by an application to the· Secretary of State, Sir George Grey, we got them released and compensated for damages. I did not carry my point in our Council at Adelaide, but I got the consent of Government to bring in a Bill expressly to abolish compulsory oaths, and leave it optional for any one to take an oath or make an affidavit at his selection. If I can carry such a Bill it will be a great protection to the liberties of people who have tender consciences.

It will be remembered that in the Constitution Act, which came into force in 1851, power was given to amend that Act according to the needs of the colony, and the South Australians were not slow to avail themselves of their privilege. As early as 1852 several sweeping amendments of the Constitution were proposed, and, as it seemed to Mr. Angas possible that they might be carried upon a bare majority, he submitted a resolution " that no fundamental change be made in the present Constitution of South Australia unless it be first recommended

by at least two-thirds of the members of the Legislative Council." After considerable discussion the
motion was withdrawn, but subsequently the principle it embodied was introduced into the Amended
Constitution.

A year later the Government brought forward a
Bill for constituting a Parliament for South Australia,
and also a Bill for providing a Civil List for Her
Majesty in consideration of the Crown surrendering
all control over the Land Fund. The former Bill
provided for an Elective House of Assembly and a
Legislative Council, the members of which were to
be nominated by the Crown. In introducing these
measures the Government gave the Council to
understand that the Land Fund would only be
surrendered upon the condition of a nominated
Upper Chamber. Several members of the Council
were strongly in favour of this Chamber being
elected by the people, and were willing to accept a
compromise rather than forfeit the control of the
Land Fund, or endanger the granting of a Colonial
Parliament as threatened by the Government.

In the discussion that ensued Mr. Angas made a
very determined stand against a nominated Upper
Chamber, and stated that rather than agree to the
proposed plan he would much prefer the continuance
of the existing Council for several years, or until
the population of the colony reached 200,000 persons.
His contention was that the elective principle, in
however small a degree, should be applied to the

Upper House, and he considered, moreover, that it was "dangerous for a handful of people to adopt machinery suitable only for a great nation."

Session after session the great question of responsible government, with two Houses of Parliament, after the English model—the Governor representing the Throne, the Legislative Council the House of Lords, and the House of Assembly the House of Commons—was the main topic of discussion, Mr. Angas invariably voting with the Conservative minority, as against the Liberals who went in boldly for "manhood suffrage and vote by ballot," points which they succeeded in carrying.

In due course the Bill passed into law, and early in 1857 extensive preparations were made for the election of members for the first "Parliament" of South Australia.

The Parliaments were to be triennial, with annual sessions, although in cases of emergency there might be more than one session in the year. Written nominations of candidates were to be substituted for nominations on the hustings, and candidates were not allowed to address the electors within twenty-four hours of the beginning of the election.

It was a busy time for Mr. Angas. Meetings of representatives were held in all parts of the country for the purpose of giving expression to their political sentiments up to the time of the issue of the writs for the several divisions and districts, after which the Act prohibited any further meetings.

It was also a time of considerable anxiety to him. The very name of the " ballot " and " universal suffrage," about to be put into practice for the first time in the province, carried with it ideas of democracy, republicanism, and anarchy.

Nothing but a strong sense of duty sustained him in the conflict, and even this failed him when, being pledged too far to retreat, he wrote in his diary :—

> After all I have seen of legislative and civil government I am come to this conclusion, that the one sure way to moralize the people and to civilize them is to preach the gospel to them in simplicity and fidelity, and that my time and means would be better spent in promoting that object than in attending the Legislative Council, or in any civil duty of a public kind.

The 9th of March was the day fixed for the elections, and a public holiday was given. To fill the 54 seats in the two Houses—namely, 18 in the Legislative Council and 36 in the House of Assembly —there were 27 candidates for the former and 62 for the latter, making a total of 89. Contrary to expectation, everything passed off quietly, not to say tamely. Mr. Angas was elected a member of the Legislative Council by 2,316 votes. By direction of Her Majesty the members of the Legislative Council and the Speaker of the House of Assembly were to have the title of "Honourable" conferred upon them, and were to be officially addressed as such while occupying seats in the said Council, and the Speaker while holding office in such capacity. The members of the Executive Council, or of the

Ministry, were also to enjoy a similar privilege or honour.*

The order observed with respect to the introduction and passing of Bills through Parliament was to be the same as that which prevails in the Imperial Legislature.

On the 22nd of April the new Parliament met, and the Hon. George Fife Angas took his seat. But the proceedings of the South Australian Parliament will not be found of thrilling interest to the general reader. The questions that came before it were of local, rather than of universal bearing. When once the great ecclesiastical question was settled, it did not trouble the Legislature again ; there were no foreign relations to intrude into the politics of the colony, and there was very little party spirit. "Measures, not men," was the order of the day, and whenever any one had influence enough to get a majority to join him on any popular question, he would at once move a vote of want of confidence in the Ministry in order that he might be sent for to form a new administration. So it came to pass that the Ministry was constantly changing, no Government remaining in office for more than eighteen months or two years, and many not anything like that time.

After the South Australian Parliament had been in existence some three or four years, the London

* The Governor in addressing the two Houses would say "Honourable Gentlemen, and Gentlemen."

Times made the following remarks with reference to the new form of Government:—

It must be confessed that it is rather an odd position for a new community of rising tradesmen, farmers, cattle-breeders, builders, mechanics, with a sprinkling of doctors and attorneys, to find that it is suddenly called upon to find Prime Ministers, Cabinets, a Ministerial side, an Opposition side, and all the apparatus of a Parliamentary Government—to awake one fine morning and discover that this is no longer a colony but a nation, saddled with all the rules and traditions of the political life of the mother-country.

Saddled with cumbersome and costly Government machinery the colony certainly was, and was subject to abuses to a great extent unavoidable. The power of governing was placed, by universal suffrage, in the hands of those who not only possessed the smallest stake in the colony, but were the least intelligent. It is amusing to remember that while the Constitution Act was under consideration, Mr. Angas and a few others endeavoured hard to establish an educational test, at least to the extent of reading and writing, as some guarantee of fitness for the exercise of the franchise, but even this was overruled by the democratic element in the Council as constituted at that time.

An early and important matter to be decided by the new Legislative Council was the order in which one-third of the Council was to retire at the end of every four years according to the provisions of the Act. This was decided by lot, the clerks of the

House drawing cards numbered from one to eighteen. The result was that six men were to retire in four years, other six at the end of eight years, and a further six at the end of twelve years. It fell to the lot of Mr. Angas to retire at the expiration of eight years.

It would be amusing, but irrelevant, to describe in detail many curious episodes in relation to this first and short Session of Parliament, during which the Ministry was changed four times. "Mr. Angas," to quote from a local paper, "took an active part in the proceedings of the Council, where his speeches were marked by a plain, business-like character, which, combined with clearness of statement, gave them considerable weight."

It was a memorable year—in many respects the most eventful in the history of the colony. Moreover, it was the year when the colony arrived at its maturity, and it was considered not a little remarkable that while in its twenty-first year it should have been entrusted with the entire management of its own affairs by the introduction of responsible government.

At the close of the Session Mr. Angas obtained twelve months' leave of absence, afterwards extended, in order to pay a visit to England, where certain matters in connection with his late father's estate demanded his attention.

CHAPTER XV.

ON the 19th of December, 1857, Mr. Angas, accompanied by his youngest son, set sail in the *Orient*
bound for the old country. Mrs. Angas was left
behind as a hostage ; had she gone too it is probable
that the colony would never have seen Mr.
Angas again, but, as it happened, she liked
the colony, had a horror of the sea-voyage, and
yet felt that the three-fold claims of health, business, and pleasure were sufficient to warrant the
temporary separation.

Prior to leaving, a public breakfast for the purpose
of saying farewell was given in Adelaide, at which
two hundred of the leading men of the colony were
present, including nearly all the members of the

Legislature and of the Ministry. The Governor,
Sir R. G. MacDonnell, a man of great ability and
energy of character, which, added to a pleasant
and genial manner, made him one of the most
popular governors the colony had ever known, was
not able to be present, but he wrote to Mr. Angas,
and in the course of his letter said :—

I take this opportunity of wishing you all manner of happiness
in your intended voyage; and for the sake of the colony a safe, if
not a speedy, return to South Australia of one so honoured here,
and who has been so eminently useful to his adopted—or rather I
might almost say created—land; for in a certain sense they who
planned the colony must be regarded as having, to all intents and
purposes, created the land by rendering it available for human
residence and civilization. These are amongst the truly great
achievements which do honour to our race, and Bacon was right
when he spoke of planting colonies as a ' heroic work.'

On all hands hearty congratulations were given
him on the realization of his life-long dream—the
prosperity of the colony—and it was no little
gratification to receive the assurance of all who
were at the public breakfast, that but for his aid
it was probable that South Australia would never
have been anything more than a dream.

A safe and prosperous voyage brought the travellers
to Plymouth by the end of March, and they proceeded at once to London. Mr. Angas was a man
of many friends, and everywhere his reception was
cordial in the extreme. In those days, when the
Australian Colonies were young, every successful

man who returned was "lionised," for in all grades
of society there were some who had sons, brothers,
cousins, friends, or neighbours who had been borne
on the great tidal wave of emigration to that far-
off land, and from the peculiar relation in which
he stood to South Australia, advice and information
were sought from all quarters.

Soon after his arrival the annual meeting of the
London Sunday School Union was held at Exeter
Hall, and it was meet that the President of the
South Australian Sunday School Union should be
the guest of the evening. He was able to tell them
that there were from 120 to 130 schools in the
colony, the diffused population of which did not
exceed 112,000. In Adelaide alone there was a
staff of 150 teachers. He brought out a curious
phase of the times by saying that although England
drafted out a supply of good and efficient men, she
had also burdened the colony with a terrible proportion of uneducated men, and that of 800 sent out
in the course of one month at the expense of the
Emigration Fund, 500 were unable either to read
or to write. This necessitated night schools for
men, and these were being successfully carried on
in many places.

Pleasurable as it was to meet old friends, relatives, and acquaintances in London, it was still
more so to tarry amongst them in his native town
of Newcastle-on-Tyne, to visit the spots familiar
from childhood, to pick up dropped threads of

memory in the scenes of his old labours, and to renew friendships, many of which were begun when the century was in its infancy.

A public soirée, organized by the friends of Sunday Schools, was held in his honour soon after his arrival in the town, and a few days later a public presentation was made to him of a handsome silver salver, together with an address and a present for Mrs. Angas.

. The visit of Mr. Angas to Newcastle will long be remembered for the extraordinary liberality of his gifts to the religious and benevolent institutions of the town, especially to the Baptist Chapels, the Sunday School Union (of which up to the year 1858 he remained the President), the Sailors' Institute, and other societies.

Sadness mingled with the pleasure in many ways, as it almost always does. His elder brother Joseph lay at death's door, and in a letter home Mr. Angas wrote :—

Newcastle, *Oct.* 25, 1858.

Yesterday afternoon I spent an hour and a half with brother Joseph in conversation, prayer, and reading special parts of the Scripture. It was a very interesting season, for the Lord's presence was with us. It was a season of joy and consolation, of gratitude to God, and rejoicing rather than of sorrow. Brother Joseph's state of mind was very happy, full of faith and hope.

A few days later he passed calmly away at the age of seventy-eight.

One of the best colonial correspondents of Mr.
Angas during his visit to England was Sir R. G.
MacDonnell, the Governor.

The position of Mr. Angas brought him much
into contact with the various governors of the
colony, who were wont in many cases to consult
him on a variety of general colonial matters, upon
which his knowledge was most extensive. Acts of
the British Parliament relating to the colonies he
had at his fingers' ends, and his memory was so
singularly keen on these particular subjects, that
at a moment's notice he could recall precedents,
or refer to episodes in colonial history which would
elucidate the case in point. In like manner Mr.
Angas used often, when public affairs were not
taking a course which appeared to him desirable,
to give his voluntary opinion with great frankness
and explicitness to the governors—not always, it
must be confessed, to meet adoption, although
always to be received with an ample acknowledgment
of the sincerity prompting them. Large packets of
such letters lie before the present writer, but their
interest, even to the oldest colonists, has now passed
away.

While in England Mr. Angas looked out for
colonial letters with the same eagerness he had
awaited English correspondence in South Australia.
The following extract from a letter of Sir R. G.
MacDonnell's relates to an important episode in
colonial history :—

NEPEAN BAY, KANGAROO ISLAND, *Feb.* 17, 1859.

I am just returned from a very rapid and successful exploring expedition up the Darling in Cadell's steamer the *Albury.* I regard all these expeditions as an extension of this colony's commercial boundary, which, after all, is its real boundary for many important purposes. It will interest you to learn that I only left Adelaide on the 23rd ult. (January), and having embarked at Blanche Town on board of the *Albury* after a ride of seventy miles (*viâ* Angaston) from Gawler through a fierce hot wind, I reached the Junction on the 26th, and slept on Mount Murchison, 290 miles by land, and 600 by water from the Junction, on the 5th instant, whilst I now write to you from Kangaroo Island on the 17th, having between the 23rd ult. and this morning steamed on Australian rivers nearly 2,400 miles, and ridden about 200.

I have just been telling Sturt how smoothly I have been gliding through scenes of his hardships and disasters. We are certainly progressing, as you may judge when I tell you that an order dated from Sydney of the 23rd of January to deliver four tons of goods at a station 400 miles up the Darling, was executed on the 3rd of February—only eleven days after the order was given at Sydney. . . .

In another letter Sir R. G. MacDonnell alluded to a branch of industry which has ever since been making rapid strides, and at the present time threatens to revolutionize the great continental trade of wine producing. He says :—

I have lately been going through the dozen duplicate samples of wine which you sent me from Tanunda, and at least eight of them are excellent. I have been quite surprised at their quality, but I have no doubt this country will be a good wine-producing country ; people are setting to work energetically planting vines in all directions, and in four years I have no doubt we shall obtain a tolerable footing in the English market.*

---

* The first vineyards were planted in Australia about fifty years ago,.

After an absence of nearly two years, much of which he spent with his daughter, Mrs. William Johnson, Mr. Angas reached Port Adelaide on the 23rd of September, 1859. Although a telegram saying he would arrive at Angaston at noon only reached that place at nine the same morning, a well-arranged and genuinely hearty reception awaited him. Some hundreds of people assembled and grouped themselves under the splendid trees which are picturesquely scattered throughout the pretty township, about fifty horsemen formed in procession, and spring carts and waggons brought up the rear. An address congratulating him on his safe return was presented, and great cheering took place when, having accompanied him to the gates of Lindsay Park, he drove away, through a triumphal arch of green boughs, flowers, and ribbons, to his long vacated home.

During his absence nothing more important in the interests of South Australia and the colonies generally had transpired than the passing of the Real Property Act. It was devised by Mr. (afterwards Sir) R. R. Torrens with the object of facilitating the transfer of property by superseding

but no trade of any importance was done with England until 1871. The colonists are now so alive to the importance of the wine industry, that the area in cultivation is being extended year by year in every direction in each of the three colonies. The wines produced are chiefly of the claret and Burgundy type, and are of excellent quality. The imports of Messrs. P. B. Burgoyne and Co. in the five months ended the 31st of May, 1890, amounted to 123,658 gallons, or 79 per cent. of all the Australian wines brought into this country, and nearly double the total imports during the year 1885.

the tedious and red-tape procedure under the old law of England hitherto adopted in the colony.

His design was not only to dispense with transferring real estate in the first instance by deed, but also in every subsequent transaction when a deed—a tiresome and long-winded document setting forth all the deeds that had ever gone before—would have been considered necessary.

" The first great principle of the Act," says Mr. Harcus,* " is the transferring of real property by registration of title instead of by deeds; the second is absolute indefeasibility of title. The system is very simple and very inexpensive. The certificate of title is registered in the official registry at the Lands' Titles Office, the owner obtaining a duplicate certificate. All transactions under the land appear on the face of the certificate, so that at a glance it may be seen whether the property is encumbered or any charges are made upon it. If an owner wishes to mortgage his land, he takes his certificate to the office and has the transaction marked upon it. If he wants to sell he passes over the certificate to the purchaser, and the transaction is registered. Any man of ordinary intelligence can do all that is necessary for himself when once his property is brought under the Act." . . .

The Bill passed the Council, was assented to by the Governor, and became law on the 27th of January, 1858. It has been amended in some of its

* " South Australia." By William Harcus, Esq., J.P.

details more than once, but its main principles remain intact. The Act has been of immense and far-reaching importance; it has been adopted in nearly all the Australian Colonies, has been copied in Prussia, and its principles are advocated by many leading men in England.

After his visit to the old country, Mr. Angas threw himself into colonial affairs with renewed vigour, and with a zeal surprising even to those who knew how hard he could work. In addition to a great accumulation of matters requiring his attention after his long absence, there was a mass of English correspondence rendered necessary by the renewal of intercourse with old friends. "I think grandpapa must have written to everybody in England," said his grandson James, "his table is all covered over with letters. I don't know how the Angaston mail would pay if the Angas family were to remove."

Much of his work was done under disadvantagous circumstances, as the heat was exceptionally severe. On one day in January (1860) the thermometer stood at 158° in the sun. Great damage was done to the gardens and vineyards, quantities of fruit having been literally roasted upon the trees and vines, and birds were reported to have taken refuge in the houses of settlers.

Into his parliamentary duties Mr. Angas entered with fresh enthusiasm, and was soon actively engaged on the Select Committee—previously referred

to in these pages—to inquire into the condition of
the natives, and to ascertain the revenue at the
disposal of the Government on their behalf, and
the manner in which it was expended. His first
words at the first sitting gave an indication of the
manner in which his share in the inquiry would be
conducted. " I know of no subject in the whole
course of the history of the colony," he said, " that
has been so shamefully shirked as the welfare of the
aborigines."

A glance at some of his labours in Parliament
during this year is given in the following extract
from his journal :—

Oct. 23, 1860.—The Session has lasted five months, and has done
more good than any previous one, although I have had my hands
full in resisting the ultra spirit of Chartism. The Upper House has
stood its ground well ; it is the safety valve of the South Australian
Constitution. I think I have laid the foundation for stopping the
Sunday trains running. I discovered that they did not pay, and
moved for a return, when I stated that Sunday traffic was a loss
to the State of £500 per year. The return proves it to be £1,000
per year, and the Chief Secretary told me that he thought the
Government would at once put a stop to the evil.

The new Government, a majority of whom are Dissenters, have
effected a saving of £20,000 per annum in the revenues.

Altogether it was a remarkable year in the history
of the colony. Towards its close some valuable
mineral discoveries were made in Yorke's Peninsula,
and it was rumoured that the famous Burra-Burra
copper mine was altogether thrown into the shade
by the Wallaroo mines accidentally discovered by a

shepherd. Claims were at once lodged for leases
of the districts supposed to contain mineral deposits ;
a further impulse was given by the discovery of
the Moonta mines, only ten miles south of Wallaroo ;
further successful discoveries followed, and on
Yorke's Peninsula, hitherto occupied only as sheep
runs, 'a series of popular townships arose, and the
whole tract of country gave promise of becoming the
most extensive mining district in the colony.

One of the most fruitful sources of interest to
early Australian colonists was to follow the movements of explorers who from time to time penetrated
into unknown regions of the vast continent, and
came back with their "grapes of Eshcol" in the
shape of voluminous newspaper reports. No
country in the world has a finer record of heroism
in the field of exploration than Australia, on whose
bead-roll of martyrs in the cause of science are
inscribed the names of men who are held in universal
esteem. That was a memorable day in the annals
of Adelaide when, in December, 1862, a mournful
procession passed through its streets, bearing the
remains of the noble explorers, Burke and Wills, on
their way to Melbourne for interment, followed by
Mr. Howitt, who, too late to render efficient aid,
had gone out to their rescue.

Only a few days later and the sorrow of the
citizens was turned into joy, the gratifying intelligence having reached them that their own explorer,
John McDouall Stuart, and his party had returned

to settled districts after successfully crossing and
re-crossing the vast continent. What followed
almost immediately is told in a letter written by
Mr. Angas :—

ADELAIDE, *Jan.* 25, 1863.

To-day there is to be a great procession through Adelaide in
honour of Mr. Stuart, who has returned with *all* his people after
crossing the continent from this city to the Indian Ocean and
back again all by land, and in the evening there is to be a great
banquet given him at Adelaide, neither of which do I purpose
attending. Stuart gains the prize of £2,000 for his exploit, and
has all his expenses paid. Our people and Government are vastly
elated with this exploit. In point of geographical discovery it has
quieted the dispute about the heart of New Holland being an inland
sea, which it is not, but there are many large lakes of salt and fresh
water, as in Scotland and Ireland. I do not think the discovery
will benefit *South* Australia, and I complain that our small colony
should have to bear the lion's share of geographical discoveries for
the *world's* benefit.

A reward was, however, in store for the colony—
but it was a doubtful one. In consideration of the
fact that South Australia had made this important
discovery an application was made to the Home
Government to place the new territory, within certain
limits, under the management and control of the
South Australian Government, and in July, 1863, a
dispatch was received from the Duke of Newcastle,
Secretary of State for the Colonies, acquiescing in
this arrangement and making over to them the
whole of the Northern Territory, or Alexandra
Land—an immense tract of country containing an
area of 531,402 square miles, or 340,097,280 acres !

From the first Mr. Angas considered that it was an unwise thing for the colony, already possessing ample territory, and with a limited population, to be saddled with the responsibility of such an enormous appanage, and he opposed the addition tooth and nail. But he was, as usual, in a minority almost of one, and the land was ceded. When a Bill for colonizing the Northern Territory was brought into Parliament he totally disapproved of the scheme and consistently denounced it, on the ground that it was far beyond the capability of the colony at that time to manage successfully, and that settling the land without making provision for the introduction of labour would not lead to the true settlement of the country. He submitted a scheme to the effect that, instead of planting a colony there, large inducements should be offered to squatters to take up the land, and that a company should be formed and encouraged to attempt the growth of tropical products. Many who wrote and spoke disparagingly of his views at the time, afterwards acknowledged that they greatly erred in disregarding his wisdom and foresight.

Many disasters attended the first attempts to settle the Northern Territory, mismanagement and failure followed, and up to the time of his decease, although acknowledging that it was a rich country with almost unlimited resources, and would assuredly some day recoup the enormous cost it had been to the colony, he saw no reason to alter the opinion he had first formed as to the unwisdom of attaching it to South Australia.

The land sales took place in Adelaide in 1864, before the surveys had commenced, and an expedition set forth to "settle the territory" almost at once. Mr. Angas alludes to his part in the matter in the following extract from a letter to one of his daughters :—

> LINDSAY HOUSE, *April* 25, 1864.
>
> The great expedition to North Australia has sailed, fitted out by our Government, and commanded by Colonel Finniss, my old opponent who sat on the same benches that I did for so many years of our first Parliament. But we were always good friends, and now part good friends. I wrote a farewell letter to him, and begged his services to patronise £50 worth of books that I sent on board for the use of the people, which he acknowledged publicly, and promised his patronage to the deputation of the Bible Society who visited him on board his ship just when he was about to sail with the expedition.
>
> It will require wise and experienced legislators to make laws and regulations for that distant land. I pray God to furnish such in our Parliament. South Australia is the largest colony in Australia by far, since that new country has been given to us by the Queen. It extends from sea to sea—from Adelaide to the Indian Ocean.

Incidentally it may be mentioned here that almost immediately after Stuart's return from crossing the continent, Mr. Charles Todd, Superintendent of Telegraphs for South Australia, conceived the idea of constructing a line of telegraph—2,000 miles in length — through the tracts of country hitherto

supposed to be impassable desert, to the northern
coast, and so . open up and utilize the newly-dis-
covered country.

The project was warmly supported by Sir James
Fergusson, the Governor, and the Hon. H. B. T.
Strangways, the Premier, and under the personal
superintendence of Mr. Todd, despite many difficulties
and thrilling dangers it was eventually brought
to a successful completion, and in 1872 communication was established between Adelaide and Port
Darwin — between Australia and all parts of the
world. "Within six months after opening the line
the colony netted nearly a quarter of a million
sterling extra on their wheat harvest through the
telegraph enabling sales to be made in foreign
markets."

At the period of which we write there were two
great subjects of interest in Adelaide, the Northern
Territory and the case of Mr. Justice Boothby.
We have seen Mr. Angas in the minority on the
former matter, we shall see him in a similar position
with regard to the latter.

The case, which dragged its weary length along
for the space of many years, was briefly this :
Mr. Justice Boothby having expressed his doubts
as to the validity of certain Acts passed by the
Colonial Legislature, on the ground of their repugnance to the laws of England, rendered himself
obnoxious to the Parliament, the press, and the
public, and this was greatly increased when he went

so far as to absolutely decide in the Supreme Court
against the validity of the Real Property Act and
other Acts which had not then received the Royal
assent. A motion for the appointment of a Select
Committee " to examine into the recent decisions
and conduct of His Honour, Mr. Justice Boothby,
and to report thereon," was opposed by Mr. Angas
on the ground that the whole matter turned upon
hearsay and newspaper reports. But the motion was
carried, and Mr. Angas was one of those chosen to
act upon the Committee.

Before this tribunal Mr. Boothby declined to
appear, and this fact, perchance, added to the bitterness of the report of the Committee—a report from
which Mr. Angas very strongly dissented on the
ground that the evidence adduced distinctly proved
that the colonial judges had power to declare illegal
and invalid Acts which had been passed by the
Legislature of the colony, assented to by the
Governor, and left to their operation by Her Majesty,
which was borne out by various decisions of the
Courts of Law in other colonies and in England,
and was consistent with the recognized and admitted
principles of constitutional law. On this and on
many other grounds he stood out in defence of Mr.
Justice Boothby, and a storm arose. So great was
the outcry that meetings were held in various parts
of the colony for the purpose of hearing the respective members give an account of the action each had
taken in the matter.

By and by a petition was sent to the Queen
praying her to remove Mr. Justice Boothby from
the Bench, but it failed of its object, as Mr. Angas
had predicted, and instead of the judge being repri-
manded, as some confidently anticipated, the
Colonial Legislature received a severe censure from
the Home Government.

Not satisfied with this, a second address to the
Crown was forwarded in 1866, to which the Secretary
of State for the Colonies replied that the *ex parte*
statements against the judge were insufficient
grounds for his removal, and that unless the colony
would agree to have the question argued before the
Judicial Committee of the Privy Council, the Local
Government must deal with the case themselves.

This they resolved to do, and in June, 1867, a
series of charges were preferred against Mr. Boothby,
who simply protested, but took no steps to defend
himself.

The specific charges laid at his door were presented to Parliament in the following resolutions :
" (1) That he persistently refuses to administer laws
duly enacted by the Parliament of South Australia.
(2) That he declines to give effect to the Imperial
Statute known as the Validating Act.   (3) That he
is accustomed from the Bench to impugn the
validity of the local Court of Appeals.   (4) That he
refuses to conform his judgment to the decision of
the Supreme Court.   (5) That he obstructs the
course of justice by perversity and an habitual dis-

regard of judicial propriety. (6) That he has
delivered judgments and dicta not in accordance
with law."

The matter was ably and lengthily debated in the
Legislative Council, but on the motion for the removal
of Mr. Boothby, Mr. Angas seconded an amendment
for inquiry and report by a Select Committee, which
was lost. In his speech he pleaded for justice and
impartiality, for calm and dispassionate inquiry,
instead of "presenting to Her Majesty's Privy
Council mere declarations sought to be proved by
newspaper reports, and even by the reports of the
very men who made the allegations."

The Government carried their point, but it was
afterwards generally admitted that it would have
been better in every respect to have acted on the
representations of Mr. Angas and the few others who
held the same views.

The whole case was difficult and delicate throughout, and was dealt with in a manner which did not
reflect great credit upon the chief actors in it, and
brought upon them the severe censure of the Imperial
Government.

The Colonial Parliament took upon itself the grave
responsibility of removing Mr. Boothby from office,
and he at once declared his intention to appeal to
the Judicial Committee of the Privy Council, but
illness, brought on by ceaseless vexation and anxiety,
supervened, and on June 21, 1868, his death terminated the controversy.

It will be remembered that one of the first duties
of the first Parliament of South Australia was to
decide by lot the order of retirement of its members.
It fell to Mr. Angas to retire in 1865, but there were
matters pending in the Legislative Council in which
he wished to have a voice—notably the questions
we have just been examining—and being returned
by a large majority he again took his seat. But
in the following year the state of his health
preventing him from giving that attention to his
duties he could wish, he tendered his resignation.

You will be surprised (he wrote to one of his daughters) when
I tell you that yesterday I resigned my seat in the Legislative
Council of South Australia, having served the colony as an M.P.
for sixteen years continuously. My eyes, throat, and memory
have become too weak with labour and old age to enable me to
discharge the duties of an M.P. to the satisfaction of my own
mind.

Special reference was made in the House to the
loss the colony would sustain by his retirement, and
men of all shades of opinion in politics expressed
their regret.

Mr. Baker, one of the most influential members,
said, " In consequence of his early connection with
the colony, his position in society, his experience,
his knowledge of mercantile affairs, and everything
connected with colonization, Mr. Angas was eminently entitled to their gratitude."

Men who differed from him on many points

joined in expressing the opinion that no other man
had done so much to advance the interests of the
colony.

Said Captain C. H. Bagot, an old antagonist, " I
always regarded him as a deep-thinking, clever man,
who never hesitated to declare what he thought was
the right view, and was never overawed by popular
clamour. This no doubt brought a good deal of
obloquy upon him, but his conduct was always
upright and consistent, and it was a matter of
great regret that they had lost his services."

The verdict of the press coincided with that of
the Parliament. "Although Mr. Angas," said the
leading journal of the colony, " was not what is
known as a popular politician, he nevertheless won
general esteem by the independence, integrity, and
painstaking industry with which his duties as a
member were discharged."

This was fair and manly criticism. He possessed
just those qualities which make unpopular politicians.
He would not be swayed by majorities, and he would
act from principle, and not for party.

During the whole of the sixteen years of his
parliamentary career he stood out consistently as
the representative of the Germans, presenting their
petitions, and looking after their interests generally.

State encouragement to the turf, it is needless to
say, met with his consistent and persistent opposition, and from time to time he found himself voting
with a minority on this subject.

The question of legalizing marriage with a deceased wife's sister cropped up on many occasions, and his testimony was always to this effect—"he failed to find in either the Old or the New Testament any injunctions of a contrary nature; he was of opinion that the Word of God did not censure the marriage of a man with his deceased wife's sister, and he felt it his duty to support the Bill in favour of it."

"I may truly say," wrote Sir Samuel Davenport many years later to Mr. J. H. Angas, "that no member of the Legislative Council felt greater interest in its proceedings, nor evinced more ardour in his desire to lay broad and sound the laws for effecting the healthy development of the colony and the common prosperity of all classes of its people than he did. In his statesmanlike view the prosperity of each individual and of each industrial class was the most logical aim and the surest path to the attainment of the greatest good of all. To a heart full of sympathy with the best interests of the colony, he further elevated the character of a Legislator by his long and extensive business experience, his high moral tone, and the consequent wisdom and prudence of his counsels. It is, however, as being specially prominent amongst the Fathers and Founders of the colony that his name will lastingly claim the grateful recognition of all who have or may benefit by being colonists."

CHAPTER XVI.

ONE of the chief pleasures of Mr. Angas throughout
the whole of his colonial life was to foster the good
works he had initiated while in the old country, to
watch the birth and development of new enterprises
for the moral and spiritual good of the colony, and
to lend a helping hand in every department of
philanthropic work. His ample fortune enabled
him to contribute largely to the funds of such
institutions, and it is no exaggeration to say that
all the churches of the colony were indebted to his
liberality, as unobtrusive as it was unsectarian, and
that every educational movement found in him a
friend and supporter.

For the erection of places of worship, liquidation
of debts upon them, maintenance of ministers, and
such like, his time and purse were always available.
He became the treasurer of the South Australian

High School; to St. Peter's Collegiate School, and,
at a later period, to Prince Alfred's Wesleyan College
he contributed largely. He provided the greater
part of the funds required for the foundation of two
large day schools, situate at Norwood and Bowden,
accessible to those who could not send their children
to other schools, the fees ranging from threepence to
sixpence per week. Many thousands of pounds were
contributed by Mr. Angas to these schools, and he
also gave liberally to two or three free schools for
the education of children of persons in necessitous
circumstances.

As an old Sunday-school teacher, and the founder
of the Newcastle-on-Tyne Sunday School Union, he
took a special interest in the religious instruction of
the young, and bore a large share in the expense of
publishing a magazine for Sunday-school teachers,
and in establishing libraries for Sunday Schools.

So also in regard to benevolent institutions. The
City and Bush Missions, the Aborigines' Friend
Society, the Female Refuge and Female Reforma-
tory, the Total Abstinence Society, Local Bible
and Tract Societies, Scripture Readers, Sailors'
Home and Bushmen's Home, the Domestic Mission
—the agents of which are known in England as
" Bible Women "—all found his help and sympathy
invaluable.

In his journals and letters there are innumerable
records, of which the following may be taken as
random specimens :—

I have formed a library at the gaol in Adelaide, and at the prison at the Dry Creek nine miles off, which I hope, under God's blessing, will do good even in such a barren soil.

The letter from the Rev. J. de Liefde was most refreshing to one's heart in these days of lukewarmness. Many thanks for sending it to us. The best evidence of the interest I feel in the labours of that excellent man and his coadjutors is my request to your dear husband to send him one hundred pounds as a contribution from me to the purposes of his Mission.

With the aid of one or two friends I am trying to pay for the foundation of a Baptist Theological College in this colony. I often feel that I fail in nervous energy to carry into operation the plans of my own mind and heart.

A movement was set on foot in 1856 to supply to some extent the want of religious services to the scattered inhabitants of the remote country districts by means of an association called the " South Australian Bush Mission." Contributions were raised, and the services of two agents were engaged to travel from station to station to deliver tracts, and conduct religious services wherever and whenever practicable.

In founding and sustaining this Mission, which did most excellent work, both Mr. Angas and his son took an active part. But their services were still more valuable in connection with one of the most interesting and deservedly popular institutions in South Australia—the Bushmen's Club, which owes its origin to the forethought and assistance of Mr. John Howard Angas.

It came about on this wise:—William M. Hugo, a relative of the celebrated Victor Hugo, was for many years a Bush Missionary, of whom nothing was known save that he was engaged in Evangelical work, travelling from station to station all over the Australian colonies, depending for food entirely upon the hospitality of those he visited, declining all pecuniary aid, and doing many kindly acts of charity for the lonely shepherds with whom he came in contact.   He called himself ' William,' and was known by no other name.   In 1866, while in South Australia viewing with pain the debaucheries of bushmen when making their periodical visits to the city after shearing time, he conceived the idea of establishing a retreat for them similar to the Sailors' Homes.   He accordingly named his project to Mr. J. H. Angas, who put the matter before his father, representing that the habits of bushmen made them, like sailors, victims to every adventurer to prey upon their weaknesses.   Mr. Angas and several other friends took up the matter warmly, and became large contributors to a fund for establishing a Bushmen's Club.   A house in Whitmore Square, Adelaide, formerly occupied by Sir Charles Cooper, one of the early judges of the colony, was secured, together with the ample grounds, and on the 20th of May, 1870, the Bushmen's Home, with " William " as Honorary Superintendent, was formally opened by the Governor, Sir James Fergusson.   Since then the original premises have received extensive additions and alterations (Mr. Angas contributing £1,000 to the building fund), and the institution is one of the most popular in the city, and the first of its kind in the Southern Hemisphere.

South Australia has always stood in the forefront of every great patriotic movement, and when the disastrous cotton famine was devastating Lancashire, subscriptions for relief of the sufferers poured in from all quarters. Referring to this, Mr. Angas wrote to his old friend, Mr. Beddome :—

ADELAIDE, *Jan.* 25, 1863.

The committee for relief to Lancashire sufferers, of which I am chairman, have remitted nearly £3,000 to the Lord Mayor of London, and we are continuing our efforts. Do you remember the time when I produced before the Board of Trade in London samples of cotton wool grown at Honduras, and urged Government to allow us to send our wool at low duty, but they would not, and we gave it up ? Oh ! how I besought the secretary, Mr. Hay, by the consideration that the day might come when a dispute with the United States might stop the supply, but they would not do that small service ! I asked them to prevent the day of calamity which now has come with vengeance.

As old age drew on, Mr. Angas, in order to allow himself more time to devote to religious and benevolent objects, found it necessary to place a considerable part of his business in the hands of his land steward, Mr. William Clark, who had been a quarter of a century in his service, and about the same time he secured the valuable assistance of Mr. W. R. Lawson.

as private secretary, who aided him in the preparation of the " History of the Newcastle Sunday
School Union," to which reference has already been
made,* and other literary work. It was at this
period that many important benevolent and religious
movements still in existence were set on foot, and
one who knew Mr. Angas well was justified in
saying :—

"I never saw a man at his age do half so much
work, or so good either—politics, business, literary
and benevolent work, and English correspondence."

In course of time Mr. Lawson joined the literary
staff of an Adelaide newspaper, and the Rev.
H. Hussey, a man of considerable ability, untiring
energy, and deep piety, succeeded him, and for several
years was the secretary and *confidant* of Mr. Angas.
It is to the able notes of Mr. Hussey on many
of the matters recorded in these pages that we are
indebted for our information.

These were among the happiest years of the life
of Mr. Angas. In regard to his worldly affairs he
could say :—

It has pleased God to give me wealth in this colony of late years,
almost without seeking for it. The lands of most value now in my
possession were bought by others at my risk, but without my knowledge or consent. The recent estimation show them to be of double
the value of my capital in 1834, when I partially retired from
business, but more than half of this was sunk in founding this

---

* See p. 47.

colony. Thus the hand of God has been manifested in what He
gave me during my mercantile life, in what He distributed during
my labours in founding South Australia, and in what He provided
for me after I came here in 1850 in my sixtieth year. To God I
give glory for what He first gave, for what He took away from me,
and for what I now possess.

In the pauses of his parliamentary duties he
employed much of his time in becoming more
intimately acquainted with his tenant farmers and
their affairs. In 1864 he made a feast in each of
the different districts where his tenants dwelt, in
every instance giving the entertainment in some
marquee or public hall in preference to hotels.
At four dinners given respectively at Angaston,
Tanunda, nine miles distant, Truro, fifteen miles,
and Mount Pleasant, twenty miles, there were
present 72 English and 153 German tenants, and
99 invited guests—324 in all.

These social gatherings were very useful. Each
guest was introduced by name, and shook hands
with the host both on coming and going. Good
speeches—loyal, friendly, commercial, and embracing
topics of general interest, such as agriculture and
horticulture—were made by local magnates, inter-
spersed with vocal and instrumental music. All
the wines and provisions were colonial, mainly the
produce of the immediate locality. And, truly, better
fare could not have been desired. In describing the
family festivities of the previous Christmas, Mr.
Angas wrote :—

We had on the table, out of our own garden, four sorts of currants, white and red raspberries, ditto gooseberries, ripe apples, red and white strawberries, very fine cherries, black and red, and a noble supply of flowers.

Although life had its full share of pleasures for Mr. Angas it had also a large proportion of sorrow. He had troubles in his own family, and from the peculiarity of his nature he felt so sympathetically for others that their troubles became his own. He wrote on one occasion to his daughter Emma :—

You know, my dearest child, how intensely sensitive my mind is, and how I feel acutely that which would not move some people's feelings at all.

The full fountain of his affection overflowed to this daughter, who was his *confidante* in everything that related to his social, business, and religious life. Many times he poured out every feeling of heart and soul to her, knowing she would respond with direct, quick, and natural sympathy.

In condoling with her on the death of her husband he wrote a very tender letter, in the course of which he said :—

Jan. 22, 1861.—Your affectionate and deeply affecting letter arrived on the 12th. Oh, how often have you administered to my afflicted mind in times past ; how often have your letters and your society been a well-spring of comfort on my earthly pilgrimage ; how frequently have you drawn water out of the wells of salvation and offered it to my parched, impoverished lips ! And now, when you so much need sympathy and consolation in your deep, very deep affliction, I feel stupefied and incapable of showing any gratitude to you in return.

Nevertheless he did pour forth strong, loving, helpful words—too sacred and private to lay bare here.

Many events in life, which to most men would be taken as mere "tare and tret," came to him with all the keenness of two-edged swords. His extreme sensitiveness caused him to exaggerate to himself the passing woes and ills of life, and in his letters there are allusions to subjects which most men would have passed over with a sigh, but with him called forth "strong crying and groans." He had a peculiarly felicitous manner of expressing these troubles and anxieties. Thus :—

ADELAIDE, *March* 21, 1861.

I often think that the powers of darkness have been let loose upon me and my family circle to confound our thoughts, wishes, and desires, and to show us all how perfectly vain is the help of man. I am sure it is good for us, even now; it is certain to be so in relation to eternity. The Lord has prospered our worldly affairs, and to prevent our boats from upsetting and drowning us and our souls, He in mercy has cast into them the ballast of worldly sorrow and deep perplexities, so that we may ride out the storms of life in safety, and at last reach the Haven where the wicked cannot reach us to trouble, and where we shall be at rest.

A great and bitter sorrow came to him in the year 1867. One day in January Mrs. Angas was in her garden-chair giving instructions to the gardeners while a cold south wind was blowing, and on the following day she was confined to her room. Nothing serious was apprehended by her medical attendants, although it was impressed upon her own mind that her last illness had come. Next day the doctor told her that there was no hope of recovery. She received the intelligence with great composure, saying, "God's will is the best! I have known Him long enough to be able to trust Him now." And so it proved; she had no fear of death whatever.

"Once while I was sitting beside her," says Mrs. Hannay, one of her daughters, "and she appeared to be in a great deal of pain, she said to me, 'I can't think how people put off seeking for Christ; I do not know what I should do if I had to seek Him now; it is quite as much as I can do to bear this pain.'"

That night, when Mr. Angas, in great distress, was praying silently by her bedside, she said, earnestly, "Let me go, oh, let me go!" as if to imply that the prayers then ascending were hindering her departure to the better land and life. Shortly after, in quiet, peaceful sleep, she passed away, and on the following Sabbath evening she was interred in the beautiful spot near Lindsay House selected by Mr. Angas for a family vault.

Writing to his daughter in England he said :—

LINDSAY HOUSE, *Jan.* 25, 1867.

On the day when I received your very kind letter of the 23rd of November my heart was full of grief and desolation, for on

that morning, about 2 a.m., your beloved mother took her departure for a better world. She slept the sleep of death with the
composure of an infant when it goes to sleep upon its mother's
breast, without pain, or sighing, or groan—she literally 'languished
into life;' no muscle of the face changed; she looked more beautiful than for years past.

Lindsay House, *Feb.* 16, 1867.

Her remains lie in a vault placed on a little hill in a peaceful,
retired, beautiful valley, not far from this house. It forms one of
the sweetest evening walks for me to wander up to the spot,
where, in perfect solitude, I can both rejoice and weep at her
grave, and where also, when the Lord wills, I hope to be placed
alongside her.

Lindsay House, *Feb.* 19, 1867.

I have just had a walk round our beautiful garden here, abound-
ing in fruits and flowers of all kinds, and still kept in perfect order
as your beloved mother left it in my hands. The broad walks, so
well disposed along the terraces, are quite dry this evening, although
we have had a constant rain for twenty-four hours. But my heart
failed me when I thought I had no one to talk with me of its
beauties, so I betook myself to my library. Solitude out of doors
I cannot get on with, so I fly to my books.

Parted for a time from his wife, his hopes went
out to his daughter in England, and he urged her
to make a permanent home with him in Lindsay
House. "I have no terms," he said, "in which to
express to you my strong desire to have you with
me here." But this was not to be. There were
children to educate, her late husband's affairs to
manage, and many other matters to make this
impossible. But eventually the wish—so strong and
passionate—to see her and her children again was
realized, as we shall see in the next chapter.

CHAPTER XVII.

Lindsay Park—The Verandah—Writing to Old Friends—Outline of Daily
Occupations—A Welcome Visit—The Duke of Edinburgh—Spread
of Roman Catholicism—Sir Dominick Daly—A Prophecy—General
Election, 1870—Last Entry in Diary—Old Age Drawing On—Interest
in Public Movements—Proposed " History of South Australia "—
Serious Illness—Recovery.

THE whole of Lindsay Park was beautiful—gardens,
lawns, drives, and paddocks ; all were kept in perfect
order, and on every hand were evidences of taste
and culture. But there was one spot that had a
charm for Mr. Angas beyond any other in all
the world—the spacious verandah surrounding his
house. From it he could gaze on hills and undula-
tions, some covered with hanging woods of rich
dark foliage, others with dwarf trees of tender green ;
here and there smiling valleys richly cultivated ;
nearer at hand the brilliant colours of choice flower-
beds, backed by the graceful and varied foliage of his
own park.

" Sixteen years have I been here," he wrote in
1867, " and yet every day when I gaze upon the
scene it has an air of novelty. The landscape
never palls upon my eyes." Ten years later he was

able to say the same thing with even greater emphasis, for every year it increased in beauty.

In this verandah he was wont to walk at eventide, or sit and gaze in early morning, and visions of the past and the future would float before his mind's eye as he meditated, mourning the loss of the one with whom for so many years he had been united, or yearning for the re-union in the " Land o' the Leal." In reply to a letter of sympathy from his old legal friend, Mr. Richard Beddome, he said :—

Many thanks for the kind sympathy you express at the sore bereavement which, as the first emotions become softened down, I find what may be called the 'joy of grief,' in the full assurance that she is not lost, but only removed to another part of our Heavenly Father's house. Sometimes I almost think her within call. Certainly the world of spirits is more homely to me than ever before. It is as if she had taken a voyage back to our Father's land and native place, and there was expecting my return to join her in the society of beloved relatives. More than ever do I feel that this is not my rest, although surrounded by a lovely, ever lovely vision of beauty in scenery, with houses for myself and children to one's heart's content, having nothing more to be desired—still it is not my rest, and I look for a better land.

In a later letter he replied to a question of his friend who had asked him how, in his altered social life and in his retirement from Parliament, he was able to keep his active mind occupied. He furnished the following singularly graphic description :—

LINDSAY PARK, *Sept.* 20, 1867.

You ask me to inform you of my daily occupations and move-

ments. To begin with, the fact that on the 1st of May next, if
I live so long, I shall enter upon my eightieth year! This circumstance ought to, and it really does, control more or less every
day's arrangements.

I live alone in this comfortable habitation, with a man-servant
to attend my horses and carriages, and female servants to manage
the domestic affairs of the house. Out of doors I have two
gardeners and two farm servants, with their wives and families, in
nice stone cottages, not far distant from me, who attend to horses,
carriages, and one hundred and fifty to two hundred acres of land.
The garden consists of seven acres, so that we have everything
produced by ourselves—large supplies of poultry of all kinds, and,
in all, four cows and seventeen horses, young and old.

In the morning, this being winter, I rise at 7 a.m., and am
ready at 8 a.m. to be called to breakfast. After that is over all
the servants come in and we have family worship, which reaches
to 9 a.m. Then I walk on the verandah until my two men of
business arrive at about 9.30 from Angaston, where they live.
These are my land steward, Mr. Wm. Clark, who has been
twenty years in the concern here, and my grandson, James Angas
Johnson. They take the keys of the offices and proceed to
business, after holding twenty to thirty minutes' conversation with
me in my library about business matters. From 10 to 12.30 I
employ my time in my library, open to calls from my clerks or
others, then the letter-bag arrives, and my chief clerk brings it up
to me to open. He and I read the business letters, and decide
upon the replies. The noted items in the daily papers also have
our attention. At 1 I dine ; then the clerks bring up letters for
me to sign and all papers on business, also cheques, drafts, &c.,
if any, as I allow no one to sign any cheque or important document but myself. All bank-books and cheque-books I keep under
my own especial control. Every Monday is the day we fix for the
tenants and others to come to the office on special business, when
I am always near at hand. At 2 p.m. to 3 I attend to a short
walk or domestic affairs, and at 3 I take a siesta on the sofa,

unless prevented by company or other matters. At 4.30 I rise with my physical frame fit for fresh work, and my eyes much the better for quiet repose. Then the clerks come up with business matters for my attention and signature, and at 5 to 5.30, as business permits, the clerks ride off to Angaston in their traps or on horses, and spend their time with their families.

I often have branches of my family call in and take tea with me without ceremony, and perhaps spend the evening; if not, I walk about or meditate in or out of doors, and look after my men, horses, and gardens, or receive calls from my friends.

At 9 p.m. I have reading and family prayers with the household for twenty minutes, and then my supper of bread and butter and glass of wine, and leave the servants to themselves, while I have my own private duties and reading, and retire to rest between 10 and 11, as I find most agreeable and convenient.

I still keep up my establishment at Prospect Hall, near North Adelaide, where I have two female and one male servant, and although I have only been there for a few days since my wife's death, branches of my family, and friends from distant parts, avail themselves of it, and it serves them as a sort of hotel when visiting the city.

Two months after this letter was written Mr. Angas had the inexpressible satisfaction of welcoming his beloved daughter, Mrs. William Johnson, and her son and daughter to Lindsay Park. But not, as he had hoped, to take up their abode permanently in South Australia. It was only a visit— bright, memorable, and helpful, it is true, but it came to an end in a little over a twelvemonth. The abiding benefit was that henceforth there was a new interest in the monthly interchange of letters. She had seen the colony, knew the people, and could

picture her father in the midst of his surroundings
at every turn.   So the correspondence, after her
arrival in England, was renewed " after the example
of the former days," but with this additional advantage.

There were stirring times in Adelaide shortly after
her departure, as the following extract from one of
the first letters shows :—

PROSPECT HALL, *March* 1, 1869.

You will see by the newspapers what excitement has been
produced by the visit of the Duke of Edinburgh and his ship,
the *Galatea;* also from the arrival of our new Governor, the
Right Honourable Sir James Fergusson, Bart., and his lady and
family, as well as the departure of our old Governor, Colonel
Hamley, who is much respected.   I ventured to dine with these
three gentlemen at our club on one evening, when we gave them a
splendid dinner.   I had a good opportunity there for conversation
with the Prince and with our new Governor of a very satisfactory
character.

About this time, and until his decease, the mind
of Mr. Angas was largely occupied with the
question of the rapid spread of Roman Catholicism,
not only in South Australia, but throughout the
colonies and the world.

As regards Adelaide, the fact that the former
Governor, Sir Dominick Daly, was a staunch Roman
Catholic may have been the incidental cause of
particular attention being drawn to the subject,
emphasized by the fact that in December, 1868,
soon after bringing one of the most important

Sessions of the Parliament to a close, and in the same year in which he had so ably performed his part in the reception and entertainment of the Duke of Edinburgh, he died very suddenly, and was buried in the Roman Catholic Cathedral, some twelve to fifteen thousand people being assembled in the streets to watch the funeral procession.

Certain it is that within a year of his death Mr. Angas, in letters to friends, records the following facts and impressions :—

My great anxiety is to stem the progress of popery in Australia, and to promote the best interests of the people and of vital religion. . . . I have been in Adelaide for several weeks, chiefly occupied in strenuous efforts against the ' Great Apostacy.' Two weekly anti-popish newspapers now work away in Adelaide. We, that is, Hussey and I, have sent into circulation from fifteen to twenty thousand pamphlets, papers, and tracts, in this and the neighbouring colonies, and this week we are very busy in founding another monthly journal for the advocacy of the Protestant Reformation principles which will, apparently, be sustained by all classes and sects of Protestants.

His views were not narrowed down to South Australia. He took a forward look into the question in its bearings on the whole world, and there are not a few who will regard the following expression of opinion as a true prophecy :—

The condition of political and religious affairs on the Continent, and, indeed, I may add, all over the world, forbode troublous times to us. I have a strong conviction in my mind that anti-Christ, in the form of popery, which, through the restoration of its Order of

Jesuits, now felt to be an organized and dangerous power in every part of the globe, will, as Jesuitism ever has done, be the grand Satanic agency employed to create confusion in every kingdom where the light of the gospel at all is seen. Next to that is the alarming degree of lukewarmness prevalent among Protestants at the increase of popery in England and throughout the British Empire! . . . To subjugate Great Britain and all her colonies to the yoke of Rome is evidently the now prevailing feeling and desire of all earnest Roman Catholics, and it appears clear as noonday to me that the next generation, if not the present one, will have to fight over again the Great Battle of the Reformation! I pray God to speed it!

In the General Election of 1870 Mr. Angas strained every nerve to overmaster the indefatigable efforts of the Roman Catholics to send members of their Church into Parliament, and confessed to a keen satisfaction when the result of the elections was declared and it was found that they had been " signally defeated, having got only one real Papist returned and another who is half a Protestant, while there is not at the present time one Roman Catholic in the Upper House of this province."

Public labours were now getting too much for his strength, and it was a source of intense satisfaction when in 1871 his son, Mr. J. H. Angas, having been returned at the head of the poll, went into the House of Assembly as representative of the Barossa District.

After the death of his wife Mr. Angas gave up the diary which had been his friend and companion for nearly sixty years, and into which he had breathed all his hopes and fears, his aspirations and confessions. Only very occasionally after that he made an entry, one of the last being as follows:—

On the 1st of May last I completed my eighty-second year, and was in the enjoyment of my mental and bodily faculties, slightly impaired by declining years, yet able to attend to my daily duties, both private and public. My chief failure is in my memory and my eyes, which somewhat interrupts my usefulness, also I feel less able to employ my mental powers with perseverance of effort as formerly. But the Lord affords me the help of others who read and write for me when I fail. . . . I find it necessary to greatly reduce my correspondence with my friends and relatives abroad, and to leave my diary to its own fate. My time on earth cannot be much longer, and there are many duties to discharge in anticipation of my departure from this world—thank God, with the hope of a better, through the Lord Jesus Christ.

Although the increasing weakness in his eyes made it necessary that he should be read to, and a throat affection kept him closely indoors during the winter months, time did not hang heavily upon his hands, and in his correspondence with old friends he frequently writes in a strain like this:—

Time passes away more agreeably with me now than ever in my past life. I have abundance of useful occupation, and everything to make me happy since I retired from the anxieties of parliamentary life. My only business now is to do all the good I can, and to manage my estate to the best advantage, so that I may have wherewith to do ' good and to communicate '—to promote the cause of God and the welfare of my fellows.

By every mail Mrs. Johnson sent him a collection

of cuttings, slips, scraps of newspapers, pamphlets, religious books—anything that she, who knew the bent of his mind so well, was sure would suit him, and these gave him infinite gratification and amusement.

As old age drew on he was in the habit of writing and speaking very freely of his growing infirmities and of his approaching end. We extract from various sources a few of his sayings as a contribution to the literature of old age, and as showing the attitude of his mind, which from first to last was without variableness.

In the prospect of his decease he wrote :—

My thoughts in England for a year or two before I left for South Australia were oftentimes engaged in getting knowledge of all things appertaining to my projected future home there, so that my mind was fully prepared to come out when I did. How unwise it would be not to act in like manner in preparing for a removal to my Eternal Home, to learn all I can about the Heavenly Land, as I tried to know all I could about South Australia.

He anticipated a long life, and based his hope on a sound argument :—

My father died in his ninetieth year, my eldest brother in his eighty-fourth, and many generations of my forefathers were long lived. Great has been the Lord's goodness to our progenitors through many generations, I may even say centuries past, who kept the faith and died in the Lord.

I am running a race with Death at my heels ! Considering the pressure upon my heart and mind ever since I began life, and the

wear and tear of the nerves and muscles, I am full of gratitude
that I can still attend to my affairs and help others also in an
ordinary measure.

All that I do in my garden now is to admire it and to thank
God that He has given me so much happiness in my old age.

It was a very remarkable old age. In 1872 he
actively protested against an attempt to get up a
Joint Stock Company to construct a railway between
Port Darwin and Angaston, and, with the aid of his
secretary, drew up a lengthy paper exposing, what
he considered, the folly of the scheme. In 1875 he
fought one of his old battles over again in watching
the passing of an Act to establish a Council of
Education with paid President, Secretary, and
Inspectors, directly responsible to a Minister of
Education — an Act comprehending these three
great principles : secular education, without ex-
cluding the Bible ; exemption to those who could
not afford to pay the fees ; compulsory attendance
whenever practicable.

No man knew more of the history of South
Australia than Mr. Angas, and it had long been his
ambition to see a comprehensive work issued from the
press, giving the story of the rise and progress of the
colony. He had collected a vast store of information
to this end, and had on more than one occasion
taken some steps to carry out his desire. But in his
eighty-sixth year he wrote :—

"I am too old now to think of writing a history,

but I have written fifty-nine private journals, containing from one hundred to three hundred pages each (but none since my wife's death — January 14, 1867), with copies of correspondence in abundance."

Like other things, to which we shall refer by and by, it was left too late; bodily and mental health were still vigorous; he could write without the aid of spectacles, and his hearing was perfect, but memory was showing symptoms of failure. "It is like a slate," he said, "which is written upon daily, and at last becomes so that discernible impressions are made with difficulty."

In April, 1875, in his eighty-seventh year, he was taken suddenly and seriously ill. It was noticed when he retired to bed that he was unusually feeble, and this circumstance induced his considerate housekeeper (Mrs. Parsons) to make inquiry some time after as to whether he was in bed. Receiving no reply, assistance was called, and he was found on the floor in a semi-conscious state as if he had knelt down and had been afterwards unable to rise. But for this timely inquiry he would probably have been found dead in the morning. On recovering consciousness he inquired what was the nature of his illness, and said, quaintly and calmly, to the doctor, "Don't allow the old house to fall down for want of a little repair."

The old house did not fall, a repairing lease was granted.

When it was thought by his medical attendant and all his friends that he was sinking, he turned to Mr. Hussey, his secretary, and said :—

"I feel persuaded that the Lord has some more work for me to do."

"Then, if so, the Lord will raise you up and give you strength to do it," answered Mr. Hussey.

"Man is immortal till his work is done," replied the apparently dying man.

CHAPTER XVIII.

IT was many months before Mr. Angas could leave
his room or resume any of his former duties, and
never again was he to have his old vigour restored.
Memory began to fail, and the principle on which
he had acted from boyhood of never putting off for
to-morrow what he could do to-day, gave place to
postponing everything which was not absolutely
necessary to do. He could still enjoy the society
of friends and of books ; the beauties of nature had
lost none of their charms for him ; and the consolations of religion and the pleasures of benevolence
were as real and attractive as ever. The old energy
of spirit often displayed itself in his closing years,
but " the flesh was weak," and he was obliged to

leave undone many good things it was in his heart
to do.

December 28, 1878—the forty-first anniversary
of the founding of the colony—was eventful in the
quiet history of Angaston. It was the day when
the Angas Recreation Park, the gift of Mr. Angas,
was formally handed over to the authorities to be
managed for the people by a committee of their own
election. It consists of a block of land about
twenty-one acres in extent in a lovely situation,
tastefully laid out and planted with thousands of
shrubs and trees, fenced, with handsome gates, and
a carriage-drive round the whole park. The cricket
oval is about seven acres in extent, with ground
rising slightly all round.

The state of Mr. Angas' health prevented him
from taking any part in the opening ceremony, but
he was ably represented, then and always, by his
son, Mr. J. H. Angas, who formally opened the park.

For the last few years of his life Mr. Angas looked
forward to his birthday with almost childish anticipation, and it was customary for him on those occasions
to receive kind congratulatory letters from friends
who could not pay him a personal visit. After the
establishment of the Angaston Band it was considered a part of its duty to proceed to Lindsay
House on the 1st of May and serenade its owner.
To this was added on the 1st of May, 1879, when
he attained his ninetieth year, the sweet singing of
the Angaston schoolchildren, and when he came

out on the verandah to see and hear them, it was with great difficulty he could restrain his emotion. It was his custom to entertain a party of special friends on his birthday, and on this particular occasion among the guests was one with whom he had been intimate ever since 1851, when he arrived in the colony—Mr. G. W. Hawkes, Stipendiary Magistrate for the Barossa District.

Mr. Angas was in wonderful spirits, and after Mr. Hawkes had proposed his health he stood and made a cheerful and vigorous speech, concluding with the simple words—"I have not done what I might have done; I have tried to do what I could."

That same afternoon he read aloud to friends, without the aid of spectacles, some of his early reminiscences. Later in the day he walked on the verandah, and as usual on his birthday, there was a great gathering of people in the grounds, over two hundred tenants and friends being present. While the band was playing lively airs, Mr. Angas said he felt in such excellent spirits he seemed as if he could dance. "And why not?" said Mr. Hawkes, good-humouredly, and commenced to *chassé*, when Mr. Angas playfully responded by making a number of light steps, amid the cheering and merriment of the much-amused guests in the garden.

Ten days after this the arrival of the English mail brought him the painful intelligence of the death of his sister in her ninety-third year. It was

a great grief to him—the breaking up of the last
tie that bound him to that generation. The affec--
tion of these last surviving members of the old
family was very great and very touching. When
they could no longer keep up a correspondence,
they would address the envelopes, so that the
well-known handwriting might be a safeguard
against anxiety, by proving that they were still in
the land of the living.

Next day was Sunday, but he had not the heart
to go to his accustomed place of worship.

" Read to me," he said to Miss Stonehouse, his
housekeeper, " the story of our Lord appearing in
vision to St. John on the isle of Patmos." As she
read those grand and solemn passages describing
the King in His beauty—" the first and the last,
He that liveth and was dead, and is alive for
evermore, and who has in His hands the keys of
hades and of death "—a quiet, restful smile spread
over his face, and he thanked God for giving him
solace and comfort. At frequent intervals during
the day and night he spoke of his sister. Next
day his medical man was called in ; on Wednesday,
the 15th of May, he was very drowsy, sleeping
calmly nearly all the day, and at eleven o'clock,
without a sigh or a movement, he passed away to
the eternal rest.

A few days later over five hundred people
assembled in Lindsay Park — relatives, friends,
fellow-workers, English and German tenants, depu--

tations from various religious and philanthropic societies, and, preceded by the Angaston Band playing the Dead March, wended their way to the family vault in the park, where a simple service was held, and all that was mortal of George Fife Angas was laid to rest beside the remains of his wife.

He left three generations of descendants, including three sons and three daughters, of whom one son and two daughters remain, besides many grandchildren and great-grandchildren.

When he died, South Australia was in a state of great prosperity, and still greater success was unfolding. There were no signs of degeneracy in the race; the intellectual and moral life of the people was well established; multitudes of those who came to the colony destitute were wealthy men, whose families were occupying positions of respectability and honour. There was a free Government, taxation was at a minimum, the population was over 900,000, and millions of acres of unoccupied land invited the industry of fresh settlers; in the previous year over nine million bushels of wheat alone was grown; the export trade to the United Kingdom was in value over three millions sterling, of which some two million pounds were the receipts for wool, and about half a million for wheat; the mineral wealth of the country was enormous, and everywhere and in everything there were not only the elements, but the signs of expansion and progress.

From the day when Mr. Angas first saw South Australia on paper to the day when he bade the colony farewell he never had the shadow of a doubt as to its ultimate prosperity; when it was plunged into financial embarrassment, and the settlers were threatened with ruin, he was ready to stake the whole of his fortune for its deliverance, and when he looked upon it in its developed and prosperous state he was more than satisfied. He was wont to describe it to new-comers in the words of Holy Writ :—

" The Lord thy God bringeth thee into a good land; . . . a land of wheat, and barley, and vines ; . . . a land wherein thou shalt eat bread without scarceness, thou shalt not lack anything in it; a land whose stones are iron, and out of whose hills thou mayest dig brass." *

When Mr. Angas passed away from the world it was like the snapping asunder of one of the few remaining links between the last century and the present, between ideas and modes of thought that had ruled the world for generations, and the new order of things which has so revolutionized the past.

Whether the times yet unborn will produce any more such men as he, is matter for conjecture: certain it is that he belonged to a type of men very rapidly passing away.

* Deuteronomy viii. 7-9.

It was the great wish of his life that if any biographical notice of him appeared it should be written in such form that it might exercise some influence upon the development of character in the generation following. It seems to us that the best way to fulfil that desire is briefly to summarize here his own characteristics.

He was a Puritan of the Puritans—of that good old-fashioned type which, when the liberties of England were threatened, struggled for the freedom we in these days possess in such ample measure. Every thought, feeling, and action of his life ran in straight lines laid down when early in his career he arrived at clear and definite religious conclusions. Those who did not understand this, did not understand him, and no just estimate can be formed of his character unless this is taken into account.

With him a sense of personal responsibility to the " Great Taskmaster " under whom he served was as paramount as with the old order of Puritans. To Him he must be faithful in matters great or small, anywhere and everywhere; for Him no duty, however slight, must be negligently discharged, no toil, however trivial, perfunctorily performed. It was this sense of accountability to God that guided his pen through all those fifty-nine volumes of diary; it was this that made him declare time after time that unless, as chairman of certain business companies, the hand of Providence was recognized in their annual reports, he would have nothing to do with their affairs, be they never so lucrative; it was this that made him personally supervise all his multifarious concerns until the growing infirmities of age compelled him to narrow the range of his activities; it was this that caused him to frame his life upon a model from which he would not depart, however urgent the plea might be, or from whatever quarter it might come; it was this that made him unpopular in the Colonial Parliament—his sense of duty impelling him to treat public monies, or public trusts of any kind, as he treated those committed to his own private control. When he was misunderstood, it was because these secret motives prompting his outward actions were not understood, or if understood were treated with indifference.

That his heart was larger than his creed it is needless to remark. He had been brought up in, and had given his thorough assent to, the old pessimist doctrine, that the world is a very bad one, and is getting worse and worse, and will do so until the great crisis comes. He had been brought up to regard human nature as vile. He believed in original sin and total depravity; of life, apart from Christian faith, as unrelieved by a single gleam of goodness. Nevertheless his interest in everything having to do with his fellow-creatures, and with the bright world in which God had placed him, never flagged. He was wont to talk of life as a weary pilgrimage, and of the earth as a vale of tears, yet he clung to it tenaciously; he loved his garden and its flowers; he revelled in all things beautiful and fair, and this "present evil world" of his old theology became transfigured and glorified when he forgot the terms of his creed.

His faith was definite, matter-of-fact, and clear. He believed in the Bible, the whole Bible, and nothing but the Bible. Against the hierarchical principle, especially as embodied in the sacerdotalism of the Romish Church, he protested with a vehemence which, to some who did not understand his principles, seemed inconsistent with Christian charity; he had a firm faith in the efficacy of prayer, and at the same time believed in an overruling Providence ordering the lives of men, and working out in them its own wise and beneficent purposes; his religious experience was removed to the utmost degree from the ecstatic or the mystical, but what he believed, he believed simply, earnestly, and with that "assurance of faith" which gave him full rest and repose of heart. As to the grave questions in Christian polemics which have been so freely and constantly discussed of late years, he knew absolutely nothing. He strove with all the zeal of an enthusiast to propagate the truth as he himself had received and believed it, and he never departed from his early standpoints by a hair's breadth, or gave heed to "new fangled notions" in religious belief from whatever quarter they came.

It followed that all the habits of Mr. Angas were
fashioned by his creed. For instance, time is
given as a preparation for eternity, therefore no
time must be wasted. Money is a trust from
God, therefore money must not be squandered. As
regards time, he felt it to be his duty to content
himself with the minimum of sleep; to rise and
retire early, so that no accident might deprive him
of morning or evening communion with God. Time
must be economized in order that he may do as
much as possible in his span of life, therefore he
dare not fritter it away in amusements or in "that
which profiteth nothing." Holding this view as
a principle, he must always let it be seen in
practice. To every appointment, all through life,
he was punctual to the moment, his calls and
engagements were all pre-arranged, and his coachman knew where to drive as well as the coachman
of any London physician. It was a curious fact
that with the multiplicity of his engagements,
especially in the days of his prime, when he was
in the thick of innumerable undertakings, commercial and philanthropic, he was never known
to be too late. If he chanced to be too early he
had a habit of sitting with his old-fashioned watch
in his hand, and in this attitude, considered the
most characteristic, he sat for the oil-painting by
Hook, from which the frontispiece etching, in this
volume, is taken.

The habit of punctuality formed in youth re-

mained with him to the end. Not long after his
arrival in South Australia he asked an old tenant
to point out to him all his land about Angaston.
On the day and hour appointed a soaking, drenching
rain was falling, with no sign of lifting. The
tenant's wife said, "No one will come to-day;" but
he, prudent man, had a horse ready saddled, and
sure enough, within a second of the time appointed,
Mr. Angas was there. He never forgot the fact
that the tenant was ready for him.

He would always, when driving to Freeling,
about eighteen miles distant—the nearest station
for Adelaide—start almost an hour before there
was any real necessity. It was upon the principle he often expressed, "It is better to be an
hour too soon than a minute too late." Of course
the hour was not wasted. If there should be any
little accident there would be ample time to set
it right, or there would be opportunity for luncheon
at the hotel after the drive, or there would be books
and papers to read.

As with time, so with money. "We are account-
able to God for its proper use" was a frequent
expression of his. Waste of any kind was repugnant to him; he would not heedlessly cut a piece
of string if it could be readily untied. In one of
his private letters he says:—

I have come to this conclusion, viz., Let a man's income be what
it may, he acts most like a Christian who avoids display of any
kind, and 'lets his moderation be known unto all men.' It is

lawful for a Christian to enjoy every comfort and convenience of
life, and beyond that he has a wide field in the world for doing
good to others.

This principle regulated all his household arrangements; he liked good plain food in plenty, but costly delicacies would have choked him if a Lazarus lay at his gates.

The principles of Mr. Angas are set forth in many of his letters. The following extract is from one written to a daughter, who was superintending the wedding outfit of a relative :—

Let me give you a gentle caution to exercise economy in whatever outfit may be recommended by you to —— for his married life. I think he is not quite complete in that science in matters out of business. ' Many littles make a mickle.' You know I am not niggardly when I can afford to be otherwise, but in beginning life a wise man will prepare for a rainy day. If I had not done so when I was in business I never should have weathered the panics and storms that a merciful God has brought me through honourably all my life.

It is the spirit of the world which induces young people to begin life with show and extravagance, and is the cause of most of the subsequent failures of business men. My maxim is 'Moderation in all things.' After a man has made a fortune, his mode of spending it is a question which he may himself decide, and no stranger has a right to interfere, but so long as a man is in active business he must consider those who have claims upon him, and that riches are not *always* to men of understanding.

In another letter he says :—

I hear that —— is dead, and that he has left his affairs involved, which is a great calamity in these uncertain times, especially to the middle class, whose prospects are so bad in the present habits of life, most of whom live up to the extent of their income, so that when the parents die little is left for the survivors. Also too many of those who are called Christians make great sacrifices to keep up for a long period what turns out in the end to be only a vain show.

His trumpet never gave an uncertain sound at any time of his life as to what he considered woman's place should be in the home. In illustration we give an extract from a letter, dated May, 1838, to his daughter Sarah, Mrs. Henry Evans, now of Evandale, near Angaston. It was written shortly after her marriage, and congratulated her on the excellent qualities of her husband, " who is," he said, " most worthy of everything you can do to show him respect and affection." Then after kindly and affectionately expressing " the great delight he has enjoyed in noticing her consistent and proper behaviour in her own house," he adds one of those neat little homilies which were highly treasured in those days, but will probably never find a place in correspondence again. He says :—

Continue to go forward as you have so auspicuously commenced, and I have no fear but that you will have as large a share of domestic happiness as falls to the lot of the most favoured of women.

Take pains to please your husband, and think nothing a trouble which will smooth his passage through the harassing and vexatious cares of business. Should he at any time appear cold, or evince the semblance of neglect, attribute it to the depressing

influence of such things, and redouble your efforts to please on
such occasions. The smiles and sympathy of a wife at such times.
have a more powerful influence in reviving the spirits and restoring
the elasticity of the mind than any other restorative on earth.
But woe to that man, when bowed down with the pressure of his
accumulated exertions to provide support and comforts for his
wife and family, if on his return for repose to his own roof his
exhaustion of body and mind should be yet further increased by
the cold look, icy sympathy, or callous indifference, if not, still
worse by the irritating droppings of contention. I have seen much
of the world and of the goings on in private families, and as the
result of it all you may take my present advice to you, my dear, as
the best proof of my affection for you, because I am sure, if you act
upon it, it will preserve for you a happy home and a peaceful
conscience.

From what I have seen, such advice does indeed appear unnecessary for you, but should it ever be needed henceforth, which
I pray God may never be, it will not be without its benefit.

On the question of amusements Mr. Angas, it
need hardly be said, had very strong views. He
objected to many, that are now almost universally
not only tolerated but encouraged, on the ground of
"worldliness," waste of time, and waste of money.
All through life, gambling, horse-racing, balls, theatres,.
and such-like were foresworn on principle, while in
early life his time was so fully occupied that, even had
he wished for these things, he would have had no
leisure for gratifying his desire. He was always a.
lover of his garden, of walking exercise, and of conversation with like-minded friends. He was a good
horseman, and an excellent whip. In South
Australia everybody knew his beautiful grey gelding.

" Verulam," and the skittish filly " Julia," which, as
his coachman testified, " he managed with activity
and agility that would not have done discredit to
a man fifty years his junior."

Like many colonists he had a great dread of Bush
fires, and frequently during the day in summer time
he would be seen on the verandah, field-glass in
hand, looking for smoke, at the least sign of which
he would dispatch some one to a neighbouring hill-
top to ascertain its exact locality. A large water-
cart, always full of water, was kept ready to send
out in case of emergency. On more than one
occasion he distinguished himself at Bush fires,
directing the efforts of the volunteers, who came
in large numbers, and distributing refreshment to
the exhausted workers. In 1862 a terrible fire
occurred, sweeping much country before it —
grass, timber, and fences, and threatening many
homesteads in the neighbourhood of Flaxman's
Valley and Lindsay Park. He was an active worker
on this occasion, and became surrounded by the
fire. But for the fleetness of the horse on which
he rode his position would have been one of extreme
peril.

In the training of his family he adhered to old
traditions, now almost universally discarded—whether
for good or ill, future generations must declare.
He held that in family life the head was to be, as
in patriarchal days, prophet, priest, and king of the
household, and of course he insisted on unques-.

tioning obedience. An incident may be cited. One
day he handed a letter to his youngest daughter,
then barely eighteen, requesting her to reply to it.
Hastily glancing at the contents, she said, laughingly,
" Why, papa, I can't answer this ; it is from some one
who has just lost his wife, and how should I know
how a man feels under such circumstances ? " " My
dear," replied Mr. Angas, rather sternly, "never
again let me hear you say ' I can't ; ' that is a phrase
that ought not to be in any one's vocabulary," with
which he resumed his occupation. Hastily brushing
away a tear, the girl sat down to write, and soon
succeeded in composing a reply to the melancholy
epistle. Whether it afforded much consolation to
the afflicted widower cannot be stated, but when in
after years the lady told the story to her own daughter, she would naïvely add, " It was the last time I
ventured to say ' I can't.' "

When, on another occasion one of his children
happened to disagree with his judgment on a controversy in family politics, he wrote :—

Adelaide, *March* 21, 1861.

I will not touch upon these controversies only to say that you
ought to believe that I should know more and better about them
than you could possibly do, and by the laws of both God and man
you are bound to honour and respect my judgment. If God has
put me at the head of my family no one has any right to put me
at the tail of it. I hope *that* controversy is, therefore, done with
and past. I have always loved and served my children heartily
and faithfully, and it would be a dangerous thing for them to dis-

place me from my position as their parent. God made the law,
not I, ' Honour thy parents.'

There was no doubt that his style was sometimes
severe, as shown in these instances, but he was
always very regretful afterwards if he felt he had
been unjust, and would often try to make amends to
the younger members of his family by presenting
them with a few flowers or some choice fruit—a tacit
way, understood by those who knew him well, of
making up for any undue severity.

When he visited England in 1858 he much
enjoyed the sojourn with his daughter Emma (Mrs.
Johnson) in her home at Bowdon, near Manchester,
and soon became a favourite with the children,
especially with his little grand-daughter, who always
claimed as her special privilege the right of sitting
next him at table.

Having brought up his own children under the
old - fashioned system, he was interested to
watch the result of the milder plan adopted by his
daughter, who, though she exacted implicit obedience in a way that might be considered ultra-strict
nowadays, yet always encouraged the confidence
of the little ones who were accustomed to come
to ' her and confess their childish faults and
misfortunes with a freedom that to him was most
astonishing, and called forth his warm approbation.

He was always very thoughtful for the welfare of
the domestics of his household, providing them with

plenty of good religious literature ; if friends came
to see them he would be greatly annoyed if they
were not hospitably entertained ; if they were in any
kind of trouble or needed help, they at once looked
to him for advice, which was always kindly and
frankly given.   In his last days the Angaston Band
had a great charm for him, and would play for hours
at a time in the park.   But he would never enjoy it
alone, and all his servants and labourers were allowed
to leave off work during their stay.   He always
recompensed the bandsmen with refreshments and
money.

" When thou doest alms," said our Lord, " let not
thy left hand know what thy right hand doeth, that
thine alms may be in secret, and thy Father who
seeth in secret Himself shall reward thee openly."

The benefactions of Mr. Angas will never be
known ; no idea can be formed of the aggregate
amount of them.   Nor is it necessary it should be,
although from note-books, kept as reminders when
certain periodical payments became due, it has been
ascertained that during his residence in South
Australia he gave away many thousand pounds per
annum.

His donations to religious and benevolent objects
were sometimes very large, much larger than he
usually received credit for, as he by no means desired
but on the contrary, as a rule, studiously avoided
publicity in such matters.   If publicity would

stimulate greater zeal in others, then, and then only, would he let his benefactions be made known.

He delighted, however, in giving, not largely to a few particular objects, but in smaller sums continuously to a vast number of deserving causes; his contributions were never based upon sectarian considerations, and they certainly were never made from a business point of view; the very idea was hateful to him.

To struggling ministers of the gospel he was especially kind, often entertaining them for weeks or months at a time, until they could get churches or comfortable homes of their own. In many cases he paid their passages from England, besides supplying them with money on their arrival. When incapacitated through illness or overwork he was always ready to give them the means for change of air.

Says one, " He was a thoughtful lover of ministers. He knew the straits and privations of many of them, and often in a quiet, unobtrusive, and sometimes in an entirely secret way he sent them sums of money." Here is a specimen :—

"I could hardly be reckoned among the necessitous ministers," writes the pastor of a Congregational Church, " but I found it hard in those days to make both ends meet when there was any extra demand on my means of living. How well I remember one of his generous gifts (and I narrate it because I know it is a sample of many). There was occasion

for a change of residence, and my household goods
were in process of removal. We were engaged, my
wife and I, in superintending the unpacking, somewhat wearied and anxious, when the postman's
knock was heard and a letter brought in. It was
from Mr. Angas, very brief, but very kind, simply
saying that ' he knew removals were costly,' and
enclosing a handsome cheque towards paying for
mine. You can well imagine how easy our toils
became after that."

"Many a time," says the Rev. J. H. Angus, of
Adelaide—no relation—" I have known him slip a
valuable cheque into the hands of a minister who
happened to call, telling him it would help his
library, &c.; and the act was so done as that it not
only took the recipient by surprise, but served right
fully to show the loving and liberal disposition of
the donor."

He took a deep and unwavering interest in young
men who were setting themselves apart for the Christian ministry in the colony. At one time he had a
desire to endow a Baptist College, but when a Union
College was set on foot, embracing the Congregational, Baptist, Presbyterian, and Bible Christian
bodies, he devoted his attention to that. He at
once gave £1000, and subsequently another £1000
to the endowment fund, on condition that an equal
sum should be raised by the Council—a condition
speedily fulfilled.

Change of residence did not produce the least

change of feeling with reference to those he had been in the habit of helping. For example, he left Dawlish in 1839, after six years' residence there, but nearly thirty years later we find from old letters that he was frequently making inquiries whether his old friends, or the chapels with which he had been associated, stood in need of funds, and subsequently forwarding drafts for considerable sums of money for them.

This characteristic is worthy of further notice. The career of his sailor-brother William was ever before his eyes. "Captain" W. H. Angas and William Penn were the heroes of his early life, and they remained so to the end. One was the principal framer of his religious life, the other of his philanthropic and colonizing career.

In 1873 Mr. Angas was in correspondence with Pastor Oncken, who in 1823 had been introduced by his spiritual father, William H. Angas, to the Continental Society, of which the good Henry Drummond, M.P., was at that time the President. Fifty years later Oncken had the person, the voice, the very words of William Angas vividly before him. During these fifty years he had circulated over a million copies of the Holy Scriptures, many millions of tracts, and two million copies of religious books, such as volumes of Spurgeon's Sermons, also his "Morning by Morning" and "Evening by Evening." During that period, to quote his own words in a letter to Mr. Angas dated January 10, 1873 :—

Millions of our fellow-travellers throughout the continent have learned of the only way of escape from wrath to come from the lips of our one hundred missionaries, colporteurs, and converts, and about eighty thousand precious souls have, to our knowledge, been led to put their trust in Christ. And it will be gratifying to you to have it brought back to your remembrance that your late devoted brother, Captain Angas, was the instrument, in God's hands, to bring me in 1823 in connection with the Continental Society.

But when Pastor Oncken wrote that letter he did not know that all through those fifty years one of his most constant and beneficent anonymous donors was Mr. Angas, who, in gratitude for his brother's influence on his own life, had been supporting the noble Christian labours of one of that brother's converts.

Of the large sums of money given in England, Australia, and elsewhere for the building of churches, the founding of homes, schools, hospitals, and especially, refuges for the friendless, fallen, and inebriates, it is unnecessary to particularize; suffice it to say that tens of thousands have benefited by his untiring benevolence.

Among the many memorials Mr. Angas has left behind him, Angaston may be cited as an illustration of the beneficent influence that may be exerted over the general condition of a place by the presence of one wealthy and God-fearing man and his household in it. No town, whether colonial or English, can present more striking evidences of the pervading influence for good that may be exerted in such a

way, in its orderliness, neatness, and general prosperity, than Angaston.

It should be stated that after his decease considerable disappointment was expressed in certain
quarters that his will did not contain any bequests
to the religious and philanthropic institutions he
had fostered in his lifetime. " It was not for want
of thought or due consideration," says his private
secretary, " that this omission occurred. Time after
time plans were talked over and devised for legacies
and endowments of various kinds, but what appeared
to be almost insuperable difficulties and obstacles
presented themselves. Foremost among these plans
was the erection of a number of cottages for the
aged and infirm. One word will explain the total
failure of all these well-meant and cherished schemes
—' procrastination.' He had left it until too late,
and when he sought to work out his benevolent
plans, headache and exhaustion would supervene
and the matter would be set aside."

Procrastination, without doubt, had something to
do with the matter, but there were other reasons.
He had been so much in the habit of helping things
on personal knowledge, that when he was no longer
able to gain or retain that knowledge, his interest
and his perception of what was needed, diminished.
Moreover there was a diminution of mental vigour,
and an uncertainty about new things which held
him back. All these causes combined may be
summed up in his own words, written not long

before his death, to an old friend : "I often fail in nervous energy to carry into operation the plans of my own mind and heart."

So lived, laboured, and died George Fife Angas— a rare man, one of the last links binding the past and present centuries together, and one of those really great men who have materially helped to make our Empire what it is.

THE END.

INDEX.

29

UNWIN BROTHERS, THE GRESHAM PRESS, CHILWORTH AND LONDON.

www.ingramcontent.com/pod-product-compliance
Lightning Source LLC
Chambersburg PA
CBHW031053110726
47900CB00003B/912